"THAT'S HARD COUNTRY OUT THERE," SAID RUFF JUSTICE.

"You've got a romantic notion about keeping a promise to your father, but the truth is there's no substitute for raw strength. If you don't have it you won't make it."

Adrienne Court just stared at Ruff, blue eyes sparkling with fierce determination. Her beautiful sister Lucille simply looked bewildered. Ruff tried to imagine Lucille with a buffalo rifle in her hands, holding back a swarm of Sioux warriors. She belonged in silks and satins in someone's drawing room . . . or in someone's bed.

Adrienne's chin came up. "I've bought wagons and hired workers. We may be walking into trouble, but at least there's three good men and three good women."

Ruff laughed harshly as he took her arm. "That only adds up to six good graves. . . ."

Wild Westerns by Warren T. Longtree

RUFF JUSTICE #12

Petticoat Express

by

Warren T. Longtree

○
A SIGNET BOOK
NEW AMERICAN LIBRARY

PUBLISHER'S NOTE

This novel is a work of fiction. Names, characters, places, and incidents either are the product of the author's imagination or are used fictitiously, and any resemblance to actual persons, living or dead, events, or locales is entirely coincidental.

The first chapter of this book appeared in *Comanche Peak*, the eleventh volume of this series.

SIGNET TRADEMARK REG. U.S. PAT. OFF. AND FOREIGN COUNTRIES
REGISTERED TRADEMARK—MARCA REGISTRADA
HECHO EN CHICAGO, U.S.A.

SIGNET, SIGNET CLASSIC, MENTOR, PLUME, MERIDIAN and NAL BOOKS are published by The New American Library, Inc., 1633 Broadway, New York, New York 10019

First Printing, February, 1984

1 2 3 4 5 6 7 8 9

PRINTED IN THE UNITED STATES OF AMERICA

RUFF JUSTICE

He knew the West better than any man alive—a hostile, savage land rife with both violent outlaws and courageous adventurers. But Ruff Justice had a sixth sense that kept him breathing and saw his enemies dead. A scout for the U.S. Cavalry, he was paid to protect the public, and nobody was faster at sniffing out a killer, a crook, a con man—red or white, at close range or far. Anyone on the wrong side of the law would have to reckon with the menace of Ruff's murderously sharp stag-handled bowie knife, with his Colt pistol, and the Spencer rifle he cradled in his arms.

Ruff Justice, gentleman and frontier philosopher—good men respected him, bad men feared him, and women, good and bad, wanted him with all the wildness of the Old West.

1

Echoes of the massacre at Paley Wells rode with the cavalry contingent. It was a sight not easily forgotten, even though Captain Hart's men had seen much savagery on the Dakota plains. The Paley family was gone. The old man, his wife, a teenage son, and a young daughter. They had been hacked to pieces, kept alive for too long. Their ghosts would haunt these plains for a long while to come.

It was Stone Hand who had done it, that was what Ruffin T. Justice, the tall, buckskinned, flamboyant civilian scout, had said. He had left his mark on the bodies.

Stone Hand was Teton Lakota. He was crazy, blood-crazy.

"What sticks in their mind is the meal," Captain Hart said. He removed his hat and wiped out the band. The morning breeze was cool across the long grass valley.

"I know it," Ruff answered.

It was the meal which stuck in Ruff's mind. Four Sioux had ridden up to the house and swung down. Inside, Paley and his wife had set the table for four extra. Then Stone Hand and his men had sat down to eat the Paleys' food, rising to slaughter them after it was over.

"I'm going out ahead," Ruff said. The captain nodded, watching the tall, lean man heel his gray and move out. Justice's long dark hair curled down past his shoulders, and it moved in the wind as he rode now. He wore a mustache which fell to his jaw line, and he was habitually clad in buckskins. He carried a Colt sidearm, a bowie riding at the back of his belt, and a buckskin-sheathed .56 Spencer carbine across the saddlebows.

And in his heart he was carrying a deep, dark anger.

He had met Stone Hand before and liked none of what he had learned about the man. His own people had kicked him out of the tribe, disgusted with his barbarisms, which could be directed at any human being or animal. There was a rumor that Crazy Horse had put a price of fifty ponies on Stone Hand's scalp, but that might or might not have been true.

Ahead lay the pine-stippled foothills north of the Red River. The grass began to give out and the trail which Ruff had been following at an easy canter to dry up.

For the first time that day he swung down and crouched, searching for sign. He led the gray forward a little way, swung left, and picked up the tracks again. Four unshod Indian ponies, two bigger horses taken from the Paley place.

Ruff glanced back, saw the blue-clad file of soldiers a quarter of a mile off, and swung up into leather again. He swung toward the low hills to his right. The tall pines swayed in the wind. The sky was a long-running thing streaked with pale pennants of cloud. A dozen crows wheeled and cawed in the air.

The first shot sang off the cantle of Ruff's saddle, and he dropped to the far side of his horse, yelling savagely to get the gray running, running into the timber as a dozen more shots echoed down the hillslope. Behind him the bugler sounded charge, and although Hart was still far behind the cavalry kicked itself into a thundering gallop.

The Indians had position, and three of Hart's men went down in the first fusillade. Ruff was into the timber now, and he leaped from the gray, unsheathing the big Spencer as he dropped to the pine-needle-covered earth. A bullet tore a chunk of bark from a tree near his right hand, and Ruff went to the ground.

His eyes narrowed as he looked upslope to his left, where the shots had come from. Glancing back, he saw that Hart had wisely broken off his wild assault and was regrouping out of rifle range.

That left Ruff alone and pinned down. To remind him of that, a dozen shots flew overhead, one neatly clipping a branch from a big pine. It thudded to the ground a few feet away.

Ruff began to move. There wasn't much hope of getting back off the hill, nor could he remain where he was. Sooner or later the searching bullets would find him.

He got into a crouch and began running uphill, weaving through the trees until he reached a narrow gully. He flung himself into it, moving again as soon as he touched bottom. Upslope again, the air in the gully close and menacing, the day momentarily, deceptively silent.

The Sioux popped up from behind a rock like one of those tin bears in a shooting gallery, and Ruff Justice fired the .56 from his hip. The bullet tore most of the Indian's head away and he cartwheeled back soundlessly. There hadn't been time to scream. Ruff crouched and waited. Sweat trickled down his throat, dripped annoyingly into his eyes. He gave it a full minute and then went on.

The gully petered out and he was up and into timber and rock again. Looking down through the trees, he could see Hart, indecisive, still out of range.

The bullet whined off the rocks beside Justice, and he scurried behind them to halt, panting, the Spencer cool in his hand, comforting. To wait, to watch, knowing that Stone Hand wasn't the kind to pull off, to leave Justice alive. The man lived to kill. Every living man was regarded as an enemy. He would come.

Ruff saw the flash of color, heard the simultaneous drumming of hoofs, and whirling around, his back to the big gray boulder, he saw the mounted Sioux charging downslope, feathers flying, mouth open in a war cry.

Ruff felt the Indian's bullet hit the rock behind him and go singing off, felt the stone chips fly against his hand and face. The .56 spoke again and the big bay the Indian rode went down, a bullet through its heart. The horse rolled and the Indian, a look of astonishment on his face, went down, the horse crushing him as it landed.

There were more shots from upslope, and Ruff took to his heels, moving through the timber, still weaving his way up the hill.

He crept up toward a rocky ridge. The serrated edge of the stony rise was shaped like a comb, whetted and polished by the winds of the eons. From there Ruff could see the Red River of the North winding its way through the trees, glinting silver and deep blue.

For half an hour as the sun began its slow descent he stayed motionless, watching, listening, the sweat cooling his body. Then he heard it—a horse whickering in the pines farther along the ridge. Stone Hand had not pulled out. He knew the soldiers could not get to him, knew he had only one man to contend with. Ruff Justice—and by now he knew Ruff Justice had teeth.

Ruff moved uphill again, his feet whispering against

the pine-needle-carpeted earth. He saw a flash of color, then made out the paint pony standing regarding him with curiosity, ears pricked, eyes alert. A second horse—one with Paley's brand—stood across the clearing, head bowed, nibbling at the poor forage.

There was no one around, and then there was. The knife striking at his throat was the first thing Ruff saw, long before his senses registered the bronzed hand which held it, the muscular body behind it. Justice jerked back, striking upward and out with the heavy muzzle of his Spencer. It hit hard, tearing the jawbone of the Sioux before him. Blood rushed from the Indian's throat and he pawed at his face, his eyes wild, dark, and savage.

He was on the ground, writhing, when Justice finished the job with his bowie.

He never heard the approaching footsteps, saw no shadow against the ground. Stone Hand's body collided with Ruff's and his ax fell as Justice jerked his head away, striking back with fists and knees as they tumbled to the earth together, rolling downslope, Ruff's bowie lying where it had landed.

Stone Hand was massive and powerful, quick and deadly. Ruff had his ax hand at the wrist, his leg hooked around the back of the Sioux warrior's knee.

They rolled down the slope, locked together in violent combat, then went off the lip of the stony shelf and dropped thirty feet to the ground below. Their faces were so near that Ruff could feel the Indian's hot breath against his cheek, see the crazed eyes, hear the grunt of effort as Stone Hand fought to tear his ax from Ruff's grip.

They hit the ground hard, and Justice felt the wind rush out of his body. He rolled away—too slowly— and got to his feet in a defensive crouch. It wasn't necessary. None of it was. Stone Hand lay against the earth unmoving, his leg crooked under him.

Walking to him, Ruff first kicked the ax away from the limp hand of the Sioux, then crouched to examine the man. Alive. Bleeding from a head wound. Stone Hand had landed against a saddle-sized rock, his head cracking against it. He lay unconscious, his savagely scarred face nearly peaceful.

Justice bent down, hefted the man, and, throwing him across his shoulder, started downslope toward the flats.

Hart was still holding back when Ruff emerged from the timber, but at the sight of Justice and his burden, the cavalry came forward, closing the distance rapidly. They found Ruff Justice sitting on the inert form of Stone Hand, arms dangling between his legs, cold blue eyes curiously expressionless.

"Is that . . . ?"

"It's him. I got four of them, including Stone Hand. That should be all. You might want to comb the hill, though. I could use my horse. Left a gun, a knife, and a good Stetson up there too if anyone cares to look."

Hart took the suggestion. The cavalrymen clustered around Stone Hand, watching as Hart put the manacles on the still-unconscious man. A lot of suggestions were made about extralegal punishment.

"Skin him. Just nail him to that tree and skin him. If they hang him it's not good enough."

"If you ask me . . ."

Ruff didn't ask. He was leaning against the saddle of his recovered gray horse, watching sundown stain the skies orange and deep crimson above the piny ridge. He ached. His shoulder with the old wounds especially. And his ribcage on the right side, his hip, left arm. He had a dull, constant headache.

"Ready?" Hart rested a hand on Ruff's shoulder, a gesture Justice didn't care for much. Hart was new at Fort Lincoln, however, new in the West—he didn't know the land or its men. He was tall, fair, competent when it came to bookwork, constantly muddled in the field.

"I'm ready."

"You'll get special mention in my report," Hart promised.

"Thanks." Ruff had had special mention—of various kinds—in many reports. It had never gotten him anything tangible. He tightened the cinches to his Texas-rigged saddle and swung up on the gray, which seemed surprised.

When Hart was ready they filed out through the dusky light toward Fort Abraham Lincoln. Stone Hand was tied onto his horse's back, swaying and lurching. He came suddenly alert in the twilight, and his blood-scabbed face set as he saw what had happened. He tried to tear himself free, but his manacles had been lashed securely to the pommel of the saddle, his feet secured by ropes tied beneath the horse's belly. He went nowhere and he sat glaring muttering in his own tongue until he caught sight of Ruff Justice riding beside him.

"You," he said, and his voice was a growl, scarcely human, deep and quite mad, "I will kill. I will kill you if I have to crawl out of my grave to do it!"

Ruff politely burped and guided his gray away from the column. He wasn't in the mood.

Fort Lincoln had been quiet when they rode in through the main gate, the only signs of activity lights in the enlisted barracks and the BOQ, a few men standing in front of the sutler's store drinking beer. Within minutes that all changed as word spread that Stone Hand had been brought in.

Men rushed out of the barracks, lamps were lighted everywhere. Somehow word had spread to the nearby town of Bismarck already, and in spring buggies and on horseback people were racing toward the fort.

Ruff had never cared for a circus, not even Bill Cody's variety. He unsaddled, rubbed his horse down, saw that it was well-grained, and headed back toward his quarters, seeing the gathering mob across the parade ground.

He shaved slowly with his ebony-handled razor, patted his face dry, washed up in the basin, then stretched out, shirtless despite the chill of the evening, on his bunk.

"Mr. Justice?" The voice sounded before the knock on his door and Justice rolled his head to glare at Corporal Willard Trask.

"Yes," he said wearily.

"Colonel MacEnroe would like to see you—in his quarters."

Ruff just stared for a moment. If MacEnroe wanted to slap him on the back or shake his hand, he wanted no part of it. Nor did he want to write a report.

"What is it? Stone Hand?"

"No, sir. I don't think so. Something else has come up."

"All right. Five minutes."

Trask, grinning at some private joke, went out, and Ruff sat up with a small groan, reaching for his shirt. Dressing slowly, he brushed his long dark hair, smoothed his mustache down, strapped on his gunbelt, and went out. Across parade something was still going on. The guardhouse was ringed by spectators, the sort of spectators who turn into lynch mobs; but MacEnroe had a dozen armed guards standing stone-faced around the place, and knowing the colonel, now that the townspeople had had their look, he wouldn't be long in running them off the post.

Ruff strode across the parade ground, achieved the boardwalk, and made his way toward the commanding officer's quarters. Passing the orderly room, he found Fort Lincoln's vastly overweight, amiable first sergeant standing in the doorway, watching the activity across the way.

"Hello, Ruff."

"Mack." Justice nodded to Mack Pierce. "Going to run them off soon?"

"Yes." Mack spat. "Although if it were up to me, I'd as soon let them have him. Tear him apart, they would."

"Vicious tonight, aren't you?"

Pierce laughed. "It's age comin' on me. Still, Stone Hand's no good to anyone. He killed his own wife, you know. Battered one of his kids until the boy's crippled."

"I didn't know that."

"You don't know Bear Foot?" Mack asked with some surprise.

"Bear Foot, sure." He was a well-known hanger-on at the fort. A kid of fifteen or sixteen who hung around the paddock all day, liked to watch the soldiers drill, and who although thrown out every evening at taps returned sharply at reveille the next day. "I just didn't know he was anything to Stone Hand."

"Yep. His kid. The colonel's banned him from the post now. Had to. Could be he'd still do something for his father; could be he'd cut his throat too. Either way, it can't be allowed."

"What's the colonel want me for now, Mac?"

"That?" Pierce smiled. "Now that's a surprise, Ruff. You'll find out."

Justice scowled, nodded a goodnight, and walked along the plankwalk to Colonel MacEnroe's quarters.

He rapped on the colonel's door and was summoned inside. MacEnroe sat with his boots propped up on a low leather-covered hassock, his tunic partly unbuttoned, a glass of whiskey in his hand. It was unusual to see the colonel looking even partially at ease, but he did on this evening.

"Sit down, Ruff. Good piece of work today."

"A lot of curiosity out there."

"I've had them all herded off for tonight. I suppose in the morning they'll be back. Stone Hand is a curiosity. He won't be for long," MacEnroe added soberly, finishing his drink. He stroked his silver mustache thoughtfully. "He's ranting over there. He wants the tall man in buckskins. Swears he'll kill you."

Ruff shrugged. You couldn't go around worrying about things like that. Besides, it didn't look like Stone Hand was going to be killing anyone again.

"He'll be hung day after tomorrow. What I called you over for," MacEnroe said, abruptly changing the subject, "was to find out if you mightn't be interested in doing something a little different."

Ruff's eyes narrowed. MacEnroe's ideas of something a little different had proved highly hazardous in the past.

"Such as?"

"Sit down, Ruff, for God's sake, and quit glaring at me like that. It's nothing like that Spirit Woman business; quite simple, really. But important—to me."

"All right. I'm always agreeable to suggestions you've got," Ruff said, and a flicker of amusement danced in his eyes. MacEnroe shook his head. Yes, he took suggestions—sometimes. Ruff was a maverick, hard-headed, sometimes whimsical, sometimes just plain intractable. He was also the best rough-country scout on the plains, and MacEnroe counted himself lucky to have him, past disagreements aside.

"A friend of mine will be arriving in the morning. Walter Court. We grew up together, separated during the war, met again at Fort Kearney—he was sutler there by that time. Now he's coming to Dakota."

MacEnroe hesitated, "He's going to set up a freight line between here and Bear Creek."

"He is, is he?" Ruff said quietly. Justice was standing next to the fireplace, studying the twisting and turning of the gold-and-crimson flames.

"I know, I know. It's damn close to the Black Hills. Very bad territory, but that's what the man wants to do, and not being able to dissuade him I promised to help. He's hoping for the mail contract, a little passenger trade and miners' supplies."

"He doesn't know the country then, sir." Ruff turned slowly and fixed those icy blue eyes on MacEnroe. "There's the Sioux for starters, some of the roughest up- and downhill country in Dakota, every hijack artist on the plains sitting out there waiting to lift whatever gold they're digging out of Bear Creek now. You mentioned mail and freight— what about Anson Boggs? He's got the mail contract right now, doesn't he?"

"Yes, and you know how well he's handling it. Half of the stuff seems to be rifled before it reaches its destination. The postmaster hasn't got anything on Boggs, but he's damned unhappy with his work. And without the mail contract the freight won't pay its way—too damned far out. So it looks as if Boggs is on his way out."

"And he's supposed to stand still for it?" Ruff wagged his head. Boggs was big, ugly, no good, a drunk with three sons who were exact replicas of the old man down to their slovenly habits.

"It—uh—may be a little difficult at first." The colonel was fond of understatement.

"It may be. What is it you expect me to do, sir?"

"I'd like you to help him set up, that's all. Locate the three stations he's planning on using, trail-blaze, guide him through the first weeks, Ruff. It would mean a lot to me. I owe this man. If I could I'd use my troopers, but you know I can't. You're next best."

Ruff had been mulling it over. There was hazard involved, but there was hazard involved in whatever a man did in these times, in this area. Boggs had had first choice of sites for his way stations, but Justice always thought he had chosen unwisely. There was no water half the time at Columbine Creek, where he had his first station. Nor could he use Walker's Pass during bad weather. That could be improved upon, and if MacEnroe's friend was any kind of a man he could easily improve the service Boggs was offering now.

"Why not?" he said at length. "Beats going after Red Cloud."

"Which reminds me," MacEnroe said, and he was off again on an idea he had for doing just that, if Regiment would lend him another company. Ruff listened politely for half an hour, then headed off to bed.

When he walked to the colonel's office an hour after reveille there were already numbers of people gathered around the stockade, hoping for a glimpse of Stone Hand. A few people, misinformed, had come and gone in disappointment. The hanging wasn't until tomorrow. That would be a big day, Ruff thought, wondering at the species.

There were half a dozen civilian mounts standing in front of the orderly room, and a spring wagon and two pack mules. Walter Court, Ruff decided, had arrived.

Mack Pierce, perspiring, harried, sat at his desk shuffling papers. The corporal of the guard sat in the corner, hands behind his head, looking at a fly on the ceiling.

"Court?" Ruff asked Pierce.

"Yes, dammit," Pierce muttered, and Ruff frowned. "Something the matter?"

"Isn't it?" Mack replied. "Go on in. There's a hell of a surprise waiting for you."

2

Ruff Justice entered the colonel's office and halted with astonishment. The room was full of women, not just women but beautiful, young women. Three of them, to be exact, two of them blond and blue-eyed, the third a Mexican girl with slashing black eyes. They all wore riding costumes—split skirts, loose blouses, high boots.

"Come in, Ruff." MacEnroe looked crushed, extremely morose despite the decorative features of his office.

"Sorry," Justice said. "I assumed this was something to do with the Court affair."

"It is," MacEnroe replied carefully, "something to do with that." He sighed heavily, "Walter Court is dead, Ruff. Drowned crossing the Missouri above Atkinson. These girls are his daughters and their companion, María Salazar."

"Adrienne Court," one of the blondes spoke up. Her voice was brisk, metallic. "This is my sister, Lucille." She looked at the colonel, her mouth tightening. "Now, can we can get down to business?"

MacEnroe looked as if he were going to explode, then he nodded. "Ruff, these young women have decided to pursue their father's project. That is—"

"Dad wanted it," Adrienne said sharply. She was tall, angular, her eyes unswerving, a striking blue without any pleasing softness. "He wanted to finish this project, wanted it to work for us, for me and Lucille. We haven't got a lot else back home. We're going to start this freight line, and we're going to make a go of it."

Ruff heard most of that. During the rest of it he had been busy looking at Lucille, a softer, more rounded version of her sister, with lovely little dimples at the corners of her mouth.

"It's a waste of time," Ruff said finally. "Can't be done."

"Who says so?" Adrienne came half out of her chair.

"That's hard country out there, Miss Court. Maybe you've some sort of romantic notion about how things are, how they should work out—the truth is there's no substitute for raw strength, and if you don't have it, you won't make it out there."

She just stared at him, the muscles at the corners of her jaw flexing, her eyes fixed on those of Ruff Justice.

"Maybe he's right," Lucille said tentatively. "Maybe we should give this idea up, Adie."

"Why? Because this—cowboy, whatever he is, suggests it?"

MacEnroe stepped in, his voice fatherly, bringing amusement to Ruff's eyes. "I've been saying much the same thing to the ladies, Ruff. I'm afraid, Miss Court, my advice would be the same as Mr. Justice's."

"Very well." Adrienne rose. Her chin was lifted, her eyes expressionless, her back rigid. "We shall find the help we need elsewhere."

"Adie!"

"Quiet down, Lucille. We've come to do something. We shall do it, and if the army and our father's dearest old friend won't help, we shall do it alone. There are, I am sure, other *gentlemen* who will assist us."

MacEnroe glanced helplessly at Ruff. "Just a minute, please. Please. You are determined to do this."

"Of course!"

"Ruff . . . they can't possibly do this alone. They need someone who knows the area well."

"What I know isn't enough to help them, sir," Justice answered honestly.

"Come, Lucille. María." The Mexican girl rose, her friendly—very friendly—eyes meeting Ruff's.

"Wait, please. Miss Court." MacEnroe looked pleadingly at Ruff Justice. "I owed Walter Court, Ruff. I owe his daughters as well. If they are determined to do this . . ."

Adrienne looked determined, fanatically determined. Lucille simply looked bewildered, and Justice tried to imagine her with a buffalo rifle in her hands holding back a swarm of Sioux warriors. She belonged in silks and satins in someone's drawing room . . . or in someone's bed. Maybe it was her helpless look more than anything which determined him, or the dark-eyed, curiously frank eyes of María Salazar. Ruff Justice heard himself saying:

"All right. I'll give it a try if you won't reconsider."

"We'll be in Bismarck. I've purchased three freight wagons and hired two men. We may need them for something," she said disparagingly. Then with a "Come, María; come, Lucy," she strode out of the colonel's office, followed by her sister and María Salazar, whose hips swayed enticingly, who glanced back across her shoulder at Ruff Justice and flashed a white, encouraging smile.

By the time the door banged shut MacEnroe had already grabbed for his whiskey bottle, and pouring a drink he sat muttering and cursing under his breath.

"Well?" MacEnroe was leading back in his chair,

his fingers drumming on his desk top. "What do you think?"

"I think I'd rather wrestle Stone Hand, is what I think. If that young woman's serious about this, and she seems to be, she's walking into a lot of trouble, taking the other two with her. She's be better off to sell the mail contract, salvage what she can, and get the hell out of here."

"You'll tell her that?"

"I'll tell her again—but it won't do a bit of good. She's determined, that one. I only wish she wasn't determined to do something so foolhardy. Anson Boggs will be having himself a good laugh when he hears about it."

"I hope he does laugh it off," MacEnroe said more seriously. "There's a streak of pure nastiness in that man. No telling what he'd get up to—which is another reason I'd like you to go along with me on this, foolishness or not."

"There'll come a time when I can't be around, sir. You know that."

"I know it. Dammit, I know it, Ruff. What else is there to do?" The answer, apparently, was to knock back another stiff drink, since that was exactly what MacEnroe did.

Justice picked up some supplies at the sutler's store, saddled the gray, and rode off toward Bismarck. His only hope was that the women had been wise enough to pick some good men to help them out, although two would hardly be enough.

The women were easy enough to find. There was a large-scale commotion at the freight yard Andy Conklin ran on Bismarck's east end. Ruff rode up and sat the gray, watching and listening.

"You can't use horses on these rigs, miss. You've got to have oxen."

"But we have no oxen, sir," Adrienne Court snapped

back. "You will simply have to give us other wagons which are suitable to horses—and I suppose we shall have some money coming back to us if the new wagons are smaller."

"I got no other wagons!" Conklin said, wiping his high forehead with his red handkerchief. "I sold you these. These are what you asked for."

"Then you will simply have to find some others for us somewhere," the blonde said, waving a hand to indicate the matter was closed.

"I'll try," Conklin said through clenched teeth. "I really will try." If it will get rid of you, his expression added.

María Salazar wasn't around—Ruff looked—but he spotted Lucille Court standing near a newly painted, newly greased Concord stagecoach, and he swung down from his horse to walk toward her. A small, ancient Chinese was sitting on the boot, watching Willie Canbury whittle a formless piece of wood into something equally formless, but apparently pleasing to both men. Willie was a moron, but he came by it honestly. His entire family bordered on the moronic.

Willie at least had a saving grace; he was a likable moron. He had a thicketlike stand of red hair on top of his bullet-shaped skull, one wildly protuberant buck tooth which emphasized the general crookedness of his features, a wild spattering of freckles, and an elfin grin. He had just about learned his right foot from his left.

"Morning," Ruff said, and Lucy Court, who had been looking the other way, nearly jumped out of her skin.

"Oh—hello." She watched her sister berate Andy Conklin for a moment longer. "I don't know how she gets away with that." She shuddered. "Such a lot of nerve."

"How's everything going in general?" Ruff asked.

He glanced across his shoulder. Willie had begun laughing, his mouth hanging open as he held up the formless piece of wood for the Chinaman's inspection.

"Oh, well enough, I suppose—are you very tall?" she asked suddenly. "You seem very tall." She touched her pale hair tentatively and then looked down at the ground as Ruff's gaze met hers.

"I'm taller than some. You have horses and your sister's working on the wagons. Is this your coach?"

"Yes." Lucy looked at it doubtfully "I suppose it is."

"Men. You have men to work for you, your sister said."

"Why, yes . . ." She blinked at Ruff and frowned. Her finger slowly lifted. "There they are."

"Who?"

"Mr. Lo and Mr. Canbury."

"Mr. . . ." Ruff looked at Willie Canbury and the Chinese. "They're working for you?" he asked in disbelief.

"Yes. Mr. Lo is a wonderful cook. We shall need a cook for the drivers and passengers, you see." She repeated that as something learned from her sister, who had likely learned it by rote from their father.

"And Willie?"

"They say he's very good with horses."

"That's true. But the rest of your crew . . ."

"Rest?" Lucy blinked again. Her soft white hand rested unexpectedly on Ruff's arm. "You're at least six foot three, aren't you?"

Ruff was saved from answering by the arrival of Adrienne Court. She stalked toward her sister and Justice, waving a piece of paper, her blue eyes afire, her mouth grim.

"It's only because I'm a woman," she said loudly. "He's trying to cheat me. If my father were alive . . . and where have you been, Mr. Justice?" She glanced at a watch which was pinned to her nicely filled white blouse. "Never mind—probably some ridiculous excuse. Here's a list of things you'll need."

"Need for what?"

"You'll have to build three way stations, won't you? You'll need saws, axes, grindstones, mortar, nails, planes . . ." The list she handed Ruff was in a man's hand. More of Walter Court's legacy.

Ruff took the list and tucked it away. "Listen, Miss Court. You need some men . . ." Willie Canbury had broken into a jig. As he danced he chanted something that sounded like a Blackfoot rain song. Dust drifted over all of them. "These two won't do at all."

"If you must know, they're all I could get. I can't find a man who'll work for a woman."

Or for this particular woman, Ruff thought without saying it.

"There are always men around willing to work," he told her instead, "if you're offering decent wages. Thing is, that's likely to be dangerous work, and they're probably not too eager to stick their necks out for a dollar a day."

"A dollar a day—I couldn't pay that."

Ruff just stared at her. "What are you trying to get them for?"

"Shares, of course. That's what my father was going to do—offer them shares in the freight line. They'll make out much better in the long run."

"Yes, except most of them would rather have silver in their pockets against starvation and such."

"They would only drink it all up—my father warned me about that."

Ruff was getting a little tired of Walter Court, whom he had never met. "You'll have to use cash or you haven't a chance of getting anyone."

"Then we'll go ahead with what we have. Three good men, three good women."

"That equals up to six good graves."

"Don't be dramatic, Mr. Justice. We shall make do." She spotted Andy Conklin across the yard, and he didn't duck quick enough. She started after him, waving a hand. "Mr. Conklin!"

"I know," Lucille said when Ruff looked away, shaking his head. "She's very forceful, isn't she?"

"That's one word for it," Ruff replied, wondering how MacEnroe would take it if he rode back to Fort Lincoln and respectfully declined this assignment.

"What are you going to do?" Lucille asked, and again her hand rested on Ruff's arm. He looked down into those blue eyes which were innocent and womanly at once.

Ruff shrugged. "Buy some tools and supplies, it looks like. Want to come along?"

"I'd like it very much. I'll get some money from Adrienne and meet you at your horse."

"Fine. We need some kind of a wagon, though. Remind your sister of that."

"I will." Her dazed eyes swept up and down Ruff, then she spun around on a dainty heel and walked across the freightyard. Ruff tried to strike up an acquaintance with his new associates.

"Hello, Willie."

"Hai-ya-ya-hai-huh!" Willie danced, grinning stupidly.

"Sure." The Chinese was smiling, his head bobbing up and down, watching the dance. "I guess you're Lo. I'm Ruff Justice." He stuck out a hand, and the Chinese took it, chattering rapidly in a sing-song tongue which made as much sense to Ruff as Willie Canbury's chanting did.

"Nice to've met you." He touched his hat brim

and walked to where Lucille waited by the big gray gelding.

"All ready." She held up and jingled a leather sack.

"How about a wagon?"

"She says we'll have to use the stagecoach if you can't figure out how to manage yourself."

Ruff grunted something Lucy pretended not to hear. "I'll see if the storekeeper will bring the load over here and deliver. Where's María?" Ruff asked as they started uptown, Justice leading his gray.

"Do you like her?" Lucille asked.

"If I don't, will you tell me where she is?" Justice asked a little grouchily.

"Men like her. She flaunts it."

"A little flaunting is all right sometimes. Where *is* she?"

"Dancing."

"Pardon me?"

"The saloon has a Spanish guitar player. María decided to dance, so she's dancing. I think she's already had a drink or two as well," Lucille said in a confidential tone.

"Has she." A phrase of Adrienne's was dancing through his head. *Three good men, three good women.* A shrew, a mouse, a Spanish dancer; a halfwit, a chinaman, a crazy scout. "Nothing to do but play along until the woman comes to her senses," Ruff mumbled.

"I heard that. She won't, you know. She's very single-minded, is Adrienne."

"I noticed. Tell me, Lucille, do you like this idea?"

"No. I didn't like it when it was my father's idea, I don't like it now, but what is there to do?" A tiny shrug lifted her shoulders. They crossed the dusty

street, and Ruff tied the gray at the hitchrail before
the general store.

Two men in their thirties dozed in the sun before
the store, hats tugged low. One looked up as Ruff
stepped onto the boardwalk.

"Either of you need work?" Justice asked.

Eyes shifted to Lucille and back to Ruff. "You
with that crazy Court woman?"

"Afraid so."

"No thanks." The other man just laughed.

"For cash money?"

"Not for love nor money." A hat was tugged down
again, arms folded, and Ruff led Lucille into the
store.

Justice was in a bad mood. He was thinking about
the three way stations he was apparently expected to
build by himself. Lucille was going to be no help; he
knew that when he picked up a crosscut saw and she
asked innocently, "What's that?"

"Horse trimmer," he said. "In case Adrienne gets
horses that are too long."

"Oh." She blinked three times in rapid succession,
but said nothing else. Ruff banged the saw on the
counter and walked among the tools, selecting a lot
of things that looked like they just might—unfor-
tunately—fit his hand.

The storekeeper said he'd deliver to the freightyard.
His little eyes gleamed with avarice. Ruff bought
tools enough for three men—optimistically—three
barrels of flour, lard, salt, dried fruit, coffee, matches,
and three spanking new Henry repeating rifles.

"What are those for?" Lucille asked.

"I hope you'll never find out." Paying off the
storekeeper, they went out again into the glare and
uproar of the day. Women's screams filled the air,
and looking down the street Justice saw a knot of
people surge out of the Bucket of Beer Saloon and

push on into the street. At the center of the distur-
bance were two grappling women, shrieking, tearing
at each other's clothes, pulling hair, kicking.

One of them was María Salazar.

Ruff loped up the street, leaving Lucille on the
boardwalk, her hands to her mouth. A crowd of
drinking men stood around the women urging them
on. As Ruff reached the perimeter of the mob, the
redheaded woman in María's grasp reached up, yanked
back on María's hair, and threw her off balance.
They toppled to the ground in a flash of petticoats
and black stockings.

Ruff shouldered into the crowd.

"What the hell are you doing?" Ruff's shoulder
was grabbed and he was spun around.

"Breaking it up. Sorry."

"The hell you are—I like a catfight."

"Better back off, Dusty. That's Ruff Justice."

"The man that brought in Stone Hand, huh? I
don't give a damn who it is," Dusty said loudly.

"Back off, friend," Ruff said quietly, but the big
man didn't read the signals right. He still had a grip
on Ruff's shoulder, and now the hand tightened.
Ruff knew how much point there was in talking to
someone like Dusty. Besides, he had given one
warning.

Justice's fist dug into the big man's stomach and he
doubled up. While he was bent over at the waist,
Justice lifted his knee savagely and the man was
slammed backward against his friends, his nose
smashed and bleeding. Ruff pushed on through the
crowd, yanked a wildly flailing María to her feet, and
shouldered her.

"I'll kill her! Let me go!"

Her dress was torn, her face dirty, her hair snarled,
but she was ready for more.

"Come on."

Ruff turned, the girl kicking and screaming as he carried her through the jeering crowd. He walked across the street and deposited her on her bottom on the boardwalk while Lucille, wringing her hands, stared.

Ruff looked at both of them for a long minute, then turned toward his horse.

"Where are you going?" Lucille asked desperately.

"To have a few words with your sister. Trail along if you want."

He yanked the gray's head around and headed back to the freightyard. Adrienne was still there, leaning over a painter's shoulder as he lettered "Great Western" on the stagecoach in gilt.

She turned, hands on hips, as Ruff swung down. "Well? Have you something to say?" she demanded.

"Plenty. You've got no business being out here. What you've got hold of is too big for you to chew. What you are going to accomplish, Miss Court, is getting your sister and yourself killed along with Lo and Canbury—and possibly me, assuming I don't pull out. There's men around who know how to handle a job like you've got in mind, but you'll have to pay them to get them to work for you. And you'll have to give up this little dictator act. You'll have to get some good advice and take it, or everything your father tried to do for you is going to be wasted, the money thrown away, you left stranded and broke in an exceedingly hostile land."

"Is that quite all?" she asked, her lips barely moving.

"That's it. And I mean this is it—I'm through if you don't get some men hired on, men who know what they're doing. Fighting men, because there's going to be a fight of one sort or another down the line. Believe me."

"Fine." Her mouth puckered up, those unwavering blue eyes settled on Ruff's. What a beautiful woman,

Ruff couldn't help thinking, but she seemed to be made out of plaster, set, rigid; there was no softness to be detected anywhere. "Now—with your permission, Mr. Justice—I should like to tell you my news. I have hired six men. Six very competent-appearing men . . . while you were off wasting time. Hardy?"

A wide-shouldered, dark-bearded man in range clothes appeared from the other side of the coach. He had his thumbs hooked into his belt, a wad of tobacco in one cheek, black eyes on Ruff Justice.

"Hardy Pierce, my new line boss. Hardy, introduce Mr. Justice to the rest of the men."

3

It was a minute before any introductions were made. Justice stood there looking at the big man beside Adrienne Court. Both of them looked pleased with themselves. Ruff was far from pleased.

He knew Hardy Pierce well enough. Pierce had drifted into Bismarck a few months back and hung on with no visible means of support. With a few cronies he would ride out of town, stay gone a week or two, and return with money in his pockets and unbelievable tales of fur-trapping or buffalo hunting to account for it. As far as Justice knew, the law wasn't after Pierce—but a lot of folks thought that was just because he hadn't slipped up yet. It was only a matter of time separating Hardy Pierce and the hangman's rope.

"What's the matter, Mr. Justice?" Pierce asked, turning his head to spit.

"You've a fair idea. Miss Court, this isn't the sort of man you want working for you."

"No?" She shrugged as if it were a matter of indifference. "He's strong and willing. At least he didn't have to be forced into it, as you did."

"No." There wasn't much to say. The trouble was, if Hardy Pierce saw a good enough reason to take this job, he was also reason to stay around. Nothing but desperation could turn Pierce to honest labor—he

33

was up to something. "Let's see the rest of them," Justice said.

"You do understand, don't you?" Adrienne Court said. "Colonel MacEnroe told you what your duties were. This is not your outfit, Justice. I'm in charge, and after me Mr. Pierce. That's the way it is."

Ruff bit down on his lip. He wouldn't say it, swore he wouldn't, but he came close. He turned sharply on his heel and followed Pierce to the wagon shed, where five men waited, three of them standing by while two soaped down the harness.

It was just about what Justice had figured on—three of them were part of Price's regular mob. Two, the Olmstead brothers, both tall and blond, both wearing mustaches, one a half-Indian named Luke who seemed to have no last name and who was very fond of a knife.

"What the hell are you up to, Pierce?" Ruff wanted to know.

"Up to?" Pierce's face was innocent.

"This isn't your type of show. Nothing that calls for work is."

"I've turned over a new leaf, Justice. The boys and I wanted to get into something with a future."

"Is that your idea or Anson Boggs'?"

"Anson Boggs? Oh, yeah. He's the man with the mail contract, isn't he?" Pierce didn't laugh out loud, but he chortled way back in his throat, sounding something like a chicken with a bass voice.

"I'll tell you about it right now," Ruff Justice said, looking from Pierce to the Olmstead brothers and the breed. "You screw this up and I'm going to be all over you. You wouldn't like that very much, Hardy."

"Mean, ain't he?" the older Olmstead said, and Justice, turning without any hesitation at all, jammed the heel of his hand against the man's nose. Blood spewed out, and when Olmstead tried to grab for his gun, Ruff backheeled him and pushed. Olmstead went down hard on the seat of his pants. He tried to rise, cussing and spitting. Ruff sat him down again, using a short right hook.

Justice spun back to face Pierce, but the big man hadn't moved. "Wally gets a little excited," Hardy said, stroking his beard. "I'll explain things to him. There won't be any more trouble."

There couldn't have been a way to say that which promised trouble more. Hardy Pierce brushed past Ruff, helped Wally Olmstead to his feet, and led the group out into the sunlight beyond the shed door, the Indian, slouching, hand near his knife, filing out last.

Ruff turned his attention to the other two, who had continued to work, rubbing saddle soap into the old harness, trying to restore suppleness.

"Which side are you on?" he asked the old-timer with the corncob pipe.

"Too old to take sides," he answered dryly. "Name's Rupert Gates. The lady hired me to work, and I'm workin' until someone tells me I'm fired. Just tell me who's ranny and what you want done."

"I'm ranny. You listen to me and we'll get along. The lady—I suppose you'll have to do what she says too unless it sounds too damned silly."

"All right," the old man said with some irritation. "We goin' to jaw all the time on this job, or be left alone to accomplish somethin'?"

"I'll leave you alone." Ruff smiled. "You can shoot, can't you?"

The old man straightened up. He took the pipe out of his mouth and said testily, "You're Ruff Justice, ain'tcha?"

"That's right."

"Son, I been shootin' since you was in diapers. Now let me be, I got some stitchin' and smithin' and hammerin' to do before this tree and harness are ready."

"How about you?" Ruff asked the last man.

"Me?" He was an open-faced, freckled kid with light-brown hair, perhaps twenty years old, broad in the shoulders, with big hands, looking like he'd been fed on milk and cornbread. "I'm like Rupert—here to work. The rest of it I don't understand, don't want to."

"And you can shoot."

The kid actually blushed. "Yes, a little they tell me. I'm Allie James."

"Kin to Rod James?"

"His brother. Baby brother."

"You can shoot."

Rod James was a scout with General Crook, and he knew which end of a gun was which. If the kid was half as good, he would do.

Justice went out into the sunlight, saw Adrienne standing with Pierce, glaring at him, swerved aside, and caught up the reins to his gray. He swung aboard and walked his horse that way.

"I'm riding out a way," he said, tugging his hat lower. "Come straight out the west road. Your route will be on it for quite a way, maybe as far as Bitter Creek. I'll catch up with you tonight."

"What exactly are you going to do, Mr. Justice?" Adrienne asked, her eyes narrowing. Pierce, damn him, was grinning.

"Check out the road. Look for Indian sign. Count squirrels." Anything, but he wanted to get away from that woman, out of town for a time. He turned the gray and walked it up the main street, looking neither right nor left. Then he was out onto the plains, the town falling away into the horizon. He heeled the gray into a gallop and let it run for a way, stretching its muscles, and when he finally halted near a nameless feeder creek and looked back he could see nothing of Bismarck, nothing of Adrienne Court, and it was just fine that way.

The horse drank from the creek, and Ruff walked along the road, looking at the crossing. Despite what he had said to Adrienne, he had been looking over the road as he came west. Boggs's big wagons had torn it up pretty bad, but then it had never been meant for anything but horse traffic anyway. People around here didn't use roads much; there weren't any. But for heavy freight wagons there had to be something approaching a road.

Here, at the creek crossing, Boggs had driven his heavy high-wheeled wagons up the bank on the far side until it was cut deeply with ruts. He had apparently made no attempt to drag it, although he was the only one who had a use for it—or had been until now.

Ruff swung aboard the gray again and rode across the creek through the willows and cottonwoods. From atop the hillrise beyond he could see far out onto the plains, see the purple thrust of the Rocky Mountains through the haze of distances. The grass was good— Adrienne would have no trouble about feed for some months to come, but someone would have to cut wagonload after wagonload of it if her horses were to be kept through a hard winter. He wondered if she realized what a freight team or mail coach would have to go through in winter out here. He expected not.

"Miss Court," he said to the gray, which pricked up its ears uncertainly, "You have cut yourself a large portion of trouble. Bad roads, bad winters, prowling Indians, Mr. Anson Boggs, uncertain water, snakes, dust, and boredom. I almost pity you, lady."

Someone with a lot of know-how and stamina would have to stick with this job, and it couldn't be Ruff even if he wanted to. It wasn't a matter of building way stations, scouting out the terrain, buying horses and wagons, cutting feed. It was a matter of staying with it, being willing and able to fight through the problems, the bad men, the Sioux, every single day, for something unexpected was going to come along on almost every run . . . and for the life of him Ruff Justice couldn't see how the lady was going to make it.

"Colonel," he muttered, "I'll try to get 'em started, but damn me, I wish Walter Court hadn't been so careless as to get himself drowned!"

Squinting into the distance now, he could see a plume of dust back toward Bismarck, and he guessed it to be Adrienne and her party. He mentally gauged their progress and decided they would probably camp at or near the old skinners' shack. Maybe it would serve as a reminder to them all—the skinners who had once lived there had been murdered by Indians.

Ruff rode on, unwilling to turn back until he had to. He had fished some salt biscuits and jerky out of his provision sack, and he chewed on these, his knee hooked around his saddlehorn as he rode through the willows and sycamores which were rife along this stretch of the creek.

He found what looked to be a better stretch of ground for the wagons to follow upcreek, crossed the stream for the third time, and again rode into the highlands. Three miles or so beyond the point where the brush and trees gave way to flat, yellow grass plains, he could make out Columbine Creek and Anson Boggs's first way station.

It was kind to call the Columbine a creek, although it ran well in the springtime, swollen with snowmelt. In the summer there was no water or the next thing to no water there.

He took a deep drink from his canteen, washing down the salt of his meal, and rode on, near enough to look down into Boggs's back yard. There was a dilapidated gray wood building which served as shelter, a second dilapidated shack for the horses—it was a toss-up which building was the better—and a rough pole corral. There was a litter of rusted cans, old tools, and broken equipment beside the house.

Justice was thinking that if he routed Adrienne's wagons up into the low piny hills to the north there was a good site near Coyote Springs an hour or an hour and a half on—it had water and grass and the advantage of terrain. Also it wouldn't be necessary to pass Boggs's way station.

Ruff thought of that with one portion of his mind; with the other portion he was thinking of his backtrail, of the man who was following him.

There was someone back there, and he was very good, but not that good. It's not easily done over open country, and twice Justice had seen the man's horse, at this distance colorless as the man was featureless.

It wasn't coincidence. Ruff had swerved sharply away from any traveled route as he considered the Coyote Springs station, and his companion had stayed with him.

Now Justice rode into the scattered timber along the hills. He unsheathed his Spencer, turned the gray, and doubled back, paralleling his trail but staying out of sight of it.

He found a deep thicket of scrub oak and pine where the insects hummed. A rattler slithered away as Ruff walked his gray into the thicket and hunkered down to wait.

He didn't have to wait long. Half an hour later he heard the crunch of a horse's hoofs over leaf litter and twigs. Ruff eased back the hammer of his Spencer, and when the rider walked his bay past the thicket, Ruff stepped out behind him.

"Hands in the air."

The hands went up immediately. "I see it's all true. You are that good."

"Quiet." Ruff walked nearer, circling the horse, staying a good distance away, the .56 trained on the somehow familiar man.

Justice faced the man, noted the position of his weapons—an old Schofield pistol thrust into his belt, a Winchester in the saddle boot.

"I know you, don't I? What are you up to, friend?"

"Just riding," Bear Foot answered with a smile, and Justice frowned. Stone Hand's son "just riding" behind him wasn't something he cared for.

"No. You're on my trail, Bear Foot. I don't like it."

"I wanted to talk to you," the kid said, leaning forward. "Can I swing down?"

Ruff nodded. The kid's English was very good. He had spent much time hanging around Fort Lincoln. His clothes were old cavalry trousers, old army shirt with a sergeant's stripes hastily cut off, a battered slouch hat with a feather in the band.

The kid got clumsily to the ground, and Ruff noticed that one leg was shorter than the other, the foot turned in.

Bear Foot followed Ruff's eyes with his own. "Yes," he said, laughing. "A cripple. My father did this to me, you know."

"Did he?"

"Yes." Bear Foot sat on the ground, holding the reins to his horse over his shoulder. "I hate the man. Tomorrow he will hang and I will be there to watch. To watch and to laugh."

"We all have our big days."

"It is you I have to thank. That is why I followed you out here. I wanted to tell you that you have done me a favor."

"And now you've told me," Ruff said. The Spencer hadn't wavered a bit. Bear Foot could look right down that tunnel-sized muzzle.

"Yes." The kid was quiet for a moment. He sighed. "I have told you now. And I will tell you this—I am your friend, Ruff Justice. I will do anything you ask. You have caught my vengeance for me. Whatever you wish, I will do it."

"Fine. Ride out then, and stay off my backtrail. I'll likely shoot next time, Bear Foot."

"I understand," the Indian said cheerfully. "It must be that way." He rose, dusting himself off, swung into the saddle, and nodded before turning his horse and walking it in the opposite direction, back toward Bismarck. Ruff watched him go, wondering. He reflected that Bear Foot could have caught up with him at Fort Lincoln if all he had wanted to do was thank him.

If he had wanted to kill him, however, it would be necessary to track him out here.

Justice recovered his gray, gave it another fifteen minutes, then headed back toward the wagon trail himself, the sun at his back sinking slowly toward the mountains, flushing the long plains to a red-violet, bringing the birds to air, winging homeward as the shadows grew long.

There were three freight wagons back under the cottonwoods surrounding the old skinners' shack, the stagecoach drawn up beside them. The horses were picketed in the long grass, though not hobbled. A campfire burned too brightly near the stack of bleached buffalo bones beyond the old tumbled-in well.

There was beef frying, coffee boiling, when Ruff Justice walked into the camp. Rupert Gates and Allie James sat to one side eating beans and beef off tin plates. The Chinese cook hovered over the fire, wearing a starched white apron. Willie Canbury sat alone, staring at one thumb for some reason.

"Welcome back, scout," Hardy Pierce said. He was slouched against a fallen cottonwood, a cigarette in his thick lips, flanked by the Olmstead boys. Ruff didn't bother to answer, and Hardy Pierce laughed loudly.

Ruff helped himself to coffee and walked to where Adrienne with María and Lucille stood eating off the tailgate of one of the wagons.

"You did come back," Adrienne said, her voice clicking metallically. "Mr. Pierce wagered you wouldn't return."

"Hello." Lucille smiled uncertainly, and Ruff nodded.

"Been off killing bad Indians?" María Salazar asked teasingly.

"Sure. Got a dozen or so. How about you? Been staying out of fist fights?"

She threw back her head and laughed, exposing white, straight teeth. "Yes. That bitch in town, she was jealous of her man, you know. Me, I was just a-dancing with him for a little fun. Got too mad."

"Most women would be jealous of you," Ruff said.

"Yes?" Her eyebrows grew together. "You bet—if you know me better, huh? I think so."

"Please, María," Adrienne said.

María shrugged. "Is just the truth."

"Did you learn anything useful from your expedition?" Adrienne asked.

"A little." He told her sketchily about the road, the site at Coyote Springs. She seemed unimpressed, and finally answered:

"Well, I suppose I have to take your word for it."

Then, picking up her empty plate, she strode off toward the campfire, Ruff watching her.

"Has she always been like that?" Ruff asked Lucille.

"She's been under a strain," the girl answered. "So have we all," she added. "Excuse me, I'm tired."

It took Ruff a moment to figure out she wanted to climb up in the wagon where the sisters had made their beds. He helped her up and watched as Lucille dropped the canvas flaps.

"You take me for a walk?" María asked, and Ruff smiled.

"Sure. Nice to have someone friendly around."

"Oh, I'm very friendly," María said, and she slipped her arm through his.

They walked away from the fire and off into the trees. There was a yellow moon rising in the east. An owl spoke from the oaks and was answered by another farther off. María held Ruff's arm tightly, her head on his shoulder.

"You were pretty rough with me today," she said with mock petulance. "You gave me a pretty big bruise on my backside. You ought to see it."

"I wouldn't mind," Justice answered.

"No?" María stepped away, turned her back, and flipped her striped skirt up. She wore nothing underneath. Ruff couldn't make out the bruise, but he had a spectacular glimpse of smooth, honey-colored buttocks, strong, tapered thighs.

"You see?" She was looking around at him, her black hair falling loose, her eyes sparkling.

"Can't really see the bruise," Ruff said.

"You can feel the bump there," she said in response. "Go ahead."

"Seems dangerous."

"I am dangerous, Mr. Justice. Very bad, very rough." Her voice changed, smoothed out and softened as Ruff's hands searched for a bump on that smooth, muscular flesh. He found none, he found nothing to mar the silky surface.

"Maybe it was a little lower," she said, her voice growing furry.

"About here." His hand slipped between her thighs and lifted slowly, and María spread her legs slightly, crouching down a little.

"Find it?" she asked.

"No."

"Make one then, Mr. Justice. Make a bump for me."

She was pulling her blouse over her head, slithering out of her skirt, and in seconds she stood before him naked in the moonlight, smooth, darkly beautiful. Her breasts, dark-nippled, full, jutted out at him. Ruff's eyes swept across her, following the contours of her finely molded body.

"So? So, you like it," she said, and she moved against him, Ruff's arms going around her. María's hand dropped to his crotch and she felt the growing bulge there. "You like it. Come on. Come on, Mr. Justice."

She led him deeper into the trees, then, getting to her knees, she slowly undid his belt and tugged his trousers down as Ruff shed the buckskin shirt. He felt her lips creep across his hard thighs, felt her probing fingers find and encircle his erection, trace patterns across the head of it.

"Nice," she said. "It is very nice. Come on, come on down to me," she breathed, and Ruff did so. They made a hasty bed of his buckskins and her skirt, and María, rolling to hands and knees, reached back between her legs, her fingers grasping, wriggling impatiently.

She sighed happily when she found him and eased him forward, fitting him into her body. Ruff rested his hands on her buttocks and moved in, slowly sinking into her as María shuddered and laid her head down on the ground. He could see her eyes, moonlit and distant, see her teeth as she breathed heatedly through her mouth. Her hand reached back again and cupped his sack, drawing it tight against her warm, moist flesh.

She began to sway, to pitch against him, and Ruff felt her alter inside, felt a rush of fluid, felt her clutching hand, heard her hectic breathing as she rolled her hips against his pelvis, searching for and finding a sudden hard sensation which brought an astonished gasp to her lips.

She collapsed beneath him, and Ruff followed her down, his hands reaching around, finding her full warm breasts, teasing the taut nipples as she writhed beneath him, panting in a deep cadence.

Ruff could hold back no longer, didn't want to, and he reached a hard, draining climax which pleasured María. She began to tremble again, her inner muscles clasping, relaxing, rippling as she came again.

Without losing him she rolled onto her back, and Ruff's lips went to her breasts, her throat, as her long fingers stroked his dark hair.

"You do it so nice. Very nice, Ruff Justice." She purred with soft satisfaction as Ruff's hands and lips roamed her body, and he felt her relax, her cramped thighs go slack, her heartbeat slowing.

"Hombre," she hissed suddenly into his ear, clutching at his shoulders. "Someone is behind us."

"You sure?" Ruff was already rolling from her. It wasn't embarrassment that caused him to move so quickly and grab for his holstered Colt, which had been within reach at all times. It was the thought of a bullet neatly piercing both of them, leaving them to lie forever in a lovers' embrace.

Ruff glanced at María, who was sitting up, wide-eyed, then he was into the trees, naked, the Colt in his hand. He heard someone ahead, running across the leaf-littered earth, and he halted.

There was no need to pursue. The moonlight showed clearly a double set of footprints. Someone with a very small foot had been crouched in the trees watching. A woman.

Ruff stood there, gun dangling. Then he shook his head and walked back to María, who was already dressed, trying to comb the grass out of her dark, sleek hair with her fingers.

"It is all right?" she asked.

"All right," he replied, snatching up his pants, dressing as María watched him with enjoyment.

"Thank you," she said. Then she went to tiptoes and kissed his cheek, walking off through the dark trees, the moon shadows, her fluid hips swaying, whistling a little tune.

4

The wagons rolled out in the morning. The dawn sun cast crooked shadows before the horses. Ruff Justice rode in the lead, his eyes searching the empty land before them. He hadn't quite shaken Bear Foot out of his mind.

Nor María Salazar. He smiled at the memory. She had been just the same this morning over coffee. Brash, cheerful, mocking. Only once did she look at Ruff, her eyes softening, the smile on her lips turning from mockery to deep pleasure.

Ruff shifted in the saddle and looked back at those following.

Rupert Gates drove the lead wagon. The old man sat the seat casually, deftly handling the reins. Allie James, who drove the second wagon, the one with the building supplies, was making more work of it, but the kid was trying.

The third wagon carried Lo and Willie Canbury. They jabbered away happily to each other, neither understanding a word the other said.

The breed, Luke, drove the stagecoach, which trailed the train. The women rode inside in something approaching comfort. The Olmstead boys and Hardy Pierce rode on the flanks, too distant for Ruff to hear their conversation, to see the expression on their faces, but he knew. He knew that something stank about Pierce and his crew. They simply weren't working men, probably didn't know what the words meant.

That was Adrienne's problem.

What came next was Ruff's.

They came up over the hillrise flanked by ranks of blue spruce, their tips lighted by the morning sun. The road was narrow, the horses straining at the harnesses, when the Boggs freight wagon came roaring down the slope, the driver's whip singing over the ears of the lead team.

The driver's eyes widened and he jammed on the brake, locking his foot against it, drawing back savagely on the reins, trying to halt the horses he had been whipping into a lather the moment before.

"You stupid son of a bitch!" he shouted at Justice. "You dumb bastards! Get the hell out of my way. Can't you see I'm rolling loaded?"

It was one of Boggs's sons, Rigger as they called him—big, mean, and ugly. Hard on his heels now came a second wagon highballing it over the crest of the hill. This one too was driven by a Boggs. This one too jammed on the long-levered brake, sloughed to a sideways stop, and sat cussing as his lathered horses buckled at the knees, tossed their heads, and whickered in confusion.

Rigger was already out of the box, striding toward Ruff Justice, his whip in his hand.

"Get down off that horse and I'll teach you something," he shouted at Ruff.

"I'd rather not," Justice answered calmly. "If you don't mind, why don't you back those wagons now. Uphill traffic's generally got the right of way."

"Why you nervy bastard, don't you know who I am?"

"Some fool trying to see how fast he can kill a team of horses," Ruff answered. He sat the gray easily, the sheathed Spencer across the saddlebow, his hat tugged low. "Back 'em up," Justice said. "Please."

"Damn you . . ." Rigger Boggs started sputtering with rage. He took another step and started to heft that long-handled whip he carried. Ruff kicked him in the face.

Rigger sprawled back, his face a mask of blood. He staggered against the lead wheel horse's shoulder, and the animal reared up in fright. From the corner of his eyes Justice saw the other Boggs boy leap from the box of his wagon, gun in hand. The rifle crack sang in Ruff's ear and he saw the Boggs boy go down, clutching his thigh.

"And you're lucky it wasn't through the brisket," Rupert shouted. The old man had been telling the truth—he could shoot.

"For God's sake!" The voice was Adrienne's. "What is going on here? What are you trying to do, Justice?"

"Just trying to get up the hill, ma'am."

"And starting a war over it? What difference does it make who goes first? We could have backed down."

"And the next time?" Boggs was crawling toward the wagon. His brother lay, still clutching his leg, howling in pain. From the rear Pierce and his men were riding up fast.

"What do you mean?" Adrienne asked, her voice edged with anger.

"I mean, will you back down again next time, and the next? You're going to be using this little piece of road for a long while. You can't back down every time a Boggs rig wants to roll over you. There's certain little rules of the road—uphill freight has the right of way. There's also rules of behavior—that means you don't come cussin' and bullin' your way past a man unless you mean to take some back. I couldn't back down, nor can you. They may as well know we won't right now."

"Madness!" Her hands flew into the air. "You're crazy, blood-crazy!"

"How is he?" Ruff asked Allie James, who had gone to look at Boggs's leg.

"I didn't even bother to bandage it. It's just a nick. Of course," the kid added, tilting his hat back and grinning, "after what he called me just now I wouldn't have bandaged it anyway."

"What's going on here?" It was Hardy Pierce, his horse lathered. Adrienne gave him her version. Ruff said nothing. "Well," Pierce said at last, "it's over. Rigger! Back that freight on up. We're coming through."

"Yeah." Boggs's voice was rough, but Justice could have sworn a look of some kind passed between the two men. It didn't surprise him a bit; he was still working under the assumption that Anson Boggs had planted Pierce here.

"Someone help my brother up!" Rigger screamed. No one would. He had to climb down and do it himself. Fifteen minutes later they had backed to a wide spot in the trail, and Justice, looking neither right nor left, led the wagon train past.

Even Adrienne wasn't displeased with Coyote Wells when they finally reached it late that evening. There was a spring high on the limestone cliffs which began a short-lived stream running from the bluff through the pines and into a natural basin in the limestone. The overflow ran off into the gully beyond the basin and was absorbed by the thirsty plains.

Ruff was beside Adrienne as she stood looking up at the gray, white-streaked cliffs where the spring had its source. The pines were thick along the rim, interspersed with occasional cedar.

"Best to build up next to the bluff," Justice was telling her. "No way for Indians or anyone else to come up on you from behind. And no way to cut you off from water, being that close to the basin."

"Yes, I see that," Adrienne said sharply.

"You're a hard thing," Ruff said. She turned toward him in the twilight.

"So are you," she responded.

"Maybe. I have to be," he said.

"So do I, Justice, so do I. Everything my father left us is tied up in this operation. If it goes bust, what do we do then? You know Lucille—do you think she's capable of making her own way out here? Or anywhere else. Yes, I'm pushing, and I'll keep on pushing—because if I don't people push me around."

"I'm not trying to push, Adrienne."

"No. You haven't been very helpful either. Although," she had to admit, "I like this site. You're sure it's close enough to Bismarck?"

"As close as you dare get. It'll do. Traveling out, you were taking your time, hunting the way. Once you've got freight wagons rolling, they'll make it in ten, twelve hours."

"You don't think I'll ever have any running, though, do you?"

"I don't think about it. I'm doing a job because your father was a friend of Colonel MacEnroe's. That's all there is to it."

"That and María," she said abruptly.

"Maybe." Ruff grinned, and Adrienne's mouth tightened again. "You shouldn't go peeping," he advised her, "if you don't want to see what's going on."

"What's that supposed to mean?" she demanded. A violent flush crept up her neck and into her cheeks.

"Nothing, ma'am. Nothing at all." He was still grinning, and Adrienne spun away, her cheeks still crimson, to walk off through the sundown light toward the campfire where Lo worked.

Ruff unsaddled, slipped the bridle and bit from the

gray, rubbed it down, and led it to water. By the time he had it picketed in the grass along the bluff it was full dark. Justice walked back toward the wagons, his head coming up at the distant mournful howl of a coyote in the hills. At least it might have been a coyote.

He sat drinking coffee in silence. No one talked much but Willie Canbury, who was telling them something about mice.

Justice walked to where Adrienne sat staring into the fire. "What's your plan for tomorrow?" he asked her.

"I thought you made all the plans," she said harshly.

"I can. We'll proceed to the next station site, leaving some men behind to start work on the station . . . Hardy Pierce and his men."

"I don't think we'll need all of them," Pierce himself said, coming out of the shadows to look at Ruff across the fire. "Maybe you ought to stay and do that. Keep the Chinaman and the half-wit."

"It won't do," Ruff answered. "I'll have to find us a trail through the foothills which doesn't include Walker's Pass, then push on toward Bear Creek. The Chinaman cooks for the ladies, and Willie has to be along to see to the horses."

"How 'bout the old man and the kid?"

"No. They're driving as of now. Your boys haven't been doing a thing but riding along. Let's put them to work."

"Miss Court?"

"Justice's plan sounds logical to me," she said as if it pained her to admit it. "There are four of you; the work should go quickly."

"I wasn't planning on staying myself. Me and the breed—we'll go along. You'll need someone to start up the other stations anyway. I'll leave the Olmstead boys, show 'em where the trees are and get 'em to it."

"All right. I'm too tired to think, to argue," Adrienne said. "That sounds all right. Mr. Justice?"

"It'll be slower, but I suppose it'll have to do. Excuse me," he said, rising. "I'm going to turn in." Hardy Pierce's expression was challenging as Ruff walked past. Beyond, the night was still and cold. Ruff sat up, blanket over his shoulders, watching and listening until the fire was doused and the others turned in. Then he rose, made one silent round of the sleeping camp, and made his own bed in a new spot. He slept deeply, dreamlessly.

The Olmstead brothers looked as if someone had marooned them on a desert island. They had a pile of tools and a keg of nails beside them, and they stood staring gloomily after the departing wagons.

"What were you figurin' for the second stop?" Ruff was riding beside Rupert Gates's wagon, a wagon he shared now with the silent Lo.

"The old trading post," Ruff answered. "It's ready-built. With a little cleaning up, it'll do. Save the ladies a lot of time and expense."

"Right out in the open, ain't it?" Rupert shouted back.

"Flat ground, wide open. But then if the Sioux decided to come down on one of these stations it wouldn't matter. They'd take it if they wanted to."

"You're right there. Hate to see these women get involved in this. Ain't only the danger—a woman gets hard, you know," Gates said.

"They do." And neither man liked them that way. They would get hard, harder yet. A lifetime of labor was what Adrienne was looking at. Maybe she could cut it, who knew, but Lucille couldn't. María—she could if she wanted to, but she wouldn't stand for it long. There were always other guitar players, other songs to be sung.

They were out onto the endless plains again, and far to the south they could see dust, a rolling wagon and outriders. A Boggs rig, and moving along a road better than the one they now traveled.

They met the cavalry patrol an hour later.

Captain Hart was commanding. He had a full platoon of dusty, sweating men. They pulled up on the side of the road, Hart signaling furiously to Justice as they neared.

"Justice?"

Ruff rode the gray to him. The horse stopped with a lot of high-spirited head-tossing and prancing, stirring up the dust still more.

"Have I been recalled?" Ruff asked with joking hopefulness.

"Afraid not. I wish you had been. He's loose."

"Who's loose?"

"Stone Hand. Someone broke him out this morning. He grabbed a horse and made a run for it, right out the front gate. Sentries were so astonished they didn't fire a shot until he was nearly out of range. He may have been wounded; probably not."

"Jesus." Ruff shook his head angrily. Allie James had gotten down from his wagon to walk over and stand listening.

"I know," Hart said. "We had him and now we don't. Security seemed to be tight enough. I don't know what happened, Ruff. The colonel's fit to be tied."

Ruff looked toward the far horizon. Stone Hand on the loose again and he was tied to this petticoat parade.

"You recall what he said, Justice? He swore he'd come after you. With a lot of men that would be just talk, but with Stone Hand, I somehow think he meant it."

"I know damn well he did."

"Well." Hart looked embarrassed. "Watch yourself, Justice. With a little luck we'll run him down soon."

"Yeah." With more than a little luck. The army hadn't a good record with Stone Hand. His bands were always small, they always kept moving. Difficult to track, difficult to pin down. There would be more blood.

Ruff sat the gray, watching the patrol move out. "Bad business," Allie James said. "I guess we'd better keep our guns close to hand from here on."

Justice nodded, deep in thought. He was bringing danger to the women staying with them, but perhaps their position was even more hazardous with Ruff gone. There was no solution but to roll on ahead.

"No sense telling the ladies anything about this," Ruff said. "It can't do any good; might just frighten Lucille."

"Sure as hell frightens me," Allie James admitted with a grin.

"Me too."

It wasn't until dawn the next day that they came up on the old trading post. Built by two German immigrant brothers, the Muellers, it had seen its day long ago. The Muellers had been convinced that the Indians needed only fair treatment and a hand of welcome and they would respond in kind. The Muellers had been wrong.

Muellers' Post hadn't seen a customer for twenty years now, but it had been built solidly of native stone. The old well was a deep one, needing a good cleanout but little else. The pole corrals had long ago fallen apart, but that wasn't much of a problem.

Justice swung down stiffly, and walked to the old building, and kicked the door open, waiting a moment before entering to let the snakes, if any, slither away.

"It'll do, I suppose," Adrienne said. She had entered behind Ruff and now stood looking over the place. Cobwebs were everywhere, there were signs of pack rats and owls, and it smelled of rattlesnake, but she was right—it would do.

Ruff turned and looked at her, and he caught a glimpse of her when she was not prepared. Her beautiful face was not set, her eyes not harsh and distant. She simply looked like a worried young woman trying to cope with a difficult task and not making much of a job of it. She caught Ruff looking at her and a veil fell across her eyes, her jaw tightening.

"It's all right to be scared," Justice said softly. He took a step toward her, and her eyes opened wide, with astonishment it seemed. Then she turned away, walking around the room.

"Sweep it out first, then get this old counter out of here. Rotten anyway, isn't it? We can wall that in over there for bedrooms, put the stove in the far corner."

"Yeah." Ruff's tone caused Adrienne to turn toward him again. The musty trading post was deeply shadowed. Through the high, narrow window a ray of sunlight, dust motes dancing through it, fell.

"You wanted to say something."

"Just that you could still sell back what you've bought, get yourself a little cash, some tickets back East."

"You don't like me, do you? Or is it that you don't like women . . ." She blushed suddenly. "No, you like women, I'd forgotten. As for the other—no. Emphatically no. My father wanted this."

"Your father's gone."

"Yes. If he were here you wouldn't talk to me like this. Disparaging everything."

"I think I would, Miss Court. Yes, I likely would. It's the sort of job that demands a certain roughness, an experience in living with this land the way it is, not the way you want it to be. Yes—that's what I'd tell your father too."

Lucille had come in as they stood talking. She blinked in that blank, childish way she had, looking from Ruff to her sister.

"Get some brooms and a bucket of water, Lucille," Adrienne snapped. "We've got work to do."

"Yes." Lucille looked ready to sag.

"I'll help you," Justice said. "Musty in here."

He went out with Lucille into the morning sunlight. She looked like a doll, a complexion of peach and cream, china-blue eyes, soft lush figure.

"I wish you'd won that argument," she said passionately, abruptly. "Oh, how I wish you could persuade Adrienne to take us home."

"Where's home?"

"Philadelphia."

"I'd have guessed the South."

"Do we still have a trace of accent?" Lucille laughed. "Yes—we're transplanted Virginians—"

"Mr. Justice!" Allie James was coming on the run. "You'd better come on over here. Looks like there's trouble riding in."

It was trouble all right. Ruff recognized the man in the buffalo coat while he was still a quarter mile off. It was Anson Boggs, looking big and ugly, one son and six riders with him.

Allie James had his rifle, and glancing over his shoulder Ruff saw Rupert behind a wagon tongue, his Winchester at the ready. That was it—all the support Ruff counted on. Lo and Willie Canbury didn't own guns, probably didn't know what they were. Pierce and the Indian weren't going to get involved—unless it was on Boggs's side.

Boggs reined up in a storm of dust, yanking back his frothing horse's head viciously.

"Mornin'," Ruff said quietly.

"Ruff Justice. Get involved in everything, don't you?" the big, bearded man said.

"I seem to."

"Stay involved in this and you won't last long," Boggs threatened. "I'll promise you that."

"Involved in what?"

"Don't give me that crap, Justice. One of my boys was shot, another beat up. You got some women or something here that want to beat me out of the mail contract, and it ain't going to happen."

"Just a minute!" Adrienne was coming on the run.

"This the one?" Boggs asked with a sneer.

"This is the one," Adrienne said, "and I speak for myself. You don't have to go through Mr. Justice. I heard you say I was trying to beat you out of your mail contract. Nothing of the sort. You've beat yourself out of it, if what I hear is true. They say you run the Bear Creek line when you feel like it or when you're sober enough to. They say there's a lot of mail that never gets where it's supposed to go—specifically, the mail that has money in it."

"Just a minute, damn you, lady—"

"Just a minute yourself. I'm telling you how it is. Quit grinning, Justice, it's not funny."

"Yes, ma'am."

"We're simply trying to build another line. A little competition, and if you can't stand the competition, then maybe you'd better get out right now. At least we have every intention of getting the freight into Bear Creek and of delivering the mail. And . . ." She faltered, then spoke strongly again. "If you want a fight, we're ready to give it to you."

Anson Boggs turned his head and spat. "You are, are you? You'd better stay ready to fight then, lady. Because you're not taking the bread out of my mouth.

I wouldn't sleep too soundly at night. Never know when you might not wake up."

"That's enough. Get out," Justice said. "If she's not ready to fight, I am. And I'm wearing a gun. Do it, Boggs, or ride out."

Boggs looked the tall, buckskinned man up and down, and for a minute Justice thought he might try it. But he was no fool. He had seven men with him, but he knew who Ruff's first target was.

"You heed me, lady." Boggs leveled a thick finger at Adrienne, suddenly laughed harshly, then turned his horse and was gone, his men following him out onto the plains.

"He meant that," Adrienne said in wonder. "He really meant it—he would kill us."

"Yes, ma'am," Justice said. "I believe he would."

5

The last way station was to be built in a pretty little valley among the pine-clad hills north of Walker's Pass. Walker had been one of the old-time mountain men—Ruff had met him once—and he knew his way around the hills, but Walker had never thought of anyone's taking a wagon through those hills in winter, and his trail, used by nearly everyone but the Indians, just wasn't suitable when the snows came. That was part of the reason Boggs's winter deliveries to the boom town of Bear Creek were practically nonexistent.

Justice had decided to follow Bear Creek itself into the settlement. The ground was lower and the trail better-sheltered.

There was water from the creek itself, and plenty of graze in the long meadows. The way station would have to be down among the trees, lower than Ruff would have liked for defense, but that couldn't be helped.

Each day now they were nearer the Black Hills, the Sioux holy land which they had fought savagely for and would continue to protect with all their strength. The great chiefs had headed for Canada after Greasy Grass—Little Big Horn—but there were still enough Sioux and Cheyenne in the area to overwhelm any white settlement.

Bear Creek, on the very fringes of the Black Hills,

existed precariously. You would find no one in the streets without a gun on, men and women alike, and many of the kids big enough to tote one without having it drag on the ground.

Pierce and the breed, Luke, had been left behind at Muellers' Post, and Ruff was breathing easier these days. Still that left only himself and James and Rupert to build this station. Lo and Canbury had remained with Hardy Pierce. That was to be the main station, the lead stop where the bulk of the horses were kept, where the passengers—if any, ever—were going to be fed.

"This is a beautiful spot."

Ruff looked up from the log he was notching. Lucille stood, hands clasped, watching him.

"It is that." He could hear the ringing of Allie James's ax in the woods. Allie was felling the timber they needed, Rupert dragging it to the site, where Ruff was progressing steadily on the way station itself.

"I thought you might be thirsty."

Lucille had a canteen in her hand, and now almost shyly she brought it forward, watching as the tall man drank the still-cool creek water down. He was shirtless, and Lucille studied his torso with a sort of awe, noticing the lean, hard muscles, the old scars traced across his chest and shoulders.

"Thank you. Happy?" he asked her.

"Happier. I wish we could just have a little place right here—Adrienne, María, and me—and forget everything else."

"Sounds nice. It takes something to make it out here, though. Can't live off roots and berries."

"The Indians do."

"Only when they have to. It's a beautiful land, but there's hard winters here, Lucille. There's a lot of Sioux about too. Rupert saw sign this morning. Three horsemen."

"Are they . . . ?" Her head spun around, and she looked to the hilltops, timbered, deeply shadowed.

"They're gone. They just had a look-see to find out what was going on, apparently."

"But they'll be back."

"I wouldn't think so," Ruff lied. "They can't have much interest in us." That is, if they didn't want guns, horses, women . . . Ruff had his Spencer near at hand as he worked. His eyes lifted constantly to the hills. Lucille was only partly relieved. She shuddered a little, and it wasn't due to the wind which drifted off the high peaks and sang through the pines.

"I wish . . ." What Lucille wished Ruff never found out. Adrienne was coming toward them, walking briskly in her tan riding skirt, white blouse, her honey-colored hair loose around her shoulders.

"We're going into Bear Creek, Justice."

"Are you?"

"We. I want you to come along and show us the trail. We'll need more supplies, more horses, more men. And I want to rent an office in Bear Creek."

"You also wanted this way station built," Ruff said, wiping his forehead on the back of his hand.

"It will wait. I want to get everything pulled together. There may be word there on whether or not we've got the mail contract too."

Ruff was pulling on his shirt, strapping on his gun. He whistled for the gray, which looked at him reluctantly for a moment, then trotted over, frisking through the long grass.

Rupert came over while Ruff was saddling up. "Watch yourself, will you?" Justice said.

"Don't worry about that. We'll keep our heads down."

"Do. There's all sorts of Indians about."

Rupert took his meaning. "We'll be wary. You've got enough of that wall up to barricade ourselves behind if need be. Maybe the kid and me will have time to get a few up on there too."

"Want anything from town?" Ruff asked, swinging up.

"You can't bring it, and I'm likely a little old to handle it." Rupert winked. "Maybe some cut plug," he added. "My last is gettin' a little hard."

The stagecoach drew up, María driving. She looked as if she could handle a team. She smiled and waved.

"Maybe we stay behind to watch the place, huh, Ruff Justice? You and me."

"I'd like nothing better." He walked to the stage and rested a hand on the box, a hand which found its way to María's booted leg.

"That all you two think of," Adrienne said sharply. Lucille was beside her, looking, Ruff thought, a little hurt. She wore a plain blue gingham dress and a blue bonnet. "Drive carefully, María," was Adrienne's last advice. She and Lucille climbed in the coach, and María made a face at her boss.

"I don't know why I don't go back to Durango," María said.

"You're having too much fun here." Ruff slapped her leg. "Drive carefully. The trail's not much, and won't be until we get a chance to drag it."

Ruff climbed up on the gray again and waited, letting María lead off down the trail. Allie James, bare-chested, gunbelt strapped on, stood leaning on an ax watching them until Rupert yelled at him. It was hard to tell, but Ruff had the idea cross his mind that the kid was jealous. Jealous of what, of who? María? He hoped she wasn't playing him up too— the kid was just inexperienced enough to take it seriously. Ruff would have to ask her.

The trees closed in, their dark ranks cathedral-like as they towered above Bear Creek, cutting out the sunlight. The trees were alive with squawking jays.

Ruff caught sight of a five-point buck which had been drinking from the quick-running stream. It lifted its water-silvered muzzle, tensed, and then bounded off into the forest, soundless, swift, lithe.

The trail wasn't as bad as Ruff remembered it. Only twice did they have to detour around narrow spots, and once clear a fallen pine, unhitching the stage horses to accomplish that.

It was most of the day before they came suddenly on the settlement of Bear Creek itself. Adrienne climbed out to have a look at it while the horses got their blow.

"Is that it?" she said in near disbelief.

"All there is of it, and as much as there's likely to ever be."

Bear Creek sat between and across the yellow-ocher hills. There was little timber on the surrounding mountains; there had never been much, and what there had been was now mine timbers, framing for the unpainted, weathered shacks along the winding main street. It was a typical Western mining town—rough, untrimmed, ugly, squat, gray. There wasn't time to paint things even if paint had been available. There was gold out there, and the only time well spent was time used to dig for it.

It was a boomer, here now, gone next year or next month perhaps, tomorrow if the Sioux came. It was inhabited by the main-chance types—prostitutes, card sharps, pickpockets, gun hands, confidence men. They too were mining for gold, and their way was a lot quicker, a lot cleaner, and sometimes rougher.

"It's horrid," Lucille said.

"It's home."

"Don't look too bad," María said, perhaps hearing imaginary guitars.

"Have you got someone you can talk to about an office?" Ruff asked.

"Father had a letter from a man named Tewes— the town banker."

"All right." Ruff glanced at the horses. Their sides no longer rose and fell frenetically. Standing there any longer they risked a chill. "Let's get on down and see what Bear Creek's got to offer."

He already knew, and he disliked it. Places like Bear Creek were scabs on the plains, boils on the mountains, and Ruff, who had been around long enough to recall when they weren't there, disliked them all. People pushed and shouted. The air was no good. You couldn't trust anyone. You invested nothing of yourself in such towns, or few did, and as a result you got nothing back. When it was played out, the countryside raped, you moved on and started up again somewhere else.

They rode down the center of the bustling main street, drawing some attention because of the stagecoach, more because of its lady driver.

There were mules and men everywhere, a lot of drinking in and in front of the saloons, two of which were nothing but tents. The street was rutted, the false-fronted buildings—all three of them—leaned forward crazily as if a strong wind would push them over. Beyond and above the town were clusters of miners' shacks and patched-up army tents. They couldn't have been much comfort in the rain and wind, but they had their golden dreams to keep them warm, whiskey to wipe away reality.

"Right there, María!" Adrienne called, poking her head out the stage window, and María nodded. The bank, of stone, was on their left.

"Pull around the corner and into the alley," Ruff suggested.

She did that and stepped down with a sigh of relief, Justice helping her to the ground. He held her for a minute as her boots touched down. She was breathing heavily.

"That's hard work!" she said.

"It can be. There's a lot of men who've tried it looking for an easy life. They didn't find it leading a team of horses up a grade in the rain and mud."

"Are you coming in?" Adrienne asked, and Ruff let his hands fall away from María. He shrugged.

"Sure."

"Not me," María said. "What do I care about the banker? I think I'll look around."

"Stay out of trouble," Ruff said lightly.

He watched María sashay off up the street, drawing a lot of attention, catcalls, whistles. Adrienne, he thought, looked for one moment nearly envious. Ruff took Lucille's arm, pleasantly surprising her.

Harold Tewes was a middle-aged man with a strong grip and a friendly smile.

"Miss Court—so you made it. And this is your sister. And . . ."

"Mr. Ruffin T. Justice."

"Really?" The banker's eyebrow lifted. "Well, well. Perhaps you won't have any trouble then."

"What do you mean?"

The banker sat down after offering the women a chair. His office was cool and dark. A wooden cabinet stood in one corner, stacks of paper on his desk.

"As you know, I told your father that I'd try to find an office for him." He frowned, furrowing his forehead. "Well, the place I had in mind, the old Pay As You Go Mine office, is right across the street, over the general store. I thought it would be convenient. The restaurant is just next door—very handy for travelers."

"The problem is?" Adrienne prompted.

"Squatters." The banker spread his hands and laughed briefly. "Can't get rid of them. There's at least six men living in that office—any kind of shelter is at a premium here with these hordes of gold diggers."

"The local police . . ." Lucille suggested.

"None. We had an election last month, voted in a man named Tom Drake for marshal, but Tom got the gold fever himself, went up into the hills, and got himself scalped. No one's asked for the job since." He looked hopefully at Ruff.

"And no one's going to," The tall man answered. "As for the squatters, we'll get rid of them."

"They're a drunken rabble," Tewes went on. "I don't think any of them has lifted a pick yet. The leader is a huge red-bearded man named McGinnty."

"I may know him."

"Then you know he's trouble."

"He'll be moved," Ruff said with quiet assurance.

"Yes," the banker nodded, appraising Ruff, "I suppose he will be." He brightened. "Then there's a matter of the lease, if you're ready to go ahead as things stand."

"We're ready," Adrienne answered.

"I thought a series of one-month leases."

"Better give us a year. We'll be here to stay," Adrienne said with confidence. Ruff wasn't sure it wasn't unwarranted, but he said nothing. Bitter and sharp as she was, you had to give her credit. She was determined.

"Fix up all of that," Ruff said. "I'll go sweep out the place for you."

"Fine," was Adrienne's response.

"Be careful, please," Lucille begged.

"You'll buy me dinner afterward at that restaurant?" Ruff asked.

"Yes." Adrienne still hid whatever she was thinking behind that tight, constant mask.

"Thanks."

Ruff nodded to the banker and started out, Lucille's

hand brushing across his arm, her soft blue eyes turned up briefly to him.

Justice went out into the cool, sunny day, stood looking up and down the street for a minute, eyes narrow and hard, then walked across the street and up onto the plankwalk opposite, finding the general store and the outside staircase beside it.

From below he could hear sounds of men shouting in the upstairs office. Gritting his teeth, he went on up. The door stood open and empty. Ruff Justice filled it, Colt in hand.

"Out. You boys are in the wrong place. Go find a hole to crawl in."

There were four of them there just then. Tin cans and bottles lay everywhere. The place stank of unwashed men. Newspapers and straw mattresses lay across the floor. A table with one leg ripped off was tilted against the stained wall.

"Who the hell are you?" one of them roared out, coming to his feet. He was huge, red-bearded, wearing a twisting scar which ran from eyebrow to chin. McGinnty, king of the squatters.

"I'm the man who's come to serve the eviction notice." Ruff gestured with his pistol. "This is it—out."

Two of them grabbed satchels and bedrolls and made for the open spaces; Ruff let them by. McGinnty held his ground, as did the narrow, dark-eyed man with him. Both wore guns, but their hands stayed far from their holsters.

"How about it, McGinnty? The nice way?" Ruff asked with a disarming smile.

"You go to hell! We're here and we're staying."

"That definite, is it?" Justice asked, looking from McGinnty to the other, who was starting to get a case of the shakes.

"Yes, dammit, it is."

Ruff fired. The bullet clipped off the corner of

McGinnty's boot, taking his little toe with it. McGinnty fell to the floor with a howl of pain, and simultaneously the dark-eyed man, panicked, drew his Colt. Ruff shot him through the shoulder. He was spun around, slammed against the wall to slide slowly down to hit the floor.

McGinnty sat howling with pain on the floor. The man with the smashed shoulder was silent, his eyes fixed on Justice as he walked across the room where the black-powder smoke rested in layered wreaths. Justice kicked the Colt on the floor aside and stood towering over McGinnty.

"Up."

"I can't get up, damn you."

"Get up and get out. You're not hurt. Take him with you. Now!"

The hammer of the Colt was drawn back, and McGinnty moved with corresponding quickness. He jerked the injured man to his feet and started toward the door, dragging his man after him.

"I'll be back, damn you," McGinnty promised.

"Don't. Not if you want the rest of that foot. Clear out, McGinnty, and stay out."

McGinnty, growing braver as the distance increased, started cursing and swearing revenge. The man in his arms moaned with pain. Justice followed them to the landing and watched as they went down to the alley below, the heels of the man with the broken shoulder bumping down the steps. There were a dozen or so men standing below gaping. Ruff ignored them.

Holstering his Colt, he went back in, distastefully picked up an armload of the miners' belongings, walked to the landing, and dropped them overboard into the alley.

Spotting a kid with straw-colored hair in the mob, he shouted down, "Want to earn a dollar?"

"You bet!"

"Find yourself a broom and clean this muck out."

A silver dollar flickered, spinning in the sunlight, toward the kid's outstretched hand, was pocketed and acknowledged with thanks. Then the kid was off somewhere, likely running home to get a broom.

Ruff waited until he was back before he abandoned the place. "Leave that window open wide, son," was his last advice. "It'll get most of the stink out."

When Adrienne and a wary-looking Lucille Court came in, he was sitting in the restaurant waiting, a cup of coffee before him on the checked tablecloth, legs stretched out, hat sitting beside him on a chair. They had María with them, and the Mexican girl was grumbling something about "this a-stinkin' town, why I don't go back to Durango, I don't know."

"Any problems with the squatters?" Adrienne asked, seating herself before Ruff could hold her chair for her.

"No, they saw the logic of it."

He told her about the boy who was sweeping up. "It will likely need a good scrubbing down with lye soap, though," he added.

"María will do just that."

María didn't look as if she wanted to do just that, but she would, Ruff knew. It was that or Durango, which despite frequent complaints and threats, must not have been that good a place for María Salazar, or she would be there.

"There's no word about the mail contract," Adrienne said peevishly. "There may be a rider in tonight with a letter from the Postmaster General, however. I'll see to setting the office up, and . . ." She sighed. "It looks as if I'm going to be stuck in Bear Creek for quite a while."

"Oh, no," Lucille said under her breath. She didn't like the town a bit, and Justice didn't blame her.

"We have another problem," Adrienne went on. "A party of six men who want to return to Bismarck. Miners who've made their stake or given up on it."

"You can't mean you agreed to take them?"

"Why not? That's the business we're in, isn't it?"

"Yes," Justice objected, "but we're not set up for it yet—way stations aren't built, and the horses are beat."

"I'll have to buy some horses here anyway."

"Who's driving, or do I have to ask?" Ruff growled.

"There's not a lot of choice—but if you don't want to help us any longer, I'm sure we can dispense with your services," she said. "After all, what have you done for us that we couldn't have done without you? Found a water hole, served an eviction notice . . ."

Justice wondered if she could hear his teeth grinding together across the table.

"I'll stick until I've seen that you're started well or you give up, whichever. If you're offering me a choice, I suppose I'll run your stage on through to Bismarck. It beats staying around here, though it's going to be a long, tough run. The road's rough, the horses few."

"You can borrow the saddle horses from each station."

"Ma'am . . ." Ruff shut up. There was no use trying to explain that it took time to break a horse to harness, and a saddle horse didn't automatically take to dragging a stagecoach around. Neither did he imagine Pierce and his men would be too happy to swap for horses which weren't saddle-broken. Maybe the wagon horses would be enough to make do with.

"I'm going to give you a note and some money," she said as if sending a kid to the grocery store. "You can go to the printer in Bismarck and get some flyers made up. Post them around town. Let people know we're running freight and passengers through to Bear Creek."

"We're hardly ready for that. The stations . . ."

"There's nothing coming in if we're not working, Mr. Justice. We'll handle what work we can get one way or the other. I'm adding a note to the bulletins explaining that we shall soon have the mail contract as well. In fact," she said, looking at the little watch on her bosom again, "with a little luck we may even have word on that before you can get the fresh horses hitched and get underway. I bought two of the nicest-looking little pinto ponies from a man who . . ."

Ruff managed not to hear the rest of it. If Adrienne Court was learning anything, she was doing it slowly. María looked off into space, leaning back in her chair, her skirt pushed down between outstretched legs, Lucille fretted with her napkin.

"I can't stay here," she said abruptly. "I just hate it. It scares me."

"You'll have to stay, Lucy," Adrienne said.

"No I don't," Lucille said with surprising strength. "I can stay out at the station with Allie James and Rupert. They'll take care of me, and I can help them. It's . . . it's nice out there." Lucille's eyes grew distant; maybe she was dreaming that dream of hers again, the one she had talked about to Ruff, living off the land up along Bear Creek, forgetting all of this freight scheme.

"It's just not right."

"I won't stay here!" Lucille flared up. Then she turned her eyes down like a child afraid of what punishment was to come.

"You'll need someone eventually to settle in there and run the place," Ruff commented. "It might as well be Lucille. As she says, Rupert and Allie are there, and they're good men. It's likely safer up along the creek than it is in this hellhole."

Adrienne was a long time responding. "Very well," she said at last. "For now then, Bear Creek is your station. You run it properly, Lucille. If you need anything, well, just ride the stage on into town. If you'd like Muellers' Post, María," she added as an afterthought, "then . . ."

María Salazar laughed deeply, heartily. "No, thank you. I'm a town girl. I'll stay right here with you, Miss Court, maybe be secretary or something, eh?"

"All right." She was actually smiling. "It won't be so bad."

Ruff got back to practical matters. "Will you authorize me to hire a couple more drivers? All of our people are tied up building right now, and I'm not looking to be a stage jockey."

"Well—I'd hoped you would make a few runs. Actually," Adrienne admitted, "the money is drying up a little. That's why it's important that we take these miners to Bismarck. Please . . ."

It was the first time she'd ever said the word in Ruff's presence. "If you could make a few runs it would help immeasurably."

Now she had to go and start acting reasonably. There was nothing for Ruff to do but agree.

"All right. Where are your passengers, and when do they want to leave?"

"They're ready now. They're at the depot."

It took Ruff a minute to realize she meant the office he had just thrown McGinnty out of.

"All right. The new horses are at that stable on the edge of town?" Adrienne nodded. "Then I'm ready. Let's get rolling."

"Lucille . . ." Adrienne looked at her sister and then at Ruff Justice. "Just be careful. Please."

"You sure, Ruff Justice," María asked, coming near to him as he rose and planted his hat, "that you don't want to quit, stay in town with me?"

"Can't quit on the lady now, María."

"No—I think that is what keeps me here too. But I am here when you come back. I wait for you." She kissed him then, her pliant lips searching his as the other restaurant customers gaped. She stepped back smiling. "To remember me by. To remind you. I will be here, hombre. *Vaya con Dios*."

6

———•••✦•••———

The stable boss was a help hitching up. "I tried to explain to the lady about these ponies," he said apologetically.

"I know how that can be. It's all right. They'll have to do, I suppose."

"It'll be some work the first few miles."

All the way back to Bismarck, Ruff thought. He had disorganized way stations, Indians on the prowl, the Boggs people, who, if they had gotten wind of this, wouldn't be above trying to stop the stage.

The miners would be no help. They moved heavily; one of them could hardly walk for the gold dust he was carrying in a money belt. They were cashing out, these men, and everyone in town was probably aware of the fact that they were carrying gold.

They were all armed, anyway, and looked determined to keep what they had. They were also unwashed, unshaven, although three of them wore new suits and hats.

"Happy to see you," one of them had told Ruff. "I'm Bronk Williams. This is my cousin, Cash. We were wondering about riding back alone. Knew damn sure we didn't want to go along with that thievin' Anson Boggs and his boys. Used to get all our mail opened and resealed. Well, if you folks can hold on, you'll have a steady flow of customers—until the ore's gone," he said thoughtfully, scratching a whisk-ered chin.

"That why you're pulling out? Claim gone dry?"

"Nope. I sold it. Don't want to press my luck. I came out wantin' to take back five thousand. That's about what I've got. Other day up along Pine Ridge, three boys lost their scalps—might even have been Indians, though they were wearin' boots if they were. I just want my skin and my poke. No sense bein' greedy."

Lucille had been standing in the ribbon of shade next to the stable. Now she came forward, head bowed, looking small and delightful.

"Ruff?" she asked in a small voice.

"What?" Then he saw she wanted him to come aside with her.

"I don't want to ride in with those men. There's six of them and . . . well, they don't look very nice."

"You can sit up top, but it'll be a lot rougher."

"That's all right." She blew out a sigh of relief. "I'd rather be with you."

"Then you can be. Bronk! Climb on in—the lady wants to ride up top."

"Can't get her to change your mind, can you?" one of the miners called, leaning far out the window.

"Guess not," Ruff answered with a smile.

"She'll never know what she was missing."

"Crude," Lucille said softly.

"I guess. Most of us are out there."

"But not you."

"No? Maybe you don't know me that well yet. Come on. Give me that little bag. Up you go. Watch what you say down there, boys. This lady's part of the management of this line. She'll have you put off."

Then with the miners aboard and Lucille up be-side him, with the gray tied on behind, its saddle atop the coach, Justice released the brake and popped the horses with the reins.

They moved out briskly, though the wheel horse, one of the pintos, tended to sidestep as much as possible, trying to step out of the harness.

A few miles settled them to the task. They wound up the grade to the east of town and into the forest, following the creek itself back toward the first way station.

Lucille looked bright and alert, finer than at any time since Ruff had known her. She had taken off her hat, and the wind now ran through her long blond hair. Her cheeks were reddened by the cool breeze. She glanced at him and smiled.

"I like this. I think I shall always ride up top."

"You'll have plenty of opportunity."

"To ride with you?" Ruff didn't hear her at first, and so she shouted it again, above the racket of the horses' hoofs, the squeak and jounce of the coach. He smiled and shook his head.

"No. Not for long."

They were two hours reaching the top of the grade. There they rested the horses, the miners stepping down to stretch their legs.

The creek was five or six hundred feet below them now, a silver thread winding its way toward the community of Bear Creek. Behind them the piny hills rolled away to the north and south.

"Let's go," Justice said after a while. The horses started again with some reluctance. Ruff had to ride the brake as they dropped down again, rejoining the creek, running at a slow but even pace through the heavy timber.

They hit them at the ford.

Ruff had halted the horses and then started them at a walk across the creek. He heard the shout to his right, and his head spun around to see the first of the bandits break from the timber.

A bullet slapped into the side of the stage, and then dozens of others.

"What . . . ?" was all Lucille had time to say before Ruff grabbed her by her shoulder and jammed her down into the box. The horses were dancing in harness, and Ruff, cursing, grabbed his Spencer. The big .56 spoke and a rider went down, cartwheeling back off his horse as it splashed downstream toward the stage. From the coach itself guns opened up as the miners fought back.

A bullet whipped past Ruff's ear, and, looping the reins around the brake, he threw himself down into the box, lying on top of Lucille, who was motionless, whimpering.

Justice tracked a masked bandit with his sights, squeezed off, and saw him blown from the saddle. He landed in the creek and was dragged by his horse up into the trees.

There were ten of them at least, and they seemed to have the advantage, but the bandits had no stomach for facing hostile guns. A third man went down as someone inside the coach tagged him in the shoulder. Ruff saw him hit the water, lurch again to his feet, and be picked up by a following rider.

Then they were gone, Justice's bullets pursuing but not finding a target as the bandits disappeared into the tall trees.

For minutes he lay still, feeling the breathing of Lucille, her slight movements, the small, frightened sounds emerging from her throat.

"Sorry," he said.

"Are they gone?"

"Yes. Give it a minute—they might come back."

She didn't answer. Ruff, glancing down, saw those

wide, wide eyes staring up at him up at him helplessly. Her hand gripped his arm below the elbow.

"It'll be all right. I don't think they'll try it again."

"Were they Indians?"

"No."

"Then . . ."

"I don't know who they were."

From below they could hear the steady, labored cursing of a man in agony.

Ruff got up slowly. "You stay down for a minute," he told Lucille. She nodded and he winked, lowered his face to hers, and tasted her lips. "It'll be all right."

"Yes." She seemed to almost believe him.

Ruff climbed down into the knee-deep water and splashed to the stage door. He opened it and peered in. Bronk Williams was sprawled on the floor of the coach. His blood was everywhere, spattering the walls and roof of the coach, staining his white shirt to a deep maroon.

"Goddammit all to hell. Damn those bastards! I had it made. . . ." His eyes rolled to his cousin, who was trying unsuccessfully to stanch the flow of blood. "I said I'd pull out when I got five thousand, didn't I, Cash?"

"That's what you said." Cash looked worriedly at Justice. It was bad, very bad. A lung shot, it looked to be.

Bronk wheezed. "Bastards." A little pink froth came to his lips. "I didn't want to risk it . . . didn't want to be greedy." He laughed then, and it was the last sound he ever made. He lay back staring at the roof of the coach for a long minute before his chest stopped its spasmodic rising and falling.

Cash said quietly, "He's gone."

They buried him beneath the pines. Justice and one of the other miners went into the icy stream and dragged out the dead outlaws. Nobody could recognize either of them, though Cash thought he had seen one of them with McGinnty in Bear Creek.

They were buried too. The money belt Bronk had worn lay on the ground. Cash picked it up and held it, staring for a long time. Then he shrugged, tugged up his shirt, and belted it on.

They reached the Bear Creek station two hours later. It was nearly dusk, the mountains gathering shadows in their valleys. Rupert and Allie James had a small fire going. Ruff could see both men standing behind the half-completed wall of the way station, rifles in hand.

Then Allie lifted a hand and waved. In a few more minutes they were unhitching the wary horses as Ruff stepped down, his face grim.

"Lucille?"

She sat there, hands folded in her lap, looking straight ahead. She shook it off, rose shakily, and got down, clinging to Justice as he helped her to the ground.

"What happened?" Rupert wanted to know, and when Ruff told him, he asked, "Boggs?"

"It might have been." Justice shrugged, drinking from a canteen, wiping back his long dark hair. "But these men are carrying a lot of gold. Could have been that they wanted."

Lucille clung to Ruff's arm, exhausted and worried. Her head was a pleasant weight against his shoulder. "I'll change those horses," Allie offered. He scratched his head and grinned. "Hell of a first run, ain't it?"

"That was the idea," Rupert guessed. "Sure, smash us like bugs at the start. You can wager it was the gold, Justice. Me, I cling strongly to the idea it was Boggs." He spoke to the miners. "You men want some stew, we got some. Can't offer you much comfort otherwise."

They accepted that gratefully enough. They were still shaky; they still carried their guns.

"How long a stop, Mr. Justice?"

"Let 'em eat and relax a little. We've got no schedule; when everyone's ready we'll get going. Miss Court is staying here."

"Did you want to eat, Miss Court?" Allie asked. She shook her head in response.

"I couldn't. Thank you."

"When you do want to, you just tell me. I'll get one of those tents out and pitch it for you."

"Thank you," she said mechanically. She was still clinging to Ruff's arm, appeared to have no intention of letting go.

"You going to make it?"

"Yes," she said in that distant voice. "Just shaky. I'll make it. Adrienne wants me to make it. Let's walk," she said.

"Sure?" Darkness was falling. The men were gathered around the stew pot, except for Allie, who was rounding up the wagon horses.

"Yes. Walk." She was trembling again now, maybe because the air was chilling. Likely it was delayed reaction to the events of the day.

They walked to the creek and stood watching it flow past in dark silky folds.

Lucille turned toward him, taking both his hands. "If you would . . . if you would . . ."

She placed his hands to her full, soft breasts. She wore no corsets or geegaws beneath her dress, needed no such help with her figure.

"I'm not sure the time's right, Lucille."

"Because I've been frightened, seen death? Because I'm just a silly woman reacting against it? No, Ruffin." She pressed his hands against her breasts more tightly. "I've wanted you since I first saw you. I need you now—can't you do me the favor?"

He drew her to him and kissed her parting lips, feeling her warm, sweet breath meet his, feeling her hands loop around him and slide down his waist to clench his hard buttocks.

"There," she said, panting, nodding toward the trees. He took her there and kissed her again. "Please," she said, "undress me."

His hands went behind her back and worked at the buttons there. Her dress fell away with a soft rustle, and Lucille, in her chemise, waited, her eyes dancing now in the faint starlight through the trees.

Justice undid the buttons at the front of the white undergarment, his lips following the buttons down as Lucille's firm, milky-white breasts emerged from beneath the chemise, blossoming ripely, their tender pink buds temping his lips and teeth.

She shuddered, her hands on Ruff's head, and as the chemise followed the dress to the ground she gave a sudden, muffled gasp.

It was cold beneath the pines. "Warm me," she whispered, and Ruff, yanking off his shirt, stepping from his trousers, took her down to do just that.

She lay back watching him, her knees coming up and parting as he slipped in between them, his thighs brushing the softness of hers, his hard chest pressing against her breasts as her mouth gaped and searched for his.

"Please," she said in a whisper. "Yes. You're touching me with it now. Put it in a little. Just a little more. Please. Yes. Hold it still there. Let me . . ." Her fingers groped for and found him, running up along the length of his shaft to her own softness, where they quivered, bring the rising sensation to a demanding pitch.

"I'd like," she panted. "In just a little more. I'd like to feel it going . . . God, it's so big, and . . . just a little more. Let me . . . give me your fingers."

Their fingers met and she pressed Ruff's against her soft opening where he penetrated. "Isn't that . . . feel me, I'm going all damp. It's . . . in a little more, I think. Now . . ."

Now there was no more talking. Her hands went behind his neck and dragged him down to her melting kiss. Her legs lifted into the air and locked together behind his waist as she began to thrust, to twist, and Ruff lifted her higher with his steady bucking, sliding in deeper, bringing a sharp, pleasured gasp from Lucille with each long, measured stroke.

He kissed her ear, her eyes, her nose, her breasts, his hand slipping beneath her to clench her silky ass, to lift her higher as he leaned back, getting to his knees to look down and watch his work by starlight as he sank into her, bringing her to a crazed, drunken, reeling climax which lifted her head and shoulders from the earth, brought her clawing hands to his neck, caused her mouth to drop open in a soundless shriek as she came undone, and Ruff rushed to join her in a sharp, trembling finish.

"Well," he said, lying beside her, holding her next to him, their clothes thrown over their cooling bodies as the night wind whispered through the pines and the stream murmured distantly.

"Better. Better than I thought." Her finger ran around his lips, traced his mustache. "I wanted you—I wasn't wrong."

"I've got a stage to keep on schedule."

"I know it." She sighed mightily.

"And you must be hungry by now."

She stretched luxuriantly. "Now," she said, "I'm starved."

"All right. Up then, lady."

"Again?" she asked, nipping at his shoulder with sharp white teeth.

"Not now. Not here. Too damned cold, for one thing."

"And the stage," she grumbled. "Adrienne's rotten stage and her rotten schedule, and her rotten . . . now I've ruined my mood. Now you'll have to do it again."

"No." He slapped her rump and stood, dressing quickly. "But soon."

"Promise?" Her voice went sulky.

"Yes."

She dressed then, and together they walked to the fire. The miners were restless, barely able to wait until Ruff had a single cup of coffee, hastily swallowed a plate of stew.

"You tired?" Rupert Gates asked, his eyes shifting only briefly to Lucille Court.

"I'll make it," Justice said.

"Want someone to ride shotgun?"

"Not either of you two. You keep your eye on that young lady. She's quite a girl after all."

"We'll keep care of her."

"All hitched," Allie said, walking up, his rifle cradled in his arms. "Have been for some time," he added.

"Thanks, Allie."

"Sure."

The kid gave Ruff an odd little look as he handed the reins up, but Justice paid no attention. The moon was rising big and golden now, and it would be a help with the driving, though it wouldn't do anything to shorten the trail.

"Sure you don't want me to take over?" Allie asked.

"No. Thanks."

Cash Williams was climbing up to the box. "This time you're having a shotgun rider," he said. "My cousin's got a wife and a kid back home. I'm seein' that this money gets to them."

"Welcome," Justice said. He glanced down—the passengers were aboard, the gray tied on behind. Lucille stood watching, arms folded, her mouth open as if she would say something, but she only lifted a hand and gave a feeble little wave as Justice started the coach out and onto the moon-glossed empty plains.

7

The stage rolled on across the dark, treeless plains, toward Muellers' Post. The moon hung white in a star-bright sky. The foothills to the south were stark and angular. Beyond, the bulk of the Rockies showed only as a mammoth, shapeless shadow against the earth.

Cash's head snapped backward and he grumbled something, coming awake. He held his rifle in his arms, cradling it like a baby.

"Was I asleep?"

"Must have been. Don't know how you managed it, though."

"Sorry."

"What for? You'd come awake quick enough if something happened. Besides, you're a passenger on this trip, remember. You've got the right to doze."

"Yeah." He stretched one arm, his mouth gaping open in a huge yawn. "Damned country," he said, looking out at the plains. "Never know when it's going to rear up and bite your head off. Most times it's peaceful, though. I always liked it."

"Why are you going home then?"

Cash Williams shrugged. "Bronk, he had the notion that he had to pull out when he made a five-thousand-dollar stake. Superstition, maybe. Like I said, he's got family back in Colorado. Me, I was going because he was going, that's all. Got tired of living in a hole in the ground too."

"Ever think of taking up stage driving?"

Cash laughed, then he said, "Are you serious?"

"There's an opening. Several, in fact. Can't guarantee how long the line will last, though."

"I'd have to give that some thought. The boss is a woman, I hear, a real devil."

"That's true."

"And a damned fine-lookin' one."

"Also true."

"I'll ponder it. Maybe. After I take care of Bronk's business for him—uh-oh, hell of a fire, isn't that!"

Ruff had noticed it at the same moment. Flames writhed high against the black sky, red and yellow, whipped by the wind.

"The station," he muttered. "Stand ready with that rifle, Cash. This looks bad."

It was bad. The fire was already dying down as Justice walked the coach nearer to Muellers' Post. It hadn't caught the grass real good, but it had taken the post, or all of it that would burn—the old stone house, scorched and blackened, still stood. The cottonwoods had gone, and Ruff could see what remained of the shed smoldering away.

He glanced at Cash, got down, and with his rifle in hand walked toward the house, the hot ashes underfoot hissing and flaring up. Cash was beside him. The other miners had clambered out and stood ready, huddling close to the shelter of the coach.

"No horses around," Ruff said.

"No nobody."

"Maybe in the house. Stand loose now."

"I get any looser, I'm going to fall apart," Cash answered dryly.

Ruff approached the front door from the side,

glanced at Cash Williams, and booted it open. It swung in eerily on its squeaking hinges.

He didn't have to go in to see Lo. The Chinese was sprawled against the floor, his fingers cut off, his eyes put out, very dead.

He came a long way to die, Ruff thought.

There was a moan from the far corner, and Justice crouched down, not trusting his ears, which told him this was a badly wounded man crying out for help. The Sioux did that trick very nicely. Justice had seen more than one man lured from shelter to help an injured buddy who was a very live Sioux in reality.

This one wasn't; it was Willie Canbury. He had his tongue in his hands and he sat there looking at it, making burbling sounds. His belly had been slit open from side to side. He was a blood-smeared dying thing who couldn't possibly understand why people would want to hurt him when all he ever did was tend to horses and carve toys.

"Willie?" Ruff crouched down and stroked his hair, feeling the blood there. "It'll be all right. We'll get you to a doctor. He'll pop that right back in your mouth. Don't let go of it now."

Cash turned away and was sick on the floor. Willie kept up his burbling.

"Was it Sioux? Was it Indians, Willie? Where are Pierce and Luke? Where's Pierce?"

Willie's head lolled to one side. He slid down the wall and ended up on his shoulder, still clutching his tongue, looking up with frightened eyes at Ruff Justice.

"Willie, can you write?" He put the kid's finger against his palm. "Can you write, Willie? Write it on my hand. Who did this?"

The finger moved down in a straight line, returned to the top, and formed a loop before it trailed off and

Willie's hand flopped to the ground and he stopped breathing.

"Christ," Cash Williams was saying. "Goddam them all. What in the hell's the matter with them?" He took a slow, deep breath, steeling himself. "Did the kid write anything?"

"He tried. A P, I think."

"For Pierce?"

"Could be." Ruff shook his head. "Might have been the start of a B. Boggs. Anyone else? Bear Foot."

"Who?"

"Stone Hand's kid. Maybe not. Maybe the kid couldn't even write, I don't know. Maybe he was just aping what he'd seen—he didn't have a full load of brains. Nice kid, though. Damn it all—" He looked at Willie Canbury's slack, bucktoothed, affable face again. "So long, kid. Sorry."

The two men tramped outside, looking across the smoldering yard. "No tracks around, I don't suppose. The fire would have been partly to cover any tracks."

"I didn't notice any sign, no."

"If I had the time . . ." But he didn't have the time to circle at a distance and see what horses, what men afoot had been approaching or leaving Muellers' Post. "Damn it all. And no horses."

"Maybe not," Cash said, "but we've got company all of a sudden."

They did. Hardy Pierce was riding in from the south, his horse lathered. Beside him rode the half-breed on his paint pony. Both men were ash-streaked, both carried rifles.

"Justice?" Pierce squinted and then swung down. "You saw it then."

"Yeah, I saw it."

"What are you looking at me like that for?" Pierce got it at length and he swelled up like a toad. "Damn you, Justice, you think I'd do a thing like that? Torturing a man? What for?"

"To make it look the way it does, I reckon, like the Indians did it."

"You're crazier than I thought. It was the Indians, damn you. Luke and me just got back from riding fifteen miles after the bastards, but we lost them up along Grand Coulee."

"What happened here?" Justice wanted to know. The miners had gathered around, and they stood looking at Pierce and the breed unconvinced.

"The Chinaman and the moron were asleep in the house. Me and Luke had our rolls spread back under the trees. First thing we hear is a scream, and when we come awake we saw this Sioux war party running in and out of the house, the corral. They got the horses, of course. Me and Luke opened up, and they scattered. By then they'd fired the place and done the Chinaman and the kid."

"And you trailed after them."

"Damn right."

"That takes a lot of nerve."

"I was mad."

"Sure they weren't white men?"

"Could have been, maybe," Pierce said, taking a moment to think it over. "Maybe in that light, if they were dressed up like Indians. What do you think, Luke?"

"Indian sign. All the way to coulee," the half-breed said. "Sioux. I know Sioux." He was positive; whether he was lying or not was anyone's guess. Justice was stumped and he knew it. He couldn't beat the truth out of them, didn't know what was the truth.

"I want your horses," he said finally.

"You can go to hell! I'll not be stuck in this country without my horse."

"I'm leaving three coach horses. I'll take yours and see if my gray will stand for the harness."

"Won't make much difference now, Mr. Justice," Cash Williams said. He was near Pierce's horse. "These horses are every bit as fagged out as ours. I don't know where these men have been riding, but they've been riding long and hard. This paint's close on to foundering."

"See?" Pierce said triumphantly. Ruff turned away. He didn't see anything except that he was in a spot: So was Adrienne. Boggs or the Indians, the robbers at Bear Creek were taking their toll. At this rate the line wouldn't last out the first week.

"See what you can do about getting the place rebuilt, Pierce."

"Aren't you forgetting something, Justice? I'm the line boss. Me! Miss Court give me this job. Don't be leaning on me. And if I ever hear you accuse me of murder again, by God, you'd better be ready to go to shooting over it."

"It would be," Ruff Justice said quietly, sincerely, "a pleasure."

"Yes, it would. And it might not end up the way you think, Justice."

"This isn't getting us much further, Justice," Cash Williams put in.

"No, you're right. Let the horses rest awhile more. There's time to bury the dead."

They did that then, burying them on the empty plains which still stank of fire and ash. Nobody knew if Willie had any people in town; nobody knew how to contact any of Lo's family. So they just planted them, got back on the coach, and started out at a very slow pace, leaving the bloody outpost behind. Luke and Pierce watched after them until the darkness separated coach and station.

"I damn near believed that man," said Cash.

"Did you?"

"Yes."

"You have reasons, I assume." Ruff slowed for a sandy gully, which the tired horses stumbled through.

"It's like this—why kill them anyway? He could have run them off with a growl or two."

"He maybe likes it."

"Maybe. Where then did they ride to? All out like that they were covering some ground to lather their horses on a night like this."

"Yes, they were that."

Ruff's eyes felt as if they were filled with sand. His hands were knotted into the reins. He had been sitting that driver's box for nearly twelve hours now. The moon was fading at their backs, the horses only dark, shambling shadows ahead and below.

"Then," Cash went on, "why the hell did they come back? Murderers don't just ride up and walk in like that, do they?"

"I've known some to. Jack Hawkins when they took him was playing poker with the sheriff."

"Maybe. I'm just saying I would have some doubts if I was on a jury and Pierce was standing before me."

"Maybe that's the reason behind it all," Ruff suggested. "To throw confusion on things. Pierce knows he would be suspected. Maybe black beard's smarter than I gave him credit for."

"Or more innocent."

"Could be." Ruff didn't argue. He was too tired. His back ached and there didn't seem to be much blood moving around. His legs had stiffened up. The trail was hard to find in the darkness once they moved off the plains again and into the broken hills to the west of Coyote Springs.

It was only an hour until dawn when they pulled into the station to find it deserted.

Ruff stopped the coach and sat looking at the station site. The Olmstead boys had actually started building it. The ground had been leveled. A half-dozen logs lay in a pile to one side.

"Maybe if you called out," Cash suggested.

Justice shook his head and climbed down, Cash beside him. He walked toward the station, listening, looking. The stage horses blew through their nostrils, pawed unhappily at the earth. The starlight was bright enough to show the bluff standing against the dark forest, the worksite, tools scattered about.

After half an hour's search Ruff was convinced there was no one there. They were simply gone. And they had taken the horses.

"That does us for tonight," Justice said, with something close to relief. He didn't have another eight to ten hours in him. Obviously the horses didn't either.

"I'll tell the boys."

"Have them stay close to the stage. I don't like this, Cash."

"Doesn't look good. Someone's sure trying to break this line."

"And doing a good job of it. There's nothing to be done now. We'll look for sign in the morning"—Ruff glanced at the stars—"and it won't be long in coming."

Justice unharnessed the horses and rubbed them down carefully. They had done more than was expected of them already. They were picketed in the long grass an hour later, and Ruff, after seeing to the gray as well, rolled his blanket out beneath the pines and was asleep in minutes.

It seemed only another minute when Cash shook him awake and he sat up, pawing for his Colt, rubbing at his crusted eyes to face an orange, piercingly bright dawn.

"It's me," Cash said. "I didn't think you wanted to sleep past first light."

"No." Justice sat there, head hanging, taking in deep, pine-scented, chill breaths. "Did you sleep at all?"

"I stayed awake. I was napping on the way, remember?"

"Anyone come around?"

"Didn't see anyone, didn't hear anything. I've walked around a bit since the skies grayed, haven't seen a track but for those of two men who spent a lot of time sitting and smoking."

"The Olmsteads."

"I guess. No one else. They headed out east late yesterday, taking six horses with them."

"You read sign pretty good," Ruff commented when he'd had a chance to look over things.

"Not much to it—they weren't trying to hide anything, were they?"

"No." The Olmsteads had simply packed up and pulled out, heading back to Bismarck.

The horses were balky when Justice and Cash hitched them again. Ruff didn't blame them, but they would have to make it somehow. He led them out at a walk and they started toward Bismarck, the sun fiercely yellow in their eyes. Above the pines the sky went to a hard crystal blue as the sun rose.

Bismarck rose slowly off the plains, dark, shapeless, as Justice walked the horses toward it. The lead pinto kept faltering, and Justice thought the animal would never be any good again except as a child's pet.

It was early afternoon when they made the town, and the miners, their spirits brightening as they realized their trek was over, that they had reached civilization and whiskey again, climbed out happily.

"Recommend us to your friends," Justice said, and got a laugh in response.

"Beats Boggs anyway. You didn't knock us over the head and leave us out there too."

Andy Conklin came out of his stable holding a pitchfork. Recognizing Justice, he came across the yard, examining the horses.

"Run these into the ground, didn't you?" he said with distaste. Conklin truly liked horses and hated to see them ill used.

"No choice, Andy. They brought us all the way from Bear Creek. Do what you can with 'em. I don't think that pinto will be sound anymore. The rest might do after a few days of grain and rest."

Cash Williams was still there, remaining behind after the others had tramped happily away in search of liquor and petticoats.

"You've got no place to go?" Justice asked, and Cash noticed the roughness in his voice, the glint in those cold blue eyes. At that moment Justice looked decidedly dangerous, and as anyone who knew him well could have assured Cash, he was.

"Still here. I want to see the end of it."

"You sure about that?"

"Yes. I want to see how the boss of this outfit handles things."

"You're sticking?"

"Sure. I'll drive a rig for you, why not? I'd just have to go down home and look for a job anyway. I'm working for the Great Western as of now."

"She pays in shares," Ruff grumbled. He had opened the loading gate to his Colt; now he spun the cylinder, slapped it shut, and jammed it back in his holster.

"Will you watch my long gun, Conklin? Grain the horses and give my horse a dip of oats too. I'll be back."

"Sure."

"Well." Justice looked at Cash. "Let's go. Just stay out of the way."

Justice started off, striding uptown with those long, easy paces of his, and Cash fell in beside him, glad of one thing—he had not been born with the name Olmstead.

8

———————•◦—◆—◦•———————

Wally Olmstead sat frowning down at the pair of sevens in his hand. He glanced across at his brother and then at Hog Higgins, whose pink face was impassive. "I'm out," Wally said. He threw his cards in, leaned back, stretching in his chair, and grabbed a dancehall girl who was passing with a tray of drinks.

The girl screeched, and the tray clattered to the floor. Simultaneously someone entered the saloon, letting in a flash of harsh sunlight. Something drew Wally Olmstead's attention to the door, and, looking that way, he swallowed a curse and pushed the girl away.

She fell to the floor, still shrieking. Wally kicked his brother under the table. The brother, who had just drawn a third ten and was raising, jerked upright angrily.

"What the hell's the matter . . ."

Wally was looking at the doorway, and now his brother swiveled in his chair to see the tall man silhouetted against the light.

"Holy Jesus!"

Ruff was striding toward the table. Cash Williams had slipped in behind him and was moving toward the bar. Heads were turning now; the saloon fell silent.

A soldier across the way called out, "Howdy, Mr. Justice!" There was no answer, and the soldier, look-

97

ing twice, gulped down his beer and headed out the back way.

"Like to step outside with me?" Justice said to the Olmsteads. His voice was quiet, even, as he hovered over the table. His expression was almost mild, but there was something in those eyes, those frozen eyes, that chilled Wally Olmstead. He knew. Knew he would have to kill Ruff Justice this day or be killed himself.

"What is it?" his brother asked.

"Where are the horses?" Justice inquired, looking at the pile of silver dollars before Wally Olmstead. "Sell them, did you?"

"What if we did?"

"Wait a minute." Wally had decided to try talking his way out of it. "We got tired of being stuck up there, and we came into town. We brought the horses along. Couldn't leave 'em alone up there."

"Let's talk outside," Justice said. "We're disturbing these people."

Hog Higgins was sliding away from the table as unobtrusively as his great bulk allowed.

"I'm not getting out of this chair," Wally insisted.

He was wrong. Justice leaned across the table with a sort of hiss escaping his lips. His hand shot out and yanked Wally toward him. Olmstead slapped desperately at Justice's hand.

I'm not going to draw my gun, he thought in panic. No matter what, he wasn't going to draw. Justice backhanded him fiercely, and blood filled Wally's mouth. His head started ringing. Behind his eyes bright lights flickered on and off.

A small moan escaped Wally Olmstead's lips as he saw with despair that his brother had kicked the table aside and was coming to his feet, his hand slapping down toward his holstered pistol.

Justice seemed to sense rather than see the

movement, and, dropping Wally, he spun and crouched, his Colt filling his hand. His pistol stabbed flame at Olmstead even as Olmstead's bullet, missing by a fraction of an inch, flew past Ruff's shoulder and slammed into the bar, throwing off splinters of wood before passing through and puncturing a beer barrel, which exploded in a gout of froth. The bartender hit the deck.

As did Olmstead. For a different reason. Justice's .44 slug had torn a jagged hole through his chest, and he was jolted back with the force of a mule kick, slamming against the table behind him, spilling bottles and poker chips before sliding to the floor, blood soaking his shirtfront.

Wally Olmstead watched it with wide, terror-stricken eyes. All the while he was telling himself, *I'm not going to draw my gun*, but then he saw his brother go down before Ruff's Colt and some uncontrollable reflex caused Wally Olmstead to fill his hand, to try to bury a slug in Ruff Justice's heart.

He was far too slow. Justice shifted to his right and fired twice. The first bullet lifted Wally Olmstead to his toes, the second spun him around and hurled him against the chair beside him, which buckled and crashed to the floor, Wally Olmstead inert, blood-soaked, on top of it, his eyes flickering weakly, his last thoughts those of anger with himself for drawing his gun when he knew, knew . . .

Ruff stood looking down at them with an expression Cash Williams couldn't read. Anger still, certainly, but it was slowly fading to a kind of regret, or even sorrow—or maybe that was all Cash's imagination, for when Ruff spoke his voice was brisk, emotionless.

"There's enough silver money on the table to pay for coffins. Anybody know what happened to the horses these men rode in with?"

No one knew, or would answer.

Ruff only then holstered his gun, spun on his heel, and walked out, Cash tagging after him.

Ruff stood outside, looking at the long-running skies, saying nothing until, realizing Cash Williams was there, he turned and asked, "Still working for the line?"

"Sure. As soon as I've gotten a bank draft off to Bronk's widow I'm all yours. Though I could use some food and some sleep."

"Grab yourself some food, get your business taken care of, then go back to Conklin's and ask him where we can find some horses. Bring them in if you can."

"I got nothing to pay with."

"I'll be back. That's where I'm going. There's a man who's made an investment in this line and now he's going to have to chip in some money to keep it rolling. Adrienne gave me some money, but it's not enough. Her backer's going to have to come through." Ruff smiled. Her "backer" wouldn't like this a bit, but that was the way it had to be.

Recovering his gray, telling Conklin that Cash would be on his way over after eating, Justice rode back toward Fort Lincoln, wishing to hell that this were all over, that he could slide into his accustomed bunk and cast aside all worries concerning this petticoat line and get back to something that wasn't so hard on the nerves, like Indian fighting.

MacEnroe was not happy.

"How much money, Ruff? God's sake, I can't support those women in this endeavor. What happened to the other horses?"

Ruff told him. He filled him in on everything that had happened since MacEnroe had sent him out to do something a "little different" as if it were going to be escorting a Sunday social to their picnic.

"You've been busy," MacEnroe said at length.

"I'm afraid it's going to get busier, but we need

horses, sir, if it's not to fold right now, before they've gotten started."

MacEnroe's fingers drummed on the desk top. His eyes met Ruff's and he sighed.

"All right. Dammit, I'll tap my reserves. I suppose I owe it to Walter Court. Think there's any chance of ever getting it back?"

"Honestly? No. Though if willpower alone can do it, Adrienne Court will pull it off. The odds are just too long out there to my way of thinking, sir, but then I've been wrong before."

"I know," MacEnroe said with some bitterness. "All right. Money for horses. Anything else?"

"Not unless you'd consider sending a patrol over to Bear Creek to kind of check out the activity out that way—could be rumors of a Sioux gathering, you know."

"I can't spare the people, Ruff. I've got the real thing up north. Red Cloud's supposed to be drifting back across the Canuck line. I might, as a matter of fact, have to call you back."

"Don't break my heart."

"No." MacEnroe managed a smile. "There's no word on Stone Hand yet; I'm sorry about that."

"How did he break out? No one's ever broken that stockade before."

"I just don't know. He has to have had help, though," the colonel answered.

"Bear Foot?" Ruff suggested.

The colonel shook his head. "I wouldn't think so. He hated the man."

"Maybe." Ruff told MacEnroe of his encounter with the young Sioux. "I'm not sure what he wanted, but his explanation seemed unlikely. Maybe he didn't hate his father all that much. Possibly when he thought of Stone Hand hanging he decided it was something he just couldn't allow."

"Maybe." MacEnroe tugged at his mustache. "He hasn't come back, our young friend."

"No, and I doubt he will." Ruff rose from his chair, sweeping back his hair to put his wide hat on. "Now then—I can't delay too long. Might get in trouble with the boss."

"That way, is she?"

"Isn't she." Ruff grimaced.

"Maybe I ought to write up a letter explaining that this is a loan," MacEnroe said as he dug into the lock box which contained his private funds. Ruff smiled faintly—so the colonel had a penurious streak in him.

"Whatever's right, sir." Justice didn't mention the fact that it was unlikely Adrienne Court would ever be able to pay anyone back, that the Great Western was in the hole and sinking fast, minus a few employees, most of the way stations, some horses, and much of its capital.

MacEnroe counted out a hundred and a half in gold, which Ruff pocketed. "Do what you can," was all the colonel said.

"For how long?"

"What?"

"For how long, sir? I can't baby-sit forever."

"I know it." MacEnroe frowned, "and dammit, I need you back. B Company lost a party of raiders in the sandhills the other day—couldn't track them, they said. Hart seems to get lost out of sight of the fort." He smoothed back his graying hair. "For a time longer, Ruff. I can't give you a firm answer. Just give it a little while more."

The colonel was pouring himself a drink when Ruff left, his expression rueful. Perhaps he was thinking how expensive friendship can be.

Justice took the time to eat at the grub hall, spent a few minutes talking with Sergeant Ray Hardistein about things in general, then started back toward Bismarck, still aching in every joint, weary and unhappy.

Cash hadn't returned to the stable yet, so Ruff rode uptown, found the newspaper office, which doubled as a print shop, swung down, and went in, dusting himself off.

There was a plain woman in a dark dress with cones of newsprint pinned around her wrists to protect the cuffs, her nose smudged with ink, furiously setting type. Nearby was a crumpled proof of tomorrow's newspaper—*DUBLE KILLING*, the headline read. A red line was drawn through the misspelling.

A back door opened and a small, hunched man wearing spectacles came through, drying his hands.

"Yes?"

"Need some posters printed up."

"All right. How many? How soon?"

"Fifty. Soon as possible. Today would be fine." The printer frowned and Ruff added, "Cash money."

"It's possible." He scratched at his ear. "If it's not too detailed."

"I don't think so." Ruff pulled Adrienne's folded note from his pocket.

"'Freight and passengers through to Bear Creek, best rates, available immediately. Great Western Transport,'" the printer read. He mumbled his way through the rest of it, eyebrows lifting from time to time. "Mail contract? You don't say! That's news in itself."

The woman had come over. In a clipped voice she said, "Mr. Justice seems to be supplying us with all of our news this week."

"Will you set this up, Ellie?" the printer asked, handing the paper to her. "Ruff Justice, is it?" he said when she had flounced away.

"Afraid so."

"Anything else happening out on the plains we should know about?"

"Nothing much. If you've got an obituary column you might mention that the Chinaman, Lo, and Willie Canbury both bought it. Also a man named Bronk Williams. I guess you can dig up the particulars if there are any."

"Lord! What happened?"

"Hazards of rough country, I guess you'd say."

It was obvious Justice wasn't going to say anything else. He scribbled a note to himself, promised Ruff the posters by four, happily took some of the gold from Ruff's pockets, and waved goodbye.

Cash was waiting at the stable when Justice got back. He wasn't alone. They waited crouched in the shade, staring at Ruff with almond eyes. Six Chinese with long queues, silk hats, slippered feet.

"What's this?" Justice asked.

"Laborers. They're stranded, Ruff. I make out that they're related to Lo or knew him—maybe he was kind of a chief or something—can't quite understand everything they're telling me. Lo, anyway, brought them over to work in his restaurant. The restaurant was burned down—maybe on purpose. Now they want work. Any work, to put food in their mouths."

Ruff stood looking down at them. Six eager, round, gold-colored faces.

"We have just a little money," Ruff said to them. "Hard work and not much pay."

"We have nothing to eat," one of them answered.

"Food we've got. You won't go hungry. It's bad out there, though. Lots of Indians. Do you understand that?"

"Indians kill, starve kills," the spokesman answered.

"I brought 'em along," Cash said with an apologetic shrug. "They were trying to get a ranch job where I bought the horses. Man wouldn't have 'em—

they can't ride anyway, I don't think. I figured you could always tell 'em no, but with the Olmsteads down, Willie and Lo gone . . ."

"You can work for food," Ruff said deciding. "Building houses, changing horses. There might be money later, I don't know."

They were up, smiling, chattering to each other, shaking Ruff's hand as if he had promised them the moon.

"Let's see those horses," Justice growled. Then he stopped and slipped the spokesman for the Chinese twenty dollars. "Buy what you want to eat. Come back here."

They went off happily trouping down the street, and Justice wiped a hand across his eyes. "It's not getting any easier," he said to no one.

With Cash he rode out to a small oak-shaded ranch house and closed a deal for eight horses, which they herded back to the stableyard. By then the Chinese were back, and Conklin told him someone from the printer's office had been by looking for him.

"All right. You know, Cash, you're going to have to stick around to take care of business."

"I'm going to what?"

"The lady's going to advertise. There's going to be freight running to Bear Creek now, maybe some passengers. We need a man to handle all of that."

"The hell with that. I'm not living in an office."

"It'll just be until the next run. I'll have Adrienne send someone through or let me hire someone here."

"Nope. I quit if that's how it is. You hire someone else now for that work."

"I'll do it," Conklin piped up.

"You?"

"Sure, why not? I can count to ten and everything. I'll paint me another sign and hang it up right there.

I get around a little. Folks looking for wagons always come here. I can guide 'em to you."

"You know the money situation, Conklin."

"I know, but damn me if I don't believe that woman's got a chance of making it now. Got you and Cash, Allie James and old Rupe, a whole flock of new Chinamen. It won't cost me much to try. If anyone needs a wagon I'll let Great Western borrow one of mine. After you get all set up proper I won't have to do much of anything, will I? Take in my pay and do what I always done."

"You're on," Cash said eagerly.

"All right," Ruff agreed a moment later. "It's probably best. If anything . . ."

"Hiyup!" The call turned their heads. A freight wagon was rolling in, and it was loaded—not with goods but with a dozen miners and their rolls. "Hey you!" The driver called out. "Where in hell's the Great Western depot?"

"Right here," Conklin shouted back, and the wagon, rolling to a stop, deposited its dazed-looking passengers.

"Who the hell are you?" Ruff asked.

"Fields, W.O." The driver was pulling off his long gloves. "You Justice?" he peered at Ruff with swollen eyes. "I'm supposed to get my pay from you, grab a night's sleep, and take back any passengers you got. I'm the stage driver, friend. Miss Adrienne Court says so."

"All right. How'd you get here?"

"Miss Court found out some of the boys were pulling out and sent up to the first station for a wagon. We stacked some mattresses in the back and set off. Rupert Gates drove the first leg while I snoozed. Then he dropped off. I went on through to Muellers' Post and got fresh horses from Pierce—he'd managed to round some of them up that the Indians had scattered. That half-breed drove through to Coyote

Springs while I slept some more, then he dropped off there to start rebuilding. Me, I came on through. Here I am and I want to be paid."

Ruff replied, "You deserve it. Tell you what," he said, fishing some money from his pockets. "You get something to eat, get some sleep. You're working for Conklin here at this end. I'm leaving the stage and the freight wagon both. If you find another driver, you hire him on as well."

"Thanks," Fields said, taking the gold. "First damned gold I seen in six months of trying to find it."

"I'll be damned," Cash Williams was saying. "She's really doing it, Justice. The woman actually might make this thing work."

"She might at that. Cash—we got a little project here." His eyes flickered to the Chinese and back to the horses. "We are going to teach these men to ride."

"Teach 'em?" Cash frowned. "Do you learn to ride? I thought it was something you just naturally did. I had me a full-grown sorrel when I was three."

"Did you?" Justice was thinking about something else. Pierce. Just what in hell was he up to? Of course he couldn't have refused to help, but he had gone out and rounded up some of the scattered horses. Maybe he hadn't planned on anyone's coming through to ask for them, though. It didn't figure however you looked at it, and Justice didn't like it.

Most of the afternoon was wasted trying to teach the Chinese how to sit a horse. Ruff left it to Cash and went off to the print shop. The ink was still wet when he got the posters. He walked around town nailing them up with his gun butt, posting them on awnings, in saloons, in the restaurant and general store.

Now they would know. Now Boggs too would know that this was serious, that Adrienne was going ahead despite the warnings. Now, Justice knew, the warnings would get a little nastier. Boggs hadn't just been shooting off his mouth—he wouldn't stand for it.

An hour before sunset they rode out, trailing down the main street of Bismarck, the Chinese jouncing around on the backs of their saddleless horses. Men stood on the boardwalks pointing and laughing. Except for one man—big, dark, his face clouded up like thunder as he watched the parade. Anson Boggs wasn't smiling a bit.

9

The half-breed stood glowering at them in the dawn light. Luke had an ax in his hands, wore a gunbelt and a sour expression. He had actually done some work, Ruff noticed immediately. Two more logs had been set in place.

Justice swung down and signaled to the Chinese, who slipped from their horses and stood around holding their asses.

"Who is this?" Luke asked.

"New men."

"More China boys?"

"That's right."

"What for?"

"To man this station."

"I don't work with China boys," the half-breed said.

"All right. Go on back to Muellers' Post then, with Pierce," Ruff said. "We'll be riding out in an hour, as soon as I show these boys what to do."

Luke didn't answer. He dropped the ax, snatched up his shirt and bedroll, and walked to where his horse was picketed. In five minutes he was saddled and out of the camp, riding west.

"Friendly bugger," Cash muttered.

"Watch yourself around him. It may be that he likes to cut off fingers and tongues and such."

"I haven't forgotten," Cash said. He looked to

where the Chinese were washing up, crouched down beside the limestone pool. "Kind of dangerous leaving them out here, isn't it?"

"Yes. It's the least likely station to be hit, though, being closest to Bismarck and Fort Lincoln."

"Yes, it's less likely, but it could happen. They haven't got any way of defending themselves, Ruff."

"No. You want to stay on for a while and help out?" he asked.

"No, I don't," Williams said honestly, "but maybe I should. I'm kind of responsible for the little buggers, ain't I?"

"Maybe. I know I'd feel better having you here. That would leave each station well manned—assuming Pierce sticks."

Cash tilted back his hat and grinned. "Me for a superintendent—maybe they'd rather go back to Bismarck and go hungry."

"You'll do." Ruff saw the Chinese carrying a log to the wall. "And so will they—they came to work, and I hope you can keep up with them."

Ruff split the horses in half and started out, riding the gray, leading the remuda behind him. He liked Cash Williams, but it felt good to be unfettered again, to be alone and silent, to watch the wind in the long grass, the clouds stacking themselves on the northern horizon, to flush the nesting birds from the grass as he rode, to shout once loudly to the wind and the far mountains.

The Sioux came up from out of nowhere. They had been in the coulee ahead of Ruff, a coulee deep enough to hide a man on horseback—or an army of them, and invisible from the flats.

They came up with a chorus of war cries, feathers flying, and Ruff flipped the sheath to his Spencer off, took the reins in his teeth, and started firing.

That was all there was to do. A man who turns

and runs just gets it in the back instead of the front. There were six of them, Teton, he thought at a glance before he triggered off, blew the first man from his horse to be trampled by the following riders, levered through a cartridge and fired again before a man could blink.

There had been six of them, now there were five, and as Ruff's Spencer spoke again, there were four. A bullet from an Indian's gun clipped the gray's ear, and it shied violently, throwing Ruff off the mark.

He was down now, riding at the side of the gray, firing under its neck. The Indians, expecting easy prey, seeing two of their men go down nearly together, had slowed up, and now they halted, sitting their prancing horses, firing at Justice as he continued past them and toward the coulee, hoping to God there were no more of them ahead.

He shot the leg out from under a paint pony and then felt the savage jerk on his line. One of the remuda horses had been hit. It went down on its head, rolling, tripping the others, and the tether line went taut.

One moment Ruff was making his run, firing from the side of the gray, keeping them at bay, and the next the line went taut, ripping the saddle from Ruff's horse, spilling him.

The gray stumbled, and Justice rolled to one side, trying to avoid the onrushing horses behind him. The wounded horse struggled to get to its feet some distance back, stirring up the dust.

The Sioux heeled their ponies, and fresh war whoops filled Justice's ears as they came on again. He rose shakily to a knee, his head spinning, fired twice and perhaps ineffectively, then rose and made a stumbling run toward the coulee not thirty feet away.

It was a long thirty feet. Stars danced in his head, and a bullet from a Sioux's gun clipped his bootheel off, tripping him with the impact. Justice spun, palmed his Colt, and fired four times, scattering the Indians.

Then he was up again, staggering on, hair in his eyes, reloading as he ran.

A bullet whipped past his ear near enough for him to feel the hot wind it pushed aside in its passing. He went headfirst toward the coulee, landing, rolling, coming to a halt in the sandy, brush-filled bottom.

He was sitting, legs spread, head reeling, when the first warrior recklessly rode over the rim. Ruff, holding his Colt with both hands, triggered off, and the .44 gutted the horse.

It rolled downslope, crushing brush, sending spumes of sand in all directions. The warrior screamed loudly and tried to drag himself away on a crushed leg. Ruff shot him again as the horse slid to a stop on its side, its thrashing head only thirty inches from Justice's foot.

Ruff tried to rise, stumbled, got to his feet again, and charged into the heavy brush, tangled blackthorn and sumac, thorns scratching at his face and hands, tugging at his buckskins.

Bullets from above clipped brush all around him, and Ruff dove to his belly, wriggling through the brush, moving with silence and not speed in mind. He found a small clearing, a dish-shaped depression scooped out of the wash, and rolled into it, lying there bathed in perspiration, thumbing fresh cartridges into his Colt.

They were near, very near. Sweat trickled down and rolled into Ruff's eyes. He hardly blinked. He heard the whispered words of a Sioux, saw the reddish haunch of a horse, saw the yellow hand painted on it through the screen of brush all around him.

There was a very good chance he could take that warrior, but it was too dangerous. He couldn't see the others. He could hear nothing suddenly but the humming of cicadas, the angry whine of mosquitoes around his head. His mouth was dry and gritty, his eyes red-rimmed and stony.

Something moved to his left; a twig cracked.

Ruff's grip slackened and then tightened on his Colt. He slowed his breathing and his heart settled into an even thumping pace.

Nothing. He could see nothing now, hear nothing. Perhaps they had given it up, collected the horses, and gotten out of there.

The Sioux burst from the brush as Ruff rolled onto his back firing at point-blank range. He missed.

Dammit all, he had time to think before the Sioux's body collided with his. The Indian's face was savagely burned from the near miss. Black powder had tattooed his flesh as it came spewing out of Ruff's muzzle half-burned.

Ruff saw that in a fragment of a second, saw the crimson and black warpaint, saw the silver flash of a downward-arcing knife.

He had time to throw his gun arm up protectively and the Indian's wrist jolted against his forearm, the knife coming up short, slashing past within inches of Ruff's eyes.

Ruff slammed his knee up and caught the Indian's groin. Rolling aside, Justice came to his feet, slipping his own bowie from its sheath at the back of his belt.

The Sioux, doubled up with pain, panting, knife held low, circled warily.

Justice wanted to glance behind him, to see if the others were coming, but he couldn't risk it. His eyes were riveted to the man before him, the man with the burned face, the scarred, painted chest, the rawhide-handled knife.

The Sioux feinted, withdrew, feinted again, and then swept up with a slashing cut designed to disembowel. The point of his knife just ticked Ruff's buckskin shirt.

Justice kicked out, wanting to break the Indian's kneecap, but the Sioux was too quick. He countered with a high kick aimed at Ruff's knife.

The sand was soft underfoot, slowing their movements; the air was close and warm. They might have been the only two men in the world, hemmed in by brush, isolated.

Justice wanted to make a move, to destroy this warrior and get the hell out of there before his friends showed up, but patience was the key to survival. A rash move could cost him his life.

The Indian moved forward, crow-hopping in, knife cutting the air as he swung it back and forth, black eyes flinty, expressionless. And then the Indian lost patience and lunged in, his knife thrusting toward Ruff's ribs.

Ruff twisted, caught and pinned the arm with his elbow, and struck back savagely, brutally. His bowie flashed in the sunlight and was buried to the hilt in the Sioux's throat.

There wasn't even a sound from the warrior's lips, nothing but the hot froth of blood, the frantic wriggling of his body as his heart pumped the life from him. The Sioux went limp, and still Justice held him up. Then slowly he stepped away, letting the warrior fall on his face against the sand. Already the flies were gathering, and Justice, blood-soaked, watched them with revulsion.

Sheathing his knife, he picked up his Colt and headed into the deeper brush, moving swiftly and silently. He halted, crouched down, and waited again. A warrior's life is filled with hours of waiting and seconds of savagery. Justice had grown used to it.

He listened and watched and waited. Gradually the shadows crept out from the western bank of the deep coulee, slowly the sun heeled over and was drawn toward the western mountains. Still Justice did not emerge from his hiding place.

Not until darkness had settled, the skies coming alive with milky stars, did Ruff creep from the brush, cold and stiff, and clamber up the sandy bluff to stand looking across the plains. The horses, of course, were gone, even his gray. Below lay the dead and before him a long, long walk through hostile territory.

It was dawn before Muellers' Post hove into view. Ruff was alone on the empty prairie; the grass stubbled red-gold in the morning light flicked against his calves as he walked into the burned-out station.

The place appeared to be deserted, which didn't surprise him in the least. Pierce had taken the stock and fled, no doubt. And the way station, fire-blackened, empty, stood facing Ruff, its windows like haunted eyes, watching.

He stayed in the scorched cottonwoods for a time, studying the place. Meadowlarks sang to each other off in the long grass. A vulture floated high against a blue-gold sky. Nothing moved within the post perimeter. No one spoke, moved out to dip water from the well, whistled with the pleasantness of a bright plains morning.

Empty. Justice hobbled toward the stone house, pistol in hand. Inside he found the dead man.

Hardy Pierce lay sprawled on the floor, not far from where Lo had been found. His fingers had been cut off, his ears clipped from his skull, his belly opened.

He had gone slowly and painfully. Fear, hatred, agony were written on his face even in death. Justice just stood there, staring down. He had never liked Hardy Pierce, but you don't wish a death like that on any man.

It tore the bottom out of Ruff's conviction that

Pierce had been working for Boggs, that he had faked the Sioux attack on the way station, that he was planning on stealing the company's horses.

"Luke," Ruff said to himself. "It has to be the breed." The breed who had ridden off alone to this station yesterday. Why, Ruff didn't know, but it had to be Luke who had killed and mutilated Pierce.

"Maybe the bastard really meant to go straight," Justice said, still looking at Pierce. Or maybe he had just come out second best in a thieves' quarrel.

He dragged the body outside and buried Pierce while the sun rose higher into a white sky. After that he stripped off his buckskins and bathed at the well, washing his clothes as best he could.

He searched for Pierce's horse, not expecting to find it, and came up empty. He looked unhappily across the prairie. It was a long and dangerous walk to Bear Creek. The Sioux were drifting in now. The Sioux were out there—and a man who got his pleasure by cutting living bodies to pieces of meat.

Without a horse, without a rifle, Justice didn't like his chances. He looked again at the old stone house, and walking to it, started searching for a broom and a bucket. He was appointing himself way-station boss until the next wagon rolled through.

Or until the man with the knife returned.

10

◆━━•━◆━•━━◆

The days were long, the nights cold and black. Justice slept away from the house, in the shelter of the cottonwoods, and he slept lightly.

He had set snares and was living almost exclusively on rabbit these days. A fat two-point buck had come creeping into the yard one evening, but Justice had left it alone—he didn't want to fire his gun unless necessary. Scenting fire and ash and possibly death, the buck had fled abruptly, even the smell of clean water from the well not able to stay its instinct toward flight.

Ruff kept himself busy cleaning up the house, rebuilding the pole corrals, but his attention was never totally on his work. A column of dust lifted by dust devils on the prairie brought his head up, narrowed his eyes as he peered through the heat-veiled distances, searching for approaching horsemen, for the first wagon or stagecoach—if there was to be any more.

It wasn't until the third day that one of those dust clouds transformed itself into something solid and defined, and Justice, peering into the sun, saw the stagecoach rolling into Muellers' Post.

He stood with his hands on his hips, his gun just beneath his fingertips, watching. He recognized it as the Great Western coach finally and then made out

Cash Williams standing in the box as he drove, studying the station.

He waved after a time and the coach came on in, stirring up the ashes which still coated the yard.

"Didn't think you'd be out here," Cash said. "No horses?" he asked, looking around.

"Nope."

"Damn. Pierce take off with them after all?"

"Climb down and we'll talk about it," Justice told him. Three passengers were climbing out of the stage— two men of middle age and an older woman.

"Is this the rest stop?" she kept saying. "They certainly promised us more than this. I shall write to the management."

Cash grinned. "I've been hearing quite a bit of that."

"Where's Fields?"

"We switched at Coyote Springs. He's with the Chinamen. Those boys have nearly got that place put together—you'd be surprised."

"Maybe I ought to bring them over here." Ruff was unhitching the horses. "We'd better cool them down." To the passengers he called, "We'll be a little while, folks. Sorry—the Sioux got our horses."

"That's certainly not very good planning," the woman prattled. "Aren't we already behind schedule? I told Mr. Dickinson to expect me on Tuesday—I just know we won't make it now."

The horses were cooled down and then watered. While they grazed at a distance from the station Ruff filled Cash in. "I don't get it, but it seems Luke must have done it."

"Guess again," Cash Williams said. "The breed never made it a mile from Coyote Springs. One of the Chinamen found him at the side of the road, his body all hacked to pieces."

"Damn."

"Yeah, looks like we've been guessing wrong. It must have been the Sioux after all—likely the bunch you tangled with."

"Maybe." Justice watched the horses graze, watched the wind shift the long grass. Two white butterflies floated above the silver-green grass blades. "Maybe so. I'm riding with you, looks like. We'll have to hire someone else to take over Muellers' Post. Sure seems we hire a lot of men," he said, dusting off.

"Yes, but you haven't had to fire many," Cash said with a tight smile. "They just don't seem to last long enough for that."

Even the old woman couldn't find anything to complain about when they reached the Bear Creek station, the horses dragging, all of them weary.

It was running the way they had all been meant to. Most of the house had been completed and there was smoke rising from the stone chimney.

Rupert Gates was at the corral, and when he saw the stage rolling in through the pines he snatched up his rifle and jogged toward the station house yelling.

In another minute Lucille appeared in the doorway, hands on hips, wearing an apron over her blue dress, her hair loose and golden in the sunlight.

By the time Cash Williams braked to a stop, Allie James had arrived, buttoning his shirt up.

"We were wondering if anyone was ever going to come again," Allie said, opening the door to let the passengers out.

"Stuck, did you?" Rupert said to Cash. "As crazy as the rest of us?"

"It looks that way." Cash handed the reins to Allie, who climbed up and drove the team toward the corrals.

Lucille stood back for just a moment, looking at

Ruff Justice, a smile playing about her lips, then in
three steps she was in his arms, clinging to him.

"I knew you'd be back," she said in a tone which
indicated she had known nothing of the sort.

"For a time. What's to eat?"

She composed herself, stepped back, and announced
to everyone, "We've beans and vension inside, hot
coffee as well. Doesn't look like it's going to rain, so
you won't mind that we haven't got all the roof up
yet."

The passengers, looking relieved to find something
going right, went inside. "You," Lucille said to Ruff,
"I'll talk to later." She squeezed his hand and went
in herself, Cash following after and casting a specula-
tive glance at Justice.

"Ever'thing all right up the trail?" Rupert asked,
spitting out a stream of tobacco juice.

"Far from it." Justice told him how far.

"Damn. Don't sound good. Haven't seen an Indian around here, but I've seen their sign from time
to time, and so's Allie—we're keeping the girl on a
close tether."

"How's she getting on out here?"

"Loves it. And she's a pleasure to have around.
Used to be she was kind of mopy, you know. She's
brightened up and got some color in her cheeks.
She's a good kid, Lucille."

"Allie think so too?"

"Allie thinks highly of her." The old man's voice
lowered. "Was I you I wouldn't carry that huggin'
too far in sight of the boy. I ain't sure, but I think
he's fixin' to ask her to marry him."

"Well, that might be a fine thing. Maybe that's the
way it should be." Ruff looked around at the pine-
clad hills, at the grassy, flower-sprinkled meadows. It
was a pretty place for two people to start out.

"Let's have some eats, Mr. Justice. You thinkin' of something'?"

"Me?" Ruff smile. "Not hardly."

Well, maybe just a little. A little of the Crow woman in the faraway mountains and of the time they had tried to start a peaceful life in the wilderness. Maybe just a little.

He tried to stay clear of Lucille while they ate, but she didn't make it easy. If she had any idea of what Allie James had in mind she gave no indication of it.

She brushed against Ruff as she served, bending over his back to the table. She sat beside him, and Justice felt the gentle pressure of her knee against his.

"Isn't Allie going to eat?"

"He already did. Just before you pulled in," she answered.

Rupert, damn him, was grinning. Ruff cut his venson roast up and ate slowly. The woman had a way with cooking, too—surprisingly. She must have marinated the meat, for it was tender, not gamey at all.

"You like it?" she asked, turning her head around, bending low until she was staring up into his face.

"Very good."

The old woman clucked to herself, and Lucille sat upright again. What Rupe had said was true—there was an animation, a life to the girl that had been lacking before. Maybe she had finally gotten what she wanted out of life, away from Adrienne and her chronic ambition.

Lucille seemed puzzled and a little hurt at the way Ruff acted. When she suggested an after-meal walk, he refused; and when the stage pulled out half an hour later she was just standing in the yard, her head cocked curiously to one side, watching after them.

The fresh horses made a difference. They moved out briskly and made Bear Creek by sundown, rolling in through the main street as the lanterns were lit in the saloons and gambling halls, as the miners streamed in from the hills to throw away whatever money they had.

Cash halted in front of the office, where another of those now-familiar Great Western signs hung, and Justice climbed down stiffly to let the passengers out.

They stood looking around at the shabby town, the forbidding hills, then wandered off after asking where the hotel was. "There's a box for someone," Cash called and tossed it to Ruff, who glanced at the label, not recognizing the name.

"Not going to check in?" Ruff asked.

"I'll leave that up to you, friend," said Cash, and with a laugh he started the coach toward the stables at the end of the street.

Justice looked up at the lighted office window, sighed, and climbed the stairs. Adrienne was there, her hair pinned up severely, wearing a green eyeshade, her pencil scratching across a sheet of yellow paper.

"You're awfully late, Mr. Justice. I've been expecting you for days." The tone was a schoolmarm's.

"I had a little trouble. I need a new horse, by the way."

"You do?" She put her pencil down and looked up, the top half of her face green beneath the eyeshade. "Well, you can get one of the stable horses."

"Miss Court, I can't ride a wagon horse. I need a good animal under me. I'd appreciate having a couple hundred dollars to get one."

"A couple . . ."

"And if the company can't see its way clear to buy one for me, call it a loan, and I'll pay you back."

"I suppose I could *loan* it to you, but you see, the expenses are just . . . well, all right. You'll have to sign a note for the money, though."

Justice looked at the ceiling and then closed his

eyes tightly. "Fine. Cash Williams just pulled in with the stage from Bismarck. He had three passengers with him and this." Ruff handed over the box.

"Fine," she said brusquely. "Now I've got some big news for you." Adrienne paused as if waiting for Ruff to jump up and down with excitement. At this point, he was thinking, the biggest news she could give him was to tell him he was no longer needed.

"What is it?" he said, answering her expectant look at last.

"We have the mail contract."

"That's fine, but—"

"Please don't interrupt, just listen." She rose and walked to the window, putting the eyeshade aside, clasping her hands behind her back. "We have the mail contract, and the first delivery will be leaving in the morning. I don't think Mr. Boggs is going to like that very much."

"No."

"He won't like this at all." She spun triumphantly toward him. "We're taking out the quarterly gold shipment of the United Mines here. It's the biggest mining concern in Bear Creek. I met the manager, a Mr. Barnes, and he's given us the job!"

She was lit up like the night sky in a summer lightning storm. Ruff was a little dark cloud across the room.

"You know what you're asking for?"

"Yes, I think so. Robbers, you mean."

"We ran into some a while back who were willing to kill me and everyone on the coach for a few thousand dollars. They'll be back with an army when word of this gets out. And if Boggs is going to survive this freight war, he'll have to stop you quick. You're getting a good price for this, aren't you?"

"Five percent," she answered, more subdued

now—or perhaps that was anger creeping into her expression.

"Yes. If you get that revenue it'll pretty well set you up."

"That's what I've been trying to tell you!"

"He can't allow it, Anson Boggs can't. Not taking him into account, we've got every holdup artist on the plains who would give an arm to get at that United gold. Word must be out around town by now."

"I know there's a hazard involved. United knows. That's why we have to do it. That's why the pay is so good. I don't care if there are a thousand armed men out there, this gold shipment must get through to Bismarck!"

But she didn't tell him how to do it.

"Can't you hire extra men?"

"Yes. I don't know how I'll be able to tell which ones I can trust, but I'll hire some." Ruff paused, shaking his head. "It won't be enough, Adrienne. Nothing will be enough."

"You can beat them." She came nearer to him, her face shifting out of the harsh glare of the lanternlight and into the shadow so that only her eyes gleamed. Eager, perhaps avaricious, desperate and utterly determined, wide blue eyes. "You can do it, Justice, you'll see. Everyone says you're the best there is on the plains."

"Sure." That didn't mean he was a one-man army. "We'll try it. That's all I can promise. We'll try. I'll tell Cash to look around for some men. When do we roll out?"

"In the morning," she said, and Justice looked to the ceiling and beyond again, grinding his teeth.

"In the morning," he repeated. "I need food, sleep, money for a horse and a new rifle."

"All right." Unexpectedly she placed a hand on

Justice's arm and perhaps even attempted a smile. Her hard face softened momentarily at least. "Don't forget to sign a note for the loan."

She wasn't joking. "No," he said. "I won't forget."

It was cool when he went out. Bear Creek was roaring. The general store was still open. The clerk tried to press a new Winchester needle gun with a seventeen-shot capacity on him—"All the men are carrying these now"—but Ruff wanted another Spencer .56. He bought a box of cartridges and examined the thumb-thick bullets, bullets designed to shoot flat over a distance and take down a bull buffalo in its tracks. They would also, some said, stop a locomotive.

Refitted, Justice went to the stable, finding nothing suitable. A little luck was bound to come his way sooner or later, and it did on that night. Passing the River of Gold Saloon he was stopped by a man in a dark town suit and white hat.

"Wouldn't be interested in buying a horse, would you?"

He was a gambler who had backed three kings too far, and the horse was a leggy, deep-chested, white-faced sorrel worth the hundred Ruff finally paid for it and then some.

"Maybe if I see you again when I'm flush I could buy it back," the gambler said.

"Sure." But Justice never saw him again and he rode the sorrel to its death.

Mounted now, he still wanted to eat, to find Cash and try to round up some help—it would be hard to come by. There were plenty of hard-luck men in town who would do anything for a buck, and Justice figured he would have to use some. But what he wanted was good fighting men, plainsmen, and they were at a premium.

He located Cash at the restaurant, explained things, and gulped down a cup of coffee. Then Justice went out looking for guards, with little luck. He hired four men, two of them much less than what he wanted, then gave it up.

He had one more piece of business he wanted to attend to before morning, and he went looking for María Salazar.

11

———•••——————•••———

She was lithe, strong, and eager. The lantern burned
low on the bureau as María shed her dress and
underthings, leaving her stockings until last. She had
laughed with joy when Justice found her in a dancehall
twirling across the floor with a miner in jackboots.

Now as Ruff lay on his back naked, watching her
by the faint glow of the lamp, she put one foot up on
the bed and slowly peeled a dark stocking down her
shapely bronze thigh. She glanced at him and smiled
from behind the silky dark screen of her hair.

The other stocking followed, and then she was up
onto the bed, straddling Ruff, throwing one leg across
him to sit on his abdomen, eyes shining as she
leaned forward and kissed him deeply, hungrily.

Ruff's hands ran along her spine, from her shoulders to the cleft between her smooth, solidly muscled
buttocks. María lifted herself and positioned Ruff,
sinking slowly onto him as she looked into his eyes,
her own expression growing sultry, faraway.

"Very nice, hombre. Know how good it feels to
have you inside me, man?"

"How nice?" She lifted herself slowly and again
sank onto him.

"Ver' nice. Ver' nice." Her voice took on the
rhythm of her body, a slow, cadenced rising and
falling which matched the rise and fall, the sway of
her hips and pelvis as she worked herself against Ruff

Justice, her hands resting on her own thighs, now dropping to run across Ruff's hard abdomen, to his lips where he kissed her fingertips and back to where they were joined, where with delight she fingered the root of his shaft.

"Ver' nice, ver' good to have it. You came back to María, eh?"

"I never would have forgiven myself if I hadn't." He grabbed her by the neck and pulled her down roughly, savaging her mouth with his own, bruising her lips against her teeth as his body began to rise to match her rhythm, as the hot blood began to pulse.

"Little higher. There, don't stop." She panted in his ear, her breath moist and soft. Her tongue touched his ear and ran around the whorl of it, sending a delicate shiver through Ruff's body.

She leaned back, bracing herself with her arms, and Ruff's head lifted to allow his lips to brush across her nipples standing taut against her round, firm breasts. María had begun to sway violently against him, to thrust her pelvis against his bruisingly as the muscles inside of her contracted and expanded, and Justice sagged back, smiling, watching her work against him, lifting herself to a shuddering climax.

She collapsed against Ruff, petting his hair, her lips kissing his nipples, working up his throat as her fingers clutched at him.

Her mouth locked against his, her tongue darting between his teeth to tease his, and again she began her pitching, swaying motion, Ruff arching his back to lift her higher, to bring a gasp of pleasure to her lips as Ruff found his own climax.

María's head was thrown back, her mouth open to reveal her white, even teeth. Her eyes were open, dream-filled, her face glowing with enjoyment.

She lay against him sleepily, kittenish in her posture, in the small soft sounds which emerged from her throat, and Ruff stroked her hair, her sleek back, her thighs before finally falling off to a deep, deserved sleep.

This time, however, it was not a dreamless sleep. The old haunting images came back. Four Dove on a white stallion riding down the blood-red falls, the archers on the shore loosing their arrows as Justice struggled to swim through the river, his body made of stone, his heart a writhing ball of snakes in his pounding chest.

He found her somehow as the stallion went beneath the crimson surface of the waters and Four Dove's arms locked around his neck, becoming snakes themselves, and when she rose again from the water her face was that of a mummy, her eyes only hollow sockets filled with amethyst, and Justice tried to fight her off, to pry her clutching fingers free, but it was already too late. The falls thundered in his ears as they tumbled down, the blood-red river washing over them, pulling them under as the distant voices roared with laughter.

It was the dark of night. Justice sat up, his body glossed with perspiration, chilled by the night. María lay sprawled on top of him, and he shoved her away with momentary anger. Then he shook his head in the darkness, kissed her exposed, golden shoulder, and walked to the window to look out at the empty street.

The stars were shimmering brightly in the black velvet sky. From a great distance an owl called twice. Ruff Justice began to dress, knowing there would be no more sleep for him on that night.

He went out into the dark streets, rifle in hand. It was somewhere between four and five and the town was locked up tight. He walked to the stable, saddled the sorrel, and led it out without waking the kid who was sleeping in the loft.

Out in the dark, chill street again, he smelled coffee brewing somewhere and started uptown, noticing the lamps which were beginning to flicker on across town.

He liked this hour, the hour before dawn when the world was still, when it seemed nothing violent could happen, when a man abroad beneath the milky stars might have been the only man walking the earth.

He hitched the sorrel before the restaurant and sat down on the boardwalk to wait, loading the weapon he had purchased, checking the action, wishing he had had the time to try the sights and see how it fired.

Ruff turned at the sound of bootheels on the boardwalk, "Howdy, Ruff," Cash Williams said. He was blowing in his hands, trying to warm them. "You're up early."

"Where are the men?"

"I don't know. Half of them I don't expect will show once they realize what we're hiring them on for. I picked up four more after I saw you last night. That gives us eight if they all make it."

"If they were eight good ones it wouldn't be enough."

The door to the restaurant clicked open behind them and Ruff got to his feet, stretching massively before he and Cash Williams went in to do a lot of damage to platters full of grits, potatoes, eggs, and ham.

It was dawning when they came out. A golden line stretched itself along the eastern horizon, and a high cloud showed like a red pennant against the sky, the stars beaming through its sheer fabric.

Ruff untied the horse and led it down toward the stable, Cash, his shoulders hunched, hands deep in his pockets, beside him.

Six of the men they had hired were waiting there.

Ruff was counting on only two of them. Ed Tower had ridden with the Texas Rangers, been a marshal in the Kansas town of Frémont. He was footloose and drank too much to hold down any job for a length of time, but he was tough and knew fighting.

The other was Handy Maxwell, a tall, lean redhead that Ruff didn't care for much. Maxwell had dabbled in peacekeeping and in rustling. He was sour and silent but deadly. When he hired on, however, his loyalty was to the brand or the company. He would do when the chips were down.

The others were drifters, out-of-work miners, men who owned a gun and little else. Three of them had horses—Maxwell, Tower, and a Jayhawker named Gant. The other three were put inside the coach.

"Ready?" Justice asked Cash Williams.

"I guess," Cash said with a shrug and a smile.

The streets were starting to fill up with people when the stage rolled down the street again and halted in front of the United Mines office. More than a few people stopped to stare after the coach, and Ruff was certain that half the town knew what was up.

Cal Barnes, the manager of United, was a big, bluff man with thinning sandy hair and a worried expression.

"You've got a hell of a lot of gold riding with you, Justice. If it doesn't get through it'll be the end for me. The owners won't stand for it."

"It'll get through," Justice said with more confidence than he felt.

"Don't know how that woman talked me into . . ." His voice fell away into an indistinct grumble. "Come on! I'll have you loaded."

There were three green strongboxes, each lettered in gold. They were very heavy. The mine-office employees who carried them to the boot of the stage-coach staggered under the weight.

"Better throw one in the box," Cash shouted. "You'll have my tail end dragging."

A few minutes later Adrienne showed up, wearing a green velvet suit and a tiny green hat with a veil. She looked over arrangements, counted heads as the guards sat impatiently waiting, and finally said, "Well, I guess we're fixed up as well as we can be. We've got as good a chance as anyone else of getting through." Spying the mine manager, she lifted her voice heartily. "I'm sure your precautions will be adequate, Mr. Justice. Goodbye, and good luck."

"Looks like rain," Handy Maxwell grumbled. "I don't have my slicker with me, either."

Ruff glanced toward the northern skies. It looked like rain, all right. For days he had been noticing the thunderheads stacked against the northern horizon, and this morning he had seen the small, frail pennant of cloud creeping over, like an advance scout for the legions of lightning-spiked clouds to follow.

"Might make it better for us," Cash said hopefully. "Keep their heads down, hide us."

"Don't count on that," Ruff answered. "If it starts to come down hard we're all going to spend a lot of time pushing. That coach is way overloaded right now. As for keeping their heads down, man, that much gold lifts them right up off their shoulders like a flock of geese in a berry patch. Handy!" He gave the man two dollars. "Get on over to the general store and pick up a slicker. You'll damn sure need it."

They rolled out fifteen minutes later. The sun was bright as it coasted into the cornflower-blue sky, but the land to Ruff's left was deeply shadowed.

He rode in the lead, feeling the mounting wind against his body. Behind him was the coach, flanked by Maxwell and Ed Tower, three men riding inside. Behind the coach fifty feet or so was the last man. It looked impressive enough, Ruff supposed, enough to scare the amateurs off, but it didn't give him any sense of security. There weren't enough guns in the territory to keep them from trying for that much gold.

It had started to rain before they reached the Bear Creek station. Allie James dashed from the house in a yellow slicker, his eyes widening and then narrowing as he saw the outriders with Ruff Justice.

"What's up?" he asked, his fingers already at the harness clips.

"Gold. Everything all right here?"

"I don't know," he said tautly.

"Lucille . . ."

"Not Lucille; she's in the house. Won't come out of her room either. What in hell did you do to her, Justice? She . . ."

"What's the trouble, Allie?" Ruff said irritably.

"Rupe. He was making his rounds of the hills like he does. He usually takes two hours or so. He's been gone since dawn."

It was past noon now. Ruff glowered, looked to the cloud-shrouded hills, and said, "Don't go looking for him. Stay in close, watch Lucille."

"That's what I've been doing, dammit," Allie snapped, "but it doesn't make me feel any better. He's an old man, Justice. Maybe he's layin' up there with a broken leg or something. With this rain comin' in . . ."

"All right. I'll have a look. Cash! See that everyone gets something to eat, but make sure this stage is guarded too."

"All right."

"Where's he usually go, Allie? Which way?"

"Along that ridge, through the high meadow, back

around toward the saddleback—that's where we've found Indian sign off and on, not much, an unshod pony's tracks or two, never more."

"Plenty enough if they took him unaware," Ruff commented, looking to the hills.

"Dammit, I know that!" Allie was really hot, very worried.

"I'll have a look-see. Finish hitching, will you?"

"Yeah, sure."

Justice swung onto the sorrel's back once more and moved out briskly. His intention was to work backward along the route Allie had described to him. If Rupert Gates had been injured, fallen perhaps, he might hear him crying out. If Rupe was down and unable to call out, the chances of finding him were close to nil.

Justice rode up beside Cash, who stood, rifle in hand, hat tugged low. Rain ran from the brim of his hat, glossed the shoulders of his slicker.

"Stay loose, Cash. It may be nothing but a fall. It may be that Rupe ran into a Sioux. Could also be that he stumbled on something else. Maybe someone wanting to hit the stage here."

"I'm not letting the coach out of my sight, don't you worry. You watch your butt, though, Justice."

"I intend to."

The grass was damp and heavy around the legs of the high-stepping, blaze-faced sorrel as Justice moved through the low-hanging clouds toward the hills, which seemed vibrant, deep green with pines.

He rode silently through the timber, taking a zig-zag course which gave him the best chance of coming across a man afoot. The trouble was, to be visible to Rupe he also had to be exposed to sniper fire, to hostile watching eyes.

The trees were heavy with rain, their scent almost

overpowering. The sorrel's hoofs were silent against the pine-needle-covered earth.

Thunder rumbled twice in the distance, and a fresh downpour began, the rain singing in the trees, the boughs swaying and creaking together in the wind.

He dipped down into a gully which was already running water, where huge moss-clad boulders bunched together protectively, and worked his way upslope again, finding many cedar trees interspersed among the pines and blue spruce.

Rupert was lying in a sprawled heap on the ground, and over him was a dark figure with a knife. Ruff fired too quickly, shot from the hip with the thundering .56 in his anger and rage, and the attacker took to his heels, almost instantly swallowed up by the low-hovering clouds.

It all happened too quickly. Recognition, attack, retreat. Justice hadn't even identified the man who fled from him.

Cottony, damp clouds closed around him like falling gray wreaths. They parted and then closed again and the shadowy figure was gone.

Justice swung down and was beside Rupert in moments, seeing the blood leaking from the stumps where two fingers had been, seeing the pain in the open, astonished eyes of the old hunter.

"Rupe?" He shook him and then sat him up. "Who was it?"

The only answer was a stream of unintelligible words. Justice laid him back gently and wrapped the mutilated hand of Rupert Gates with his scarf. Blood stained the white cloth to crimson in seconds. Ruff shouldered Rupe and apologized:

"Sorry, old-timer. There's no gentle way to do this. I'll get you down to the station. There's whiskey and Lucy's care. You'll be up and on your feet next week."

Maybe. He had lost two fingers and his cheek was knife-scarred. There was blood leaking from his scalp as well. He must have been thumped over the head initially—but with no attempt to kill. No, this one, whoever he was, liked to work on a live victim. Maybe it was more fun that way—seeing the terror in their eyes, hearing the screams of anguish.

Ruff sat Rupe up before him on the sorrel's back and started down the piny slope, rifle in hand, eyes darting everywhere as the damp, gray wool clouds swirled around him, moving like ghostly fingers through the trees.

"What happened?" Allie came running to meet them, and Lucille finally appeared. She walked slowly toward them, the rain drenching her hair; then, seeing that it was very serious, she started to run. Handy Maxwell had drifted over to help. His mouth was grim as he and Allie carried Rupert Gates inside.

"What happened?" It was Lucille who asked this time, and Justice shook his head.

"I don't know. Someone was laying for him. Come on—he needs you now."

Rupert was laid out on a cot near the fire. Allie was holding the scarf against his hand, his eyes wild with anger and helplessness.

"For Christ's sake, it's his fingers. Can't someone do something?"

"His fingers . . ." Lucille looked and then pulled back, one hand going to her mouth. "Just like the others, isn't it? Just like . . . ."

Ruff brushed past her and tossed his rifle to Allie. Rupert would bleed to death before anyone did anything. "Get some bandages," he snapped at Lucille. "Handy, get back outside, watch that coach, dammit. That's what you're being paid to do."

Justice had his bowie unsheathed; now he held the blade in the fire, watching the flames curl around it. Rupert's eyes were open and he glanced down at his hand, sucking in his breath angrily.

"Did me, did he? Dammit it all. Justice? You know . . ." then he was out again, and it was for the best. Justice pulled the knife from the fire and lifted Rupe's hand. Then they heard the hiss and crackle, smelled the singeing flesh as Justice cauterized the finger stubs. Lucille made a little gagging noise and buried her face in her hands.

"That's not helping anybody," Justice said roughly. "His face and scalp have been cut. Set some hot water started, and get those bandages! Allie!"

"You'd better do it," he told Lucille more softly than Ruff had, and she nodded, starting toward the bedroom where she had a new petticoat she could tear into strips.

"Now what?" Cash asked as Ruff straightened up.

"Now he either gets well or he doesn't."

"Us, I mean. Now what do we do? There's someone prowling around this station, Justice. If we pull out that just leaves the kid here to protect the woman and the old man."

"Yes, and if we leave anyone, we're weakening ourselves."

Allie made the decision for them. He glanced at the roof, completed only that morning, and then at the solid log walls of the way station.

"They can't root me out of here, Justice. No matter how many there are and there's only one so far as we know. I'll hole up with Lucille and Rupe. Once I draw the latch string no one's going to get in, and they're not going to burn me out in this weather."

Ruff looked toward the bedroom door, then back again at Allie. "All right. It's the only way to do it. If it helps, you can tell Lucille I got him."

"I don't have to lie to her," Allie said. "She's stronger than any of you realizes."

"I hope so." Ruff looked at Cash and shrugged. "Let's get rolling, son. That high pass is going to be a mud trough soon."

The rain was really coming down now, silver buckshot peppering exposed flesh. There was a chill wind behind it. The trees on the ridges moaned in misery. Ruff stood for a moment looking back at the tiny house, not sure he had made the right decision, not knowing what else he could have done.

"Ready, boss?" Cash asked.

"Yeah." Ruff tied the sorrel on back, clambered up in the box beside Cash, and said, "Give 'em a taste of that whip, Cash. We'd better keep it rolling."

They moved out up the pine-lined trail toward the ridge, the lightning crackling around them, the wind lifting the horses' manes and tails, whipping the fringes on Ruff's buckskin shirt around. Justice turned in the seat and looked back, seeing Maxwell, Tower, and the Jayhawker, Gant, close up to the stage. There was no point in their hanging back. They would lose sight of the coach in this weather.

Justice leaned forward now, rifle on his lap, eyes trying to peel back the harsh weather, the low, roiling clouds. The higher into the hills they rode, the worse things got. Twice they had to stop to clear blown-down trees. The wind positively shrieked through the trees now, pelting them with pine cones and dry twigs. The clouds were below them as well as above, and the coach seemed to be floating through a gray, tossing sea. At times Justice couldn't make out the lead team, so bad was the weather.

This was the most hazardous part of their trip, he felt. Here in the hills where bandits could hide so easily, where they could strike without warning, hit hard and make their getaway. Once over the hump and onto the plains running into Muellers' Post, they would have a tougher time coming up on the coach unseen.

"Getup!" Cash yelled, and not for the first time. The team was slogging its way through hock-high mud now, the coach sloughing wildly along the narrow trail. Below there was a drop of five hundred feet or so, above piny ridges revealed only occasionally by the angry clouds.

"Getup! We're not going to make the pull like this!" Cash shouted.

And they weren't. The lead team off horse went to its knees suddenly, whickered in panic, and struggled up as Cash tried to check the horses behind it with the reins. He had to hold up, and once he had done that there was no way to get started again.

"We got to get down!" Cash called above the wind roar. "One of us anyway," he added with a grin.

Justice grunted, poked his rifle in the boot scabbard, and got to the ground, sinking to his calves in red, slimy ooze. The rain came in with a rush, stinging his face with steel pitchforks as Justice trudged forward, gripping the harness to keep from going down himself.

"Maxwell! Tower!" They couldn't hear him, but they eventually made out his waving arms and they rode forward, squeezing between the bluff and the stagecoach team.

"Tie on here somewhere. These ponies need some help. Damn wagon's too heavy."

In five minutes all three outriders had lassos on the coach, and with Cash rising in the box to pop his team with his whip they gave it all they had, Justice trying to lead the horses forward, to encourage and bully them up the long grade.

They finally felt the motion, saw the coach, sliding and digging deep furrows in the red mud, start forward. As they built up momentum it seemed they

would make it. Cash was still standing in the box of
the coach.

"Looks like . . ." he shouted and then he was
blown from the stage by a rifle shot they never heard
above the roar and lash of the storm. He was there
and then he wasn't, his body tumbling through space
toward the bottom of the white-water gorge below.

Ruff spun, Colt in hand. There were no targets
but muzzle flashes like winking red eyes from the
shelter of the cloud-bound forest.

The horses reared up behind him, and from the
corner of his eye Ruff saw a man go down—he
thought it was Handy Maxwell, but couldn't be sure
in the confusion.

The guns from the pines bellowed, their mingled
thunder continuous, pealing. From the coach itself
guns answered back as the three Great Western men
emptied their weapons, shooting at an enemy they
couldn't even see.

Ruff went low and ducked under the horses, con-
scious of the cutting hoofs, the sweating bodies of the
animals, the splat-splat as bullets ripped the coachwork
apart; the walls of that stage had never been designed
to provide protection against flying lead. Someone
inside screamed in agony as Ruff reached the far side
of the stage, the horses still dancing in panic.

The earth fell away inches from his feet, and he
clung to the harness as he worked his way to the
wagon box and stretched out an arm, wanting that
.56 in his hands more than anything on earth.

Lightning arced overhead, illuminating the rolling
skies to bone-white brightness for a brief moment
while thunder like a cannonade echoed up the long
canyon. A gust of wind, angry, violent in its intensity,
shook the stage.

Ruff felt the sting in his hand like getting tagged by
wasps and when he withdrew his hand he saw that it

was filled with splinters kicked up by a bullet which had come that close to taking his hand off.

Angry now, feeling a cool recklessness come over him, a resignation, he climbed up, exposing himself from the waist up. He grabbed the Spencer and withdrew, knowing that bullets were flying all around him—bullets which could not be seen, could not be heard.

He had the rifle but still had no target. He inched along the edge of the trail behind the coach, grabbing the yellow spokes of the front wheel, then the window frame.

"It's Justice," he yelled, not wanting to stick his head up for someone inside, someone on his own team to shoot off. "Justice!"

There was no response but the rattling of the coach, the creak and sway of it as wind, rain, and gunfire assaulted it. He reached out, turned the handle, and peered cautiously in.

They were all dead, tangled together in a bloody, many-limbed mass. Three men. Men Justice had placed inside a fish barrel and allowed to be killed. They hadn't had a real chance. One entire panel of the stage wall had been shot out during the assault.

He dropped down and worked his way toward the back of the coach to where the sorrel, rearing up, tearing angrily at the tether, slipped and whinnied loudly. From the front of the stage he thought he heard more activity, but it was impossible to be sure as the wind screamed down the canyon.

How many were alive? No one inside; one down up front he thought. Maybe by now all of them. And the Jayhawker? He was down. Ruff saw his horse, blood smearing the saddle, limp past. The rain had stained the horse darkly.

Justice had two choices. He liked neither. Wait them out. Hold fast, try to outgun them when they came down—that was unlikely to happen. They would send a man or two down first and if there was any attack from the stage the guns would open up again.

The second choice was to run—but run where and how was the question. He was crouched behind the boot of the coach, watching the sorrel work itself into a panic. To untie the horse and try to get down the backtrail was the longest gamble. The gunmen were upslope—that left only over the side, down a five-hundred-foot bluff. That was the direction Cash Williams had taken, but Cash was dead or dying.

There was another choice, he thought, and his lip curled back, his mouth twisting into an unconscious and nasty smile as he thought of it. There was the alternative of attacking.

Cross the road, get into the timber. If he could do that without getting himself killed in the first twenty feet, he would have some sort of a chance. A chance to do close combat with a dozen or more men in the woods. A chance to do some damage to them, to hurt them before they finally cut him down.

It wasn't a good choice, not even a smart choice, perhaps, but it beat waiting, hiding, running away, letting them have the gold, letting them do murder without payment of any kind.

Justice lifted his eyes to the wind-battered trees, took a deep slow breath, and made his move.

12

Justice was ankle-deep in mud, and when he started to run it seemed infinitely slow, seemed that his feet were made of lead, that someone had tethered him with an elastic rope. Lightning struck so near that the air was filled with the overpowering scent of sulfur. It was blindingly white for just a moment, the clouds which drifted up the canyon silvered eerily. The bullets followed.

The first volley cut the sorrel down, and Ruff saw its wide brown eye staring wildly out at a human world it didn't comprehend, saw the blood rushing from a terrible, jagged wound in the throat.

Then he saw nothing, allowed himself to see nothing but the ranks of timber, rain-heavy, swaying, across the road. Why they didn't get him then Ruff didn't know. Perhaps it was simply unexpected. A man suddenly appeared and rushed directly at them, and although shots were fired they missed, splatting up mud all around Justice, but not hitting him.

He slipped, nearly went down, lunged onward, and then he was onto grass, darting upslope, zigzagging as he went, the cold rain driving against his back, the fire in his lungs, the drumming of his heart, intense, violent.

With a last desperate leap he flung himself into the trees, seeing but not hearing above the wind roar a bullet tear the bark from a pine a dozen inches from his head, seeing the pink-white meat of the tree trunk gape open like a mocking mouth as the bark was blasted away in a hundred fragments.

Ruff kept moving. He had no idea where he was running, but he couldn't stay put. If he ran right into them, so be it; he wasn't going to sit and wait for them.

Them—who? Boggs, it had to be Boggs, didn't it? It wasn't the Indians; he was sure of that, somehow sure on a subconscious level that it wasn't the Sioux, who would have filled the air with their challenging war cries, burst from the trees to show themselves, to demonstrate their personal courage.

Justice hit the ground. Ahead of him through the murky clouds, he had seen a shifting shadow. There were only the trees and the bandits, and this shadow had moved like no tree.

He wiped the rain out of his eyes and snuggled in behind the familiar curved butt plate of the Spencer, watching, waiting. The bandit moved first, running down the slope toward Justice, wearing a red scarf across his face. He never saw Justice but Ruff had no mercy on him. They had come to kill from ambush, and they had killed, killed better men than they were. The steady finger squeezed the curved, cool trigger of the Spencer and the buffalo gun spoke its deadly message, its unmistakable voice communicating righteous anger and savage death.

The outlaw never heard it. He felt only the impact of the .56-caliber bullet, like an avalanche of stone against his chest, the shock of the bullet destroying all thought, all possibility of reaction as it tore apart heart muscle, severed the spinal column, and hurled its victim back in an unstrung marionette's sprawl.

Ruff felt no emotion. You don't go out killing unless you're ready to die. This one had forgotten that. Justice was already up and moving, this time to the right, slightly upslope.

It was a hard place, a hard time for battle. Targets were only wavering ghosts among the clouds and rain. You could not hear the rush of boots over the sodden pine needles, could not hear the bullets flying. The enemy was a ghost, the weather a common enemy, a third adversary to be considered by both sides.

The battlefield was a difficult one, and to Ruff's way of thinking, it favored him. He knew what he was doing here. He was alone with no one else to think of, to protect, to try to identify. The odds, he figured, had shifted dramatically when he entered the woods. They were close to even.

He was running now, running upslope as fast as conditions permitted, weaving through the timber, his legs aching as he ran on, the Spencer in hand, the rain driving against his face through the gaps between the pines. Clouds blotted out the day, flooded the forest, moving across at ground level, making shadowy specters of the pines.

He was far above the bandits now, perhaps as much as five hundred feet. He turned and continued east, to his left. His way was blocked by rocks, by underbush and thick timber with many young trees, but he ran on, his buckskins heavy with water, the trees creaking and groaning from out of the cloudy mist.

Ruff halted, sagged to the earth, and sat breathing in deeply, taking the cold, damp air into his starving, heated lungs. He sat there for ten minutes, calming his body, gripping the Spencer, reloading it as he watched the clouds drift and part, intermingle, twist and fold, the occasional sparking thrust of lightning as the gods of the storm attacked the earth with fiery arrows.

Then, quite calmly, he rose and started down the slope, his eyes a hunter's eyes, those of a big cat on the prowl. There was acceptance in those icy blue eyes and the knowledge of death.

It was a killing time, and someone would have to pay tribute to the vengeful mood which was upon the man in buckskins.

He walked the edge of a stony bluff, catching just a glimpse of the road far below him, seeing a patch of color which was a horse, nothing else. Across the way the sun had managed to pierce the mass of frothing clouds and light one peak miles away, showing the water which ran down its green and jagged flanks brightly, like molten silver flowing to the mile-deep gorge below.

Then he saw something else. A blue roan. A yellow slicker. He didn't even hesitate. He shouldered the Spencer and fired before the clouds could cut off his line of sight and the gunshot racketed down the slope, delivering yet another message of sudden, violent death to the men who had come out to kill and were now learning about the price.

Justice was already moving before the answering fire, if there was any—and it could only have been inaccurate, a panicked response—could probe the trees. In battle, Ruff had learned long ago, most men were picked off by chance, by the random shot, by a ricochet, a stray bullet. He didn't discount the menace of these shots, but he knew that the moving target was less likely to be hit.

They had no idea where he was, he knew that. Their nerves had to be frayed by now. For they knew *who* it was, and they knew that their people were going down, going down and staying there, dying in the mud and rain on this mountain peak.

Ruff slipped, went to his haunches, slid down a grassy slope, holding his gun overhead, regained his balance, and ran on downslope, his legs momentarily out of control. During a lull in the rainstorm he did hear shots. Shots aimed blindly at a position forty or fifty degrees from where he now was. He smiled thinly and tried to think ahead for the bandits.

Get out. That was their next move, had to be. Get the gold and move before any more of them could be picked off. Use the coach? Yes—the strongboxes were unwieldy, impossible for a single horse to carry, and it would take too long to break them open and redistribute the gold.

The stage then—uphill or down? Uphill, Ruff guessed, away from Bear Creek and toward the plains. Accordingly he moved to the east, running through a straggly stand of cedars, dipping into a wash heavy with manzanita and mountain sage, climbing up the far side and then on into the yellow-lichen-covered boulders and tangled oaks beyond, glancing constantly downslope, and when the trail was visible through the parting clouds he stopped, chest heaving, found himself a firing position prone on the damp gray rocks, and settled in to wait.

The bandits were now in precisely the position Ruff and his men had been. They had to get the heavy coach moving up the grade while hostile fire could pepper them at will. Justice was within fifty yards of the road, and no one was going to pass by without paying a price.

Gradually they came into view, a lead rider, a rope tied to his saddle, struggling and cursing, whipping the buckskin horse he rode as he tried to lead the exhausted team forward.

Ruff held his fire. Another rider came into view, this one in a black slicker mounted on a roan, his every movement frantic, indicative of panic. Then came the coach itself, two men in the box. They must have been sitting in Cash Williams's blood.

In another moment they were sitting in their own.

Ruff laid the front sight on the driver's chest and squeezed off. He was driven back and sat against the coach wall as if spiked there by the impacting bullet. Justice had shifted his sights before the rolling echo died, and he fired again as the shotgun rider made ready to leap from the coach. He leaped, all right, but by the time he hit the ground he was nerveless, bored through by a twisted, nearly molten hunk of spinning lead. The coach rolled over him, crushing ribs and organs.

There was panic, disorganized reaction at the coach. Guns were discharged in all directions; horses reared up as panicked riders yanked savagely on the reins, digging into mouth and tongue with hard bits. The coach sideslipped and began rolling back.

Ruff settled in on another target. It was then that he discovered he had underestimated his enemy.

He thought at first that it was a peal of thunder, the near striking of lightning. Pain filled his upper arm, the loud crack rattled in his eardrums.

Behind me, he thought, rolling away before the second shot could be fired. His arm was suddenly filled with surging pain. His sleeve was already soaked in blood.

They had left a man up there after all, a man with sense enough to get higher, a man with a shooting eye.

Ruff threw himself off into space, his rifle clattering away down the rocks as two more shots peppered the boulders around him, as below, seemingly miles distant, a horse whickered in agony.

Ruff hit the ground below the boulders hard, and he kept rolling, getting to his feet as more shots stitched their way across the earth under his feet. He hurled himself toward the trees and began crawling, crawling into their cover, his arm on fire, his head aching insistently. He must have cracked it when he fell. He halted, rolled to a sitting position, and looked back upslope, but there was no pursuit he could see, no target offering itself as he sat gripping his big blue Colt, teeth clenched with pain and anger and determination.

He hadn't counted on that—hadn't counted on it at all. He had spent a lot of time hunting men, and that wasn't the way things happened.

They won the skirmish, rushed to their booty, and got the hell out of there. They didn't leave a man behind!

But they did, you dumb bastard. You listening to me, Ruffin? By the way, you're bleeding badly. You might be bleeding to death, Ruffin. Dammit! Are you listening?

Yes, he replied to the small voice finally. I am bleeding—all right. Leave me alone.

Fumbling fingers found his skinning knife in its sheath inside his boot, and he cut the sleeve of his buckskin shirt away, his eyes flickering toward the slope above him as he worked, wondering where the son of a bitch was.

The wound was not good, was not as bad as it might have been. The bullet had clipped past beneath the bone on his upper arm, missing the bone and major artery, yet it had cut a deep slot in the flesh and the blood refused to be stanched. There hadn't been enough resistance there for the bullet to mushroom properly, and that had helped. The wound was clean. It might have been made with a meat cleaver.

Justice wrapped his scarf around it, wincing as he did so, knotted his crude bandage tightly, and sat a moment longer, trying to clear his head.

He touched his skull and found an egg-sized lump there. That bothered him more than his arm, though his arm would be more dangerous in the long run. He didn't recall cracking his head, but then he hadn't been analyzing things when he left the boulder stack. He had thrown himself into space as an alternative far preferable to being blown off the rocks.

Move, Ruffin, the little voice inside said, and Ruff realized it had been repeating that message for some time. He was sitting there in the rain, head bowed, hair hanging across his face in a tangled dark screen, staring at his arm and the rain-jeweled pine needles.

Get up!

He did, bracing himself against the trunk of a huge, woodpecker-pocked pine tree. Then, moving cautiously, silently, he began to filter through the trees, knowing now that there was someone above him, someone who was a woodsman, who knew the silent ways, who would require caution.

He angled down toward the trail, knowing that a wounded quarry almost always fled downhill. Still he wanted to see the coach again, have a chance at stopping it, of following if possible. Perhaps a horse had been left behind. There were several men who would need one no longer.

He emerged from the forest on a bluff which overhung the road, and already he could see he was too late. There were deep furrows cut in the muddy trail, furrows the heavy rain had not yet washed away. The coach was past—over the hump and on its way down toward the plains.

Ruff hesitated, then leaped to the road. He wanted a horse, and so he backtracked, keeping to the forest verge, his eyes shuttling upslope to where danger presumably still lay.

Was he there? Had he too pulled out? You can't take the chance, Justice reminded himself, and so he clung to the trees, to the hem of the blue-green, cloud-locked forest which ran into the rambling, twisted hills to the south.

It wasn't any good. Reaching the spot of the ambush, he found no horses. No live animals. There were two down, a third crippled. The rain drove down as Justice cocked his Colt and placed it next to the ear of the thrashing dying horse.

He shouldn't have fired his weapon, but he couldn't stand to see it. The Colt bucked in his hand and the horse lay still in the mud and rain.

He crossed to the edge of the trail and looked down, spying Cash Williams on a rocky ledge fifty feet or so below. He wasn't moving, was likely dead, should have been dead, but again Ruff was compelled by honor. He holstered his gun and with a last look at the forest where a stalker prowled, he started climbing down, knowing he was dead himself if caught on that bluff.

It was a hard climb, considering the length of it. Handholds pulled away in the mud. Rocks showered down. He slid twenty feet past Cash before he was able to crawl back up. He hunched over the body, seeing the eyes staring up at him through the rain. Dead and there was nothing to be done about it, nothing but find those responsible.

It took fifteen minutes to climb the fifty feet up and out, then, heavy with mud and rain, he started on, jogging up the slope, again keeping to the trees, his Colt in his hand.

Crazy, Justice, he told himself. What are you going to do—run down the stage in weather like this, afoot?

If that's what it takes, he thought with force. Yes, if that was what it took he would run through the storm, across the mountains, and out onto the plains as long as his lungs would suck in new air, as long as his heart would keep pumping blood into his weary body.

It wasn't quite so incredible as it might seem. The coach, heavily laden, had already proved it was going to have difficulty along the trail. And it was going to have to keep to the road. There was only one way through those hills. Justice knew that—it was his trail. His. Scouted for the Great Western, for an impatient overbearing woman who was probably sitting in Bear Creek just now complaining about the rain. . . . Justice wasn't keeping to any trail. He was going up and over the high ridges, down the white-water washes, through the trees. And he would run it down. He would run it down and more of them would pay, perhaps many more before they managed to fill him full of enough lead to drag him down to the cold, sodden earth.

13

Night came on too quickly. It shouldn't have been dark, Ruff thought, but the world had grown steadily more deeply shadowed, the wind increasing, the flashes of bridged lightning more brilliant, striking nearer and with greater intensity.

It was coming on to night, and still he ran. He had stopped a time or two, nearly dropping from exhaustion, but always he had risen again, stiffly, wearily, to stumble on through the deep timber where ghostly trees thumped his body with outstretched arms, slipping and falling down the gorges where the water ran now with enough force to sweep a man away. Whitewater rapids formed in the canyons, carrying driftwood and debris along, undercutting the banks, washing down to the plains in a roaring, defiant rush.

Justice felt a knee buckle, and then he went down hard. He was halfway up a rain-slick, rocky bluff, and he knew he couldn't make it the rest of the way. He knew it and he cursed his trembling body, cursed his shaking legs, legs which seemed to have no sensation in them anymore.

He tried to rise and couldn't, and so he crawled back farther on the rocky shelf to prop himself up and sit staring down at the dark, rain-shuttered valley below him while the wind whipped his long dark hair around his head, and his legs, made of wood, simply lay there stretched out before him, useless, infuriating.

There was a brief gap in the clouds, a glimpse of a burnt-orange sunset, then that too was smothered up by the clouds as the wind shrieked mockingly through the canyons.

He had his gun in his lap. He sat staring, simply staring, and then he opened his eyes to find himself on his side, the rain falling again, or still, or eternally, battering at him, and he dragged himself back to search along the rock face, finding a crevice scarcely big enough for him to crawl into.

There it was drier, there, for a time, he could rest, but not sleep. No, not that, because he was back there—the stalker.

How Justice knew it he couldn't have said. There had been no sounds behind him on the trail, none audible above the lash and crackle of the driving storm, nothing to be seen, but he had known.

The man who had gotten above him at the ambush site, the one who had come so close to doing him, to putting Justice down for the last time, he was back there.

Justice sat in the crevice, listening to the wind pipe in the rocky crevices, feeling the drip of icy water down his back and neck, once feeling something slither away beside his knee.

He sat there, gun held beneath his shirt protectively, and with red-rimmed aching eyes he stared out at the impenetrable darkness, listening, waiting until at last the body surrendered to the night, the storm, the exhaustion, and his eyes protestingly closed, the fingers unclenched from the butt of the blue Colt .44 on his lap, and he fell off to sleep, knowing that he had failed, knowing that the stage was far away by now, not—for the moment—caring as he gave in to the demands of exhaustion.

He awoke to a gray, tumbling day. Clouds drifted past the mouth of his tiny cave. Thunder still rumbled distantly. Nothing had changed. Ruff didn't feel refreshed at all by his night's sleep. He could hardly come to his feet; his legs were knotted into aching cramps, his eyes refused to focus properly.

He stood there for a long time on the ledge confronting the day. Then, turning his eyes up to the bluff, he began to climb again, to climb across waterglossed surfaces where there were only tiny fingerholds between him and a drop of a hundred feet, to clamber over broken, jagged shale which tore the knees and elbows out of his buckskins until he was at last atop the ridge where he could look down on the stage trail, or what the rain had left of it, and out onto the empty gray plains where the wind shook the grass until it seemed all of the earth was trembling.

When he had his breath, he started down again.

He ended in a sliding, rock-accompanied jolt which brought him onto the stage trail once again. He followed it eastward, finding the wheel tracks and hoof imprints in the sheltered areas and then finding no more tracks at all for a way when the trail arrowed out across the smooth granite plate where the pines dwindled and became stunted as the vast plains began to dominate the landscape.

The clouds held back for a while. Sunspots danced across the grass of the prairie. Scarlet trumpet flowers and purple aster stood out starkly against the grayness of the day.

Then the rains closed down again and the flowers lost their color. Justice plodded on.

He had lost track of time. Usually he had a good sense of time, a fine sense of direction, but now he couldn't have said if it was noon or dusk. He didn't give it any real thought. He had found the wagon tracks again, lining out southward toward Columbine Creek.

Ruff felt a humorless grin lift the corners of his mouth, expose his teeth in a nasty expression. Columbine Creek. Anson Boggs's way station was there, and unless Ruff was badly mistaken that was the only destination the driver of the coach and the dozen outriders had in mind.

And he would be there. Maybe not in time, but he would be there, and then there would be no more Columbine Creek station. He would destroy it as they had destroyed his work; and if there was anyone in the way, he would kill them as they had killed his people.

The horse appeared from out of nowhere. Ruff turned his head as he ran and saw the big bay driving toward him. An army horse it was, regulation bay, regulation size. The rider was no soldier.

Stone Hand. Ruff felt his heart flutter, with trepidation, with eagerness, with a knowledge that this would have to be done one day and it might as well be now. Now he knew who the woodsman back there was, and he turned to face the crazed Sioux warrior.

He saw the puff of smoke, heard the racketing of Stone Hand's gun, but the shot missed. Ruff brought his Colt up, but before he could trigger off, Stone Hand dropped to the side of his horse and began to ride in a wide arc from Ruff's left to his right, the horse lathered up even on a day such as this had been—the man had had a long, difficult ride. Stone Hand, they said, pursued his own death.

Maybe he had found it.

Stone Hand's rifle cracked from beneath the bay's neck, and the army horse shied, not used to that, not liking it. The shot again was a miss, but too near, remarkably so considering the circumstances. Ruff heard the little splat as the .45-70 bullet impacted with the low hummock behind him. Justice sighted, one hand behind his back, the rain pelting down, half-blindingly. He hated to kill the horse, he could have used it himself, but it was the larger target, and while Stone Hand was mounted he had the advantage.

Ruff squeezed off; the .44 kicked against his palm and he saw the horse go down, rolling over, its neck tucked under. Stone Hand dove for safety, holding his rifle high, his long hair flying in the air, his red breechclout the only splash of color against the gray and twisted day.

Then he was down. Down and silent. The horse pawed at the earth in its death run. Justice moved toward the hummock behind him, his eyes shifting, searching. The man had burrowed into the earth, it seemed. Gone. Deadly as any rattler lurking in the grass.

The stalker was there. Now. He had come to kill and he would have his blood.

Ruff began to move in. There was no point in waiting for Stone Hand to make his move. Have done with it now. One way or the other.

Justice moved in a half crouch through the long grass, the rain like a leaden net cast over him and all of the world. High overhead a strange dull-red spot moved across the clouds. The water was ten inches deep, creeping into his boots, but his feet were too cold and damp already to notice it.

He felt the chill which crept up his spine, however. He might be walking in front of the sights of a man who hated him, who felt his pride injured by having let Ruff take him in the first place, who would do anything even to dying himself to kill Ruff Justice.

Justice halted suddenly. He was near the downed horse. The animal's carcass steamed against the chill air. Rain ran in rivulets across its still flanks, across its face. Lightning crackled distantly. And there beside the horse was Stone Hand's rifle.

Ruff frowned. He had seen Stone Hand leap free, seen the rifle in his hand—or was that all an illusion? It seemed already to have happened long ago, far away.

He walked to the rifle, seeing now that the stock was broken. Ruff noticed the feathers tied to the barrel, the brass studs hammered decoratively into the stock.

He leaned over to pick it up and saw from the corner of his eyes a thrusting shadow, like a cloud shadow gusting across the plains, but then Stone Hand's body impacted with Justice's.

He had come up from nowhere, from the ground, and now he hit Ruff like a mauling big cat. A forearm was looped around Ruff's throat and a jolting blow landed low on Ruff's back, above the hipbone, to the right of his right kidney.

Ruff threw an elbow back hard and it smashed into Stone Hand's face, spewing blood down the Indian's bare chest; and it was only when Stone Hand fell back that Ruff realized he had been stabbed. That blow low on his back was a knife thrusting for vital organs. Stone Hand had missed the kidney as Ruff twisted frantically away, but he had cut deeply, dangerously.

Now the pain came as if by realizing what had happened Ruff had willed it to come. Sharp, sawing pain, dozens of severed nerves screaming out angrily, and Ruff staggered.

Stone Hand came in again, his eyes lighted greedily, his hair washed across his face, the bloody knife rising again.

Justice shot him full in the face, and as he touched off an immense satisfaction flooded him. As he saw the back of the Sioux's head blown away, saw the face cave in like a boneless mask sucked in by implosion.

The Indian went down and stayed down. He was dead. Like that. Dead, his black little heart stilled forever.

Justice got down on his knees beside Stone Hand, pressing a hand to his back where the blood leaked out and the pain continued unabated. He felt a fresh wave of jagged pain tear through him as he did so, but there was something that had to be done, must be done.

Effortfully Ruff slipped the skinning knife from inside his right boot. Then he leaned over the dead Sioux, yanking his head up by the forelock, and the sharp, narrow blade of the skinning work slid under Stone Hand's scalp and began peeling it back, exposing blood-smeared ivory. The rain washed the blood away, and as Ruff sat back on his heels panting, the matted scalp in his hand, there was only the white skull, the shattered face.

"Another one," he muttered. He shook his head, trying to clear the dizziness away. The images leaped into his mind briefly, mockingly. Blood-red rivers, armies of the dead rising off the plains, the long rows of yellow flowers sprouting along a grassy sunlit rise while Ruff behind the sights of his incredibly long, incredibly heavy black rifle picked them off one by one and Four Dove screamed with each report.

Justice opened his eyes. He was flat on his face against the grass, his back spasming, his head filled with shocking pain. He retched, but there was nothing for his stomach to throw up. It took an hour to get to his knees, another hour to get to his feet. He still had the scalp in his hand. Now he tucked it into his belt and started walking. Walking through the wind and pelting rain.

There was somewhere he had to go . . . he shook

his head again. Somewhere . . . and then he remembered. He remembered and the anger came back, fueling his determination.

It was dark again. The ground kept falling away from beneath his feet. A dozen times he fell and lay, knowing he could not get up again, but somehow he did, his back filled with liquid fire. Then he would touch his scalp, stroking it almost lovingly, liking the comfort it gave him. That at least was finished. Stone Hand was not behind him. The stalker was dead.

It was black, the wind snapping at him like the dark teeth of a blacker beast. He saw the red glow and stopped, puzzled. It was no place for the sunrise. No place for lanterns. He walked toward it, realizing suddenly that it was a fire, that he wanted warmth more than he wanted anything in the world.

If it wasn't Boggs—and if it was he would put a finish to it right now. Walk in blasting and let them kill him. At least then he would be warm—if what they said was true.

The fire was low in the coulee, but still the wind whipped it into a red-and-yellow frenzy. Ruff stood blinking at it, staring through the rain. His leg felt oddly numb. One eye seemed to be locked shut, and fingering it he found a huge welt and knot above the eye.

"What was I doing . . . ?" He stood numbly in the rain for a long while before the red glow caught his eye again and he remembered.

He pushed through the brush as a fresh cannonade of thunder echoed across the tortured plains. And then he was into their camp.

They sat staring at him as he dragged his blood-soaked, battered body toward the fire. The tall man in torn buckskins with a long mustache drooping down past the jawline, his face swollen, blood still soaking his shirt in back. There was a fresh scalp hanging from his belt, and the Sioux just watched as Justice crossed to the fire and sat down next to it, staring into the flames.

He thought one of them spoke his name, but he could not be sure. He didn't care. There was a vension haunch hanging over the fire, and he managed to get to his knees, take the skinning knife from his boot, a knife still stained with Stone Hand's blood, and cut himself a slice of meat, which he ate ravenously without looking up at the dark figures of the Indians who sat around him in the rain, staring.

"They may kill me." He said it aloud. He looked at them, still chewing his meat, still close to the fire, the smoke of it in his lungs, the heat of it causing his face to glow warmly. His buckskins steamed. He ate, wolfishly, ravenously, and the Sioux stared at him. This time his name was spoken distinctly by a tall, scarred brave who sat hunched in a red-and-yellow-striped blanket to Ruff's right.

Justice looked up, still eating. He thought again, almost casually, I suppose they'll kill me. Perhaps not. Strangers are not murdered in an Indian's camp out of hand. It is inhospitable. They let you get a mile down the road before they come after you. It didn't seem to matter much. So long as he had a full belly, so long as he had a minute more before that fire. He keeled over abruptly, his head banging against the ground. The pain in his back had risen up like a striking serpent and struck with jagged fangs.

None of the Sioux made a move. Justice sat up again, his head thrown back, gasping for air, his mouth gathering rain. He ripped his shirt off angrily and tried to twist around to see the wound, but he couldn't make it. He scooped up a handful of mud and plastered it against his back to stop the bleeding, sat with his stomach convulsing with pain for a minute, then tugged his shirt back on.

Again he began to eat. Still the Sioux watched silently.

One man rose finally. He walked to where Ruff sat and crouched down, his eyes meeting Ruff's. He touched the scalp, his fingers working through the long, coarse hair. It was an Indian's scalp, quite obviously.

"Whose?" he asked.

Justice looked up. Something about this warrior was familiar. He wore a beaded vest and an earring made from a gold coin. It was too difficult to make out his features through the rain, to identify him.

"Whose?" The voice was not commanding, but soft, wondering, it seemed.

"This?" Ruff took the scalp from his belt and he lifted it toward his lips. Then he spat on it and threw it into the fire. "Stone Hand," he said. His eyes glittered. His throat worked soundlessly. "Stone Hand."

The Sioux stared at him. His mouth seemed to twitch into the beginnings of a smile, but he said nothing, never completed the expression. He went back to his semi-sheltered position against the bluff of the coulee and seated himself, saying nothing. Justice had finished eating. Now he curled up by the fire, thinking as he dropped off into the deep padded tunnel beneath him that there were worse ways to go than in your sleep.

14

The fire had flared up. It skipped across the clearing regardless of the rain and leaped over Ruff's body, searing him. He could hear his flesh crackling, smell his hair burning—but it wasn't his own hair he wore. It was bloody, straight, coarse, and when he touched it trying to understand this his scalp came away and lay on the ground, crawling across toward the laughing flames.

Justice sat up from out of the nightmare. His side exploded with pain and he bit at his lip, cursing loudly, violently. He sat, arms hanging across his thighs, staring.

He realized eventually that the sun was shining. He glanced skyward to see the schooners of cloud sailing across the clearing skies. Somewhere a meadowlark sang out, greeting the sunshine.

"The Sioux." He blinked and looked around. Another nightmare? Another pain-inspired delusion? No, there was the fire, now dead, there the hollows where men had sat.

And beside the fire a singed and disgusting scalp.

They had left him meat. Ruff groaned as he crawled toward it, cut another huge slice of venison, and chewed it, the sun shining down warmly, and at intervals blocked by the massive drifting clouds.

He was shaking, he realized now. Touching his face he found it hot, clammy. He was feverish, and with anger he considered the possibility that he had blood-poisoning.

He sat upright, frowning. His memory of the previous night's events came back sharply. He recalled it all. The scalp, the dark eyes of the man who had spoken to him. The man who had left him the meat, who had given him his life. He knew him now. Knew him and was not surprised at the generosity.

Colonel MacEnroe should be told; but MacEnroe and the army problems seemed far away and unimportant as long as Anson Boggs existed, as long as his scalp had not been taken, the dead avenged.

When he could eat no more, Ruff Justice struggled to his feet, looked around once more at the empty coulee, at the dead fire and the scalp. Then he started down the long trail south once again, leaving the deserted camp of Crazy Horse behind.

He slogged on. Seeing nothing but a damp, stoic buffalo herd of three or four hundred which didn't even look up as he passed. All traces of wagon traffic, of horsemen, were erased by now, but Ruff didn't hesitate. He knew where he would find the stolen coach and gold. Columbine Creek.

Unless he was wrong—no, he didn't even consider it seriously. It was Boggs. Adrienne was taking the bread out of his mouth, he had said. He should have gone hungry.

Ruff was laboring as he entered the piny foothills, as the rain came in again, this time lightly, a sheer silver mist drawn finely across the world. His back was an old agony, one he had grown used to. He moved now in a certain way, took a shorter stride with his right leg, protecting his back unconsciously.

He had stopped once that day to bathe it in an icy, quick-running rill and to pack the wound again with moss and mud. Maybe he would make it, maybe not.

It was a deep and angry wound. His arm hardly troubled him.

Going upslope was unimaginably torturous, but he had to climb and he knew it. The rain misted down, swirling in the wind, and he grunted aloud with each step, dragging his right leg now.

And then he was there.

He stood in the shadow of the pines looking down into the Columbine Creek yard of Anson Boggs' freight line. He could not see the coach, but no matter—it was there, somewhere. Perhaps in the arroyo to the south or back in the trees, smashed into kindling.

There were seven saddle horses arrayed around the house itself, and smoke rose from the chimney. How long had they had? They couldn't be that many hours ahead of Ruff. They too must have halted at darkness to rest. They too had traveled slowly. Had they divided the gold yet, Anson Boggs counting out the blood-smeared shares?

He was in no hurry to move now that he had caught up with them. Slowly he searched the hillsides, the creekbed where water now ran with force.

He saw one and then another. Two men left out to watch in the rain. Their spirits would be low by now. One was in the cottonwoods behind the house, the other watched from the window of a rickety shed— watching the coach as well? With his Spencer he could have picked both off before they knew what was happening and begun to punch the house apart board by board; but the Spencer lay back above Bear Creek. This would have to be close-in work, and Ruff wasn't exactly at peak agility.

He saw a man come to the door of the house, peer out, call back over his shoulder, then reenter the house, banging the door shut. Nothing else happened for an hour, and after that time Justice was convinced there were only the two guards.

He made his move.

It had to be the one in the cottonwoods first. Otherwise there was no way of crossing the yard to get to the shed. The corner of the shed itself seemed to cut off the view of the man inside toward the west, where the cottonwoods were, so Justice thought he could take that man unobserved—if he hadn't changed position.

It was growing darker again; perhaps the sun was going down, although it seemed the clouds were just thickening, drawing a heavier drape between earth and sky.

Ruff pushed all thought of pain, of difficulty, aside. He was a killing thing in the woods, a wounded panther, which is more dangerous, not less, because of its injuries.

He dropped down through the trees to the Columbine, splashed across the creek, and crawled up onto the muddy, willow-strewn bank. And he saw something there which strengthened his resolve. It wasn't much—only a green strongbox which had not quite been buried when they caved the bank in over it.

He waited, only his eyes moving, and when he saw his target, back to him, he rose into a crouch and moved toward the trees, closing the distance on cat feet, his bowie dangling from his right hand.

He clapped his hand over the guard's mouth and dug the bowie into his back. He did not make Stone Hand's mistake. Ruff's bowie severed the spinal cord, and the man went down shuddering, twitching spasmodically, before Ruff finished him with a *coup de grâce* which found the jugular. He wiped his knife on the grass and slipped it into his scabbard, then snatched up the guard's Winchester and started his wide circling movement toward the shed above and south of the house.

There were no windows on the far side, and Ruff came up to the wall itself, smelling the damp wood, damp hay, hearing the drumming of rain on the sod roof. He edged his way to the corner, looked through the rain at the big house, satisfied himself that he was not watched, and slipped toward the door.

He rapped softly.

"What?" a surly voice demanded.

"Relief."

" 'Bout damn time."

He swung the door open, and Ruff thudded the butt of the Winchester against his face, caving it in for him, and the outlaw went down. Ruff stepped over him and dragged him in, glancing behind him. Still there was no alarm sent up from the house.

He bound the guard with his belt and scarf and straightened up, angered to find the old wooziness had returned. He had lost blood, run and walked a long way, had little enough rest, and his body was simply rebelling.

What do you want me to do, sit down? he asked himself. He was fiercely angry for a moment, and then a calmness returned and he was able to smile at himself.

He leaned against the wall for a moment, and it was from that position that he noticed the kerosene.

It was in two fifty-gallon drums, and Ruff straightened up, his eyes narrowing. He looked at the drums again and then out the door at the rain. He walked to the doorway, showing himself briefly, looking down at the house, watching the rain from the roof of the shed drip to the ground and wriggle away down the path to pool around the foundation of the house.

He crouched down over the bound man, hoping he was a smoker and not a chewer. A tin of matches and sack of tobacco were in his right-hand vest pocket. Ruff took the matches, opening the tin to examine them, finding them dry.

Then he went back to the door, watching again as the water ran down the slight incline to the house below.

Placing his rifle aside, he walked to the kerosene drum and tilted it, finding it nearly full. He lay it down on its side and rolled it to the door. There he pulled the bung and let the kerosene slither away down the slope, watching the oily stream it left. When the drum was empty he switched for the fresh one, pulled the plug on it, and let it run.

Now he could see a dark stain in the puddled water around the house. Still no one had come from the way station. Now perhaps no one would.

He stood the heavy drum up and worked it out the door. There was still a gallon or two inside, which was just about right.

"You shouldn't have killed my people," Ruff was muttering without realizing it. He felt hot all of a sudden, awfully hot. He was aware of fresh blood leaking down his pantleg, of stabbing pain.

He struck a match, its brief glow brilliant in the gloom of the day, and dropped it into the bunghole of the drum, kicking it away to roll and bang downhill.

It had no sooner splashed to a stop next to the wall of the house than the fire caught. There was a red flash, fiery arms suddenly embracing the house as the kerosene spread on top of the water. Black smoke rose curling into the dark skies, and Justice, rifle in hand, watched it as he stood in the doorway of the shack.

They had only to wait, to identify the smell, the source of the fire, and they would be safe enough. The walls of the house would never catch, not in this weather. But panic set in, wild-eyed panic.

The door was flung open and a man splashed across the fiery pond, firing his weapon blindly. Ruff shot him.

The man fell and lay there on the ground face down, his pant legs burning brightly. The kerosene fire was smoking heavily. Vast clouds of wind-drifted smoke floated across the yard. A second man burst through the cloud of smoke, backlighted nicely by the glow of the wavering fire. He saw the dead man, realized where any gunshots had to be coming from, and looked up at the shed, raising his rifle before Ruff stopped his heart with a .44-40 bullet.

Justice's face was a devil's mask in the firelight. The flames now danced above the eaves, writhing red and yellow.

"It's only a foretaste, boys. This, damn you, is your eternity. Better get used to it."

Two men rushed out together, one from the front door, another by way of the window. Ruff sighted on the man using the window and then switched off as that one slipped and went down into the flames to rise again painted with living fire. He rushed out of the burning lake and was desperately rolling on the muddy earth, screaming to the heavens for help. There was to be no help for him. Ruff squeezed off, watching the man who had come out the door go down nearly on top of another dead bandit. Meanwhile the burning man screamed out prayers and curses, and Ruff, taking pity on him, finished him with a head shot.

None of those he had gotten had the bulky form of the Boggs men, nor had Ruff recognized any of them. He only knew they had participated in a savage slaughter which had left Cash Williams, Ed Tower, Handy Maxwell, and the others dead. They had killed from ambush all for the sake of gold. Well, they had their gold now.

Cooler heads prevailed inside the house. Rattling gunfire exploded from the windows, and Ruff was driven back inside the shack as fifty rounds were unleashed, the bullets singing off the eaves, walls, and doorframe, smacking harness from the wallhooks, ringing off steel tools, the anvil in the corner, as Justice, beside the door, tucked himself into a protective crouch.

When he peered out again the fire had nearly extinguished itself, but the smoke was doubly bad. The house had vanished behind it and black streamers rose into the sky to be whipped away by the wind.

There was a lull in the firing—a lull caused by the smoke. Ruff got out of the shed then, moving lower to a grassy knoll slightly to the left, thirty feet downslope.

As the smoke cleared, the guns from the house opened up again, peppering the shed. Ruff let them fire away as he lay there on his belly, his eyes stinging, his head throbbing madly, his side flooded with pain as if he had set fire to himself inadvertently. His pulse seemed to expand his skull with each beat.

"Damn you, Stone Hand," he breathed, "you've killed me anyway. You and that filthy knife of yours."

The firing stopped again. The flames had nearly burned out, the smoke nearly cleared away. There was ten minutes during which nothing moved, nothing changed except that the skies, as the sun dropped slowly beyond the clouds, went darker still. Then a man's head appeared in the window to the left of the door and Ruff triggered off, seeing the head vanish, hearing a loud, broken howl of pain.

"Now they'll wait until dark," Ruff told himself. God, it was hot! How could it be so damned hot in the rain? Oh, yes. Stone Hand. That filthy knife of his. He closed his eyes and lowered his face, feeling the rain run off it, feeling the prickly, damp bristle of the grass.

What are you going to do, Justice? Die on me? His head lifted and he looked around. "No," he muttered, "not just yet."

It grew dark, as dark as only a stormy night can be. There wasn't so much as a candle anywhere for a hundred miles, no faintly glimmering starlight, no distant lightning.

Move! a small, imperious voice inside his head shouted, and he got slowly to hands and knees, wondering where his gray horse was, where Casqual was leading him, but Casqual was far away, buried in a heap of rocks in Mexico—the Apache would never rise again; and the gray was dead. Everywhere Justice went death followed in his wake. It had happened in Denver, in Paris, in San Francisco, in Bismarck. You can't elude it—touch me and you die, he thought.

He was standing up, wavering, in plain view, but the darkness cloaked him in invisibility.

Very bad, Justice, he told himself as he moved into a shambling trot downslope. A little moon and you would have been dead.

I'm sick. Why shouldn't I die, anyway?

He fell, crawled forward through the wet grass, found he couldn't rise again, and just lay there. He was within twenty feet of the front door, smelling the dead kerosene, the stagnant water, the rain, the grass, the wood of the house, the death beyond the door.

He sat up with great effort, swept back his hair, and waited. The door swung slowly open, but no target appeared. Inside they must have a candle, for he could see faintly the outline of a table and beside it a steel chest. A chest filled with gold.

The bulky man appeared momentarily in the doorway, pulled back, and then appeared again, rifle in hands. Ruff let him come. Someone inside whispered savagely.

It was a Boggs that emerged, which he couldn't say. Perhaps the old man himself, perhaps Rigger. Now Justice noticed the slight limp and he knew it was the other, the one Rupert Gates had shot. Poor Rupe—Stone Hand had clipped his wings for him.

Now two more men appeared, and Ruff let them creep out into the night. They weren't coming hunting, they were trying for their horses, for freedom. They were moving slowly; men always move slowly with canvas sacks filled with gold in their hands.

Ruff fired twice. He got the first man, missed the second. Tongues of flame flickered out and were answered. Ruff rolled to one side, heard the hammer of the Winchester fall on an empty chamber, and hurled it angrily aside. Gunflash illuminated the dark pool of water, marked the targets, and Ruff brought his Colt up, firing twice, hearing a scream of agony, a muffled splash.

An enraged roar filled the night and a huge shadow burst from the doorway, and before Justice could switch to him, the body collided with his, slamming him back.

"Justice! Damn you, you son of a bitch!" Anson Boggs bellowed.

The muzzle of Ruff's Colt was against Boggs's belly and he triggered off, blowing the big man back, smelling the gunpowder, the singed flannel, the sweat of the man simultaneously. He groaned and tried to crawl away, but Boggs made it only as far as the pond, where he lay face down in the water, inches from a money bag, a few feet from his two dead sons.

Ruff tried to rise, fell back, feeling agony wash over him. The fire had spread, it was licking his body, burning him. The others would come and he couldn't do anything about it. He didn't care. Finish me, he thought, grinding his teeth together as he arched his back in pain. I'm through. I've had enough.

The pain ebbed slowly, and he sat up, gun in his lap. Sweat poured from his body—or was it raining again?

A voice called from the house.

"You! Whoever you are, we give up. We're coming out. Don't shoot!"

Ruff didn't answer at first, couldn't. Then he swallowed a deep breath of air and managed to croak, "Guns first, boys. Let's have those guns."

They splashed into the pond, and Ruff simply stared at the dark ripples.

"We're coming out, all right?"

"No!" he screamed at them. He wiped his face, sweeping away the rain. "Light a lantern first. How many of you are there?" Someone had already struck a match and the lantern went on.

"Three. There's only three of us. And one dead."

"All right. One of you tie up the other two. Hands behind the back. Use your belts. A nice tight figure-eight. First two back out so I can see they're tied, last man with his hands high."

"All right." There was a little panic in the voice, a shadow of arrogance. The speaker wanted to be a hero but he wasn't willing to die for it.

Ruff sat until they called that they were ready to come out, then he got to his feet, using the empty rifle as a crutch. They emerged, two tied, the third hands raised high.

Justice staggered forward. "Hold it. You now," he said to the last man, "hands behind you."

The man complied, and Justice tied him himself. "All right."

They turned then, and by the lanternlight they took a close look at Ruff Justice.

"Dammit all," one of them grumbled, "if we'da

waited another little while he woulda been dead hisself."

"Down on the grass," Justice said, noticing to his annoyance that he was trembling again. They complied, slowly. He went to the doorway and peered into the lanternlit room, seeing the dead man, the sacks of money, the empty strongboxes. Satisfied that there was no one left alive, he began the laborious task of herding the bandits around, letting them squat to pick up the gold sacks with bound hands, transferring it all to the saddle bags of the ten horses behind the house. The dead they left to the buzzards and the coyotes, the prairie wolves and the worms.

It was dawn suddenly, the skies clearing. There was a lot of excitement over something Ruff didn't quite understand as he rode into Bear Creek trailing his heavily laden horses, convoying his prisoners up the main street. People were all around him shouting questions which echoed in his head like voices hollering down a barrel. He would have answered them but he didn't know what they wanted. He knew he handed the lead rope to someone who looked an awful lot like Allie James and then he knew nothing else. He nodded to the mob, tried to swing down from his horse, and stepped right into a deep, black, silent hole.

15

When he opened his eyes it was white. Everything white. White sunlight, piercingly bright to the eyes, beaming through white curtains which fluttered in a gentle breeze. The walls were white. A white sheet across his naked body. He assumed he was dead.

Turning his head, he saw her sitting there, erect, pale, golden hair loose around her shoulders.

" 'Lo, Adrienne," he said weakly.

"Hello." Her head turned slowly to him. She placed aside the book she had been reading. There was a softness in her eyes. The sunlight highlighted and streaked her hair. For a moment as she moved nearer there was a pale halo hovering around her head.

"Well, darn you, you're going to make it, are you?" she asked, and her voice, half mocking, half gentle, was as enigmatic as ever. As was her expression—warm, yet stiff around the edges. Her smile only went so far; the light in her eyes dimmed if he looked long enough at her.

He lifted his hand, put it behind her neck, and pulled her face to his, kissing her. When she pulled away, Adrienne said:

"That gold was supposed to go through to Bismarck. Why on earth did you bring it back here?" And Justice sighed, closing his eyes, sleeping deeply, down where her voice could not reach.

Lucille was there when Ruff came around next, and with her Allie James.

"How goes it?" Allie asked.

"I'm starved," Ruff answered. "You two always stand that close together?"

"We're married," Allie said a little defensively.

"Are you now?" Ruff smiled and looked at Lucille, whose cheeks reddened slightly as those blue eyes met hers. "Fine. I'm happy for you. You staying with the line, then?"

"For now," Allie said. "Maybe later we'll drift on west. The line's running full-bore. Freight nearly every day, mail twice a week. We've taken on six new drivers, five more station personnel. Rupe says hello—he's doing all right now. Said to tell you it was the Indian who got him if you didn't already know."

"I knew."

"The Chinamen stuck—they're running that Coyote Springs station by themselves, and doing a damn fine job of it. Fields is still driving. No one else you know, I don't suppose."

"No." Everyone else was dead. But the damned line was running. Well, maybe that was all right. The freight would run in, the passengers out, until the gold dwindled and stopped, and then there wouldn't be a Great Western anymore, and that would be all right too. "Can you get me something to eat?" he asked.

"It's on the way; the nurse is bringing it along." Allie looked impatient suddenly. He wanted to leave, and Ruff realized he was making him nervous. "The army sent down a letter, Ruff. Colonel MacEnroe's thanks and orders to get back to the post when you're able."

"Sure."

"Well . . ." Allie stuck out his hand and Ruff took it.

"Goodbye, Ruff," Lucille said, and she smiled once, briefly, before they left and Ruff was left alone in the white room, the open window letting in a soft breeze. He wished to hell that nurse would show up. When he had eaten last he didn't know—he didn't know what day it was, how long he had been in that bed. He heard the clink of china against china and she breezed into the room, smiling widely.

"Now you want to eat, eh?" María Salazar said. "Sure—I been trying to feed you for a week and you knock the tray out of my hands. I coulda dump it over your head, Ruffin Justice."

He just lay there looking at her. She looked fine. Sleek and dark, well molded in her light-blue dress and white apron. Her hair was coiled up on her head, revealing those small round ears Ruff had liked to kiss.

"Now what?" she asked, still smiling as she sat the tray on the bedside table and scooted a chair up beside him. "What are you looking at?"

"Just you, María. You look good to me, very good."

"Yes?" she was pleased. "But you're a sick man. No exertions, the doctor said."

"It wouldn't take much exertion." She was propping him up, stuffing a spare pillow beneath his shoulders. "I thought you'd have gone back to Durango."

"Durango? Is a stinkin' place, Ruff Justice. No, I stay here for a time anyway. But not with Adrienne Court. No more of that. I'm working at the restaurant when I'm not taking care of the big mustached baby."

She was cutting his meat for him, and Ruff watched her, liking the concentration on her face, the sparkle in her dark eyes. His hand found its way to her thigh and just rested there, and her eyes brightened.

"I think you eat a lot, get well pretty soon, eh?"

"I think so." He opened his mouth like a good patient, and she started to place a bite of meat in it, changed her mind, and kissed him first, her tongue flicking between his lips briefly. Ruff responded, but she pulled away, nostrils flaring, lips parted, breathing tight. "Aye! Eat, eat, hombre, we better make you strong pretty quick."

"Very damn quick," Ruff agreed.

The steak was tender and thick, the potatoes cut thin, fried crisp. After that he had about a gallon of coffee and lay back just watching María.

"I'd like to have my gun in here, María."

"Gun?"

"You know—bang-bang," he said with a smile.

"What for? Fight the women off or something?"

"Just to look at. You can hang it on the bedpost here."

"You got strange habits, Mr. Justice."

"Maybe so. Cater to my whims, okay? Bring me my Colt."

"Okay." She was picking up the dishes, Ruff's eyes following the grace of her small movements. She bent low, gave him one last kiss, and said, "I got to get off to work, Ruff Justice. You sleep for a while, okay?"

"Don't forget my gun before you go."

"You going to shoot someone while you sleep?"

"Never know," he said. "Please?"

"Whatever pleases you. Anytime whatever pleases you, Mr. Ruff Justice."

Then she was gone, Ruff watching the empty doorway for a time afterward. He looked at the open window, seeing a mockingbird perch briefly on the

sill, cock its head at him, and then flutter off, squawking loudly.

Ruff yawned and closed his eyes, the meal resting
comfortably on his stomach, his thoughts warm and
distant. Something brought him back sharply to reality,
to the present. Some deep instinct which had seen
him through years on the plains and in the mountains,
some warrior's knowledge, and his eyes flickered open
to see the dark figure hovering over him, to see the
flash of the knife as he stepped toward the bed.

Ruff kicked out savagely and rolled to the side,
tearing open his wounds. He landed on the floor
with a thud, heard the simultaneous thunder of a
gun, and slowly raised himself to one knee.

"He . . ." María stood in the doorway, holding his
Colt, still holstered. She had fired it that way and
had done the job with it. "He . . . God, hombre, the
dirty bastard wanted to kill you!"

Ruff got to his feet, his head swimming. He moved
stiff-legged across the room, still naked, warm blood
trickling out from under the bandages on his arm,
around his waist. He put an arm around María and
took the gun from her.

Bear Foot lay on the floor, his eyes staring up
expressionlessly at them. In his hand was the knife.
Ruff walked to him and kicked it aside. He helped
the kid to sit up against the wall. Bear Foot clutched
his stomach, his stomach where the life flowed from
his twisted little body.

"It was you who worked over Pierce and the half-
breed and the old man."

Bear Foot nodded. "You were the great warrior,
Justice. . . ." His eyes closed briefly in agony. Sweat
rolled off his dark face. "The best. The man who
captured my father. The man who beat Stone Hand.
Me, I wanted to beat you! To be the best, to be a
warrior my father would have been proud of. . . . I

wanted to show him I was strong too." He clutched
Ruff's arm, his eyes pleading. "He called me 'cripple.'
My own father kicked me until I was bent and twisted,
then he called me 'cripple'! He said I was not a man,
Ruff Justice. Do you think he knew that it was Bear
Foot who ruined the great Ruff Justice's work?"

"He told me he did. The last time I saw him. He
told me he was proud of you, Bear Foot. That he was
sorry he had called you a cripple. I swear to you that
it is so."

There was no answer. Bear Foot was dead. Ruff
stood up, his mouth twisted into a distant, hard
expression. He was dead. But the woman was still
alive, and Justice turned toward her, seeing her taking deep slow breaths, trying to steady herself, and he
went to her, feeling as weak as she did, needing her
as much as María needed him, and to hell with all
the doctors in the world.

WESTWARD HO!

**The following is the opening section from the
next novel in the gun-blazing, action-packed new
Ruff Justice series from Signet:
RUFF JUSTICE #13: POWDER LODE**

There couldn't be more than three of them in the
cabin below the bluff. Three outlaws left from the
Morgan gang, which had stormed into Bismarck six
days earlier and tried to open up the bank. Five of
them had been left dead in the streets. Armed, irate
citizens had objected strenuously to losing next year's
seed money or the nickles put painstakingly away to
buy a new mail-order corset.

Five outlaws dead in the streets of Bismarck and
three townspeople, including the banker and a twelve-
year-old kid. Marshal Shearer hadn't wasted any time.
With ten men behind him, he had ridden directly to
neighboring Fort Lincoln and marched himself into
the commanding officer's office.

"The Morgan gang just hit the bank," Shearer had
said, leaning across Colonel MacEnroe's desk. "I
want you to give me a dozen men to go after them."

It wasn't a good way to approach MacEnroe. The
colonel's color darkened, and he narrowed his eyes.
"It's not up to us to provide you with a posse, Shearer,
and you know it."

"Damn you, MacEnroe, this is your town too. I've

got a twelve-year-old boy dead and the Morgan gang making a run for the foothills. They've got our money; they've killed our people."

"You've got no one in town who'll ride with you?"

"I've got ten men right now. It won't be enough. Once we get out into Indian country they're going to get almighty shy. They won't stick it out."

"Then they don't much deserve to get their money back, do they?"

"If we had soldiers with us—"

"I don't have any soldiers to spare, Shearer!" MacEnroe rose behind his desk. He was a tall, imposing man with a silver mustache. He was annoyed with Shearer—sorry for him, but annoyed nonetheless. "I've got Captain Markham up near the Canuck line chasing down that animal Sky Warrior; I've got Lieutenant Cooper out with two platoons on the western perimeter, trying to locate that Sioux force which is drifting along the Heart. That leaves me one officer and three platoons. That officer is Lieutenant Harkness, who just came in yesterday from three weeks in the field, and who took an arrow in the thigh. I'm sorry for you, Shearer, I'd like to help, but I can't strip this post for you. No, I don't have anyone."

"All right." Shearer stiffened, his mouth compressing into a tight line. "If that's the way it's going to be. Just don't you forget that you've turned your back on the people of Bismarck—"

"For Christ's sake, Shearer, shut up."

"Yeah, I'll shut up." The marshal mopped his forehead with a red handkerchief. "Listen, MacEnroe, I've got myself a situation. I'm not a bad town marshal, I think people will tell you that, but I'm not cut out for that wild country. If you could give me a hand— like an Indian scout, maybe." Shearer looked worried now, more concerned than angry. He had a town depending on him.

"They're all out," MacEnroe said. "Except for one who just came in with Lieutenant Harkness and is due some leave. I don't think he would want to ride out with you. He was leaving for Denver."

"You can ask him," the colonel added.

MacEnroe was looking beyond Shearer, and it was only then that the marshal realized there was another man in the room, sitting in a wooden chair against the wall. He was a lanky man with long, dark hair which curled down past his shoulders; he wore his mustache drooping to the jawline. He had icy blue eyes, a somewhat narrow nose, a mocking mouth. He wore a gray suit, and his black boots were highly polished. On his knee was a new white stetson with a low crown. His shirt had ruffles down the front. Someone less observant, less knowing, might have taken him for a dandy, but Shearer had been around some. He knew the look in those eyes. He thought he knew the name.

"Ruffin T. Justice?"

"Yes. So you've got a little problem."

"I've got myself a large problem, Mr. Justice. And I guess I made a fool out of myself by not coming in here and admitting it. I need a scout and need one bad. The Morgan gang's got a good start, and they've got good horses under them. I shouldn't ask you to delay your trip to Denver, but if you could possibly help us, I'd be forever grateful. So would all of Bismarck."

Ruff smiled thinly. He didn't believe in eternal gratitude. "A twelve-year-old was killed. Who got him?"

"They say Rufus Morgan. And it wasn't no accident. It was Hugh Thomas's kid, the blacksmith. He had a squirrel gun and tried to stop them."

"I'll change my clothes," Justice said. He exchanged a glance with Colonel MacEnroe. "Fifteen minutes."

In fifteen minutes Ruff Justice, wearing fringed buckskins, a gunbelt which held a Colt revolver and a back-slung, razor-edged bowie, carrying a buckskin-sheathed Spencer .56 rifle, was leading the posse out onto the Dakota plains.

Colonel MacEnroe stood on the plankwalk before the orderly room with Mack Pierce, his massive first sergeant, beside him, squinting into the harsh sunlight, watching the horsemen.

"I don't think I'll ever be able to figure that man out," MacEnroe said. "He's been badgering me for months to let him go to Denver."

"I read him," Pierce said slowly. "Justice knew the kid, you see."

"The Thomas kid?"

"Yes, sir. Justice knew him. He used to take him fishing. It's personal, Colonel. It's personal, and I can damn near pity Rufus Morgan for what he's got coming now."

Ruff Justice was pressed against the rim of the bluff, looking down upon the shanty where Rufus Morgan and two of his men had taken refuge. The sun was dropping lower, glinting orange through the willows along the river beyond the shack.

Justice felt the sweat trickle down his cheeks and throat, felt the prickly heat on his flesh. His mouth was dry, his eyes hard and cold. The Colt was clenched, thumb hooked around the curved hammer, in his right hand.

There were three outlaws below, only three. Of the posse, there was only Ruff.

Six members of the posse had turned back the second day after the Indians' sign became prolific. A hundred Sioux warriors had crossed their trail only the day before, and the townsmen didn't have the heart to continue.

"Let the Morgans have the money. They won't live long enough to spend it."

On the following morning the posse had run right into the Morgan gang, almost literally. The outlaws, believing themselves safe from pursuit, had been late in breaking camp, and the posse burst through the trees practically on top of them.

Three outlaws had gone down in the first barrage. A horse had cried out with pain; Marshal Shearer, holding his shattered thigh, had been thrown to the ground. Five of the Morgan gang had plunged their horses into the river. Bullets from Ruff Justice's big .56 repeater had stopped two of them before they had reached the far bank.

There were only two of the posse left alive: Shearer and a cowboy named Wright. Only Shearer didn't look as if he was going to last long. The color had washed out of his face. He was sitting propped up against a fallen cottonwood when Ruff returned, Wright trying to stem the flow of blood from a jagged wound.

"That's done us, I guess," Shearer said.

Ruff smiled. "Done you anyway, Marshal." Justice had helped splint the leg. They couldn't do much about the bleeding.

"Maybe if we get him back to town, he'll make it," Wright had suggested.

"Maybe." The kid looked anxious to get himself back to town. "That's all there is to do. We can rig up a travois, maybe."

"Justice!" It was Shearer who spoke, his voice weak and dusty. "We can't let them get away."

"We won't."

"I won't go back to town."

"You'll have to, I'm afraid. Don't fret. I'll get them. Every single one."

"You're going on alone?" Wright asked in disbelief.

"Oh, yes." Justice stood looking across the glimmering river. "I'm going after them." Then he helped Wright fashion a travois out of two long willow poles and a saddle blanket. When he had last seen Shearer the marshal had been unconscious, tied to the travois, jouncing back toward Bismarck.

Ruff tensed—the door of the shack below had opened a bare inch. Someone was peering out. He would see nothing. Justice was out of the line of sight, fifty feet above the cabin on a sandy bluff, a hundred feet away. The door closed again. They would wait until dark undoubtedly.

Fine. That suited Justice.

He lay there staring at the cabin, the glare of late sunlight in his eyes. A red ant crawled across his gun hand, but Justice didn't move.

Only the eyes moved. The eyes which restlessly searched the land, returning periodically to the cabin. He hadn't forgotten the Sioux sign. They were out there as well. Perhaps the gunfire had chased them off; perhaps it had drawn them nearer, piquing their curiosity.

The sun had dropped another degree or two, the orange rim of it disappearing behind the willows. Still Justice held his position. He could see movement in the trees behind the shack—a hobbled horse restlessly moving around.

The breeze rose at sunset, cooling Ruff's heated flesh. Doves winged homeward and the night birds began to appear. An owl swooped low, following the river as it searched for insects.

The first star blinked on, shining through the orange haze of sunset, and Ruff Justice began to move slowly from the bluff, backing down toward his horse, bringing a stream of sand with him.

He left the horse, circling on foot through the

cat's-claw and sage, the willows, toward the trees behind the shack. The outlaws were going nowhere without those horses.

If Ruff Justice had his way, they were going nowhere at all.

He came up slowly, silently, on the horses, not wishing to startle them. A roan lifted its head and began to quiver as if it would whicker, but it did not. Perhaps it was just too weary. Some of the horses still wore saddles. All of them were sweat-streaked, beaten. The outlaws had ridden them hard.

To one side, seen dimly through the shadows the stars cast beneath the willows, was a very tall chestnut gelding. Saddleless, it alone looked fresh.

Justice had only a moment to glance at the chestnut before he heard a twig crack under someone's boot. The sound was loud in the night. Ruff's eyes shifted that way, toward the cabin. The outlaws were coming out.

Justice hunkered down, the big Colt in his hand, and sat watching. It was time for Rufus Morgan to pay.

The first man entered the thicket cautiously. The starlight glinted in his eyes. He wore a leather jacket, jeans, a red scarf. The outlaw looked around cautiously, moving forward on tiptoe into the thicket where the horses were picketed. But he was no woodsman. He never saw the tall man in buckskins.

Justice still waited, and in another minute two more men appeared, each carrying a canvas sack.

The bearded man was Rufus Morgan. Justice's Colt automatically shifted that way. Morgan was the first target. Justice waited until they had assured themselves that no one was there, and when Morgan was busy tying the sack onto his saddle, his hands busy, Justice rose and took three silent steps forward.

"This is it, Morgan. Judgment Day."

Morgan flinched but did not turn around. The man in the leather jacket did. He flung himself aside, grabbing for his holstered pistol. He fired wildly at Ruff from the ground. Two rapid shots sang past Ruff's head, the pistol spitting flame. Ruff's big Colt spoke in reply, and he saw the outlaw buck from the impact of the .44 bullet.

He dropped to a knee and turned back toward Morgan, but he was gone! The big man had taken to the brush, leaving the third outlaw to fend for himself.

"You can go back to Bismarck," Ruff said, moving toward the outlaw, who looked very young.

"And get hanged?"

"I reckon," Ruff answered quietly.

"What the hell's the percentage there?"

"You've always got a chance with a jury," Ruff said. His eyes restlessly searched the willows beyond the kid. Where was Rufus Morgan? Had he taken to his heels, or was he circling back? There was little time to fool with the kid. He had to decide now where he wanted to do his dying.

"What's it going to be?" Ruff asked him.

"I've got more chance with you than with a hanging jury," the young outlaw said. Then he drew his gun.

He was wrong. He would have had much more chance with a jury. He was young and scared and desperate. His gun spewed flame and lead, but in his haste he wasn't even close. Justice answered his fire with one heart shot. The kid went to his knees, already dead, although his eyes were still open, his mouth still working.

Justice stood there in the darkness for a minute, the rolling echoes dying away, the scent of burned powder still in his nostrils, acrid, smelling of death and the promise of death.

He heard something—the slightest of sounds, a

whispery movement to his right—and he backed out of the thicket, circling left, a shadowy, substanceless thing as he moved toward the sound.

The stars were bright and blue now through the lace of the intertwined willow branches. Far off a coyote howled. The wind rustled the leaves of the willows and was silent.

Ruff was nearer the river now. He could smell it in the night, hear the tinkling of water over stones. And ahead was something moving which was not water.

"Morgan," Justice said quietly. "You can't win this game. Let's go on back."

The answer was the near bellowing of a large-caliber rifle, and Justice flung himself to the earth as a bullet cut willow brush over his head.

He was on his belly, and wriggling forward on elbows and knees he reached a small cut which led down to the narrow river. Ruff was over it and down in seconds, then running south, wanting to get back to the thicket where the horses were kept. Morgan had no chance without the horses, and he was smart enough to know it.

Panting, Justice clambered up the bank, stifling a grunt as his knee knocked against an unseen rock in the darkness. Then he was into the trees again, moving like a ghost toward the thicket, his sense of direction leading him unerringly to it.

The skies were lighter now, and as he glanced across his shoulder he saw the rim of the moon, orange, huge, appearing above the dark Dakota horizon.

He saw the horse move in the thicket, saw simultaneously the man mounted on its back, and he fired as the rifle spoke again. Justice had missed, but he didn't miss the second time, and as the thicket was lighted by the yellow-red muzzle flash, a gurgling scream split the night. The horse went to hind legs, whinnying shrilly, and Rufus Morgan slid from its back to thump against the earth and lie there, still and dead, dark blood pouring from a savage wound at the base of his throat.

Ruff glanced at the outlaw and moved toward the horse. He untied the canvas sack, which proved to hold bank notes in various denominations and a quantity of newly minted gold coins.

Justice found the second sack and shouldered both of them. With extreme caution he moved toward the cabin—he and Shearer and Wright had believed there were only three outlaws left, and those three were now accounted for—but men had been killed by assuming too much.

Besides, the Sioux were around still. They could use that gold as well as anyone else.

The moon was rising higher, becoming round and golden. Justice reached the cabin, and approaching it silently, opened the door. He went in, leading with the muzzle of his Colt, but the place was empty.

There was a jug of corn liquor still on the table, a few tins of beans, half eaten, the scent of tobacco. In the corner were empty mail sacks, a broken shotgun, a bit of harness, a rusted shovel and pick, rags and bottles.

Justice dropped the canvas moneybags he held and sat down, his back to the table, reloading his pistol, watching the moon glimmer on the river through the open door of the shack.

His hand, he noticed, was trembling slightly. Justice smiled thinly, rose, and holstered his pistol. He poked around the shack a little, moving the mailbags in the corner. They were all empty. In the fireplace was a heaped pile of fine ash. Paper had been burned in it. The mail, undoubtedly, searched for valuables and then tossed away.

Ruff took one of the empty mailbags with him and

went back out. The night had grown chilly. A ground fog crept across the river toward him.

Morgan and his friends were still there, growing slowly cold, slowly stiff, nothing but a memory and a heap of bones. Justice crouched beside Morgan's body and searched it, coming up with a buckskin sack full of ten-dollar gold pieces and, from an inside vest pocket, three pieces of mail, which Justice stuffed into the saddlebags on one of the horses.

A search of the other two outlaws yielded one pocket watch and two more sacks of gold. Justice left the bodies there, unburied, unmourned, and leading the horses, he started slowly back toward Fort Lincoln as the pale moon rose higher above the empty land. Behind him the coyotes yipped excitely as they crept nearer the dead objects lying in the willows.

JOIN THE RUFF JUSTICE READER'S PANEL
AND PREVIEW NEW BOOKS

If you're a reader of RUFF JUSTICE; New American Library wants to bring you more of the type of books you enjoy. For this reason we're asking you to join RUFF JUSTICE Reader's Panel, to preview new books, so we can learn more about your reading tastes.

Please fill out and mail today. Your comments are appreciated.

1. The title of the last paperback book I bought was: _____
   _____

2. How many paperback books have you bought for yourself in the last six months?
   ☐ 1 to 3   ☐ 4 to 6   ☐ 10 to 20   ☐ 21 or more

3. What other paperback fiction have you read in the past six months? Please list titles: _____
   _____
   _____
   _____

4. I usually buy my books at: (Check One or more)
   ☐ Book Store   ☐ Newsstand   ☐ Discount Store
   ☐ Supermarket   ☐ Drug Store   ☐ Department Store
   ☐ Other (Please specify)_____

5. I listen to radio regularly: (Check One)   ☐ Yes   ☐ No
   My favorite station is:_____
   I usually listen to radio (Circle One or more)   On way to work /
   During the day / Coming home from work / In the evening

6. I read magazines regularly: (Check One)   ☐ Yes   ☐ No
   My favorite magazine is:_____

7. I read a newspaper regularly: (Check One)   ☐ Yes   ☐ No
   My favorite newspaper is:_____
   My favorite section of the newspaper is:_____

For our records, we need this information from all our Reader's Panel Members.
NAME:_____
ADDRESS:_____ ZIP_____
TELEPHONE: Area Code (   ) Number_____

8. (Check One)   ☐ Male   ☐ Female

9. Age (Check One)   ☐ 17 and under   ☐ 18 to 34
   ☐ 35 to 49   ☐ 50 to 64   ☐ 65 and over

10. Education (Check One)
    ☐ Now in high school   ☐ Graduated high school
    ☐ Now in college   ☐ Completed some college
    ☐ Graduated college

As our special thanks to all members of our Reader's Panel, we'll send a free gift of special interest to readers of RUFF JUSTICE.

Thank you. Please mail this in today.

NEW AMERICAN LIBRARY
PROMOTION DEPARTMENT
1633 BROADWAY
NEW YORK, NY 10019

THE Avenger #3

Chet Cunningham

COLOMBIA CRACKDOWN

WARNER BOOKS

A Warner Communications Company

WARNER BOOKS EDITION

Copyright © 1988 by Chet Cunningham
All rights reserved.

Warner Books, Inc.
666 Fifth Avenue
New York, N.Y. 10103

A Warner Communications Company

Printed in the United States of America

First Printing: July, 1988

10 9 8 7 6 5 4 3 2 1

Chapter
One

Lieutenant J.G. Willard Kline growled as he swung his small-chase Coast Guard chopper around and pointed it seaward. His radio chattered at him.

"Here it is, Watcher. Radar shows six, I repeat six, targets now moving away from Mother Hubbard. A surface craft is on the way. Close with and identify if possible."

"Six!" Lieutenant Kline wanted to swear, but he couldn't on the air. "Jeez, base, they'll be all over the Atlantic before I can tie down one of them."

"Sorry, Watcher, best we can do. The *Bell*, using call name of Hunter, now at flank speed for a rendezvous. Good hunting!"

Lieutenant Kline glared at the radio and looked ahead for the small boats. In a year and a half of chasing these crack smugglers, it was always the same. Some rust bucket of a freighter came plowing up the Florida coast, and a small boat pulled away from it with twenty million dollar's worth of cocaine on board and made a fast run for the shore.

They caught some of them and proscecuted. But most of the bastards slipped through. There were hundreds of miles of coastline and thousands of small bays, ports, and harbors where a twenty-four-foot motorboat could come ashore. There was no way to watch every mile and every landing every hour of the day and night.

Six of them! How could he track six small boats scattering for the shore? It had happened once before with three. They picked out one, nailed it, and it happened to be the right one. Sometimes the smugglers sent in decoys. There might be four boats, only two of which carried the goods. If he and the cutter picked the wrong one, the good guys came up empty and the bastards got away with it again.

It just plain made Lieutenant Willard Kline angry. He had known two people who had died as a result of cocaine. One young Coast Guard officer had perished in a car crash when his wife insisted on driving home. She had snorted two hundred dollars' worth that night when they were at a party.

He shook his head and stared across the clear Florida seascape as the six specks on the horizon came into sight. They had been well outside the three-mile limit, probably outside the seven-mile zone.

His radio crackled again.

"Watcher, this is Hunter. Good morning. I'm about a mile out. You spot them yet on visual?"

"Right, Hunter. Just got them. They're heading at different angles for the shore. They're about a quarter of a mile apart already. This is going to be a nightmare."

"Pick one, your gamble. You still toothless?"

"Right, no stingers. Love to have a pair of rockets on my landing frame."

"Maybe next time, Watcher. We have the backup fire-power that you don't, and we're coming."

Kline snorted and put his binoculars on the six boats, now little more than a half mile from him. The second from the far end was the largest, maybe a thirty-six-footer. That one should be the fastest as well. As he watched, the six small boats gunned their engines, and two spurted out faster toward shore. The thirty-six-footer was one that surged away head of the others.

Kline dropped away to the left and raced toward the large, fast, blue-and-white boat making a big wake.

"Picked out one, about a thirty-six-footer, blue-and-white. Second from the end on your left. I'm going down for a closer look."

Kline raced the small two-man chase chopper down almost to the wave tops as he closed quickly on the motorboat that raced directly toward him. At the last moment he veered to the left and let the craft flash by under him.

He saw no one on the small deck. Only a shadow showed in the little cabin. Kline had been hoping he would draw fire. That would pin this craft down as dirty. But he had no such luck. He swept the bird up in a steep, climbing turn and overtook the boat. He guessed it was doing about eighteen knots, maybe more. A jolting proposition for those riding through the light chop that had developed on the always unreliable Atlantic waters below him.

For a moment he hung right over the blue-and-white boat fifty feet above. He saw the man jump on deck, lift a long object, and Kline waited no longer. He cut the chopper to the left and down, gaining speed, then kicked it up in another turn. The booming sound of the rifle never made it to the chopper, but two bullets did. One ripped into the strut below the bird's cabin, and the second shattered the Plexiglas side window.

Kline was unscratched. He hit his radio button.

"Hunter, just took rifle fire from that blue-and-white thirty-six-footer. I'd say that's our target of choice."

"Right, Watcher. Got him on my scope. He's doing about twenty, and we're closing at twenty-four. Estimated time of contact is about four minutes. You still flying?"

"Nothing serious. Break out that .50-caliber MG of yours and treat the little son of a banana to some hot lead!"

"Yeah, but not too many holes. We can use a good thirty-six-footer when we confiscate it, so we don't want to have to make a lot of repairs."

Kline lifted the chopper up to a thousand feet and circled over the ships below. It always looked like a giant puzzle, or maybe a TV game-show set. The sleek, small Coast Guard cutter slammed through the light chop straight for the smaller blue-and-white.

At about four hundred yards he saw a man on the bow with a .50-caliber machine gun. A moment later the small blue-and-white craft went dead in the water.

The two men in the blue-and-white boat, now bobbing in the Atlantic swells two miles off Biscayne Bay, knew they were blown the minute the Coast Guard craft showed up on their own radar.

They had turned on the afterburners heading for shore. One of the boatmen was called Bear. He had a last name, but no one ever used it. He stood 6'8''' and weighed in at 290 pounds. His playing weight when he bounced around the National Football League had been 280, and he was still in great condition.

4

When Bear was sure the Coast Guard cutter was coming and that the little whirlybird was a spotter, he waved at Phil DeLuca, a thin, wiry man with a beard and an M16 in his hands.

"Pop the guy a couple of times," Bear said. "Drive him off our back. We need some room to maneuver."

DeLuca pushed out of the cabin and fired twice at the chopper just behind and above them, then came back.

"Pegged him twice and he's up and away," DeLuca said.

"Yeah, okay. What you get paid for. Your other toys ready? Looks like we're gonna need them. No way we can outrun that cutter."

He could see it now, the obvious red diagonal stripe covering half the side of the Coast Guard craft making it unmistakable.

"This sumbitch is cutting us off, he's got the angle," Bear bellowed. "Just get it ready, DeLuca. First you'll have to take out the machine gunner on the bow. They think those .50s across our bow are gonna work wonders. Not this time, Boy Scouts!"

The two craft sliced through the light blue Atlantic, coming closer and closer. When they were four hundred yards apart, the heavy .50-caliber machine gun chattered, and the slugs slammed across the path of the blue-and-white cruiser, churning up the water twenty yards to port.

"I'll pull her down," Bear said, killing the throttles. "DeLuca, now you really start earning your money."

Phil DeLuca pushed the cabin door open and wedged it with a briefcase. He laid out his two weapons and waited. The small cutter edged closer. At two hundred yards the bullhorn boomed.

"You, on board the blue-and-white craft. This is the

Coast Guard. You're under arrest for attempted murder for shooting at the aircraft. I want all on board to come on deck one at a time with your hands clasped behind your heads.''

The blue craft swung around in the current just enough so DeLuca had a shot out the cabin door at the machine gunner. He flipped the selection lever to full automatic, and just like in Marine Corps advanced training, he fired.

The six-round bursts of 5.56-mm slugs ripped out of the M16 at a thousand meters a second muzzle velocity, and at a rate of nine hundred rounds a second.

Three bursts around the machine gun on the bow of the cutter jolted the gunner off his feet and slammed him halfway to the far rail, where he died before the officer in the wheelhouse could react.

The cutter had just started to move away when DeLuca picked up his second weapon, stepped on the deck, cleared his back blast, and fired a LAW missile at the Coast Guard cutter.

At less than a hundred yards, the ship was a perfect target. The experienced shooter dropped the round on the side of the wheelhouse, blew the crew off the bridge, and killed the engines.

DeLuca's second round caught the listing craft just at the waterline, created a secondary explosion in the hull. The cutter began taking on water.

''You earned your goddamn money,'' Bear said as he hit the throttles and surged away from the scene. Now get on deck and see how far you can keep that damn chopper away from us.''

Kline circled the rapidly sinking Coast Guard ship. He had reported the first hit of the missile to his base. Now he confirmed.

6

"Yes, sir, the cutter is down, almost under water. I see one body floating. There's one survivor! Get a rescue chopper out here fast. I can't help him a bit. He looks wounded. I can't do any more here, I'm going after that blue-and-white!"

Kline shivered as he thought about the crew on that cutter. Six or seven men! He watched the blue-and-white craft ahead and wished he had a Drug Enforcement Agency channel on his radio. Even a tie-in channel with the Dade County Sheriff's Department.

He hit the radio talk button again. "This is Watcher. Isn't there some way we can tie in with the local law? I can tell them where these varmits are headed and—"

"Sorry, Watcher. Can't do. No tie lines, no cooperation with those folks. We're on our own out there. We've got a another craft on the way to pick up any survivors. They lifted off about three minutes ago."

"Yeah. I'm gonna tie down for damn sure where this boat puts in. Just for the record."

Twice he had taken evasive action when he edged too close to the blue-and-white boat, and the rifle on deck fired. He could see the muzzle flash and he backed off. Only one bullet hit his craft in the exchanges, and it was not in a vital spot.

Damn, but he hated this! They had this outfit in their pocket, and now they were getting off free and clear, and with multiple murder raps on their heads!

Below, in the blue-and-white boat, Bear had slanted past Old Rhodes Key at the southern end of Biscayne Bay's protective line of keys and tiny islands, and slid slowly toward the shore. He found a small bay with thick, over-hanging mangrove branches and powered the sleek blue-

and-white craft under the foliage until it couldn't be seen from the air.

Bear kept the engine running just enough to hold the thirty-six-footer pressed against the hanging branches and mangrove roots. He eased back and caught a cold beer DeLuca tossed him from the refrigerator.

"Damn good day's work half done," Bear said, and grinned. He had four front teeth missing, two upper and lower, football mementos from his college days. He hadn't bothered to put his bridges in this morning.

"We gonna sit here all fucking day?" DeLuca asked, his Brooklyn accent showing plainly.

"Relax, kid. This ain't a New York action. We wait him out a couple of minutes, maybe five. Then he'll get tired, or low on fuel, and haul ass. Worked before a couple of times."

"What if he calls in the local cops?"

"Not a chance. They don't work together that good yet. Day they start doing that, we'll have to figure out something else, night drops, probably."

Bear snorted at the young Italian. He had been highly recommended and was an expert with the new Army weapons they had recently picked up. This operation was outfitted damn near as well as an infantry company.

Bear leaned back in the pilot's chair and relaxed. Christ, but it had been beautiful! Usually when that .50-caliber chattered, the game was over. He'd been chopped up by a .50 once when he wouldn't stop. He'd been close enough to shore to swim for it when the boat went down. The darkness was all that saved him that time. He'd give a thousand bucks to see the expression on that swabbys' face when the fucking missile went off in the wheelhouse.

Bear looked out the cabin and listened. The chopper was still there, but he had pulled back, trying to fool them. Bear shut down the engine and tied one line to some mangrove roots. Now he could hear the chopper engine. He'd give him another five minutes.

Bear grinned at the murky mangrove swamp as he thought about his life so far. He'd had a good career in the pros. For six years he'd played ball as a guard and tackle. He'd never made the really big money, but he got by and even saved some. Rather, his agent saved some for him. He didn't have a Super Bowl ring, but his team made the playoffs twice.

Lately money had been no problem, not since he signed on with Vito Labruzzo. Vito had been running about half the goods in the Miami area for years. The last five years, when the market had gotten so good, Vito had cleaned up in a rush, and he didn't mind paying good wages now for people to run the business for him.

Bear had fitted in nicely when he came to work. He loved boats and could handle people. He'd made more than fifty runs into the Atlantic this way and had never been burned except that once. He figured he'd go back to night runs. They were harder, more dangerous on the tie-up and transfer.

When you're picking up ten to twelve million dollars' worth of goods, it isn't just dropped overboard into the Atlantic Ocean with the hope that it'll float.

Bear went on deck. He couldn't hear the chopper at all. Back in the cabin, he grinned, finished the beer, and had DeLuca cast off the one line. He applied a little power and edged away from the mangrove roots.

He had just cleared the overhang and headed into a channel when a shot slammed through the mid-morning sultry stillness. A slug ripped a half-inch groove in his shoulder, and Bear dropped below the open windows.

"Get the bastard!" Bear roared at DeLuca. "That damn chopper pilot must have landed close by and walked down the shore. He's trying to be a hero. Make him a dead hero!"

The small man dived for his M16 as five more rounds slammed into the windows and sides of the sleek powerboat. By then DeLuca had his rifle out the open door and saw a figure slide behind a big tree.

He sent a burst of six beside the tree and waited. A head bobbed out on the other side, and DeLuca jolted six more rounds where the guy's head had been.

Bear hit the throttles, peered over the top of the console, and worked out of the small channel toward the open bay. Another round from a heavy gun thunked into the hull.

DeLuca rattled off a dozen shots, then all was quiet except the engines. They powered into the bay itself, raced half a mile south, and slid into a mangrove-covered inlet that was totally hidden.

Bear eased the craft up to a wood dock that was moss-covered and seemed about to dissolve into the mangrove swamp. A small man with pimples on his forty-year-old face stepped from behind some mangrove trees and waved.

"What the hell took you so long? The other guys have docked and left already."

Bear lifted a .45 from his shoulder leather, and the pimply man jumped behind the tree again.

Twenty-five miles north of the mossy dock, Matthew Hawke worked a lock pick on the rear door of a warehouse owned by WIPEOUT! the manufacturer of the most popular make of surfboards, sailboards, and catamarans in the nation and according to the information Hawke had gathered, a leading cocaine distributor.

Matthew Hawke, now also called The Avenger in San Diego and Houston newspapers, had been in Miami for two days, getting reacquainted with the lowlifes of the drug trade. When he was an agent for the DEA, the Drug Enforcement Administration, he had worked there for two months three or four years ago. But the contacts he'd developed then were now gone, dead, or in jail.

His new life as The Avenger began in San Diego when Colombian drug suppliers had kidnapped his wife and tortured her for three days, slicing her flesh, breaking her bones, tearing her body to gain maximum pain, keeping her alive. At last the pain-saturated days of torture were over and she died of shock and loss of blood.

Hawke had found her on a table, with three druggers still in the room laughing and drinking. He had killed all three, the last one slowly, first blasting apart his knees with rounds from a .45, then his genitals.

Hawke's former partner had rushed in just as Hawke executed the sniveling Colombian drug wheeler-dealer. Then Hawke left the agency, struck out on his own where he would not have to follow the spirit or the letter of the law to bring these monsters to justice.

He had taken a million dollars in payoff money from the druggers in San Diego to use as his war chest. He had been a six-year veteran of the DEA, and now he fought the drug kings, the smugglers, the wholesalers, even the pushers, wherever he found them. He meted out justice his own way at the end of a smoking gun.

When the druggers had made turkey meat out of his wife, Connie, they'd freed him of all the rules. Now he fought them the way they lived, down and dirty, using the only language they understood: a death for a death; a bullet for a bullet; a blasted car or a burned-down cutting room for every kid or adult hooked on narcotics.

He had been called The Avenger by a sympathetic San Diego press as he waged his unrelenting, bloody war against the druggers who had tortured his wife in the U.S. and nearby Tijuana, Mexico.

He was wanted by the police in both cities, and in Houston, where he had rescued a former partner from a drug cartel that again understood only violence when it came to doing business.

Now he was in Miami to spread his brand of justice, to bring down some of the operators who had made Miami the funnel of ninety percent of all the cocaine, and its highly concentrated derivative known as crack, that entered the U.S. If he could stop the poison here, it couldn't kill and maim and cripple on down the line.

Hawke hit the last touchstone on the lock, and it clicked open. He slid inside and closed the door without a sound. Hawke was not a huge man. He stood an even six feet tall and weighed 185 pounds of solid muscle. He worked out, ate just enough to keep his weight stable, and didn't smoke. He seldom drank alcohol.

He looked around the warehouse end of WIPEOUT! At two A.M. there was little activity in the far end of the huge plant where WIPEOUT! had been born fifteen years ago and taken the nation by storm. It also had made a multimillionaire of its creator.

During his surfing days he'd picked up the nickname of Pipeline because of the way he loved to ride into the overhanging wall of water just as a wave broke but before the water came all the way down.

The name stuck, and soon he had his name legally changed to Pipeline, a monomial, a taxonomic name consisting of a single word.

Pipeline worked late that night in his office. Which part of his work he did was not important to Hawke. He was interested in only the drug side of Pipeline's business.

Hawke worked around stacks of unfinished surfboards, pushed past molds and areas where the blanks were fiberglassed. He came to a small door in a high wall and listened through it.

He heard nothing.

He tried the door and found it unlocked. It led to a carpeted hallway. Oil paintings dressed the walls. The thick carpet led him forward to an open door at the far end. He could hear a radio playing softly somewhere. Light showed from the corner office but not from any of the other doors.

Hawke moved silently, efficiently, like a large cat stalking its prey. Through the pauses in the music he heard a soft hum. He identified it as a computer sound.

Hawke dropped to his knees and looked around the edge of the door into the office. It was a large one, with surfboards decorating the walls. A man sat hunched over a computer with his back to Hawke.

The Avenger drew his .45 automatic from shoulder leather.

"Pipeline!" Hawke roared.

The slender man jumped, then turned around, his face tanned, his T-shirt showing a WIPEOUT surfboard with a topless girl printed on it. He was shorter than Hawke, with good arms and shoulders from years of paddling out to sea for a big wave. His eyes blinked, closed, and he shook his head to come alert.

"Who the hell are you?"

"St. Peter. Welcome to hell."

Hawke made sure of the ID from pictures he had, then he shot the man in the right shoulder. Blood spurted. Pipeline screamed, grabbed his shoulder.

"You crazy? You crazy bastard! Call an ambulance!" When he saw Hawke standing still, he lunged for a phone on the desk in front of him. Hawke swept the handset off the desk to the floor.

"Your name is Pipeline, previously Harold Shumway, and you made a million dollars in surfboards and sails and boats before you discovered coke and crack.

"In the last ten years you have been one of the major distributors of crack and coke in the Miami area, working the kids for boards and crack at the same time.

"You have been found guilty of a capital crime and now face sentencing."

Pipeline's face turned pale. He was about to faint. "Chrissakes, help me! I'm losing too much blood!"

"I hear you keep your crack supply away from your boards. Let me tie up that shoulder, then you're taking me to your other office, the one with the packaging setup and the distribution list of names and addresses."

"I don't know what you're talking about."

Ten minutes later they pulled to a stop in front of a small office on Trenton Street near Miami's shopping district. Hawke got out of the Ferrari and slammed the door. Pipeline had insisted on driving. He opened the door himself. There were lights on in the front of the building even though it was nearly two A.M.

Pipeline opened the door and dived to the left.

"Kill the bastard!" Pipeline screamed. Just ahead, a huge black man hovered over a desk, a double-barreled shotgun in his hands. He looked at Pipeline in wonder.

"Kill who, Pipeline? Nobody else here."

"Outside!" Pipeline screeched from where he lay on the floor.

The shotgun came up as the big man waddled toward the door.

Hawke pushed his .45 around the door frame two inches from the floor and fired twice into the big body. It lumbered forward another step, then turned and fell, both rounds from the shotgun blowing two foot-wide holes in the hanging ceiling.

Hawke came in the door, kicked the shotgun away from the dead black fingers, and prodded Pipeline with his toe.

"Now, big crack wholesaler, I'd like a tour of your facility."

Pipeline pushed up to a sitting position with his good arm. "Who the hell are you?"

"You've never heard of me. You killed my wife. Now it's pay-up time. An eye for an eye. Show me the goods."

Hawke prodded Pipeline up. He made a lunge for Hawke's .45 but missed, and Hawke kicked him in the left kidney. He went down in a limp pile of arms and legs.

"Up," Hawke said. "No more problems. You have to do this yourself."

In the back, Hawke found the packaging room, several tables where crack crystals were put in plastic envelopes holding from a gram to an ounce. A pickup truck stood at one side of the building. Hawke backed the rig up to the packaging table.

"Load all of the crack into the pickup," Hawke ordered.

"Can't with one arm!" Pipeline bellowed.

"I'll help with the heavy stuff," Hawke said.

Ten minutes later they had all of the crack in the pickup. There were three five-gallon white buckets full, a small box, and three plastic-wrapped bundles. Hawke guessed there were a thousand of the small gram- and ounce-filled envelopes with flaps that didn't seal. It would all work.

"Let's go for a ride," Hawke said, pushing the smaller man into the passenger's side of the pickup. Hawke remembered the city well enough to find the water. He parked beside the bay on a low dock with no safety wall and slit open the plastic packages of crack. Then he told Pipeline to get out of the truck.

Hawke released the parking brake and steered the pickup as it jumped the low curb and plunged into the bay, which was ten feet deep there. The pickup hissed a moment, then sank slowly by the front. Hawke could see the crack in the box melting away as the pickup sank below the dark waters.

"Looks like we better find a taxi back to your digs," Hawke said. Pipeline looked pale in the streetlight.

"You just melted down half a million dollars worth of good crack, you maniac!" Pipeline screamed.

Hawke's big fist smashed into the pale face, just over his jawline, breaking bones in the drugger's cheek. He went down on one knee. Hawke grabbed his arm and pulled him up the street to a phone booth where he called a taxi.

A half hour later they got out of the cab a block from Pipeline's WIPEOUT office and when the taxi had driven away, Hawke prodded the drugger back to his building. They went in the front door, and Hawke pushed Pipeline down in front of his desk.

"All of your distribution records, now! Every pusher you sell to, every one. Names, addresses, phone numbers. Now!"

Slowly Pipeline went to filing cabinets and drew sheets from selected files in half a dozen different places. At last he had them all.

"The cash. Where is it stashed?"

Grudgingly Pipeline pulled out another filing cabinet that was locked. He took off the bar and lock and showed Hawke a false back on the file. Behind it were grocery sacks filled with bundles of bills. Hawke took two bundles of twenties and slipped them in his pocket. Then he stacked the paper sacks of cash on the big desk. He put the list of pushers and suppliers on the desk beside the money.

Hawke screwed the silencer on his .45 and watched Pipeline.

Pipeline's shoulder began to bleed again.

"Who is your supplier, Pipeline? You don't bring this much junk in by yourself."

"I do. Make more profit that way."

Hawke punched Pipeline's shot-up shoulder. The drugger groaned, his teeth biting into his lip to stifle a scream.

"Your supplier, Pipeline. I can keep this up all night, or until you run out of blood. Who is he?"

It took Hawke five minutes to coax the name out of him. Then it came over a keening of pain.

"Christ! Tony Labruzzo . . . the Labruzzo family. Nobody deals in Miami without Tony's help."

Pipeline looked at his bleeding shoulder. He sighed. Hawke figured the guy was about thirty-five, playing that he was twenty-five.

"I'm not getting out of this, am I?" Pipeline asked.

"How many teenagers do you think you've killed, Pipeline? Kids who get stoned and then try to drive home and kill themselves and a few innocents on the road besides? How many?"

"Some, I guess."

"In ten years? There's no way you can pay back all those parents and sisters and brothers. No way, Pipeline. But this is a start."

Hawke shot Pipeline in the forehead. The big .45 slug slammed through his skull, expanded as it sliced into vital brain centers, and jolted out the back of his head in fragments.

Pipeline, the man who had created WIPEOUT! sat slumped in his big executive chair, dead for all time.

Hawke picked up the phone and called the police. He was half a block away in his rented Grand Am Pontiac when the first police car whined to a stop in front of the crack cutting room. As Hawke pulled away in the other direction, five more patrol cars skidded to a stop outside the office, and the Miami cops raced into the building.

Hawke nodded grimly as he pulled away. Now all he had to do was find Tony Labruzzo, one of the biggest Mafia hoodlums in town, and the man who ran dope for the Labruzzo family.

Chapter
Two

Hawke caught six hours of sleep in a nondescript motel on the edge of Miami, and the next morning he stood in a phone booth making calls to former reliable contacts. One remained at his old haunt, a sidewalk hole-in-the-wall deli halfway downtown.

A little after ten A.M., Hawke walked in. The place hadn't changed a bit.

"Who ever heard of a Polish deli?" Hawke demanded in a loud voice. A small man with a white-haired fringe around his head looked up quickly and grinned. Joseph Silokowski looked the same way he had four years ago. Small blue eyes peered out of a pale face now beaded with sweat from the heat of the grill.

"Hawke, you ugly bird of prey. What the hell you doing back in God's country?"

"Swatting mosquitoes and bargaining with cockroaches to see who uses the bed, and trying to keep out of the way of marauding gators."

They shook hands over the top of the counter.

"Got one coming for you, the lunch special . . . so it's a little early. You don't look like you been eating too well lately."

Shortly they sat at the only table in back by the counter and talked. Hawke looked at the Warsaw Deli lunch-special sandwich. It was on a round slab of rye bread eight inches across. Piled on that were four inches of filling. He could see ham and cheese, Polish sausage, sauerkraut, kippered salmon, a big stack of lettuce, and half a dozen other kinds of meats and cheeses, all topped with two big round slices of tomato and another rye slab.

"I eat this, I'll sink," Hawke said.

"Eat or you'll starve," Silokowski shot back and went to wait on a customer. When the little deli owner came back, Hawke had made a start at eating the mountain of a sandwich.

"You still chasing the damn druggers? Hope so. We got twice as many now as when you was here. That devil juice is everywhere you look."

"Tony Labruzzo," Hawke said.

Joseph looked up sharply. His face a scowl. "Don't say that monster's name in my establishment! One of his hoodlums tried to get me to sell for them. I threw a cup of coffee in his face and threw him out on his ass! Three of them came back and tried to beat me up, so I shot one of them. The other two ran like plucked chickens. Now they leave me alone."

Hawke grinned. "Just like old times. I need to know exactly where Tony lives, where he does his business, and any of the drops or stash houses he's using."

"Easy. So cut off my left leg," Joseph said. "You don't

want much. They find out about this, you got to promise me you come to my funeral mass and maybe light a candle every month. I'll be so dead, not even St. Peter will know about it.'' He nibbled on a dill pickle. "Let me make a couple of phone calls.'' He shrugged. "What the hell, I'm an old fart. I've lived. Now maybe it's time I pay back a little for all the good times. Yeah. Let me make some calls.'' He looked down at the paper plate. "Now finish your sandwich like a good boy. Don't you know there are lots of children in Warsaw who are starving?''

Hawke ate the sandwich.

A half hour later Hawke parked the Grand Am on Seafront Street in Miami Beach and looked across at the plush Sea Arms condominiums. They were the luxury kind, facing Biscayne Bay with lots of white sand and palm trees. It had underground parking and all the glitz that spelled money.

Tony Labruzzo was trying to show a legitimate face to Miami. He owned a bowling alley, two trucking firms, a big nightclub and restaurant and two hotels. He also owned the Sea Arms Condos, where he lived on the top floor. The condos sold for $1.5 to $1.75 million each. There were only thirteen of them in the seven-story building.

It was a high-security operation: key-card gate with a gateman, two security guards on both parking garage floors, private keyed elevators that stopped only at the floor keyed in by the tenant, TV security monitors on the first-floor security office that checked all entrances and hallways twenty-four hours a day. In both garage floors were dayrooms for chauffeurs, and six rooms that could be used by the drivers if they got stuck there on late trips for one of the residents.

Hawke had no idea what the security was on the beach side, but it must not be quite so tough.

Forty-five minutes later Hawke found his ticket on the beach. She was about forty, tanned, sleek, her tummy-tuck scars barely showing around her high-rise bikini bottom.

She had been watching him ever since he walked up the beach from the park area half a mile down. He had slipped his watch into his pocket as he walked toward her. She stared at him all the way, a smile, half curious, half disbelieving, on her face. She was blond, pretty in a manufactured sort of way, and more like forty-five.

The woman did not flinch or show any touch of embarrassment as he came up and smiled. He looked up and down her tanned body, stretched out on a beach towel.

"Beg your pardon, miss. But could you tell me what time it is? My Rolex is in the shop . . ."

She laughed delightedly. "I win a bet with myself. I knew you'd use the what-time-is-it line."

"No really. I'm in town from New York and have an appointment at two-thirty. . . ."

"Oh, maybe. Actually its only ten-fifteen in the morning. We have almost four hours." She laughed. "Now I know I shouldn't have said that, but I've been sitting here for a half hour feeling sorry for myself."

Hawke frowned. "I don't understand. You're pretty, you're slender, you must live in one of those expensive condos back there, which means you're rich. What could you be feeling sorry about?"

"You silly boy. Haven't you heard of the idle rich? Too much money and not enough to do."

"That's never been my problem. Thanks for the time." He had moved off two steps when she called out.

"Like a drink at my place?"

He stopped and turned. "Actually, I've always wanted to see the inside of this place. I walk by here every trip down. Would it be any trouble?"

She laughed again, low in her throat, and started to get up. As she bent over to pick up her towels her bikini bra top slipped off one breast showing a crescent of brown areola. She shrugged back into the slip of cloth, gathered up her beach towel and backrest.

As they walked the twenty yards to the built-up patio in front of the condos, he took the towel and backrest from her.

"Are these places really as expensive as they look?" he asked.

"Depends on what you mean by expensive. We paid a million and a half for ours. Some are bigger." She watched him closely. His brows lifted, and he looked at her.

"That much? Jeez. I could live the rest of my life on the interest."

"Lots of people could. Oh, I'm Millicent. That's all you need to know right now. Let's go upstairs and have that drink I promised you."

They went through the patio, which was grandly laid out with built-in sunning platforms with umbrellas, glass-topped tables, benches, and fancy brick barbecues big enough to cook for a company of Marines.

Big double doors at the rear center of the condos were watched over by an armed guard. An electronic beam opened the doors. Millicent never even glanced at the guard as she walked into the building. It evidently was beneath her. Hawke followed her like a faithful servant and didn't look at the guard, either.

23

Once inside the lobby, Hawke saw it was smaller than he had guessed, with a few pure white upholstered chairs and couches in conversation groups. The carpet matched the whiteness of the couches. Millicent turned to the right to the elevator. She slipped a plastic card from the bikini bottom and pushed it in the slot on the elevator console.

The door opened at once, then closed when it sensed no one else enter after them. The box glided to the fifth floor with no sense of movement, and the doors opened. The elevator had doors on three sides, so it could open on whichever condo had been keyed in, or the lobby.

"Home sweet home," Millicent said, and walked into the eight-room luxury living quarters. The elevator opened directly into the living area. It was plush, expensive, and professionally decorated.

"I feel so much freer here," Millicent said, and slipped out of her bikini bra and tossed it on a couch. "What do you think of my humble home?"

"Beautiful," Hawke said. "Both of them." They laughed.

"You want a guided tour first, or what?"

"I didn't come here to seduce you," Hawke said.

"Maybe, but I didn't invite you up here to seduce you, either." She paused, her chest held up to negate the slight sag of her breasts. "Nor did I bring you up here to pay you, if you're one of those." She looked at him and shook her head. "Not a chance you're one of that ilk."

She slipped back into her bikini top. "Not that the damn thing covers much." She looked up, her face curious now, softer. "I saw you walk up and down the beach twice before I went down. You must be an investigator or something. Are you FBI? Or maybe you're with the IRS. He's scared shitless of both of them."

"Who is scared?"

"Tony, of course. He tries to be so straight, such an honest businessman. But we all know who he is. The Labruzzo Mafia family. It runs half of the Miami underworld, including dope. We bought here because his place was actually a good buy, about twenty percent under most of them on this stretch of beachfront. So who do you work for?"

"CIA," Hawke said. He saw her eyes widen. "But I can't tell you that because we aren't supposed to work inside U.S. borders."

"I'll never tell. It is Tony, then, right?" Millicent shivered. This was delicious. She'd never actually talked with anyone who was a CIA agent before.

"I can't say that it's Tony, you understand that. Do you know if he's home?"

Millicent grinned. "I can tell you that. He's always home in the mornings. He has three women up there. The man must be ready for a heart attack. He's thirty-five and not that macho. Honestly, three girls, one of them barely a teenager, the other two early twenties, and he *does* use them. Each one every day, I've been told."

"I know your elevator key won't get me up there. Two more floors, right? How do I get to Tony 's floor?"

"I can't tell you this, but there's a fire escape, a fireproof stairway. It opens with no locks into each apartment. Goes right up beside the elevator shaft. Our secret escape door is in the closet. That's where my neighbor's is too."

"Do Tony's girls ever go out?"

"Not often. We call them his sex slaves."

"Where's the closet?"

She showed him, pushed past him, and after separating

the coats and jackets, she opened a sliding door. Behind it was a regulation metal fire door with an unlocked doorknob.

She pushed back past him. In the tight quarters her breasts brushed against his chest. She stopped, still in contact with him.

"Hey, you never told me your name."

"Hawke."

Her face lit up. "What a wonderful name. It fits you." She reached up and kissed his passive lips. "You know, I wouldn't mind at all . . . if you wanted to take a look at my bedroom." She kissed him again. When he didn't respond, she backed away.

"Just a suggestion. I was dreaming, an old lady having a fantasy about a young, handsome man like you." She shrugged. "Sorry. Damn!" A tear formed in her eye and ran down her carefully made-up cheek.

He kissed her cheek. "You're a gorgeous lady. I'm out of my mind for passing you up. But I have to. I'm the one who's sorry." He kissed her lips softly, then pushed away and turned the knob on the metal fire door. It was unlocked, and he opened it into the stairway.

He paused and looked back at her. "Hey, if I don't see you again, thanks. The security around this place was giving me fits. I appreciate the help."

Millicent blinked back tears, nodded, and then touched his hand. She closed both doors as soon as he slipped through.

In the concrete stairs with steel railings, he checked his tools. The .45 rested in its shoulder leather under his light-weight jacket. The holster had a built-in flap that held the eight-inch silencer. He had no explosives or other violent tools of the trade that he often used. There had been no time to find any since he'd arrived. He had the sawtooth wire, a garrote, and slender knives strapped on both wrists under his shirt sleeves.

Hawke screwed the silencer into the barrel of the .45, made sure it was snug and tight, then checked the twelve-round extension magazine for the .45. Usually a magazine holds seven rounds, with one more in the chamber. He had a special magazine that extended out the bottom of the .45's handle and held twelve rounds. With one in the chamber, he had thirteen without pulling the mag.

The Avenger moved up the steps silently, went past a landing marked 6A on one side and 6B on the other. Up one more flight and the stairs ended. The door was unmarked. He tested the handle. The polished brass turned easily, and the door opened toward him a crack. Behind it, he saw the sliding panel. It had been left open an inch.

Hawke accepted any luck that came his way. He paused, not breathing, listening for any sounds from the closet or the rooms beyond. He heard nothing.

Hawke eased the sliding door open. There was no alarm he could hear. The closet door was closed. He parted the coats, mostly men's, and stepped into the closet. He closed the door and then the sliding panel behind him. He paused again. Now he could hear music playing. It was a radio or stereo or piped-in music.

He took the door handle and turned it slowly, deliberately. When it stopped, he edged the closet door open an inch. The slit of light that came in showed him that the door was open, and he could see a slice of the living room.

Two men sat on the couch watching a TV set somewhere to the right. Both were muscle-and-gun men. Both had Mafia goon stamped all over their five-hundred-dollar suits and two-hundred-dollar shoes. Both had their jackets off, and hardware showed in shoulder leather.

As Hawke watched, a man in his thirties came onto the scene. He could be Tony Labruzzo. He was small, slender, nervous, and took small steps in a frenetic fashion. He stopped for a minute to look at the TV screen, snorted, then turned back to the men.

"The car in five minutes. Jocko, you stay here this time. You even think about touching one of the girls and I'll chop your whang off, you hear?"

"Yes, sir, Mr. Labruzzo. They're off-limits for damn sure!"

"Remember that this time. Don't let them tease you. Lock them in their bedrooms if you have to." The small man shook his head and continued his short, nervous steps out of sight.

Hawke heard a door close somewhere and eased out of the closet. Both men stared straight ahead at the TV screen. Hawke had out his silenced .45 and jumped to the left by the wall for protection so he could cover both the hard cases.

"Don't move an eyelash, either one of you, or you're dog meat!" Hawke spat at them.

They jumped and turned. The nearest one swore and dived for the rug, pulling a weapon from his left side. Hawke put one round through the top of his head. The silenced weapon made a soft cough, and then the muzzle swung up on the second goon, who sat frozen in his seat.

"Don't try it!" Hawke hissed. "Put your piece on the coffee table and then set up your buddy there so he doesn't look dead."

The goon stared at the muzzle of the silencer and nodded

slowly. The message at last got through to his pea-sized brain.

Hawke had just grabbed the .357 Magnum off the coffee table when he looked up and saw Tony Labruzzo come back into the big living room. The goon looked up, too, and let go of the dead one, who promptly fell on his face on the floor.

"What the hell . . ." Tony yelped, seeing Hawke.

Even before Hawke had shifted his weapon's muzzle to Tony, the Mafia big shot dived behind a couch at the far end of the living room and fumbled with his shoulder rig.

Hawke slid behind a couch on this end of the room.

"Who the hell is this joker?" Tony screeched. "Bruno, you asshole! Where'd he come from?"

"I don't know, Mr. Labruzzo."

Bruno made a small mistake. He tried to move from where he lay in front of the couch, just beyond Hawke, his back toward his boss. His head came up and he lunged forward.

Hawke's snap shot almost missed, but clipped the side of his neck, severing the right carotid artery. Blood pumping up the artery at more pressure than the average city water supply suddenly found the leak and spurted ten feet across the room. It came sixty-nine times a minute as Bruno's heart pumped furiously. Twelve seconds later the flow stopped.

Bruno had bled to death.

"Bruno! Stay down. I'll call some of the boys."

Hawke threw a pillow down the room. It knocked over a lamp, crashing it to the floor from a low table. Two shots slammed into the area from Tony's .357.

"Bruno, get the bastard!"

"Bruno can't help you much, Tony," Hawke called. "Give it up."

"Not a chance!"

All was quiet for a moment.

"Who the hell are you, some muscle from DeAngelo's bunch of bastards? You guys don't stand a chance. The Labruzzos run everything down here. Go back to Chicago while you're still alive."

"I'm not with DeAngelo, Tony. I work for myself."

"Yeah? Then you're dead meat!"

Nothing happened for a moment. Everyone held his spot on the floor.

"Betsy, baby, come out here!" Labruzzo screeched. "Bring Tril and Lonnie with you. Right now! Nobody is going to get hurt. Just get your little asses out here. I don't care if you've got your pants on or not. Get out here now!"

Hawke could see part of the hall off the living room. Five or six doors opened from it. Now he saw two of them open and lifted his .45, then lowered it. Three women stepped into the hall. Two were naked; the third wore only red bikini panties. They moved down the hall slowly. All were young, slender, and big-breasted.

"That's right, girls, right up here by me. Move your tits, I ain't got all day!"

They walked faster then, and stood there watching someone on the floor. Male hands moved the three women until they formed a shield in front of him.

"Now, smart fuck! You man enough to blow away these three innocent little ladies just to get at me? I'm betting a big chunk of my life that you ain't!"

Hawke could see Tony now as he bent over behind the three and told them to walk backward. They formed a complete shield for the mobster. He went down the hall, then darted into one of the doors, taking the three women with him.

Hawke scurried down to the side of the door and kicked it flat against the wall. The room was empty, but a door across the way stood open.

Hawke slid into the room, raced across it to the far wall, and peered out the open door. It led to another room and into a living room that was nearly a duplicate of the one they had just left. It was the owner's second living room, the one on the other half of the double-sided condo.

Hawke saw the three girls standing beside the rose-colored furniture. He tore into the big room, looked around, saw the elevator panel, and ran to it, but the car was moving down already.

"He went down in the elevator?" Hawke demanded.

The smallest nodded. "Was Bruno dead in there?" she asked, her voice breaking into a sob.

"Probably," Hawke said. He jumped to the side, found the closet, and ripped open the sliding door. A moment later he was in the stairway, taking the steps down five and six at a time as he raced the elevator. In his ride up in the elevator before, he noticed that it sacrificed speed for smoothness. He might just beat the damn thing down.

Hawke passed floor one and went to the first basement. It was marked G-1. Hawke slid the door open and looked around. Just then a Jaguar engine roared into life, and tires squealed as the rig slashed past Hawke toward the exit.

Hawke's big .45 came up, and he pumped eight rounds at the auto. One hit the left rear tire and blew it. Another round went into the gas tank, and the next screaming lead slug produced a spark that ignited the gas.

Tony bailed out of the Jag and leaped over a low wall at ground level that fronted on the beach. He raced toward a private pier that pushed out into the bay, with Hawke right behind him. Hawke had just cleared the parking garage when the Jag's gasoline tank blew up with a roar, spreading Jaguar over half the concrete parking floor.

The force of the blast sent Hawke into a front roll on the grass. He jumped up and saw Tony gain the pier and then vanish. By the time Hawke legged it down to the pier, he saw a powerboat gunning away from the dock with a huge man at the throttle of the blue-and-white thirty-six-footer.

Hawke raced down the pier. There were six boats moored there. One had its motor idling, the owner sprawled on the bow, painting a new name on her.

Hawke jumped on board, cast off one line, and ran up to the front.

"Police business, sir. I have to appropriate your boat for a while." The man looked at him in surprise.

"Tony finally mess up, did he?" the man in his late fifties yelped. He jumped off the boat and untied the forward line. "Get the little bastard, the boat's insured."

Hawke took the controls, spun the wheel, and raced after the vanishing powerboat with the red stripe on the stern.

They were in a series of shallow waterways, false bays, and marinas that fronted the fancy, built-up inside of Miami Beach facing Biscayne Bay. On the far side lay Miami itself. The charts listed the long bay as part of the Intracoastal Waterway.

Hawke pushed the throttles forward and began gaining on the other boat.

As he raced after the other boat, Hawke unscrewed the silencer from his .45. Any device that muffles the sound of a handgun also decreases its power and range. Hawke wanted all the range he could get.

Suddenly he saw the boat ahead make a sweeping turn. They had come up against a small bay, and now Tony's boat had to turn to swing back into the passage.

Hawke took the angle and cut him off, roaring to within twenty yards of the other boat. Hawke put three rounds into the small flying bridge where the big man spun the wheel frantically. Tony wasn't on deck. There had been no chance for him to slip off the boat—unless he was swimming, and Tony didn't look like the type to get wet unless he had to.

Hawke ducked as the big man at the wheel fired a handgun at him. The round went wide and Hawke fired again, then the smaller boat spun to the left and roared in close to shore across what Hawke saw was shallow water. He wasn't sure how much water he needed under his larger boat to stay afloat. The area closer to shore looked too shallow.

For ten minutes he had to lay off, let the other boat meander in the shallows. Once Hawke edged in, felt the bow touch a sandbar, and reversed the engines, and pulled off it.

The other powerboat wandered along the shoreline, then revved its motor and jumped over a narrow, grassy levee into a marina. There was no entrance to the marina from this area. Hawke gunned the forty-two-footer around the outer boundaries of the marina, and its houses and canals and boat slips.

After five minutes he found the only inlet from the bay to the waterways and he nosed in, then turned around and came out. There was no real land contact. No roads. The other boat would be coming out. Hawke left the marina and idled his engine just outside and behind a showpiece grouping of specially planted palm trees.

It took an hour of waiting. Hawke had his man figured right. It had been so long since Tony had walked three blocks, he wasn't about to try it now. The blue-trimmed thirty-six-footer gunned out of the marina, swamped a rowboat, and slammed around a small island.

Hawke raced after them. This time the blue-and-white boat headed for the far side of the bay, and the commercial docks. Hawke caught them in the middle of the half-mile-wide waterway. He roared alongside, put six rounds into the little bridge's console, and trashed enough instruments and wires so that the charging blue-and-white craft's engine cut out and she coasted to a stop.

Hawke had kept out of the way of the big man's .38, and now he circled the stalled craft just out of range. There was only one way to do the job right. Since he didn't have a rocket launcher, he'd have to resort to primitive measures.

Hawke slumped down in the cabin and checked out the window, gunned the motor, and then pushed the throttles forward. He held the wheel steady, checked the angle again, and then braced himself.

The sharp bow of the forty-two-foot powerboat sliced through the rear half of the smaller boat. Hawke jolted against the forward controls, then careened backward as the larger boat's engine stopped suddenly and then eased away from the fatally struck boat.

Hawke lifted up and looked over the edge of the console at Tony's boat. Half the stern was gone, and water poured into the rest of it. Already the bow had dipped from the surge of water.

"Bastard!" somebody shouted, and Hawke heard a splash.

Two minutes later the blue-and-white boat sank in the bay. Hawke looked around and found Tony swimming slowly toward the larger boat.

Hawke pushed a new magazine in the .45 and watched him come. Tony caught hold of the diving platform at the stern of the big boat and looked up.

"I'm hurt," Tony blurted. "God, let me get on board."

"Tony Labruzzo, is it true that you run half the drugs in the greater Miami area?"

"Run drugs? What is this, Twenty Questions? I'm a businessman. Maybe some crack comes my way now and then."

"Half the drugs, last year some hundred and fifty million worth?"

"Yeah, yeah, all right. So I'm a good businessman. Now get me on board. I can take care of you. I can use smart people like you in my organization."

"You also are a member of the Labruzzo family, with Big Daddy Vito Labruzzo the capo?"

"So he's my uncle. So we stick together. Damn Chinese do it all the time." His face went underwater. Tony floundered until he grabbed the railing. Then he screamed, "Let me on board!"

"You've sold your last kilo of crack, Tony. You were part of the big syndicate that killed my wife. None of you were good enough to hold open a door for Connie."

"What the hell you want? Money? You want money? I can give you ten million dollars . . . in cash. Now give me a hand."

For a moment Hawke's eyes clouded. All he could see was Connie lying there on that stainless-steel operating table, her naked body so slashed that not a square inch of her skin was left unviolated. Her arms and legs had been broken, her hair cut off and then singed down to the roots. Her fingers had been broken, her fingernails pulled out. Her breasts had been cut off, and blood was everywhere, spattered on the walls, on the floor.

"You killed her!" Hawke roared. He shot Tony Labruzzo once in the chest, then twice in the face, then watched him lose his grip on the diving platform and slowly sink under the emerald-green waters of the bay.

Hawke shook his head, trying to blank out the memory of his wife's tortured body in that abandoned San Diego office building. He would never forget it.

He saw the body sinking slowly. If the sharks didn't eat him, Tony would surface in three or four days. There were no boats around. Evidently nobody had noticed the unsilenced shots.

Hawke moved back to the controls, started the engine with no problem. There was nothing left of the other powerboat except two floating cushions. What happened to the pilot, the big man at the wheel? Did he die in the crash? Hawke made a slow circle around the area but saw no one in the water.

He shrugged, pushed the throttle forward, and started back to the big condominiums on the shore. A noise behind him made Hawke turn. He was just in time to lunge out of the way as the big man who had been driving Tony's boat charged forward like an NFL tackle trying to sack the quarterback.

Only this one had a six-inch knife that he slashed at Hawke, nicking his right hand, which still held the .45. The pistol jolted from Hawke's hand and slid down the deck.

Hawke cut the throttles and darted away from the confining space of the little cabin.

Bear roared with delight.

"Don't know who the hell you are, but you gonna die. You just killed Tony and for that you gonna die hard and you gonna die slow, as I slice you to little pieces of meat!"

The big man charged with the blade poised and ready.

Chapter
Three

Hawke jolted backward a fast step to avoid the slashing knife wielded by Bear, the 280-pound ex–pro football player who enjoyed slicing people into small chunks. Hawke tripped on a tie down on the motor cruiser, nearly fell, hit on his hands, and vaulted to the other side of the deck.

He caught a three-foot fish gaff from a rack, its four-inch hook gleaming and sharp. Bear laughed.

"You gonna bother me a lot with that little stick."

Hawke made hooking motions with it but missed an arm. Bear started one way, cut back, and a moment later slammed the gaff out of Hawke's right hand. Bear's knife blade put a bloody scratch on his arm.

"Getting interestin'!" Bear growled.

"You like working for a bastard like Vito Labruzzo?" Hawke tried.

"He pays good, that's all I want. Good pay and all the coke and crack I want." Bear charged like he was after a quarterback, cut off Hawke on the narrow deck, and lunged, grabbing Hawke's arm. Hawke kicked at the big man's crotch, but Bear shifted his leg, taking the blow on his thigh and laughing.

Hawke tried to unfasten the knife on his wrist but didn't have time. He grabbed a short fishing rod in a rack and reversed it, swinging the rod, which had a heavy Penn 6/0 reel on the handle end, like a club. The reel bounced off Bear's shoulder, and he roared with pain and frustration.

"Stand still, you little wimp, so I can smash you!" Bear bellowed.

Hawke grabbed a ballpoint pen from his shirt pocket, opened it, and dropped the cap. He closed his right hand into a fist and put the barrel of the pen between his second and third fingers, with the butt of it resting in his palm.

Now the point of the pen jutted four inches from his fist. He kept the pen in a straight line with his wrist and arm and had a potent stabbing weapon.

Bear saw the pen and guffawed.

"You gonna hurt me with an ink pen? Damn, but you are dumb."

He came at Hawke again, this time forcing him to the stern where there was nothing to hide behind. Bear moved in.

"Getting yourself killed out here won't help you any," Hawke said, snarling. "Why don't you cut out and swim to shore while you're still ahead?"

"Oh, hell yes. Go and tell big Vito Labruzzo I let some asshole kill his nephew? I'd be fish bait by morning."

He charged.

Hawke faked one way, then the other, but the ex–pro

football lineman knew all the moves. He caught Hawke's arm and spun him around. Bear stopped. Faster than Hawke thought possible for a big man, Bear changed directions and charged again.

Hawke waited until the big man was almost on him. Then Hawke threw out his left arm to deflect the vicious swipe of the sharp blade Bear swung and rammed his own right fist straight at the huge chest. His arm was frozen from wrist to elbow.

Bear's knife arched in at him, but as a target had only Hawke's arm and the light material of his sport coat sleeve. The blade bit it, cut through the fabric, and Hawke felt the sting of the blade as it sliced deep into his left forearm.

His right hand punched forward with the pen-weapon, and the force of the 280 pounds charging toward him resulted in tremendous force.

Hawke felt the pen point lance through the light shirt Bear wore, then hit flesh and slant off a rib, then it plunged deep into Bear's chest until Hawke's knuckles jolted against his ribs.

Nothing could stop Bear's forward momentum. He smothered Hawke, and they both went down near the bait tank. Hawke rolled to escape the massive weight and, coming to his feet, realized he had lost the pen.

Bear lay facedown on the deck of the boat, which was bobbing gently in the warm Bay of Biscayne swells.

Hawke watched him a minute, found the gaff hook on the deck, and stared at the big man, who still lay where he had fallen. He hadn't moved since he'd crashed into the wooden planking.

A trap. He was playing possum, waiting for Hawke to get

close enough to him. Hawke prodded the big body with the wooden handle of the gaff.

He didn't move.

Hawke moved closer, but still out of reach. He hit Bear's wrist sharply with the wooden handle. There was no reaction.

Slowly Hawke moved in next to his head. The big man's eyes were open but not moving. Dead? Slowly Hawke turned the massive body over on the deck. Blood soaked the man's shirtfront. Sticking out from his chest was an inch of the blue ballpoint pen. It had rammed four inches into Bear's heart, killing him instantly.

Hawke shivered, letting the pent-up tension flood out of him. He looked around. No one seemed to be paying attention to him or the boat.

It took Hawke a nervous two minutes to roll and shove and push the big body overboard. At last Bear hit the water and sank at once. Hawke found a bucket on a line and dipped up seawater to wash down the blood on the deck. He had to brush it with a short, stiff tool to get all the blood off the varnished wood.

When he was satisfied that the blood would not be noticed in a cursory inspection, he went to the bow and looked at both sides of the craft. It had a gash a foot deep on one side, but it was two feet above the waterline. There were a lot of red paint smears and some long scrapes on the other side, but as a battering ram, the larger boat had come out the winner.

He stripped off his coat and checked his left arm. Blood still oozed out the three-inch-long cut that slanted down his arm. He found a first-aid kit and put some healing ointment on it, then some square pads, then clumsily wrapped it with

41

a two-inch roller bandage. He checked it. No more blood. That should hold it until he could get some stitches.

He put on his light jacket and went to the console. Hawke started the engine and looked around. At last he found the seven-story Sea Arms condominium on the skyline and motored slowly toward it.

The boat owner sat on the dock with a fishing pole when Hawke brought the launch into its slip ten minutes later. The senior citizen reeled in, looked at the plastic worm, and shrugged. He stared at the hole in the bow of his boat and snorted.

"What in hell you hit?"

Hawke tied up and shook his head. "I'll explain later. No time right now. My watch commander will give you a call and get it all straightened out. Tell him Lieutenant Johnson is still after them."

With that Hawke ran up the short dock, past the security guard and down the street to his rental car. He pulled away before anyone came to check him or his license number.

Two weeks before Hawke came to Miami, another visitor arrived. She was from Shelton Bend, Mississippi, and it was her first time in the big city. Her name was Sue Beth Townsend, and she already had a job. She had answered an ad in her hometown newspaper for drivers to transport cars from Miami to points north and west.

Sue Beth was a good driver. She'd had her license since she was fifteen and a half and hadn't had a single ticket or even a fender-bender accident. She was nineteen and promised her mother that she would find a modest apartment and write every week and send home twenty dollars a week to help pay on the loan at the bank.

Sue Beth had long brown hair, straight bangs over soft green eyes, and enough bounce to make the rally squad in high school. After a year of trying to get a job around Shelton Bend, she had seen the ad and telephoned.

Her first trip for Labruzzo Transport had been easy. The friendly manager, Mr. Marcello, had explained everything to her about what she had to do. It was easy. All she had to do was drive a nearly new Cadillac up Highway 95 to Washington, D.C. She'd never driven that big a car before and it was a little scary, but she made it without a slip and took the bus back down with the ticket Mr. Marcello had given her.

Sue Beth made a hundred and fifty dollars for the ride. Mr. Marcello had paid her as soon as she got back, in cash. She had worked all week at the Shelton Five-and-Ten for a while and made only half that much. It took her two days to drive up and two days on the bus coming back.

Now, in a small office on Harbor Street, Manny Marcello smiled at her like her Uncle Charley used to.

"Sue Beth, you did fine on that trip. I've got three more lined up for you, and since you did so good, we're going to fly you back from the far end, so you can drive more trips."

Sue Beth's eyes widened. "Oh, glory, Mr. Marcello, that's just ever so good. I sure appreciate it. When do I go next?"

"Not until tomorrow, so you've got all the rest of the afternoon and night."

"Good, I do need to go shopping for some things. And then I'm looking for a good little apartment, not too expensive."

"Hey, what's the apartment thing? I told you. Stay here

as long as you want to. We have a couple other women drivers who stay here when they're not busy.''

"Lordy, Mr. Marcello. I couldn't do that, impose on you and all. Glory be, Mr. Marcello, you sure do sell a lot of cars up north.''

As she spoke, Manny poured a pinch or two of white powder on his desk and used a razor blade to shape it into long, thin lines.

"Well, glory now. What in the world are you doing, Mr. Marcello?''

"You don't know?''

"Well, sure, we get the TV and everything in Shelton Bend, but I never seen . . . I mean. . . . I better be going.''

"No!'' His voice came sharper than he had intended. "Sure Beth, there's some things we need to talk about.'' Manny rolled up a ten-dollar bill and loudly snorted the two lines of cocaine up his nose. His eyes watered, he shook his head, then his grin broadened and he nodded to Sue Beth.

"Time you know the score, little poon. That white wonder dust was what you drove to Washington. Hidden in the spare tire were two pounds of pure cocaine, worth a little over a hundred thousand dollars.''

"Weren't no such thing!'' Sue Beth said. "That's illegal. I could get put in prison. . . .''

"Exactly, Sue Beth. And you're going to go right on driving for us, because if you don't, I'll tell the police you're a mule and let them catch you. Then for sure you're in Florida Women's Correction Prison for ten years!''

Sue Beth had stood when she saw the cocaine. Now she backed toward the door.

"Stay right here, Sue Beth. You and me have other things

to talk about.'' He came up in front of her and put his hand on one of her breasts. She bristled, then stepped back.

"Damn, your tits ain't so big, but what the hell, nobody ever fucks tits.'' He grabbed her arm and pulled her toward him. He pushed his free hand down the loose top of her blouse and worked under her bra.

"Damn, but they feel bigger this way.'' He saw the look of terror and disbelief on her face.

"Look, sweet tit. Don't go getting upset and stupid on me. You've got a nice little body, and right now, right here, you and me are gonna look it over good. We gonna see how good you are naked and flat on your back with your legs spread and your heels high in the air over my backside.''

He felt her breasts a minute more, then took his hand out and slapped her bottom.

"Oh, yeah, Sue Beth, we gonna have us one hell of a good old time here on my couch. You notice I got inside bars on the door. Ain't nobody gonna bother us. And with you a law violator, I guess you ain't gonna do nothing stupid and scream or cry or anything.

"See, little darlin', you be nice to me and I won't tell the Miami narcotics squad about your trip north. I bet you understand just about everything now, don't you, sweet tits?''

Sue Beth stared at him, her eyes wide. "You . . . you mean you're gonna do it?''

"Hell, yes. Goes with the job, only we don't tell the poon that right up-front. Scare some of the sweet young things like you off. Now, don't tell me you never been fucked. Not in this day and age.''

She let him lead her over to the couch. Sue Beth wanted to cry, but she knew she couldn't. Easy money! Sure it had been easy. She was delivering cocaine to Washington! She could have gone to prison! As soon as she got out of the office, she was going to grab a bus right back to Shelton Bend. All the way? He was going to! She and Billy Joe had . . . you know . . . messed around some, and he said he'd come, but she never let him put it—inside! Oh, glory, she wanted to die!

Manny liked them young. He was forty-five himself, and these damn young ones were what made it all worthwhile for him. Jesus, but this one was scared. Maybe he had a real-live, honest-to-God cherry here! He snorted. Not these days when kids are having sex in junior high school. Not a chance.

Still, she was so scared that she couldn't talk. After a few times she'd loosen up. She was a little on the chunky side, with some meat on her bones, the way he liked them. He took off her blouse and bra without any real fight from her.

For a minute he looked into her eyes. They were scared but resigned; she knew there was no way out. Yeah, he had hooked another one, and this one wasn't getting away.

Manny pulled her skirt and panties off, and he was up and ready. New, fresh, unused, and he bet she'd be so tight that it would hurt on every stroke. Damn, what a way to make a living!

Two hours later Manny lay exhausted on the couch. Four times in two hours! It was a new record for him, and she had been tighter than he guessed. Maybe she had been a cherry, but no fucking more! He laughed and heard her moving around. His door was locked from the inside; she couldn't get out. He sighed, tried to get some of his strength back. He figured he had another five years of really wild whanging around, then he'd have to slow down.

His desk drawer opened, and he figured he should watch her, but he was still too bushed. Christ, four times in two hours! When Manny Marcello looked up, he stared into the muzzle of the 9-mm Walther P-38K automatic that usually lay in his right top desk drawer.

He jolted upright.

"Now, Sue Beth, you just put that down! You enjoyed it, I could tell. This ain't nothing to get yourself in trouble over."

"Mr. Marcello, nobody ever done that to me before, and I'm gonna kill you. I can't go to prison but once, I reckon. I'm a farm girl, Mr. Marcello. I know all about guns."

Manny stood up; he had to get closer to her.

"The hell you do. The safety is on. It won't fire even if you try."

Sue Beth looked down at the weapon.

Manny dived at her, swatting at the pistol.

Sue Beth fired.

Hawke drove safely and legally from the bay front to a downtown office building. His destination was the Central Miami Holding Company on the fourteenth floor of La Ronde, a semicircular building. All of its offices had an ocean view.

In the lobby he had paused to look at a statue. It commemorated Caesar Labruzzo, the grandfather of the whole Labruzzo clan and the man who had founded the family in Miami. The "family" was now strongly situated in the Miami business community.

The deli owner had told Hawke that the Labruzzo family owned at least ten percent of the better Miami real estate of which this building was a prime example. A conservative estimate of that real estate's worth would be somewhere around eight to ten billion dollars.

Hawke took the elevator to the top floor and found that the Central Miami Holding Company had the whole four-teenth floor. The elevators opened on a gardenlike reception area with a small fountain running down rocks and through a fish pond and under a small bridge. Across the bridge sat a girl who looked like she was fresh from *Vogue* magazine. She was dressed in a miniskirt that looked impossible to get into, let alone out of.

Hawke stared at the girl through his mid-darkness-range sunglasses and grinned.

"I'm looking for Vito Labruzzo. Is he in?"

"Do you have an appointment?" the girl asked. Her face was oval, almost part Oriental, eyes widely set, delicately made up, her hair a mass of dark mane flung out to one side, giving her head an off-balance appearance.

"No appointment, but I have a message from Tony I'm sure he'll want to hear."

"I'll ring his secretary, but I'm sure he's out." She flicked a switch and talked in a low voice he couldn't pick up.

"Miss Gina will be here to see you shortly. Would you care to sit down?"

"Got a spare lily pad?"

The girl looked up, not understanding. Hawke waved at her and checked out the modern-art painting, an original, on the wall. It was a square set in a field of wavy lines, circles, triangles, and trapezoids; each set of boxed lines held a weird human face. At least, Hawke *thought* they were human. He sensed her behind him and turned.

"I've always preferred Miró, myself. More body, more

substance, not just some flight of fancy. You wanted to see Vito Labruzzo?''

''Right.''

''Why don't you come down to my office and I'll see if I can locate Mr. Labruzzo for you. Usually he's a hard man to find this time of the week.''

Hawke let her lead the way. She was small, three inches over five feet perhaps, not the five-ten and six-foot females who swarmed all over the continent these days.

In sharp contrast to the fashion slave on the reception desk, this girl wore a mid-knee skirt, a light sweater, and a heavy knit coat sweater with the sleeves pushed up and open down the front. It looked exactly right on her. Her black hair was just touching her shoulders.

She checked over her shoulder to be sure he had started to follow her, and he caught up and paced beside her down the softly carpeted hallway. Leaving the lobby, they had come through an ornate single door, and it had closed with an electronic click behind them.

She went two more doors, then opened one on the left and motioned him inside. He waited for her.

''Not many men do that anymore,'' she said, walking into the office in front of him, going behind a remarkable cherry-wood burled desk with a free-form top made from the whole burl slice. She settled down in a chair and looked out the window, which stretched the length of the room. Below, Miami and Miami Beach spread out along the sunlit coast.

''Now,'' she said, folding her hands on the leather-bordered calendar and blotter on her desktop. ''How can I help you?''

''I have a message for Vito Labruzzo.''

"I'm sure you do, but Mr. Labruzzo is almost impossible to locate these days. He had a week's vacation scheduled in France but had to postpone it due to business. Two days ago he flew to Rome to take his vacation. I'm afraid we won't see him for at least two weeks. He loves Rome."

"The old country."

"Yes, his grandfather was born there."

"So, my message?"

"You could give it to me orally, or you could write it down and seal it in an envelope and I'll forward it to Italy."

"What if my message can't wait?"

"Then it won't do us any good to send it, will it? I'm sorry, I didn't catch your name." Her smile was perfect, teeth gleaming, capped, small earrings. Everything muted, precise, exactly right for her.

"In Colombia they call me El Halcon."

"In Miami we still speak some English, even with the invasion from Cuba. I'd prefer to call you Mr. Hawke."

"Fair enough. So my options are to give you the message and hope it gets delivered, or just forget about it."

Gina stood, came around the desk, and paused near him.

"I'm afraid so. Mr. Labruzzo has a lot of interests. This is just one, and he's spread terribly thin right now. I've suggested that he needs some help, but you know how the older generation always is about that idea."

Her smile came through again, frankly honest.

"Any suggestions?" he asked.

"I'd say write out the message and I'll bust my little bottom to get it to Mr. Labruzzo."

"Good."

She found a legal yellow pad in her desk drawer, and Hawke asked for a pen. His was still rammed into the big goon's heart somewhere in the middle of Biscayne Bay. He leaned forward in the elegant chair and wrote. Hawke used a series of coded words, phrases that meant absolutely nothing and wouldn't, even if there had been a key. It looked like code, but it was actually jumbled non sequiturs from years ago. He finished, pushed it into an envelope, licked the entire length of the glued flap, and sealed it.

Gina wrote "Mr. Labruzzo" on the outside and looked up.

"Is there anything else I can do for you?"

He grinned and watched her, his eyes dancing. She laughed.

"Now, El Halcon. You know what I meant."

"I could ask you out to dinner."

"It's too early for that."

"I could wait."

She smiled, turned, and went behind the desk again. Her friendly, bantering smile of a few minutes before was gone. In its place was a formal, cold smile that was remarkable for the change.

He took a step back without thinking.

"Yes, I see what you mean, Miss Gina. All you have to do is fold your arms across your chest and cross your legs, and the body language will be exhaustingly complete." Hawke turned and walked to the door. There he looked over his shoulder. Her arms were folded as if protecting her breasts.

"You don't even have to steam open the envelope. It says that Tony wants to go south on the next trip, the first-class kind. That's what he said." It was a stab in the dark. South could be almost anywhere.

Hawke left the room at once, then walked down the

hallway and over the bridge to the elevator. Once there, he paused and scowled. One minute she had been a beautiful, warm, friendly girl, but in an instant she had changed into another person. Amazing.

Something bothered him. As he rode down in the elevator he went over the office scene again. She had been friendly, then changed. Why? He hadn't come on too strong, just a mild, innocent little flirtation. She had frozen up. Hawke tried to recapture the moment. She had come around the desk and stood in front of him.

Hawke had then faced the dividing wall. It had a large bulletin board with items on it. He had been watching her to remember much of what had been on the board. But long years of training meant that his subconscious still had gathered up, as much as possible, the evidence in sight and recorded it. What had he seen on the wall?

He went back over it. A calendar with a sunset scene, a personnel chart with mug shots too small to see. To the left had been pull-down maps, such as he had seen in schools.

Yes, a map was down, a large-scale map that he had noticed first. What country? As he concentrated on the wall, the synapses closed and snapped and created new paths, and suddenly he could read the large print: "Honduras."

He remembered. She had turned away from him, smiling, pleased about something. Her line of sight must have swept across the map, and at once she retreated behind the desk, behind her business mask, and he was out the door moments later.

The map. She had been afraid that he'd seen it. What was so important about that map? He was sure it wouldn't be there if he tried to go back into her office. Not reasonable to try to break in for something like this. Was it important?

He stopped at a phone booth in the lobby and checked through the directory. At last he found a Labruzzo listing for this building. He dialed.

"Labruzzo. How may we help you?"

It was a woman's voice, but not Gina's.

"Yes, hello. I just paid a business call on a very nice young woman in your office named Gina, but I didn't get her last name. I want to send her some flowers as a courtesy, but I need her last name."

"I'm sorry, sir, we have no one in this office named Gina."

"Oh. Isn't this the Central Miami Holding Company?"

"No, I'm sorry. That's really been a problem. We've just had a group of phone changes, and then they got confused again. I don't even know how to get that number for you. Sorry."

She hung up.

Hawke stared at the phone a moment, then went outside. He knew the U.S. was using Honduras to snipe at Nicaragua. What else had he heard? He'd have to go contact his Polish deli listening post. Joseph must have heard something about Honduras being tied to the Labruzzo operation.

Hawke stepped into his Grand Am and headed for the deli. As Hawke pulled away from the curb, a young man ran out of the building Hawke had just left, stepped into a new Lincoln town car waiting for him in a no-parking zone at the curb, and pulled into traffic two vehicles behind Hawke.

Sue Beth Townsend's aim was not as good with a pistol as it had been when she was thirteen; still, the round from the 9-mm automatic hit Manny Marcello high in the chest just under his shoulder bone, broke a rib, and slanted upward, lodging in the fleshy part of his upper back. He bleated in surprise and fury and drove forward before she could fire again.

Three men pounded on the door a few seconds later. Manny had knocked Sue Beth down, kicked his revolver from her, and gotten the door unlocked before he passed out.

That afternoon twelve men were in and out of Sue Beth's room. At first they had to hold her down as the men worked out their sexual fantasies without her permission. Finally she stopped struggling. Toward the last, she wasn't even sure where she was or what was happening.

Manny came back from his family doctor, who had treated his gunshot wound and would not report it. The family sawbones dug the slug out of Manny's chest, bandaged it, and gave him tetanus and penicillin shots and some pills to take. The doctor told Manny to get a week's bed rest.

"Where is the slut?" Manny roared as soon as he came into the room. One of the drivers showed Manny where Sue Beth huddled in the room that had been hers. She was naked, eyes wild, sometimes screaming, sometimes babbling words that made no sense.

Manny eased into a chair, his head still light from the anesthetic. How else could he punish her? How else could he make her sorry she ever went for his gun? He snorted. Then Manny chuckled. He pointed at two of his drivers.

"Put her in a car and take her downtown. Drive in an alley, then back up, walk her down the alley, and push her out into the street. Then haul ass out of there. Don't let nobody spot your plates."

"Dump her . . . naked?" one of the guys asked.

"Damn right! She'll make all the papers."

Hawke talked with Joseph Silokowski for two hours while he had the vegetarian special: avocado, alfalfa spouts, lettuce, and green pepper strips on rye.

"Sure, I've heard talk about Labruzzo and Honduras. I hear it's a major point along his private drug pipeline. He don't pay no fancy importer mule to get the stuff in here. Works the whole thing himself—or so I've been told."

"Where? Honduras is a good-sized country. I can't take a survey of the place."

The fat little deli owner began to sweat. Hawke finished the sandwich and worked on the beer.

"Stop sweating, Joseph. You tell me what you know, and nobody ever finds out about it. They won't touch you. My word on it."

"Sure, your word, with you three or four thousand miles away and this whole damn town swarming with Labruzzo muscle and hit men."

He popped the cap on a Perrier and took a long slug, wiped his mouth on his hairy arm, and shrugged.

"Hell, you only die once. Place I heard about they called El Centro. Spanish for 'the center'."

"In the capital city, right?"

"Right. Tegucigalpa, wherever the hell that is."

"Probably the only town with a jet airstrip. If I have to, I can find it."

Joseph looked up. A lot of horn honking and yelling came from out in the street. "What's all the fuss about?" he walked to the front door and looked out. Hawke went with him.

"Christ! Look at that," Joseph said.

A naked woman half stumbled, half walked down the street, weaving from side to side, cars swerving around her. She seemed unaware where she was, or that she was naked. Nobody offered to help.

She came to the sidewalk on the deli side. A well-dressed couple made a wide detour around her. A teenage boy ran up and stared at her.

"Isn't somebody going to help her?" Joe asked.

"Yeah, get ready to close up, Joe." Hawke pushed out the door, ran twenty feet to the woman, caught her around the waist, and picked her up in his arms. He carried her into Joseph's deli. Joseph swore in Polish, dropped the blinds, and cut the lights.

"So what the hell happens now?" the Polish deli owner asked with more than a little concern in his voice.

Chapter
Four

Joseph Silokowski shook his head as he frowned at the naked woman Hawke had just carried into his now closed deli.

"Bring her in back. There are some clothes, a cot." Joseph snorted. "Probably stoned out of her skull. Happens now and then around here."

Hawke put her on a cot, and they covered her with a blanket. Her eyes were still staring vacantly, then for a minute they were wild with fury, then she shook and whimpered. Hawke sat beside her, knowing he should call the police or some psychiatric unit. But he waited.

She slept for two hours and came awake at about midnight. Hawke put down his cup of coffee. She seemed to be smelling the brew.

"Would you like some coffee?" Hawke asked.

"Yes, I shore would," she said.

"I'm Matthew Hawke. What's your name?"

"Sue Beth," she said automatically.

"You have a last name?"

"Townsend. Sue Beth Townsend from Shelton Bend, Mississippi."

Hawke poured the coffee. She sipped it half sitting up. For the first time she realized she had no clothes on under the blanket.

"Oh, glory," she said softly.

"What happened to you?" Hawke asked. "Do you want to talk about it?"

She shook her head.

Joseph came in with a pair of pants and one of his work shirts. He put them on the blanket. "My wife is coming down with some clothes for you," he said. "Nothing fancy, but they'll do."

She nodded, pulling the blanket up to her chin.

"Hey, relax," Joseph said. "I've got three daughters older than you are." He frowned for a minute. "How long since you've eaten? You have any lunch or dinner?"

Sue Beth shook her head.

"I'll bring you something. Best deli in town. Half a person's problems are gone the minute she gets something to eat." He grinned, patted her on the shoulder, and hurried out to the deli.

"I'll leave so you can dress," Hawke said. He went out into the deli for some fresh coffee.

"Vito Labruzzo," Hawke said. "He still the top dog in the family here, the capo?"

"Vito is the man. Been running the mob here for twenty years. Longest anywhere in the country. Hear he's not in the best of health."

"He ever travel to Honduras?"

"Used to be down there a lot. Lately he's going to Rome

more. Still trying to get an audience with the Pope, I hear. He must be worried about his soul. No good Polish Pope would talk to that bastard!''

Joseph finished the sandwich. It was his light special with cheese and sliced ham and mustard and lots of chopped lettuce and a few sprouts. He took a coffeepot and knocked on the door.

When they went in, Sue Beth was sleeping. She had dressed and pulled the blankets back over her.

An hour later she woke up screaming. Mrs. Silokowski came with clothes. She was about the same size as Joseph, short and chunky with gray hair and a smile that brightened the whole block.

Denise Silokowski talked softly to the screaming girl. She flailed out with her fists and clawed at the restraining arms, but after two or three minutes she quieted and went to sleep again.

The sandwich sat uneaten near the cot.

When Sue Beth woke the next time, she was calm. She hugged Denise Silokowski, and the two chatted about clothes. Denise had brought underwear and a bra and skirts and blouses for her to chose from. The sandwich was a bit soggy by that time, but Sue Beth pounced on it and ate it quickly with two cups of coffee.

Hawke had gone back to his hotel, but he returned shortly after seven.

Sue Beth shook his hand. ''You . . . saved me last night, Joseph tells me. Thank you, Mr. Hawke.''

''Is there anything we can do? You mentioned some men.''

Denise shushed him. ''We talked about it. Soon we go to the hospital for a checkup, then Sue Beth comes home with me for a few days to rest before she goes back to Shelton Bend.''

''I could pay a call on those men,'' Hawke said. ''Was it where you worked?''

Sue Beth nodded. ''The Labruzzo Transportation Company.''

''They tricked her into driving crack and cocaine up the highway to Washington,'' Denise said.

''Labruzzo!'' Hawke said coldly. ''What's the address where you worked? Who was the man you contacted there?''

She told him.

Hawke's face went grim. He reached in his pocket and took out one of the packages of bills. They were all hundreds. He turned his back and counted out ten, folded them, then took off five more. He gave the five to Denise.

''That's for the hospital. You know how they are these days.'' He turned to Sue Beth. ''This is a little something to help you get back to Shelton Bend.''

She looked at the top bill.

''No, no, I couldn't. I've never seen so much money.''

Denise closed Sue's hand over the bills. ''You can, Sue Beth. You will.'' She smiled at Hawke. ''Time for us to go. I've got my car.''

Hawke had a Danish and more coffee out front where Joseph was deep into his breakfast trade. Then Hawke marched, full of anger, to his Grand Am, which was parked on the street. His car looked unscathed. The radio hadn't even been ripped off. But as Hawke pulled away, a driver in a Lincoln town car just down the block purred into traffic and followed him.

Hawke found the address Sue Beth had given him. There didn't seem to be anyone there yet. He waited until slightly after eight-thirty, then went to the door and turned the knob. It was open.

Inside, a man looked up from a desk in the small entry room.

"Yeah?"

"Finster, I'm a driver. Just got in from New York with the Oldsmobile."

"So you want a medal? See Manny, first door to the left. Careful, he had a tough time yesterday."

Hawke walked down the hall and went through the first door to his left and into Manny's office.

A man sat behind a desk. A couch stood on the far side of the room. The man at the desk looked up slowly, as if his head hurt by just moving it.

"Manny Marcello?" Hawke asked.

"Yeah. Who the hell are you?"

Hawke was across the room before Manny could get his piece out. The Avenger's big fist connected solidly with Manny's jaw, smashing him backward out of his chair and dumping him on the floor.

Hawke picked him up and pounded a right fist into Manny's soft gut; then, holding him up, Hawke backhanded him four times across his face.

Hawke dumped him on the floor, jumped back to the door he had come in, pushed the bar locks in place, then went back to Marcello.

"Sue Beth sends her regards," Hawke said. He picked up the limp excuse for a man and slammed his fist into Manny's nose, breaking it, spurting blood all over his face.

"You must remember Sue Beth. She was the girl you raped yesterday. Then she shot you, and you set twelve men on her in a gang rape. Too bad her bullet hit you so high."

Hawke pushed Manny against the wall. "Don't worry about the cops. There won't be any trial where a smart mob mouthpiece can spring you. It's between you and me, right now. How long do you want to live?"

"Oh, God! I never hurt like this!"

"How long, Manny?"

"Years, years!"

"Then talk. Where is Vito Labruzzo?"

"Don't know."

Hawke slapped him hard, and Marcello's head swiveled.

"Christ! I don't know. Nobody does. Nobody seen him for three, four months. Somebody said he's sick. But the family operation goes on."

"Okay. What is El Centro in Honduras?"

"Damn, they'd castrate me!"

"I'll save them the trouble."

"No! no! Okay. El Centro is the coordinating office in the capital down there where the shit is collected and then brought to the States. Mostly cocaine and crack."

Hawke had all he needed: the next step in the crack pipeline. Hawke turned away from Manny, took out his .45, and screwed the silencer on it. When he turned back, Manny saw the silencer and he lifted his hand in protest.

Hawke shot him once through his forehead. The heavy slug bored a neat round hole in his flesh, expanded as soon as it got through the skull, and pulped six vital brain centers as it plowed through the mortal remains of Manny Marcello.

Blood and bone fragments splattered on the wall, then Manny slid slowly to the floor. He'd never ship another pound of coke north, and never rape another innocent girl.

Hawke looked around the office. No records, no lists, no cash. There was nothing of value to him there. He unscrewed the silencer and put his piece away in its holster. Then he unlocked the door, walked into the hall and out the front door, not even bothering to look at the front-desk man.

An hour later Hawke slid out of the rental car at Miami International Airport. A Lincoln town car stopped three slots behind him, and the driver and a watcher waited. They saw Hawke turn in his keys at the rental desk and pay the tab. He walked to the information booth and found which airline flew to Honduras.

It took only five minutes in line to buy his ticket, which Hawke paid for in cash. The flight would leave just after noon. Hawke called Silokowski.

"Doctors said Sue Beth is fine. A little battered and bruised, but no real damage. No danger of pregnancy, either. She's staying overnight there, then we'll get her on a plane first thing in the morning to Jackson. She lives about thirty miles away from there."

"I'm going to see our friends in the south," Hawke said. "You'll hear from me again."

Two phone booths from Hawke, another conversation took place.

"That's right. He's booked for Honduras. Leaves in about two hours. Plenty of time for you." The caller listened to his instructions, said good-bye, and walked back to the Lincoln and drove away.

Hawke was no expert on Honduras. At the airport before he left, he found a small tourist book about Honduras that told some of the fundamentals. Spanish was the main language, so tourists were encouraged to learn the language before they came. A few phrases were given that were close to Tex-Mex and border Spanish, so Hawke felt he could communicate.

He perused the small pamphlet: Honduras is about the size of the state of Tennessee and is one of six nations that make up Central America. Wedged between Nicaragua to the south and east and Guatemala and El Salvador to the south and west, the Caribbean sea laps gently at four hundred miles of its northern border.

What he read in the section on agriculture surprised Hawke. For years he thought the cocaine that was sold in the U.S. in its pure form and in its concentrated form, crack, came from "somewhere down there south of Mexico." But, according to the brochure, coca was not grown in Honduras. "Honduras has no significant drug trade," he read. "A few smugglers may use some of our ports or airfields, but the number and amount is insignificant."

As Hawke read on, he felt the airplane begin its descent. It was still light as its wheels touched the runway and it rolled to a stop. Hawke deboarded, and since his only luggage was a small carry-on, he moved directly into customs, was cleared in ten minutes, and hurried outside to find a line of waiting taxis.

The first two taxi drivers in the line were arguing about something, and Hawke motioned for the next one to come around them. Just as he opened the door, a man surged out of the cab at him with a knife.

Hawke swung the soft bag he carried, and the knife penetrated it. Hawke ripped the blade from the man's hand and followed through with a round kick to the man's stomach. When the attacker bent over in pain, Hawke surged forward and rammed his elbow hard downward into the back of the man's neck, dropping him to the paving.

Two more men ran from the sidewalk at him, one waving a handgun. The other had out a knife, and both looked dangerous.

Hawke leapt into the taxi.

"Get out of here!" he bellowed in English. "*Vamos!*" he added, and the driver gunned away from the airport parking area. When Hawke was sure the men were not following him, he told the driver in Spanish to take him to the Americana Hotel. The brochure said this hotel was the one the foreign journalists all stayed at, and usually someone from your home nation could be found there, no matter what your nationality.

The driver nodded and drove down the paved highway toward the capital city. As he rode along, Hawke took an ordinary padlock from his pocket and opened it with the key, then snapped the ring around his belt buckle. It might just come in handy until he could find a firearm somewhere. Reluctantly he had left his .45 and silencer with Joseph, the deli man in Miami.

Suddenly the taxi turned off the road and bumped fifty yards to a halt behind some trees. The driver turned, and in his hand was a revolver. Hawke unbuckled his belt and drew it out of the loops and caught hold of the end of it a foot from the buckle, which still held the heavy padlock.

"Out of the car, *Señor*. It is best no funny business."

Hawke eased out of the cab and held his belt in his right hand behind his leg.

The driver got out and grinned, holding the gun on Hawke. He looked behind him on the road, then back at Hawke. The second time the driver looked away, Hawke lunged forward and swung the belt with the padlock on the end.

The square, rough edges of the padlock slammed into the taxi driver's gun hand, bringing a scream of protest as steel broke four bones in the back of his hand and spun the revolver away into the dirt.

The smaller man scrambled for it, but Hawke swung the padlock again. This easy-to-carry non-weapon is best used in a slashing manner, and Hawke knew the technique. He swung the padlock on the end of his belt again, hard. It hit the taxi driver on the cheek, continued downward, ripping an inch-wide swath of skin from cheek to chin.

The next blow from the padlock caught the gunman's nose and tore off an inch of it.

"*No mas!*" the driver said, whimpering.

Hawke threatened him with the weapon.

"Who hired you to hold me?" Hawke asked. The man shook his head, screeching that he didn't know. Hawke picked up the revolver, a make he was unfamiliar with, which had six rounds in the six cylinders. He slammed the butt of the weapon down on the drivers's head and looked for the car keys. They weren't in the ignition.

Just then a car turned off the highway and started down the dirt road about fifty yards away.

Hawke sprinted into the trees, and when the car came to them, he waited to see what the three men in the rig would do. The car stopped at the taxi. After a series of shouts and accusations, the three men rushed back into the car and slammed the rig up the road to the highway. It roared off toward town.

The driver still lay in the dirt. Hawke ran back, found the keys in his pocket, and drove the cab on toward the city. He had to ask twice to get instructions to find the Americana

Hotel, but at last he located it. He parked the cab six blocks away and walked to the hotel.

The room clerk spoke English, and soon Hawke relaxed in his room on the third floor. Hawke had time to try to think it through. Only Silokowski knew he was flying to Honduras. How did someone on this end know he was arriving?

A telephone call. But who could do it? He had obtained a forged and altered passport while he was in Houston, in the name he used as a cover in San Diego: Brian Barlow. It had cost three thousand dollars but was authentic, not hot, and would pass any inspection.

Nobody had called him by name in the airport, or in the taxi. He had used the passport name and the passport to get his international ticket. Still, somebody knew he was coming— and wanted him dead. It must be Labruzzo. Hawke had used his real name with them at the big office building. But at the airport and here, he had used Brian Barlow. Yet somehow Labruzzo was on to him.

Hawke took out different clothes from his small bag, put them on, and got out a golf cap and a pair of large, reflective sunglasses that were impossible to see through from the outside. The change of clothes and glasses just might allow him to slip by Labruzzo's watchdogs.

Hawke decided that he'd have no chance of finding El Centro unless he set out before dark. He pushed the revolver he'd borrowed from the cabbie into his jacket pocket and checked the mirror. The jacket was loose enough, so the heavy bulge was not noticeable. He left by the side door and found a taxi after a two-block walk.

When he told the driver he wanted to go to El Centro, the cabbie shook his head. In slowly spoken Spanish he said there were three streets with that name, and a bazaar and two big office buildings.

Hawke said to take him to the smallest of the office buildings. The taxi driver did. For a town of nearly half a million people, the capital city looked like nothing more than a small village that got bigger and bigger. Streets were mostly tracks and trails.

Only the downtown section had larger buildings, many made of stone and brick. The Catholic churches were large, well made, and profusely decorated. He passed the Church of the Virgen de los Dolores, then cut off into a series of narrow cobblestoned streets that ran between the walls of stucco houses, solid doorways, and iron balconies with window grilles.

At last they came into a paved street with rows of three- and four-story buildings and streetlights. The cabbie pulled up in front of a tall structure. It was an office building but with a plain front and big double doors at the top of concrete steps.

Hawke saw the man hold up two fingers. He gave him a U.S. dollar, and the cabbie didn't offer any change. He'd have to get some of his money changed into lempira.

Hawke walked up the steps and into the building. It had a small lobby, two elevators and a directory. The name Labruzzo did not show on the directory. He checked the other names but could find none indicating an import-export business.

He went back outside and found the same cabdriver waiting for him.

"The other building?" the cabbie asked in Spanish. Hawke shook his head, then got in and told him to go back to the hotel. What he needed was a local contact, somebody who knew the local scene. At the hotel he sat in the lobby and watched and waited.

An American couple came in, but both were loud and demanding. He passed on them. Fifteen minutes later a man came out of the elevator and talked a moment to the room clerk. He spoke English, British English, and Hawke moved toward the desk.

The Englishman started to leave.

"I beg your pardon, but I heard you speaking English. I just arrived, and I wondered if you'd been in the country a while?"

"Indeed I have. You're American. Not many of you left here now, you know. I say, would you care to have dinner? It's about time, and I've been hungry all afternoon. The food here is quite good, for Honduras. My treat—to welcome you to town. Oh, I'm Preston Smith-Jones, originally from Tunbridge Wells, down toward Brighton on the Channel."

He held out his hand and Hawke took it.

"Great! I'm starved myself. My name is Brian Barlow, from San Diego."

"You're a tourist? Oh, this way to the eatery."

"No, business, rather hush-hush."

"Quite, I understand. I don't blabber about what I do myself. I usually spend six months of the year here, then try to get in some skiing during the winter, Mt. Hood, Aspen, Big Bear, the Canadian Rockies. Do you ski?"

"Poorly." They laughed.

Dinner was pleasant but not exceptional.

"They have a leg of lamb here that is quite good. It's cooked in a special sauce, and then a second sauce is added when it's served. I'd like you to try it."

Lamb is lamb, and not one of Hawke's favorite foods, but

this went down easily. During dinner they talked. Hawke probed and asked innocent questions. He brought up the name El Centro.

"A friend said I could find the person I need to talk to at El Centro, but it doesn't look easy. The cabbie said there are three or four streets named that, and two office buildings and some other centers."

"He's right, but few of them are known outside of town. If your friend was an American, he was probably referring to a kind of flea market and auction yard where anything and everything is sold. It's a combination farmer's market, swap meet, and auction barn. I've heard it said that if you want to find someone, go to El Centro and wait. If the person is in Tegucigalpa, sooner or later he'll come to El Centro."

"That's some help. I knew this wouldn't be easy. So what else do I need to know to survive in this country?"

The Englishman hesitated. Their dinner was over. "Why don't we go up to my rooms and continue talking. I have some excellent brandy, and there aren't so many ears."

"Done."

When they had settled into chairs in the two-room suite on the fourth floor, Preston Smith-Jones poured the brandy.

"A carryover from the homeland, I'm afraid. You can take an Englishman out of England . . ."

The brandy was apricot, delicate, potent.

"You must remember this isn't the U.S.A. This is a banana republic but with little democracy. There is always a strong man around the corner or behind the powers-that-be, and there's a colonel ready with an instant coup at almost any given moment. It makes the authorities nervous.

"For all practical purposes, you're guilty until proven innocent. The Napoleonic code, not English Common Law."

"So I should be careful where I put down my feet."

"Precisely. A little money goes a long way down here when it comes to greasing the official skids. Bribery is a way of life. The standard of living is extremely low, especially in the villages. My business is repairing jet-engine turbine blades. You might think this is a poor spot for such work, but on the contrary. I gather up blades from all over South America here and ship them to my plant in Dallas."

"Turbine blades? They repair them?"

"Oh, quite. A pigeon or a duck or just a robin might get sucked into a jet-engine turbine and cause all sorts of old billy hell with those rapidly spinning rotor blades. Lots of those highly sophisticated blades are no more than two feet long and six inches wide and can cost over ten thousand dollars new. I can repair most of them for about a thousand dollars. Big savings to the airline companies."

"Interesting."

"What line of work are you in, Barlow? Oh, right, you said it was hush-hush."

"Not all that secret. Insurance investigator."

"Well, now, I say, that *is* exciting."

"Mostly routine, tracking down backgrounds, digging out facts about the recently dead or some claim. Not really exciting."

"What case are you down here—" He stopped. "Sorry, I know you can't say. Would you like to do a line or two?"

Smith-Jones took the lid off a fancy silver candy dish on a small table in front of them. Inside was white powder, maybe a half a cup, and a small silver spoon with two diamonds set in the handle. There had to be four to six thousand dollars' worth of cocaine in the dish.

Hawke shook his head. "Not me. Tried it once. It put me to sleep and I had nightmares I still remember. My system just can't take it."

"Do you mind if I . . ."

Hawke shrugged. Smith-Jones had a habit of leaving sentences unfinished. "Every man to his own poison."

Hawke watched as the Englishman spooned out one measure, put it on the glass tabletop, and then moved the white powder into one long thin line with a pocketknife. He took a short glass tube from a drawer in the table, unwrapped it from a tissue, and calmly snorted the line of cocaine.

The whole operation took maybe two minutes, and neither of them talked during the time. Smith-Jones snorted the coke and grimaced, then sniffed loudly a few times before he wiped his nose with a linen handkerchief. When he turned back to Hawke, his eyes were bright and his reserved expression was replaced with an open and friendly smile.

"I say, that is better. None for you?"

"Not really, the nightmares. I was wondering why you're needed here for the turbine blades? Couldn't they just be shipped straight to Dallas?"

"Could be, but fast service is our claim to fame. We keep an inventory here of three hundred blades, all sizes to fit all makes of jet engines. Usually when I get a box of six blades in for repair, I can send out by return air freight six duplicate repaired blades. They go out by same-day air and the airline doesn't have a delay. Most of these small South American airlines can't have a big spare-parts inventory. They can't have twenty spare engines in their shop ready to be dropped into a plane.

"All of our blades are inspected and approved by the Federal Aviation Administration of the U.S. government. Just seems to work better this way."

"You can see why I was never any good at business." Hawke finished his drink. "Well, big day tomorrow, and some research to finish tonight. I better get cracking."

At the door, Hawke held out his hand. "Thanks for rescuing me, and for the dinner and brandy. My turn next time."

They shook hands, and Hawke went along the hall to the stairs and down to his own room.

There was something off-key about Preston Smith-Jones, but he wasn't sure what it was. Honduras was only four or five hours more by air to Dallas. It didn't make sense having a facility here. What troubled him most was that much cocaine in a candy dish. He must have a wholesale contact and buy it cheap. What a risk!

Hawke thought of going to El Centro to look it over, but he decided tomorrow would be time enough. Instead, he checked the revolver. It was a .38, and he had six shots. How would he get more ammo if he wanted it? He'd have to ask Smith-Jones—he'd know.

Hawke checked the lock on his door and pushed a chair under the handle for added protection. Then he lay down on the bed with his clothes on, the revolver nestled in his right hand. He had left a small light on but pushed a towel against the bottom of the door so no light would show in the hall.

About two A.M. Hawke came alert. He sat up without a sound and looked at the door. Someone in the hall turned the knob to his door slowly, then pushed inward. The lock had been picked, and the door pressed against the chair.

Chapter
Five

In a modern, luxuriously appointed apartment in the Presidente section of Tegucigalpa, a phone rang. After three rings a slender hand came out of a rumpled bed and knocked it off the cradle, then picked it up and dragged it under a thin silk sheet.

"Yes?"

"We've found him. He's staying at the Americana. Any change in your orders?"

There was a pause. The woman under the sheet sighed. "No, the same plan, but be careful. We're not sure of anything yet. We must be positive. Too much has been left to chance lately. Vito said it was past time when all that had to stop."

"Be easy just to dump him in the river with an incision across his neck."

"No!" the woman under the sheet said. "I told you, same orders. Don't wake me up again unless it's damn important."

She threw the sheet back and stared at the ceiling in the darkness. Now she'd never get back to sleep. She always had trouble sleeping without her own personal pillow.

Without thinking about it, she reached out to the other side of the king-size bed. She drew her hand back at once. Dominic was not there. Her Dom might never be there again. Vito had sent him to Sicily to "manage" one of the businesses Vito had there. Now there was a murder warrant out for his arrest in Miami. If Dom ever tried to come back into the U.S. on his own passport, he would be arrested immediately.

Vito never said a word to her about Dom, but somehow he had found out. Her bed had been empty ever since. Jesus, it had been good with Dominic! She had never realized that sex could have anything to do with tenderness or loving someone. It had been wonderful.

Now this crazy madman was charging around. They had a definite description of him from the boat owner at Tony's condo. Two witnesses had seen the boats collide in the bay, and Tony's go down. Tony now had been missing for a full day. The same big man with the dark hair had visited her office, then yesterday Manny Marcello had been executed in his own office by the same man.

This man who said he was called Hawke was the same one who barged into her office asking a lot of questions and who had made a gentle pass at her. It had been enticing for a moment. He was a handsome hunk of man, but she had noticed the map of Honduras rolled down, and she had to get rid of him quickly. Then he had taken a flight to Honduras under the name of Brian Barlow. What the hell was he up to?

Gina rolled over, got tangled in her silk nightgown, threw

the sheet back and pulled the offending garment off, sliding under the sheet naked.

Ten minutes later she still couldn't sleep. She knew she shouldn't. But, damn it, sometimes this was the only way. Gina got out of bed, turned on the light, and went to the bathroom.

It always seemed to be the same. She was worried about something. She couldn't sleep, and the urge, the *knowing,* came to her. She stared at herself in the mirror. She knew every part of her body. Her soft brown eyes looked back at her. She never wore makeup, for with her olive skin, ebony hair, and high cheekbones, she never needed it. She had even modeled a while when she was a teenager before Vito found out. He stopped it with one word.

She reached in the small box from her travel makeup kit and took out a single-edged razor. It had to be somewhere that it wouldn't show. Dom had known; he had seen the scars on her hips. The bikinis she wore never showed them.

She took the razor, unwrapped it from the paper and cardboard, and stared at her right hip. The last time had healed. Gina trembled, then she took the razor in her left hand and gritted her teeth as she made the cut. Always the same: two inches long and deep enough to draw plenty of blood.

It never hurt. She always thought it would, but somehow it didn't. Gina stared down at the blood that seeped from her slashed hip, then moved to the shower when the blood ran down her leg.

For two minutes Gina watched the blood surge from high on her left hip, then run down her leg to the shower stall tile. Already her breathing slowed, her heart stopped racing.

For just a moment she yawned and she grinned. It always worked.

Gina turned on the cold water and let it beat down on her thigh and leg, washing away the blood. Then she worked quickly, holding a small towel over the cut as she expertly took three butterfly bandages from her kit and pinched the cut flesh together. Then she put on ointment, and a larger bandage to cover the slice.

Gina nodded as she turned out the light and went back to her bedroom. She found her nightgown, pulled it on over her head, and slid under the silk sheet.

She was so sleepy. In the morning everything would be wonderful again. She knew it would. Gina had no thoughts about why she hurt herself, why she was a self-mutilator. Nor could she remember when it had started. When she was in high school, she thought.

Her Uncle Joe had been involved in some way. She refused to think about it. Nobody knew. Not Vito, not her mother, not Tony. None of her other uncles. She had been a sophomore in high school, and for three months she had lived with Uncle Joe when Vito had been in Italy.

Uncle Joe had always been her favorite. He was about forty at the time, a widower who lived alone in a big house.

The second week she was there, Uncle Joe had walked into the bathroom just as she stepped out of the shower. She had forgotten to lock the door. He had seduced her right there on the bathroom floor. Every day for the three months she stayed there he had violated her, taught her everything about sex and intercourse he knew.

She didn't know what to do. To her family this was the biggest sin. The family structure was sacred. She knew any of his three brothers would kill Uncle Joe if they knew about it. She had no close girlfriends she could tell.

The day before Vito came back from Italy, Gina had tried to kill her Uncle Joe. She had cut him bad, but she also cut herself. He patched them both up, and nobody ever knew a thing about it.

Gina knew that Vito would have killed his brother Joe without a second thought if he ever found out. He would also send her to Italy to the Sisters of Blessed Silence nunnery. One of her cousins was there.

That might have been when it started; Gina couldn't remember.

The sight of her own blood always relaxed Gina. She could watch the blood flowing and let all of her frustrations and worries wash away. Then she could concentrate on what she needed to think about, often something as simple as going to sleep.

Gina didn't think about Hawke—Brian Barlow—as she slid into a deep, dreamless, refreshing sleep.

Hawke watched the chair under his hotel room doorknob being pushed backward across the carpet, then the pressure increased and the wooden back broke and the door slammed open. He had the pistol up, but no one charged into the room.

A paper airplane glided through the door from the hallway, made a gentle turn, and landed on the bed. Hawke darted to the door, dropped to knee height, and looked into the hall. No one was there, either way.

He looked at the chair, kicked it aside, and closed the door. To his surprise it fit tightly and locked. Hawke scowled at the door, then went to the paper airplane. He had made them himself when he was a kid, the swept-wing variety.

He unfolded the paper and turned on his light to high. The writing was in block letters, in English: "Barlow: You are a dead man. We can kill you whenever we want to. Go home. We don't want you here. *Vamos!*"

There was no signature.

So he would disappear. He packed up his clothes, cleaned out everything he owned from the room, and went up to the fourth floor where he knocked on Smith-Jones's door. He came after a time, bleary-eyed and angry.

When he saw Hawke, his scowl softened. Hawke pushed the note at him and walked inside the room.

"Damn unsporting of them!" Preston said. "You're leaving first plane out?"

"No. I don't let people push me around. I came to do a job. Can I hide out here for a couple of days, until I move on or find a spot to go underground?"

"Of course. Can you use the couch?"

"Gladly. Without at least four hours of sleep I'm not a functioning human being."

Preston was gone when Hawke woke up about eight the next morning. He changed clothes, pulled down the hat, and added the reflector glasses. It was raining outside.

Hawke looked in the closet, hoping to find an umbrella. He didn't, but on the shelf he found a brown bag. Curiosity had always gotten Hawke in trouble. He opened the bag and stared at a plastic-wrapped package. Inside was white powder. Chances are it wasn't sugar. Hawke ripped open one of the plastic bags and took a taste of the powder.

What in hell was Preston Smith-Jones doing with a kilo of pure heroin in his closet? A kilo cut and on the street was worth about $90,000 in the States. At wholesale it still must bring a third of that down here. Wasn't it two for one? The importer buys it for one third, sells it to the jobber for twice that, or $60,000, and the jobber puts it to pushers on the street where it brings in 50% more, or $90,000. He would have a short talk with Smith-Jones soon.

Hawke hit the street out the side door, walked in the gentle rain for six blocks, then made sure that no one followed him with a series of cutbacks and vanishing acts through a big store. When he was sure no one trailed him, he caught a taxi to the El Centro marketplace.

It was all Smith-Jones said it would be. But this was retail. Labruzzo would be buying here, collecting, not selling. He worked the outside markets, the bazaars under small tents and shelters. It was still raining. In back were permanently housed stores, shops, and offices. They were getting most of the trade.

Hawke bought two more hats and a native jacket. He had found a money-changing booth at a bank and changed two hundred dollars into Honduran lempira. The clerk had been unimpressed with the hundred-dollar bills. He must see a lot of them.

Hawke found the man he needed. He walked the hallways with a small broom and dustpan, sweeping up trash. Hawke motioned to him and waved a ten-lempira note.

In an alcove he talked quietly with the janitor in Spanish. He asked if the man knew where the American business was. "A *norteamericano*, big business, buys things, has an office. Sells nothing." At last the man nodded and reached for the money. Hawke pulled it back.

"Show me first, then you get the lempira."

The small dark-skinned man led Hawke down some steps,

to the other side of the large square of permanent buildings and back to the third floor.

"End of the hall," the man said. Hawke gave him the bill and walked toward the door. He was still fifty feet from the office when a door opened just in front of him and a large man with one arm and a hook for his other hand stepped out and shook his head at Hawke.

"You're not allowed here," the man said.

"I have an appointment," Hawke said in his best Spanish.

"Not true. Go away."

"Who are you to turn me away?" Hawke asked.

The man grinned and swung out the hook. The point had been filed into a delicate point.

"I am El Cancho, the Hook. You want to argue?"

Hawke laughed. "I am called the Gun," he said, taking out the revolver and cocking the hammer. "You want to argue?"

"*Si*, because you won't shoot. You fire the *pistola* and twenty *policia* will be here in two minutes. You gringos forget that *pistolas* are *muy, muy* bad in Honduras!"

The Hook stood six feet from Hawke.

"This is a bad place for you to be, gringo. Go."

Hawke thought about the one that went, "Discretion is the better part . . ." and put the revolver back in his pocket and walked away. Tonight he would visit the place again.

In a heavily draped window twenty feet down the corridor, Gina watched the confrontation. She touched neutral polished nails to her forehead. How in the world had he found this place? This was enough. He was a threat, and Vito would have eliminated him two contacts ago.

She had made a minor mistake, but it could be corrected.

Gina went to the phone and dialed. When the phone on the other end was picked up, Gina spoke quickly.

"Ramona?"

"*Si.*"

"My office, now."

Thirty seconds later a small, slender woman barely five feet tall, dressed in a modest blue dress, pushed through the door to Gina's office and smiled.

"Some work, I hope."

"Yes, Gina. A gringo, about six feet, pale yellow jacket and rain hat. The rain has stopped. He shouldn't be hard to find. Look for El Cancho. He's following your target."

"Eliminate him?"

"Yes, quickly. A bonus if he doesn't live past siesta."

Ramona nodded grimly, hefted the shoulder bag she carried, and hurried out the door.

It took her five minutes to spot El Cancho, the big man with the hook for a hand. He stood outside a small shop that sold maps.

He saw Ramona and winked. She lifted her brows. She looked in the window as she stood beside him.

"Yellow jacket at the cash register. He's all yours."

Ramona moved quickly into the store and was looking the other way when she bumped into the tall gringo. She lay sprawled on the floor, her short skirt hiked up to her crotch.

Hawke caught himself before he fell down, then looked at the victim.

"Hey! Sorry," he said, reaching down to help her up. She caught his hand and chided him grandly for being such a big lummox and moving too quickly. Then she laughed, grinned, and almost smiled.

"American?" she asked in English.

"Yes, and you're right. It was my fault."

"My fault too. You are a guest in my country. Let me buy you a soda or a beer or something. I am Ramona."

She held out her hand, and he shook it.

"Hello, I'm Brian. Come to think of it, I could use a beer."

She took him to a small, dark cantina half a block away where the beer was served in big mugs.

"It is good for my English to talk to you," Ramona said. She was delightful, tiny, vibrant, excited, her dark eyes sparkling as she talked.

"But I should be using my poor Spanish," he said. "Do you work in this area?"

"Yes. I am secretary for exporter. I do the English letters for him to America."

"What do you export?"

"Straw hats and leather purses. Many, many leather purses."

She drained her beer. "We go now, siesta time. Cantina close."

"Oh, right, I had forgotten. Just like in Mexico."

"We go out back door. I take you to pretty place. I not do siesta."

He shrugged. It was siesta time, so he couldn't do much for an hour and a half, anyway, with the shops and stores all closed down. He nodded.

The back door led to an alley. Hawke saw no one. Ramona jumped up, locked her hands around his neck, and kissed him wetly on the lips.

"Ramona hot for you! You come to Ramona's place, I take off clothes and dance dirty hoochi-koochi. Then we bounce on bed!"

As she hung there, Hawke worked one hand inside her shoulder bag, which hung half open, and came out with a .38 automatic. He pushed it in his pocket, lifted her up, and set her down on her feet.

She must have felt the difference in her purse at once, because she glared at him, then reached in her bag and came out with a knife with a wicked-looking four-inch blade.

"Bastard!" she screeched, and lunged at him. The blade nicked his jacket but missed flesh.

"Labruzzo," Hawke said.

She looked up, surprise on her face. Then she tightened her mouth and moved toward him. He let her come, then did a quick *mae geri keage*, a front snap kick aimed at her knife hand. He missed and caught her in the side instead. It threw her off-balance, but she recovered quickly and lunged at his leg. It was gone as quickly as it had come.

"Bastard gringo!" she shouted.

"So you do work for Labruzzo. I got too close down here and they sent you after me. Hit men come in funny packages these days."

"You one dead bastard!"

"You'll need more than that little sticker. I'm gonna take it away from you and use some injections in your arm and find out everything you know!"

"Gringo son of a bitch!"

"You're even running out of swear words. The Labruzzo headquarters here is in El Centro, isn't it?"

She stood staring at him a moment, hatred blasting from her eyes. Then she turned and ran down the street. She was not a sprinter. Hawke kept up with her, cutting her off when she tried to turn. She would tire soon.

She did, panting, her small breasts heaving as she backed

up against a building that ended at the alley. It was a concrete-and-steel affair, four stories high. The lower floor was half finished, but only the floors had been built on the second and third levels.

Ramona turned and raced into the construction, pushed aside workers, and darted up the unfinished steps until she was at the fourth floor. Here, only the concrete slab was in place, with steel beams rising where the roof would be.

Hawke walked toward her. She was on the fourth floor, and she had no place to go.

"You no kill Ramona. You chicken Yankee. Ramona dance naked for you and you let her go, no?"

"Not a chance. Tell me all you know about Labruzzo's operation here, and then I'll let you go."

She tried to spit on him but wasn't close enough.

"Fucking gringo bastard!"

"Now you're getting the hang of it. There's a cadence you need in swearing to make it sound natural."

Ramona glowered at him. Then her right hand moved back, and in a quick motion she threw the knife. Hawke had little warning. He stood six feet away from her and kicked his feet outward and dropped to the raw concrete on his hands and knees just as the blade slashed through the air where his chest had been.

He was up at once, and advanced on her. There was nothing to hide behind. The raw concrete ended four stories above the alley, with only a few reinforcing steel rods pointing up like bones on a beached whale.

She looked down at the alley thirty feet below, then she unbuttoned her dress top and pulled it off her shoulders and down to her waist. Ramona unhooked her bra and threw it into the alley. She moved her shoulders so that her breasts bounced.

"You want some good chewing?" she asked, and giggled. "Come chew on Ramona, and then we do poke-poke and you be one happy guy!"

"Then you tell me about Labruzzo."

"No fucking way, gringo!"

"I've still got my needles and the truth serum."

"No chance, they kill me."

"Things are tough all over."

"You not kill Ramona. You soft chicken."

"Who sent you to kill me, the Hook?"

"No, he just guard-type loony head."

"This is a cocaine collection point for the Labruzzo operation, right, Ramona?"

"I tell you, you let me go? I hide easy in town from Labruzzo."

"Hide, I'll help you get out of town with some money, say five thousand dollars?"

"Ten thousand, Ramona spill her guts."

"Might work. For starters, who's the top boss here?"

"Franco Rosales. Run office in El Centro."

Hawke moved closer. This might work out. He reached in his pocket and pulled out two loose hundred-dollar bills, then held them out to her.

"We're making progress."

She snatched up the bills and grinned. "Two hundred! You good guy, Brian."

"You ever seen Vito Labruzzo down here?"

"Last year. Not for long time now. Somebody else comes down."

She stepped closer. Her hand scratched her leg under her skirt.

"Now we're getting somewhere. How is the dope sent up to the States?"

"That easy. Airplane. Fast."

Without warning she pulled a knife from under her skirt and thrust it at Hawke. They were only three feet apart. The move caught Hawke by surprise, and he jolted back a step. She dived toward him, slashing with the knife.

It tore through cloth but missed skin, and she hit the concrete on her shoulder and tried to stop. Only the yawning drop-off was ahead of her. Ramona couldn't stop a half roll, and that put her over the edge. She screamed as she teetered a moment, then slipped over the rough concrete as Hawke grabbed for her foot.

She hit the hard ground thirty feet below on her head and shoulders with a deadly smack that cut off her wailing scream. Hawke didn't look over the side. He heard voices below as the workmen ran to the site. He hurried down the steps, went past a few workmen, and walked quickly to the street and back toward El Centro.

They knew he was here, and they wanted him dead. If he had agreed to go to bed with the little spitfire, he would be dead by now. Women assassins worked best naked.

What now? He'd go through every door on that third-floor hallway where he was before until he found Labruzzo's operation, and he'd bring it down around their heads. It all depended on the situation and the terrain. He grinned at the old military cliché. But it was a cliché because it was true.

Hawke had just climbed the steps to the second floor of the El Centro permanent building structure when he heard a roar behind him. He turned to see the Hook storming toward him. The big man's face was a mask of fury.

"You killed her!" he screamed, and raced toward Hawke, his hook held in front of him like a lance. Hawke put his hand around the revolver but kept it inside his pocket. He could point the gun at the big man without his knowing it.

Hawke turned to meet the angry man.

He didn't want to talk. The Hook did a "Pearl Harbor"— attacked without warning, hoping to eliminate his opponent with one telling blow.

Hawke sidestepped the battering thrust of the hook, then barely escaped from the second swing, a slashing move with the hook that would have torn Hawke's throat from his body.

There were too many people watching here. Hawke ran down the steps into the paper-strewn alley, seeing only a few drunks and small boys there.

The Hook attacked again as soon as Hawke stopped. This time the back side of the hook hit Hawke's left shoulder, numbing it. For a minute he couldn't raise his arm. The big man lifted the hook, ready to jerk the shiny point back into Hawke's chest.

Hawke fired through his jacket pocket. The round bored through Hook's left shoulder, and he roared in pain. Hawke fired again. This lead messenger was aimed to kill. It came up under his chin, blasted through the soft flesh into his mouth, through the roof and into his brain where the punchless .38-caliber slug spent itself, but not before it permanently turned off the power on the big man with the hook.

He jolted backward a step, then his eyes froze open, staring at Hawke, and he tumbled sideways into a dumpster.

His hook swung sideways, and the point was embedded in a six-by-six piece of lumber on the side of the building.

Hawke pulled his hat lower, turned, and walked through to the street, losing himself in the El Centro crowd. He paused inside a shop and turned the golf hat inside out so that it was blue. He did the same to his yellow jacket. When he came out of the shop, he had a blue jacket and cap, just in case anyone was searching for a tall gringo in a yellow coat.

Now he would charge back to the third-floor offices and see if he could root out the Labruzzo connection in Honduras.

Just before he started up the steps, someone touched him on the shoulder. When he looked around, Smith-Jones stood there grinning.

"Brian, I've been looking all over for you. Your stay in Honduras wouldn't be complete without meeting the Shooter. He's a Yank, a sometime friend of mine who said he wants to show you something. All you have to bring is an American M16 and plenty of ammo."

Chapter
Six

Hawke looked at the Englishman with surprise.

"I'll need an M16? What the hell are you talking about?"

"Defending yourself. This friend of mine, called the Shooter, works the back country. I'm not sure what he does, I don't ask. But he's out along the border quite a bit between Honduras and Nicaragua. It's not a friendly border. People shoot each other out there now and then. He says he wants to show you something. I think he has an idea you're a newspaperman or a writer or something. Whatever it is, should be wild."

"You have an M16 for me?"

Smith-Jones chuckled. "Matter of fact, I don't. But the Shooter can probably find a spare. I've got my jeep outside. He says the sooner we get out there, the better."

"How far is this place?"

"Forty, fifty miles. We go around this little mountain range and then up a valley toward Yuscaran. The border is close by."

"They still shooting at each other along there?"

"Now and then."

The paved road quickly disintegrated into gravel, then the road surged up across the other side of a mountain and the gravel was replaced by ruts the width of the jeeps' wheelbase.

Preston shifted to four-wheel-drive, and the rig crawled over the edge of the mountain, then down to the valley on the far side.

After three hours Hawke felt like he'd had his liver jarred right out of place, and that he'd lost his kidneys somewhere twenty miles back.

"How much further?" Hawke asked.

"We're getting there."

It was three more hours before they left the small town and snaked up a bulldozed road into the hills.

"Most of the border between the two countries is marked by the Coco River," Smith-Jones said. "It runs northeast and crosses more than ninety percent of the country. The part we're going to is almost at the start of the river, where the man-made border is more than a little uncertain and indistinct."

"In this wilderness, I can imagine. Are these jungles?"

"Close enough. Ah, the way station is just ahead. I's also the end of the line. I always bring the Shooter a bo of goodies when I come—beer, cigs, smoked fish. He says sometimes he lives off wild bananas for weeks at a time."

The road ended at an unpainted shack. It had been pounded together with whatever material was available. Smoke rose from the chimney.

"The bloke must be home."

Just as they stepped down from the jeep, six rounds of

automatic rifle fire slammed over their heads. Hawke hit the dirt. Smith-Jones looked down at him, laughing.

"You win, Shooter!" he called. "He hit the dirt proper."

A man came out of the shack with an M16, complete with the army issue M-203 grenade launcher nestled under the barrel. He was in his late twenties, six-four, with blond hair and a light-colored beard that could not be seen from a distance. He carried the rifle by the top handle and strode down the trail to the car with a big grin.

"Twenty bucks you owe me, Englishman." He looked at Hawke. "You must be this Brian guy I hear about. You don't do coke, but you pack a rod in Honduras. Some kind of guts. They catch you with a piece on you, it's good for ten years, no trial, no questions asked. If you can stand the rubber hoses, you stand a chance to get out in seven." He held out his hand. "Call me Shooter. Used to do the needle bit, but I'm clean and pure now. Security chief for this coffee plantation."

"Who the hell tries to steal coffee?" Smith-Jones asked.

Shooter grinned. "Some do. And other kinds of things." He looked back at Hawke. "Let's go on a hike. Ain't far, maybe five miles. You in shape?"

"We'll see. What we going to look at?"

"Surprise, Barlow. Damn big surprise. I didn't figure you came down here to this armpit of a nation just for the mineral water. You can't be running from the law. So, if you ain't interested in this, I'll just shit my pants."

"Will I need an M16 too?"

"Hope not. I only got one."

"You got rounds for that launcher?"

"We'll take six in a bib. You can pack 'em."

He went to the shack, came back with six candy bars and

an olive-drab "bib." It was an ammo pouch with a hole in it to fit over the head. The ammo carrier used extensively in 'Nam could hang in front or back.

Hawke looked inside. There were six 40-mm grenades, four HE and two WP. "Should take care of a platoon of dinks," Hawke said.

Shooter looked up. "Yeah, dinks, crispy critters, 'Nam. I missed it. Tried to get in when I was fifteen, but somebody squealed. My sister, I think. Fuckers jerked me right out of boot camp. Had one hell of a lot of fun before that. I loved the damned army. Okay, let's move. See you later on tonight, Pres, or tomorrow if you visit the hot stuff down in the village. Come to think of it, I've never known you to pass up that dusky poon down there when you could get it."

Without another word Shooter took off down a path through the light growth of the rolling Honduran hills that lay due south. The pine-covered hills seemed to go on, one after another. They walked past fields of tobacco that had been carved out of narrow valleys. More coffee groves, and now and then tall plants that looked vaguely familiar.

"Marijuana plants?" Hawke asked.

The Shooter shrugged. "Damned if I know. They ain't coffee or tobacco, I know that. They hire me to protect the coffee and tobacco."

Hawke thought he detected a little tongue-in-cheek tone, but he let it pass. Honduras was not a big producer of pot. This could be for local consumption. He was more interested in what the Shooter had out front.

Twice they heard rifle fire. Both times they hit the dirt and waited. Once there was a small firefight ahead, and some shouted words, but they were too faint for either man to understand.

"Locals get bored, so they try to work up a firefight now and then," Shooter said. "Almost nobody gets hit up here, mostly because they are lousy shots."

"Then the war is all politics?"

"Mostly." Shooter stopped and eased up to the crest of a hill on which dozens of young pine trees grew. Over the ridge they looked down on a valley.

"The locals call that *Valle de Oro*. No lie. There's lots of gold and silver left in Honduras, but no gumption to go out and get it. Right down there with a six-foot sluice, I could come up with at least five ounces a day. That's two thousand a day!"

"Big trouble is, that's also the headwaters of the Coco River, and the boundary between Honduras and Nicaragua."

The Shooter looked over at Hawke and grinned. "Hey, you want to live forever? Let's go take a look."

Hawke hesitated. "Don't they have security down there? Patrols, fire zones?"

"Naw, we'll be as safe as if we were home in our little beds." Shooter grinned and headed over the ridge and down through a thick stand of pine that ran almost to the river.

Hawke shook his head. Must be the gold. Gold fever could strike anyone. Just the thought of panning gravel and sand and coming up with gold dust and maybe a small nugget hooked almost every man who lived.

They came to the edge of the woods, and Shooter paused. "Now, friend, from here to them rocks we're in the open. Best if we rustle our asses across that thirty yards at a right smart pace. You savvy?"

"Exposed area, I get it," Hawke said. Before he could continue with his objection, Hawke watched Shooter lift up and charge ahead. Hawke went after him, and they both slid to a stop next to some eight-foot-tall slabs of rock that had been disgorged in some volcanic burp millions of years ago.

Just as they jolted to a stop behind the rock slabs, an automatic rifle blasted two six-round bursts into the rocks from the Nicaragua side.

Hawke looked at Shooter. "What the hell! Thought you said they didn't shoot much over here."

"Them guys get bored, they got to have some fun. No sweat, man. It can't get hairy unless both sides start to shoot at us at the same time."

He leaned around the rock and fired a seven-round burst from his M16 at the Honduran side, and then they both dived between the big slabs of rock that would give them protection from both sides of the gully.

A moment later, machine-gun fire blasted the rocks from both sides.

"Damn, but that gets them excited! Sounds like a good old-fashioned war out there, don't it?" Shooter's face had flushed; his eyes were bright, snapping; his breath came in gulps and gasps. Hawke figured his blood pressure and heartbeat were at the top end of the scale. This crazy loved being shot at!

"I hope they don't have mortars, or we're in a lot of trouble," Hawke said.

"Naw. They can't afford any heavy stuff like that. Grenades're about the biggest bang they can muster. Even those are carried only by the officers."

Rifle and machine-gun fire hit the rocks from both sides again.

The Shooter relaxed against a rock, and it was evident he'd done this before.

"Just how the hell do we get out of here? There's at least

thirty yards of open country before we get back to the pine forest, and enough cover to save our asses.''

"Relax," Shooter said. "It'll be dark in half an hour. Then we walk out like we're going to church. What I want to show you won't go down until after dark, anyway. They're a little sensitive about people shooting pictures.''

Shooter looked up. "You CIA?"

" I couldn't tell you if I were, could I, Shooter?"

"True. It's a possible. Were you in 'Nam?"

"Yeah, marines, two tours. I was just out of high school and gung-ho. Figure I did my part over there and lived to tell about it. Which means I was just dumb-ass lucky.''

Forty minutes later it was dark enough to move. They went around the nearest escape route. Every five minutes a machine gun blasted twenty rounds into the open spot between the rocks and the closest cover north. Hawke was glad they weren't on that path.

When they were in the pine forest and moving back up to the ridge line, Hawke was still mad at the crazy expatriate.

"I'd guess you've played that trick on more than one or two people," Hawke said.

Shooter nodded in the darkness. "Yeah, this is a lonely and damn boring job, so I like to do a pretend war once in a while. Makes it just a hell of a lot more fun to surprise some tenderfoot when they start blasting at us with live ammo.''

They hiked along the ridge, moving downstream, not making any noise, and staying in good cover.

An hour later the trail widened, and they moved with greater caution. Ahead, they heard an engine whine into life, but the headlights moved the same way they did.

Shortly before nine o'clock that evening, the Shooter called a halt. Less than a hundred yards ahead in the bright moonlight, they saw a small road that went down to the very edge of the Coco River. There had been a bridge there once.

Now trucks from the Honduras side rumbled down the road. Men and machines went to work. In the moonlight Hawke could see them throwing a bridge over the water. The span of the bridge wasn't more than thirty feet. Soon the spanners were in place. Squads of men quickly rolled out steel mats to form the roadway, and the truck and men withdrew.

"Now watch!" Shooter said.

A truck came out of the pine forest on the Nicaragua side, tested the roadway, then eased across the new bridge and drove to a cleared spot seventy-five yards from Hawke's hiding spot. Less than a minute passed before Hawke heard a chopper. It swept in, two signal fires were lit at the sides of the chopper pad, and the bird settled down.

Generators whirled into action, floodlights snapped on, and within a minute men started unloading packages from the truck and into the chopper.

"Cocaine and crack," the Shooter said. "Interested?"

"Damn right!" Hawke spat. He reached for the M16, checked to be sure the grenade launcher was lashed on right, then took out a high-explosive (HE) round from his bib and pushed it in the loading tube.

"You ready to haul ass?" Hawke asked.

"Ready when you are."

Hawke estimated the distance again, laid out the other five rounds in order—one more HE, then a white phosphorus, then two HE, and a final WP. He sighted in and fired.

The HE landed ten yards short of the truck but still sprayed the truck and some of the workers with shrapnel. There were shrill cries of pain and snapped orders. Gunfire exploded into the hills around the valley, but none came near them.

Hawke adjusted his sighting, loaded again, and fired the WP. It hit just short of the chopper, splattered the furiously burning WP all over the bird, and in minutes the helicopter gushed with flames.

Without waiting to watch, Hawke reloaded and fired two more HEs. By that time, the screaming below intensified. One officer ordered a squad of riflemen toward the suspected shooters.

Hawke's last WP landed directly under the truck that had come across the border, setting it on fire. Just then the fuel tanks on the chopper blew, and flaming aviation fuel turned an area thirty yards in diameter into a sea of fire.

Two men tried to run out of the flames. Hawke paused to watch. Their steps became shorter and shorter, until at last the fire storm sucked the last of the oxygen out of the air, seared their lungs, and the dead men toppled over in the fire, now little more than additional fuel.

Hawke shifted his sights to the men coming up the hill and fired a magazine of the 5.56-mm whizzers from the M16 rifle. When the magazine ran dry, he jumped up.

"Let's haul ass," he said.

Shooter had watched Hawke in awe from the first move he'd made to take the rifle from him. Then with each shot he got more and more excited.

"Christ! Now that was a war. We took incoming fire, and you shot back and blew up that truck and the fucking chopper and just everything!"

Hawke pushed him forward. "Yeah, and if you don't get your butt in gear, we're gonna be two more corpses for somebody to count. Let's move!"

They ran back up the ridge, mostly moving west. The sounds of shouts from behind them became weaker, and at last they could hear them no more.

"Who do you think was chasing us, Honduran or Nicaraguan troops?" Shooter asked, his voice still high and charged with excitement.

"Both, probably. Did I see right back there? The two sides called off the war long enough for a load of cocaine to be delivered across the border and picked up in an official Honduras military chopper?"

"You saw right. It looked like cocaine in those packages, and it was. Two kilos to a bundle. I got real close one night, just to make sure. Happens every two months or so. From what I can tell, some general uses an army chopper and an engineering outfit to put in the bridge. Then they take it out and wait until next time. There's a good-sized exchange of money, too, I'd be damned sure."

"We shortstopped them once, at least," Hawke said. "This going to mean any trouble for you?"

"Hell, no. That isn't even my area. I work six miles to the other side of the mountain."

By the time they got back to the shack, it was nearly midnight. The jeep wasn't there, so Hawke stayed overnight. His accommodations included a bunk made of two logs, strung with electric cord across the logs to form the springs and a sleeping bag. He was surprised by how comfortable it was.

Hawke and the Englishman arrived back in Tegucigalpa the next morning before noon. Smith-Jones said he had to go directly to his office to get a shipment ready for Dallas. Hawke tagged along. As he sat in Smith-Jones's office, where the Englishman had left him, Hawke was trying to figure out how to get into the El Centro Labruzzo offices without shooting his way in or waiting for darkness.

If Vito Labruzzo wasn't here, where was he? The crack king had to be working on his supply route. Everyone he had talked to so far about Labruzzo was a company person: Gina, the hit "man" Ramona, even Hook. They would lie right down the line.

Hawke speculated that Vito could be in Honduras working on his supply pipeline. Or he could be in Colombia tying down a supply. Either way it was a good bet that the crack king would use his El Centro facilities for shipping.

It was all speculation, but it was damned logical. And it meant that Hawke's next move would have to be a quiet entry after dark into the Labruzzo offices in El Centro.

Hawke looked at the magazine Smith-Jones had left him with. Preston said to hang tough there for an hour or so, and he'd be ready for a great lunch just after siesta.

The magazine was a Spanish edition of *Playboy*. The girls were all at least partly draped, but the photography was artless. Hawke paced the office for a minute, then pushed through a door through which he had seen Smith-Jones vanish. He found a big warehouse, with a loading dock to one side. In back were racks and racks of metal gas-turbine fan blades, all arranged according to the engine maker and the size of the blade.

At a bench on the far side, he saw Smith-Jones and two men working over a four-foot-high wooden crate. They carefully inserted two foot-long turbine blades into slots cut in wooden crosspieces to protect the sensitive air pushers.

Hawke approached the men who were so involved in packing the crate that they didn't notice him. He frowned as he saw the last blade fitted in, then two brown-wrapped packages pushed down past the blades in the box.

He got closer and stepped behind a stack of the wooden shipping boxes and waited.

"Bring two more," Smith-Jones told one of the men helping him. The Honduran man went to a room down the line and walked inside. A minute or two later he came back with two more of the brown-wrapped packages.

One more turbine blade was fitted in the wooden crate, then Smith-Jones took the foot-long packages and placed them in the bottom of the crate and taped them down solidly. Then Hawke made the connection. The brown paper around the packages was identical to the brown paper he had seen the day before around the kilo of cocaine in Preston Smith-Jones's closet at the hotel.

He was smuggling cocaine to Dallas in his engine-blade boxes.

Hawke drew the .38 and remembered that he had only four more rounds. He moved up to within ten feet of the three men getting ready to strap the cover on the box.

"Hold it," Hawke said. "Take that last bundle out of the box, Preston. Do it now."

"Now wait a minute, old man. That's personal, private business. You've got no right."

"We'll see how much right I have. Take out the goddamn package!"

Reluctantly Smith-Jones pulled out the brown-wrapped package and threw it at Hawke. He let it fall to the floor and bent, watching the Englishman.

"Nice little operation. Customs probably doesn't even bother to unstrap the boxes of blades going through on a quick turnaround.'' Hawke sliced open the package with his knife and saw the white powder.

Smith-Jones charged him. Hawke shot him in the right knee and saw him go down. "*Vamos,*" he told the two workers. They scurried out the side door without even looking back.

"I wondered how you got so much cocaine in that candy dish," Hawke said. "You bought it cheap and made millions."

"Bastard! You ruined my knee! I might never walk again!"

"I'd say you have figured that one out. Did I tell you that druggers like you tortured my wife for three days until she finally died? Did I tell you that they slashed her body everywhere but her face, so she bled for three days before she passed out from loss of blood and died minutes later? I guess I didn't.

"Did I tell you that I'm on a one-man vendetta against all drug dealers, jobbers, suppliers, shippers . . . everywhere? You fit the pattern. I hope you have a good partner on the other end who knows nothing about the dope."

"Yes! Yes! Willy is clean. He'd have a heart attack if he knew. One of my men takes each incoming shipment and slips out the goods before anyone else sees them. My partner is blameless."

Smith-Jones sat on the concrete floor. Tears seeped down his face, which was distorted with pain. He tired to hold his bleeding knee together

"I don't imagine you're going to call an ambulance."

"Not a chance. Where's all of your goods?"

"In the office. Big safe in there that's open. If you're hunting Vito Labruzzo, he hasn't been down here for six months. The word is that he's sick."

"Somebody told me he was in Italy."

"He wishes. He's a sick old man."

"He's older than you'll ever get. Who do you contact in Colombia for your goods?"

"Why should I tell you?"

"You still have another knee and two elbows."

Smith-Jones's eyes went wide. He groaned as another wave of pain shunted through him from his knee. He nodded.

"All right. My contact is the Grasshopper. He's a man in Bogota with many connections. Some people say he's the richest man in the world."

"He deals only in cocaine and crack cocaine?"

"What else does he need?"

"When I get through with him, he's going to need a priest."

Hawke shot Preston Smith-Jones in the forehead. The force of the round slammed him backward. He died before he hit the concrete.

Hawke went to the big wooden boxes. It took him an hour to open and take out the four kilos of cocaine from each of the boxes. In the front office he found a small bathroom for the owner. He carried the cocaine in, slashed each package, and emptied it out in the shower stall. The cold water kept melting the poison down the drain a bag at a time.

There were twenty packages. He melted down over forty kilos of cocaine—about four million dollars' worth on the street. It probably had cost Smith-Jones a million to buy in Colombia.

He went through the records in the office. Most were legitimate. He left them undisturbed. It took him another hour to find the hiding place. It was a false bottom in a window seat. The lid lifted, and inside was storage for office supplies. Under them was a foot-tall space built halfway into the foundation.

Most drugs are paid for by cash at all levels. Since banking large amounts of cash in almost any nation causes the person trouble, large amounts of cash are usually hidden around safe houses, and the smuggler's digs.

Hawke found two suitcases in a closet, and packed the stacks of U.S. currency and Honduran lempira into both bags. There was no easy way to get the money out of the country. Customs would find it in a moment. Outside, he hailed a taxi and told the driver to take him to the closest Catholic church. It turned out to be a poor parish near the business district.

Hawke climbed out of the cab, gave the driver a two-lempira tip, and carried the suitcases into the front door of the church. He found a nun, who smiled and said she could take him to the parish priest.

He was middle-aged, a mestizo, mixed Indian and white blood, as more than ninety-percent of Hondurans are. He watched Hawke, curious and smiling.

"What can I do for you, my son?" he asked in Spanish.

"You can take a great problem off my hands, Father. Can we go into your office?"

The priest lifted his brows, nodded, and led the way. Hawke carried the two suitcases and put them down on the priest's big desk.

"*Presente, padre,*" Hawke said. He opened one suitcase and showed the priest the money. The long-suffering cleric's eyes widened, then he sat down in his chair.

"Why? I don't understand."

"You don't need to understand, padre. It's yours to do with as you like. Bad men owned it. My only requirement is that you keep it here, do not put it in any bank, and use it only for good for your parish, sharing it with every poor family."

The priest couldn't stop the tears. He came and hugged Hawke, then shook his hand. He put down the top of the suitcase, covering the money before he walked Hawke back to the church door. When Hawke looked back, the stunned, delighted padre still stood watching his surprise benefactor. Hawke figured there was more than two million dollars in the suitcases. It should last the poor parish a long time.

Hawke walked around Tegucigalpa as he waited for darkness. He ate, bought some new clothes, rented a room at a small hotel, and took a shower. He put on the new clothes and threw away everything he had worn before to make it harder for Labruzzo's killers to spot him.

He abandoned the flight bag and clothing he had left in Preston Smith-Jones's room. There was nothing in it to identify him or tie him in any way to the Englishman.

"Grasshopper," he said softly as he planned his upcoming trip to Bogota, Colombia, the source of ninety percent of the cocaine that came into the U.S. That was where the traffic had to be stopped.

He walked through El Centro just after dark. The place was deserted. He was not sure if there were any night guards on duty. At the third-floor offices of El Centro, he found the windows dark. A set of picks provided easy entry through a locked door. Inside, he looked for alarms but found none. The outer office was dark. He used a pen light he had bought earlier and checked the other rooms. Nowhere did he find any narcotics. He found no record of any narcotics shipments.

There were records of the Labruzzo Fresh Fish Company. All of the shipments were by air or by boat. He took a list of large oceangoing freighters that had carried the Labruzzo "fish."

Hawke slipped out the door and went to his hotel. In the morning he would fly to Bogota and find the Grasshopper.

Chapter
Seven

Hawke had no trouble at the Tegucigalpa airport. He bought a ticket for the morning flight to Bogota. The distance was a few miles less than to Miami, and they made one stop in Panama before continuing. At the airport in Honduras he had kept in groups of people. He tried never to be alone to give a hit man a shot.

Hawke saw no one he had seen before, but any agent from the Labruzzo clan would be a stranger to him. He was relieved when he got on the flight, and again when he got off safely in Bogota.

This time he had no tourist's booklet. He knew Colombia was Spanish-speaking, that there was intense coca-leaf growing in the mountains, and that most of the processing of the coca leaves for all of South America was done in Colombia.

He knew that big drug money had practically taken over the political and judicial systems of Colombia. Jurists who tried to crack down on drug czars were shotgunned to death on the streets. Politicians looking for monetary support had quickly lined up behind lax law enforcement dealing with cocaine.

It was a vicious circle. The more money the drug runners made, the more they had to use for bribes and "fixes" with police, politicians, and the military.

Hawke found Bogota a much more modern city than those in Honduras. The city's economy was obviously booming, Hawke figured, due to the cocaine profits. Money seemed to flow everywhere.

A few minutes later he registered at the best hotel in town, the Casa Colombia. After a quick shower and a change of clothes, he went to the bar and heard a lot of English being spoken.

It took him a half hour and two beers to find the man he wanted. He was a foreign correspondent for the Chicago *Tribune* who had been covering Colombia for ten years.

Hawke bought drinks for both of them and listened to the man, Alex Contreras, who spoke Spanish like a native and liked rum and cola.

"This country is heading straight down the road to absolute chaos, destruction, and anarchy," Alex said over his drink. "Hell, ten years ago there was a lot of cocaine pumped through here, but it was low-profile, underground, smuggled out. And law enforcement, while not excellent, did a pretty good job at trying to stop it. Not so anymore."

"How much more goes out now?" Hawke asked.

"Twenty, fifty, maybe two or three hundred times as much. It's damn big business, and it's controlled by three or four huge syndicates who call the tune. Somebody starts up a new processing plant for the coca paste without the approval of the syndicates, it gets burned out and anybody there is gunned down with Uzi submachine guns."

"What does the government do?"

"*Do*? Like any government, it tries to stay in power and live off the graft, the bribes that they take on almost every level. That means the cop on the beat and right up to the President himself. I'm convinced that this is the most corrupt government in power today anywhere in the world."

"That bad?" Hawke probed.

The reporter's glass was empty. Hawke signaled for another one. By now Hawke drank straight cola.

"Look at what our illustrious *Presidente* did. The great President Virgilio Barco Vargas. He said he was declaring war on the narcotics trafficking after a prominent Bogota newspaper editor was slaughtered in the street by thugs. The editor had the nerve to criticize the drug bosses.

"Now, a year after the president's 'crackdown,' there is twice the cocaine flowing out of Colombia as before! The whole antidrug campaign has been stopped dead by the cash the druggers throw around and the violence they are not afraid to use if money can't buy the official they need."

"This has happened in other countries," Hawke said.

"Not like it has here. Soon cocaine will be seventy-five percent of the total export of this nation. That, even though the possession, processing, and sale of cocaine is against the law. Now the court system has made decisions to protect from extradition to the United States the prominent drug kings. Warrants and extradition requests here from the U.S. are no good."

"You say there is a syndicate here in Bogota that controls most of the action?"

"All of it, ninety-nine percent of the export goes through the big three. They cooperate, even help supply each other when one source might dry up. They control things with an absolute iron fist.''

''Didn't I hear something about a judge down here?''

''Judge Delamba. He approved an extradition request by the U.S. for one Carlos Estrada. Estrada was wanted in Miami for murder, arson, and drug trafficking. Two hours after Judge Delamba signed the extradition order, he walked out to his car in the parking lot where he and his driver were riddled by four blasts of double-ought buck from two shotguns. They had to sew those two back together with staples to get them in caskets. The next day another judge rescinded the extradition order.''

''You're telling me that these guys don't mess around.''

''These guys make the Mafia organization look like kindergarten kids swiping lunch money from little girls.''

It was nearly six o'clock by then. Hawke asked if he could take the reporter to dinner, and Alex grinned and said fine. They walked two blocks to a moderate-priced restaurant, and Alex ordered for both of them. Two drinks later Alex was still on a roll about the drug bosses in Bogota.

''What about a guy called the Grasshopper?'' Hawke asked.

Alex looked up at him, his eyes widening, and finished the rest of his drink. Their dinners arrived at the table. Alex motioned Hawke closer and barely whispered.

''The Grasshopper is also known as El Cigarron, which means grasshopper in Spanish. He's the most vicious, most deadly man I've ever seen. He's highly excitable, flies into rages if anyone questions him. He's been in the business since he used to be a mule in the backcountry, carrying the coca paste out of the hills and running it to the processing plant.

"The Grasshopper is the junior member of the big three who run the whole operation called the Medellin Cartel. Right now he's probably worth more than five billion dollars. Owns half of Bogota and rents the rest. He has more personal residences and apartments than anyone can count, with a mistress in each one. He went through only the fourth grade, can barely write his name, and can't even read a newspaper.

"He's personally killed more than a hundred men, and some women, who crossed him in his rise to power. He's the best man to stay away from in the whole country."

When he finished, Alex began eating his dinner and picked up his coffee. He sipped it, looking over the top of it out of sad brown eyes.

"Don't mess up. I knew a guy down here who decided he'd do a factual book on the Grasshopper. He was a reporter for *The New York Times*. I told him to keep the idea quiet, maybe do some research but all on the sly. Then go back to the States to write the exposé. He didn't.

"Three days later they asked me to identify him. He had been run over by a macadam roller, one of those big ones that squashes down hot mix. He had been smashed between six tons of steel and a concrete street. His gold pocket watch survived, and they said that was enough to identify his body. They scraped his half-inch-thick remains off the concrete with grain shovels."

"Sounds pretty grim."

"Worse than grim. I seldom write a story about drugs anymore. If I do, it's noncritical, fairly benign. It's old news, and besides, I want to stay alive. It's good advice for anyone who wants to stay in Colombia long."

He hit the drink again and looked up.

"The experts say that more than eighty percent of the world's cocaine is refined in clandestine labs here in Colombia. It comes from coca paste and coca base smuggled in from Peru and Bolivia, where most of the coca plantations are.

"These guys are so powerful that they control the business from small airstrips in Peru's upper Huallaga River Valley and Bolivia's Chapare region. They work the goods here to Colombia, turn it into crack or powdered cocaine, and then run it all the way to the distribution points on American street corners."

"I got the picture. So how do I find this Grasshopper guy?"

Alex stared in amazement. "You haven't heard a word of my warning, have you?"

"I've heard every damn word of it. Two months ago a Colombian drugger and two from San Diego tortured my wife for three days before she finally died. The Mafia calls it making somebody into turkey meat. I killed all three of the bastards who tortured my wife, Connie.

"I don't care if I walk away from this town or not. Before I leave or get buried here, the drug bosses are going to know that I've been hitting them. You can be damn sure that I'll take as many of the big shots with me as I can."

"Good God! You're serious! These men have armies of security around them. They can spend a million dollars a month on security and protection and never even notice it. It's like trying to blast your way into Fort Knox with a water pistol."

Alex held out his hand across the table. Hawke grasped it.

"I want to shake your hand while you're still alive. You're either the stupidest man I've ever met, or the bravest." He took a deep breath, polished his glasses, and stared at Hawke again.

"I would guess that Brian Barlow is not the first name that you've used."

"Correct. It's the name on my passport."

Alex started to reach for his drink, then pushed it away. He was suddenly totally sober. "Christ, I should have my head examined. The first time you make any kind of a move against any one of them, there will be a network out that won't quit." He lowered his voice. "My suggestion is to keep a low profile. Play tourist or buyer of coffee or something benign. Then, if you can strike at one of them, do it fast and be on an airplane less than an hour later."

Alex shook his head. "Christ, now I know I'm loony. Is there any way I can talk you out of this strange form of suicide?"

"Not unless you can bring my wife, Connie, back alive and sparkling the way she used to—"

Alex held up his hands.

"All right. The easiest one would be the Grasshopper. He lives in a beautiful former hotel just off Benedicto Park. He took it over, rebuilt it into his own palace. He holds court there and drives around in armored limousines—two Caddies and a Lincoln.

"He isn't social. Doesn't try to put on a cultural front the way the other two do. He's a thug and knows it. Money can't turn a mule into a thoroughbred racehorse."

"Thanks. I won't talk to you again, so I don't involve you any more than I already have. Now, one more bit of help, then I'll vanish. I need a good, reliable underground arms dealer. I don't even have a water pistol."

Alex Contreras groaned. "You're really trying to get

yourself killed. The penalty for possession of a concealed weapon in Colombia is ten years. No appeal, no defense, no trial. A quick hearing and off to the slammer."

"I can't go after them without some hardware."

"That's not my usual beat." He stood and walked to the bar and back, then sat down in the booth again. "You're dead set on getting yourself killed?"

"If I have to. I'm going to get to this guy one way or another. If I have the right tools, it will be easier and safer for me."

Alex wiped his hands over his face, peering out from one eye.

"What the hell. If some bastards cut up my wife . . ." Alex nodded. "I have to make a phone call to check on a guy I talked with two or three years ago. Have another cola, I'll be right back."

Ten minutes later they drove in Alex's Volkswagen down a crooked little street deep in the poor section of Bogota. Alex knew the town like the inside of his shirt pocket. He had splashed mud over half of his license plate, and wore a slouch hat that covered most of his face. He drove past the few streetlights quickly.

At last he nosed into an alley and stopped. They walked halfway down it. Alex made sure no one was looking, then he pulled Hawke into a doorway and into the back of a building.

They went along a dimly lit hallway to steps, then down to a basement. At the first door Alex knocked. A peephole opened, and a moment later the door swung wide.

A small, thin man stood there in a white T-shirt and military fatigue pants. He wore glasses and stared at Hawke critically.

There was a gush of Spanish between the man and Alex that went too quickly for Hawke to follow, but it was pleasant talk, the haven't-seen-you-in-months kind.

Alex did not introduce them.

"My friend needs some personal protection and perhaps other devices. I'll leave him with you. He's a good friend. Treat him as you would me."

"Alex, thanks," Hawke said, shaking his hand.

"Do me a favor, gringo. Stay alive." Alex hurried out the door.

For an underground arms dealer, this one's stock was limited. But this was Colombia. He had six pistols, two rifles, one hand grenade, and a quarter of a pound of American C-3 plastic explosive.

"This is all you have?" Hawke asked.

"For these weapons I would not go to prison if I was caught. I would be killed trying to escape. The authorities are making a big show of cracking down on illegal weapons, which means anything that uses gunpowder. Of course, they don't touch the drug bastards."

Hawke selected a well-used U.S. Army Colt .45 ACP 1911. It was worn but functioned perfectly. He got two extra magazines and a box of fifty rounds of standard ammunition. It looked fairly new.

He took the C-3 as well.

"Fuses, detonators?" Hawke asked.

He had only one, which he kept on the other side of the room from the C-3. It was an impact-type detonator. When he asked the man how much the items were, he figured on a pad of paper for a moment.

The peso was the monetary unit here. Hawke had none.

The most recent exchange rate was about two hundred pesos to a dollar.

"Seventeen thousand pesos," the dealer said.

Hawke could figure that one in his head, eight hundred and fifty dollars. At least fifty percent too much, but he was in no bargaining position. He took out the greenbacks, turned around, and peeled off nine of the hundreds. When he gave the money to the man, he frowned for a moment.

"That's nine hundred U.S. dollars, worth at least eighteen thousand pesos," Hawke said. "Close enough." Hawke put the detonator in his shirt pocket, the block of C-3 in one jacket pocket, and the .45 in the other. The small, dark man showed him to the alley, where Alex stood smoking.

"Figured I better get you back to the hotel or you might never make it. Took me five years not to get lost in this town. Nearly five million here now. That's a lot of bodies."

As they drove, Alex shook his head. "No, don't tell me what you bought. I don't want to know. Nothing illegal about my taking you to a friend's place of business.

"Christ! Best story I hit in a year, and I can't write it. I called San Diego while I waited. Christ! They really want to talk to you. They're up to their asses in warrants on you."

"I remember something about that."

"This lady records cop said you were a legend in that area. Said you took on the druggers the cops couldn't touch and just blew them away, burned them down, blasted them with a .45. She said they call you the Avenger."

"Newspapers started that."

"Christ, best damn story in my life, and I can't write it."

"Send it in without a byline."

"Yeah, but I'm the only reporter down here from my paper. I'd be dead meat by noon."

"See what happens. I might strike out."

"Not with your batting record. She said you were in Houston raising hell as well."

"Yeah."

They were back at the hotel parking lot where Alex kept his car.

"Thanks for the help. What's your phone number? Next time I'll phone you. Are they tapped here?"

"Doubt it. I'm in Room 604. That's the number."

Hawke thanked him and went in the hotel by the side door and up to his room. First he hid the explosives and the pistol and ammo. Then he had a shower and dropped on the bed. He needed a good night's sleep. Tomorrow was for recon and for laying out his attack plan on the Grasshopper.

Hawke's phone rang at five-thirty the next morning. He finally found it and mumbled into the receiver.

"Wake up, Cowboy. This is Alex. I got a night wire from my boss. He wants an in-depth story on the little guy in the drug trade. The legal types here who never break a law. That's the peasants who strip the leaves off the coca tree and sell it to feed the kids. Want to go on a run into the high country with me?"

"Is the Pope Polish?"

"Meet me in the café downstairs in fifteen minutes. You don't even have to shave, we're going informal. Got any jeans? A pair of boots would be good. Might have some hiking to do."

They left the hotel shortly before seven that morning, and Alex had the café pack them a noontime lunch: sandwiches, fruit, and beer.

They drove west out of the city, and soon the road narrowed and they were climbing into the sky.

"The Andes," Alex said. "There are some very tall mountains around here. One a little to the north is over seventeen thousand feet."

Two hours later Alex parked in a small village. There were only four houses and a tiny store. Hawke had been seeing trees all the way up the mountain. Most were scrubby, twelve to fifteen feet tall, and bushy. In places they had been planted in long rows, closely spaced. They seemed to thrive on the poor mountain soil

"Welcome to El Timano, population fourteen, altitude about twelve thousand feet. Don't try to run very far or you'll be gasping for oxygen. It's a bit thin up here, but the coca trees love it. That's where it all starts, right there."

He indicated a tree that had been stripped bare of its leaves. Right beside it was one filled with leaves.

A woman came out the door of one of the houses, built partly with sawed lumber and partly native stone six feet up from the ground. The woman was about thirty, with dark skin and brown hair under a scarf. She waved at Alex and held up a chicken.

He ran to her and hugged her, twirling her around until she dropped the chicken, which ran off squawking, thankful for its life.

Alex laughed at something the woman had said, then came and introduced her to Hawke. Her name was Maria Folores.

"She wanted to have a chicken for our dinner, but I told her no, she had to sell the chicken in town to buy clothes for the *niños*."

Four children ran out of the house and grouped around

Alex, their big brown eyes wide with hope, sly smiles showing. He gave each of them a candy bar, and they ran off shrieking and squealing.

"Kids up here don't get candy, almost never. They'll make that one candy bar last for at least a week."

Maria waved at them, and they followed her. She carried a small cloth bag with a piece of wire holding open the top. At the second coca tree in the line, which still had leaves, she began stripping off the oval-shaped greenish-brown leaves and dropping them in the bag, which now was tied to her waist. She stripped all the leaves off the branches.

When the bag was filled, she emptied it out into a three-foot-tall woven wicker basket that sat next to the trunk.

"Do this whole tree," Maria said. She picked up the wicker basket and carried it to an open place where a large canvas had been spread out on the ground. She dumped the coca leaves from the filled basket on the canvas and spread them out.

"Dry in the sun," she said. "Every three months take leaves from tree and dry."

"How many trees do you have?" Hawke asked.

"Only a few—twenty, maybe."

"When the leaves are all dry, what happens to them?" Hawke asked.

She led them to a small shed where she had large brown bags full of coca leaves. The leaves were dried brown and crisp.

Maria popped two into her mouth and chewed.

"You chew?" she asked. "Make you feel all peppy, full of energy."

Hawke shook his head.

"Leaves all legal," Maria said. "We sell them to a mule, who picks them up and takes them to his house. Alex show you where."

Back at the car, Hawke rummaged around in the lunch box and pulled out a can of beer. He handed it to Maria. She looked at it and giggled.

"Enjoy your beer," he told her, and they drove down the mountain. Five miles back toward the city, they turned off at a small village of thirty houses. It had two stores. At the end of the lane stood a house that was better than the rest. It was larger, newly painted.

Alex stopped and honked twice, then twice more. A man came around the far side of the house holding a shotgun.

"Ah, Alex. Much time between your visits."

"This time I want pictures," Alex said. "Oh, Bacilia, this is my friend Brian, from *Estados Unidos*."

They shook hands.

"Brag to me how well you're doing, Bacilia," Alex said.

The short, slender Colombian led them to the back of his house where a new aluminum-roofed building stood. They went through the door, and Hawke saw that the floor of the building was filled with metal pans six inches deep and three feet square. Some were empty, others had a disintegrating mass of leaves in them, and some had nothing but an inch of colorless fluid.

The odors that assaulted him were fierce. Alex did a double take and then held his breath.

Bacilia laughed. "It is the smell of success, my friends. I pick up the coca leaves from families all over the hills, the little ones who have twenty to fifty trees. In my pickup I bring the leaves here. They are bulky, light, hard to carry, very many.

"Here I pour kerosene over the leaves. Soon the leaves dissolve and what's left is called coca paste. Maybe fifty pounds of leaves makes one pound of paste. Easier to transport."

He showed them some of the paste, which was about the consistency of peanut butter but a dull gray-brown.

"Stays wet, so I wrap it in heavy plastic and sell it to the processing plant or to a buyer for the plant. Very good work. All the poor people in the hills make money, I make money, everyone happy."

"Don't you ever think about the people who use the crack and cocaine?" Hawke asked. "This stuff winds up ruining lives and killing people."

Bacilia shrugged. "The man who makes a knife cannot be blamed if someone uses it to kill."

"It isn't that simple," Hawke said.

Bacilia moved the shotgun in his hands. "To Bacilia it is that simple. Maria, up the mountain, makes ten times as much money now as when she and her husband both dug potatoes for a living. Then they half starved and had no money for clothes. Now they eat well, are dressed, are warm in the winter, and even save a little money."

As they talked, Alex shot pictures of the pans, the packages.

"No face pictures," Bacilia said.

"But in the States this stuff is killing people, ruining lives, putting people in prison." Hawke paused. "What you're doing right there is illegal in Colombia, right?"

"Yes, but it is accepted. I am a very small—how do you say?—small fish."

"But I would net you if I could."

"Then fifty, sixty families in this area would be without any income. You would ruin our cash crop."

"Tough shit!" Hawke snapped, and walked out of the processing shed.

He waited for Alex in the car.

Alex got in a few minutes later and put his camera away.

"That's the end of the tour. I have no contacts any higher on the chain. I'd like to get into a processing plant, a refinery or laboratory, whatever they call them.

"I know the process, just never seen it. The paste is taken, and chemists add several compounds to it and cook it for a few hours. This concentrates the mixture more. At this point they call it coca base.

"The base is washed, strained, and treated with hydrochloric acid and acetone. Then it is dried in an oven. At this point it comes out as a grayish crystal. Last couple of years, they've been selling some of it that way—crack. It's one step from being finished powdered cocaine, so it's cheaper.

"The rest of the goods are powdered, then bleached to a pure white and ready for sale."

Hawke hit the dashboard with his hand. "So it all starts out 'innocent' and 'legal' up there in the hills, and before it's done, it's killing judges and policemen and pushers and thousands of cokeheads way up north in the States."

"That's about the size of it. I got a request for a story about the innocent beginnings. You've seen it, right down to the paste, where it changes from 'innocent' to 'illegal.' "

"I almost wish I hadn't gone. No, I'm glad I saw it. It's all part of the same cancer, and I'm going to do what I can to make it less profitable. If we could take the profit out of cocaine, the supply would dry up overnight. Why try to smuggle the stuff into the States if it sells for a dollar an ounce instead of three thousand dollars an ounce?''

''But how can that happen?''

''It can't, not with the current demand. They could charge ten times as much if they wanted to. It's a monopoly, with the price controlled at the point where they think it's as high as people can afford, yet high enough for outrageous profits for them. Damn!''

They ate their lunch as they drove back. On the outskirts of Bogota they found a small restaurant and had dinner well off the beaten path. After that Hawke caught a cab to the hotel so he wouldn't be seen with the reporter again.

On the way he asked the driver to go around the park where the Grasshopper lived. Hawke asked the driver to stop at the edge of the park, just across from the Grasshopper's big mansion. It was only four stories high but nearly half a block square. Lots of room for protection inside there. He wouldn't have a chance breaking in.

He sat staring at the mansion for a while, then asked the driver to move on. Just as they drove past the place for the last time, a woman came out the big front doors and was escorted by the doorman into a waiting stretch limousine.

Hawke had to look carefully, but then he was sure who the girl was. Slender, short, with dark hair and a pert Italian face. She was Gina, from the Labruzzo family office in Miami. What the hell was she doing in Bogota?

Chapter
Eight

Hawke stared in surprise at the stretch limo that carried Gina away from the Grasshopper's mansion. What was a girl from the Labruzzo family business in Miami doing in Bogota?

It was obvious: She was setting up a drug deal, to buy for the Labruzzo pushers.

Gina was more than a secretary to Vito Labruzzo—Don Labruzzo!

"Driver, see that limo up there, the light blue one? Follow it but stay three cars in back."

"No, no! That's a Grasshopper car. I might get machine-gunned."

Hawke pushed a hundred-dollar bill across the front seat. The driver grabbed it. "Five cars back. I won't lose it, but I don't want him to see my license number."

"Lose him and I'll kill you myself."

The cabbie sweated but stayed with the big car, which was in no rush. It meandered through the downtown section, then stopped at the same hotel where Hawke stayed, Casa Colombia. Gina got out and went in.

Hawke ran up the steps right behind her, and when she started for the elevators, he cut her off at the pass, bumping into her gently.

"Oh, *me siento*," he said.

She looked up in anger for a moment, then grinned.

"Yeah, I bet you are. Hawke, what are you doing in Bogota?"

"Following you. I still want to take you out to dinner."

"Some guys just can't take a slap in the chops for a no."

"I'm a glutton for punishment. What are you doing in Bogota?"

"Business. I work for a worldwide company, remember? Labruzzo International has interests here. Mr. Labruzzo sends me down here now and then. I'm a management specialist."

"I'm on vacation. Trying to hit the capital cities of all thirteen South American nations. I'm up to four."

She watched him from deep brown eyes that he couldn't read. Her smile was tentative, and her snub of a nose twitched once. She wore a sleek, form-fitting light green dress.

"I like your dress," he said.

A quick smile broke through her formal one. "Thanks. Since you're on vacation, maybe I'll see you around. You staying here too?"

"Right. When I'm on vacation, I go first-class. Afterward it's back to beans and peanut butter."

She laughed, waved, and moved on to the elevators.

He still didn't know her last name.

Hawke went to the room clerk. He explained his position.

He had just seen this beautiful girl in the lobby who was registered there, an American with the first name of Gina.

The room clerk took the U.S. five-dollar bill and smiled.

"Ah, an affair of the heart. I remember Gina. From a very good family. Just a moment." He went to his computer and in a few moments came back.

"Yes, I have the information." He waited.

Hawke dug out a twenty-dollar bill and slid it across the counter. The room clerk took it and grinned.

"Her last name is Labruzzo, Gina Labruzzo, and she is in Suite 404. A most attractive young lady."

"Thanks." Hawke walked toward the elevators. Labruzzo! She wasn't just a secretary. She must be a daughter of one of the brothers, or maybe the wife of one of the sons? She wasn't wearing rings. If she had them, she would wear wedding rings.

A Labruzzo! This put a new twist on the whole damn picture.

By the time he got to his room, it was a little after seven and getting dark outside. It was too late to do anything about the Grasshopper that night. He had ruled out any break-in. Too risky, and he was sure the Grasshopper had bought the best gunmen on the continent to protect him.

His money would buy all kinds of electronic listening and warning devices. The place would be like trying to break into a missile silo.

Hawke turned on the television and was surprised when Spanish came out of it. He looked again and saw the Fall Guy up to his usual Hollywood tricks, only this time from his mouth came Spanish. Dubbed. He'd even seen that episode. He snapped it off, checked his new .45, which he left in the room.

At last he went down to the bar to see if Alex was there. Hawke had a beer and made it last. There were several groups speaking English. Alex had his head near a blonde at a far table. A waiter brought a note to Hawke. He read it but held it under the table top.

"Batista," the note said. "Young kid in the Hawaiian shirt. You should meet him." It was not signed. Hawke looked over at Alex, who was watching him. Alex nodded and went back to the blonde.

There was only one person in the bar wearing a Hawaiian shirt. He was maybe five-ten, slight, with a full beard that was closely trimmed. Hawke watched the two others he was with, and when the party broke up, Hawke moved toward him.

"Batista?" he said when the man looked his way.

"Yes, suh. One name good as any. What can I do you outa?"

The Southern drawl was natural, not put on. Hawke held out his hand.

"Name is Barlow, Brian Barlow, from San Diego."

"Yes, suh. Batista, Buddy Batista. We're both a pair of BB's."

"Buy you a drink?"

Ten minutes later they had broken through the first fumbling-around conversation.

"Buddy, the locals think I'm here to buy coffee. Actually I'm trying to learn as much about this country as I can. A friend of mine said I should meet you, that you are in an interesting line of work, and that you could show me something most people can't about Colombia."

"Damn right. If I wanted to." He finished the beer and signaled for another one. Then he scowled and studied

Hawke. "You sure ain't no CIA man, or a fed law officer. Hell, they ain't got no extradition treaty worth a shit down here anymore, anyway."

He gulped at the new beer, wiped his mouth, and nodded. "Yeah, there's a sheriff back up in Texas who would like to get his mitts on me. It was only a little damn argument—I popped the guy a couple and he goes down, has a heart attack and dies, and they try to stick me with murder.

"Shit! A man can't even defend hisself no more. So I came down here as a permanent tourist. Run out of bread and took a job." He nursed the new beer. "What the hell you really after down here?"

Hawke grinned, and catching the bartender's eyes, ordered another round of beers. "Background, local color, details, on-the-spot descriptions, and the *feel of a place* that you can't get out of a book. Okay, I'll tell you, but don't let anybody know. I write men's action books. Shoot-'em-up, carve-their-guts-out kind of stuff. Not literature, but it buys my bread and a Caddy or two."

"A real writer? No shit? Magazines?"

"No, novels. I've had about twenty published. Running out of material, so I travel. I'm looking for the down-and-dirty underbelly and asshole of this country."

Buddy Batista laughed. He slammed his hand down on the small table and called for two more beers.

"Hell, I was *hoping* you did something like that. I can show you some of the shit-stomping places around town. You probably want to see where I work too. I got to get back tomorrow. You want to come? Leave at five A.M. and drive to hell and gone up into the hills. You wanna come?"

Hawke put his arm around Buddy and whispered in his ear.

"Buddy, what the fuck could I see up in some damn hills?"

Buddy laughed. "See? I'll show you a fucking coca plantation, and a fucking laboratory where they refine the shit into coke and ship it to Miami. How's that for a fucking underbelly and asshole of a country?"

"I'll go. Five A.M.—where?"

Buddy arranged to meet Hawke at the side door of the hotel in his car. Buddy stood and weaved his way out the door. Alex had left a half hour ago with the blonde. Hawke thought of calling Gina, but it was nearly midnight. He had to be up and ready to go at five.

Ten minutes later he was in his room taking a shower. Then he slept like a kitten until his wakeup call came promptly at four-thirty. Damn, what a short night!

Hawke wore chino pants and a light knit shirt with short sleeves and a slouch hat. He expected a beat-up Chevy to roll up for him. Instead, it was a year-old Mercedes convertible, in the States it was worth at least fifty grand. He had no idea what the tag was down here.

Buddy Batista wore slacks, alligator shoes, an imported French sport shirt, and a Miami Dolphins billed cap. He took off sixty-dollar shades and grinned.

"Ready to see how the workingman lives in Colombia, the real asshole of the nation?"

Hawke stepped in and laughed.

"Not what I expected," he said.

The trip wasn't as far as he had gone the previous day. They were not even an hour out of Bogota when they had climbed from the 8500-foot plateau on which the city is situated, to more than 10,000 feet. Hawke saw more and more coca trees. The hills were covered with them, growing wild in the small valleys and ridges.

Here and there he found regimented rows of trees in cultivated plots. These areas were dotted with men and women stripping leaves from the branches.

Where there weren't coca trees, the hillsides were covered with coffee trees. Not really trees, more like shrubs, but many showed bright red coffee beans.

Soon Buddy swung the Mercedes off the main track of a road into a rougher lane that led to a country mansion. It was built of stone and wood, designed to fit into the hillside, and he guessed it had about fifteen rooms. To one side he saw the blue-green of a swimming pool, and as soon as the engine quieted, he heard shouts and laughing.

"Home sweet home," Buddy said. "This, too, might not be what you expected. The people I work for believe in taking care of the hired help."

"Looks like it," Hawke said, impressed.

"I manage this place."

Two big dogs of uncertain breed raced out from the house area to greet him. They ignored Hawke. A moment later a slender Colombian girl in a well-filled bikini ran from the pool. Her hair formed a dripping wet trail of black that hung to her hips.

She ignored her wet body and suit and hugged Buddy, kissing him thoroughly.

"Nothing like the pets and a little woman greeting you," he said in English, then told the girl to get back in the pool; they would join her soon.

"First we take the guided tour. What do you want to see—the leaf picking, the paste, or the refining?"

"I've seen the first part. Where is your lab? I don't see it."

"They planned it that way. This is a long-range operation. If the government suddenly changes, we have to be ready to swing with it until we can get to the top men. It's illegal in Colombia to make coca paste, or base or cocaine. So that's in our hidden plant."

They walked to a nearby well-constructed building that had a padlock on the door. Buddy unlocked it, stepped inside, and flipped on a switch. It was a workshop, armory, machine shop, and held a jeep with a mounted .30-caliber machine gun behind the driver's seat.

"We need some firepower, so the natives don't get restless."

Two walls of the building had racks. One held a dozen rifles, two Uzis, and about twenty handguns. Buddy pulled off two rifles and tossed one to Hawke.

"Ever handled one of these? That's an AK-47. The genuine article. Let's make sure it's new and in operating order." He picked up four magazines and handed them to Hawke. "I never like to walk around here without some firepower. I have a guard who goes with me most of the time, but today you can play the part. You know how to work that critter?"

Hawke punched the thirty-round magazine into the AK-47 and pulled the lever, charging a round into the chamber.

Buddy nodded. "Guess you know what to do with one." He took an M16 and three magazines of rounds, and they went outside and down a steep trail in back of the house.

A paved road showed ahead that led into a heavy growth of pine trees. Under the trees, and painted to blend in with

131

them with camouflage, sat a well-made frame building a hundred feet long by sixty feet wide.

"The old salt mine," Buddy said. "That's the heart of the operation. We even have our own power plant so nobody knows how much juice we use. Come on, I'll give you the tour."

Hawke knew nothing about cocaine laboratories, but this one was what he expected: tubes coming out of bottles; cooking vats; more tubes; tables; areas for bleaching, crushing, and powdering.

Buddy stopped at a table covered with what looked like broken gray glass.

"You probably call it crack. It's cocaine in one form, the crystals formed after the first drying. Not white at all, is it? To get it white we have to bleach it. Yeah, bleach. We can sell the crack for almost the same price as powdered coke now, and we save about twenty percent in the processing costs on this end."

"How do you ship it out of here?" Hawke asked.

"Vans. I can put fifty million dollars' worth of crack and cocaine into one van and send it to town where it will be placed on the next leg of the trip, by air or by sea."

"You've got everything worked out nice and neat."

"Fucking A, man. We don't fart around when this kind of bread is working. Hey, guess what I make a month?"

"A thousand?"

"Ha! I make twenty grand a month. Almost a quarter of a million a year! Hell, some of the middle-management types make two million a year. The bosses rake in three or four billion, I'd say. Hey, you want on board? Give up that writing crap and get a real job? I can get you on at five thousand a week, no problem."

"Tempting. What about fringe benefits? Any more sweet little things like that one who greeted you?"

Buddy guffawed. "Hell, you can have two or three like her just for feeding them and buying some clothes. Bimbos come cheap down here."

"Now your offer is sounding better. Where's your power plant? I don't even hear a diesel engine banging away."

"Hell, you won't. Got them in back all soundproofed, nothing to look at, just two working and one on standby. Damned efficient operation."

"So where are the bimbos?"

Buddy grinned. "I figured you were getting cock-happy. I could use some relaxation myself. We'll swim awhile, then flake out and see who's anxious."

"Hey, I got no swimsuit."

"Hell, then none of us will wear swimsuits. Come on."

Hawke enjoyed the swim. There were just four of them, the two men, the girl Hawke had seen before, and another girl, about the same size, not as pretty but with a better figure. Hawke swam six laps, then floated. When he looked up, he and the naked girl were alone in the pool. She grabbed his hand and led him into one of the bedrooms of the main house.

This was his chance while Buddy was busy. Hawke grinned at the girl and pushed her down on the bed. She laughed and started talking sexy in Spanish. Hawke quickly tied her hands. She thought it was a game until he put a gag in her mouth and tied her ankles together.

"Don't worry, nothing is going to happen to you. Just relax."

He dressed and made sure his AK-47 and the ammo were still in the room. Then he grabbed them and slipped out the poolside door and ran toward the lab. The power plant had to be first.

Hawke found it with no problem, near the lab. There was a hasp on the door, but the lock had not been snapped shut. Inside, he found the sound intense. Two diesels pounding away. This would be a great spot for his C-3, but it was back in the hotel. At the far side of the building sat a diesel fuel tank that would hold two thousand gallons. Beside it were three butane bottles, the round, ten-gallon size.

Hawke checked them and found that two were full. He searched farther and found an old shirt someone had discarded. He opened the top filler of the big diesel tank and dipped the shirt in the diesel, then carried the wet shirt to the door. He arranged most of it outside the loose-fitting door but made sure a foot of the diesel-wet fuse would be inside the room when the door closed.

He checked the door and found it would close and not squeeze the shirt at all. There was room underneath. Now he went to the two butane bottles and opened both valves fully so that the volatile gas gushed into the building. He left them open, held his breath, and ran for the door.

Hawke squeezed out, closed the door, then bent and lit the diesel-soaked shirt with his pocket lighter. It didn't want to start at first, then blazed up, and the flame crept forward along the material as it burned up the oil. Soon it was almost to the door.

Hawke ran for the protection of the rear wall of the laboratory. He had just skidded around it, AK-47 in hand, when the flames reached the inside of the generator plant. The twenty gallons of butane had turned to butane gas and almost filled the small building. The first touch of flame coming under the door ignited the gas, which now was like a giant bomb.

The building, the generators, and the diesel-oil tank all exploded in one massive ball of fire that slammed Hawke to the ground even behind the building. The diesel fuel splattered a hundred feet in all directions, some of it still burning. Hawke saw that much of the burning oil had hit the back wall and the roof of the laboratory. The painted surface caught fire, then the shingles, and soon the building was burning brightly.

Screams of surprise and pain had come from the lab as soon as the explosion hit. Hawke jerked open the back door, his AK at the ready.

Inside, it was a mass of confusion. A section of glass windows facing the power plant had shattered, driving shards of glass forward, cutting up the half-dozen workers in the plant.

Most of them were gone. One man lay dead on the floor near the windows, his face and neck bathed in blood where he had taken the full shock of the shattered glass.

The blast had tumbled equipment, smashed some of the tall towers of glass tubes and bulbs, shattered jugs of chemicals. In one section chemicals spilled together, creating a dense fog that soon burst into flames.

Two men with rifles stormed in the far door, looked around in wonder and then spotted Hawke. They shouted at him in Spanish and lifted their rifles.

Hawke cut them down with one ten-round burst from the AK-47. He ran out the back door. The Avenger checked around and saw Buddy charging down the path from the big house. Buddy saw him at about the same time and lifted a pistol and fired. Hawke was far out of range for the handgun.

"Your gravy train ride is over, Buddy," Hawke bellowed at Buddy. Then he brought up the AK-47 and chattered off two bursts of five rounds each. The last five 7 .62-mm slugs cut across Buddy's chest and pitched him off the path into some wild coca trees that were barely a foot high. He stared unbelievingly at the coca leaves, and they were the last thing he saw before he died.

Hawke saw two of the workers from the lab stumbling down the hill. Another one sat away from the lab, which now burned with an unusual intensity from all the chemicals in the building. A small explosion rocked the plant, then the roof fell in.

Hawke prowled around the plant and the house. There must be more protection here, more workers, someone. He found no one else. He explored the house. The girl he had tied up was gone, along with her clothes. No one else was there.

In the garage he found a new Chevrolet van. The keys were in the ignition. He backed it out and checked the gas gauge—full.

In the house, the two girls had come out of hiding and now sat side by side on one of the big couches, smoking and staring at him.

"You going to kill us too?" one asked him.

"Why should I? You're just part of the entertainment, part of the furniture. Now get outside and get moving. Your meal ticket here just ran out."

Hawke set the house on fire in three places, made sure it was burning well, then drove the van down the mountain, found his way across the plains thirty miles to Bogota, and left the van on a side street. He wiped his prints off it everywhere that he remembered touching it.

A half hour later he was back in his room at the hotel. There was a note for him under his door. He opened it and read: "Dinner? Why not. A girl has to eat. Find me."

It was unsigned. He went to the phone and asked for her room number. The phone rang ten times—no answer. He checked his watch. Two-thirty, local time.

Hawke took a taxi to Benedicto Park, fed the pigeons, and walked up past the Grasshopper's mansion. On the way back he spotted three big limos lined up outside. A whole group of people came out. About a dozen seemed to be bodyguards, surrounding a small man in the middle. He waved them aside and looked across the street into the park where a juggler was doing his street-entertainer act.

The small man watched the juggler intently, then sent one of his guards over with a wad of bills. The guard handed the roll of bills to the juggler, who juggled the roll along with two rubber balls. The old man laughed, got in his limousine, and drove away.

It got Hawke to thinking. Protection plus for the big drug czar. But he showed a bit of human weakness with the juggler. If he did it once, he might do it again. It could be a handle on the Grasshopper!

Did the man have a schedule? Did he move out of his mansion every day about the same time? Hawke would find out.

Back at his hotel room, Hawke phoned Gina's room. She picked up the phone.

"*Hola*," Gina said.

"Hi. Glad I tracked you down. Dinner about six?"

"Five. We've got a party to go to at seven, and I need an escort. Are you available?"

"What kind of party?"

"A stuffy, dress-up party. Most of the people there will be high government officials, and a scattering of big-shot businessmen."

"So why are you going?"

"Contacts. I'm in business, and contacts are as important as having a good product or a good price."

"Dinner at five. You pick the place, I'm new in town."

"I hope you brought a necktie."

"For dinner?"

"For the party."

They ate at the hotel. She recommended the game hen with wild rice. He settled for a side order of fried bananas and the two-pound steak. Both were delicious.

She asked Hawke a lot of questions he fielded flawlessly, then Hawke probed with a few questions, but she cut him off.

"This is not a quiz show, and you're not a contestant," Gina said. "I just wanted to know something about you before we went to the party. I have to tell them something. I mean, I know most of these people."

"Okay, okay. I'm here on vacation. My passport says I'm Brian Barlow, but you know that already. My friends call me Hawke, and I have an extermination business in San Diego. Yes, I am not married, and my vacation is almost over. It's a fine little country, but I wouldn't want to be a policeman here, and I'd much rather live in the good old U.S.A. where the policemen don't wear army uniforms and carry automatic rifles."

Gina laughed. "Sorry, I guess I asked for that. When you

are in management, you tend to get a little bossy. At least I do. Forgive me. My name is Gina Labruzzo, which you must know now because you found my room number. I work for one of my father's small companies, Labruzzo Transportation, with worldwide operations. Last year billings of a little over $2.5 billion, and a net profit after taxes of $11.7 million.''

''Not bad.''

''Far too low a percentage for the business we did. I intend the profit figure to be much better...'' She laughed and looked over at him. ''Why on earth are we talking bottom line and profit picture?''

''I'd much rather talk about moonlit beaches and soft music and a convertible with the top down, maybe a nice gentle breeze.''

''Instead, we'd better hurry. I have to change for the party. We just have time to make it.''

He waited in the outer room of her suite as she changed. When she came out, she was breathtaking. The evening dress was right out of some French designer's shop. It was cut low, showing the tops of both her breasts, and it had no back at all. It glittered and glistened and swept almost to her ankles but showed off her lower body as if she wore a bikini.

''Fantastic! Absolutely stunning!'' He rushed up and kissed her on the cheek, and she turned slowly for him.

''When I seduce you, be sure to wear that dress,'' he said.

She smiled. ''Change that *when* to a very iffy *if*. Thanks for the nice words. Now come on. A car is waiting for us.''

It was a limo like the one in which he had seen her arrive at the hotel. Inside, it was plush, luxurious. A small TV set played a local variety show. There were wines on the side. She said nothing to the driver, who worked his way through the traffic. He knew where he was going.

They spoke little on the ride, and when Hawke looked out again, he saw Benedicto Park. He looked on the other side just as the limo rolled up and stopped in front of the Grasshopper's floodlighted mansion.

"What's this, a museum?" Hawke asked as they got out.

"No, this is the home of Señor Marcus Bocodado. He's a very big man in this town. Some people call him El Cigarron, but not to his face. That means the Grasshopper."

"If he has this much money, I'll call him anything he wants me to," Hawke said, and laughed. Inwardly he was in a turmoil. How was Gina involved with the Medellin cocaine syndicate? Was she just a messenger girl for her daddy, or was something else going on he knew nothing about?

"Come on, silly. It's time we walk up the steps and meet our host, Mr. Bocodado. Remember, that's with a soft *c*. Please don't embarrass me."

"I'll be a perfect gentleman," Hawke said. What a chance. He would be right inside the bastard's mansion. Maybe he could figure out a way to cut down the Grasshopper tonight, or see a way to do the job for sure tomorrow. Watch and wait.

Hawke took Gina's arm and walked the beautiful woman up the steps where they were greeted by the same small man who, earlier that afternoon, he had seen give the juggler a roll of bills and enjoy the show.

Chapter
Nine

On the way up the steps, Gina held his arm. She was smiling as she whispered to him.

"This dirty old man likes me because I'm not a blond bimbo. He probably will feel my boobs, but try not to notice. He's rich and powerful, so he can get away with it."

When they were almost there, she whispered again. "Oh, I'm touting you as the best nature photographer in the U.S. The Grasshopper is a photo nut, too, so don't blow your cover and get me in lots of trouble."

They were there on the top of the steps outside a pair of thirty-foot-tall double doors with large gold handles.

Two huge men bristled on each side of the drug czar. When his shortsighted vision made out Gina, he chuckled gleefully. Now Hawke saw that he was in his seventies but spry and alert. He had close-set eyes; deep, sunken white brows; wisps of white hair that couldn't cover the brown liver spots on his white scalp. His body was thin and he was short, about five-four, but dressed in the best silk suit Hawke had ever seen.

"Ah, Gina, my little Italian sweetheart!" He kissed her on the lips, and his hand fondled one breast as he held her. Then she edged out of the embrace.

"Señor Bocodado! It's wonderful to see you. You're looking so strong and healthy these days." She turned to Hawke. "Señor Bocodado, may I present Mr. Brian Barlow from the States. He's an expert nature photographer."

Hawke shivered for a moment. He wanted to strangle the little man, to bash his brains out on the steps. Instead, he put on a pasty smile and took the offered hand. The grip was surprisingly strong, the handshake loose and quickly released.

"I understand you do some photography as well, Señor Bocodado?"

"Some, some," he said, glancing at Hawke quickly, then back at Gina's cleavage. "Yes, we'll have to talk later, young American."

More people came up the steps, and Hawke and Gina moved on inside the art museum–like entranceway. It had paintings, statues, and artifacts of early Colombia on the walls and in glass cases.

"Where does this guy get his money?" Hawke whispered to Gina.

She smiled. "He's in shipping. Has a large fleet, I understand. Much bigger than the group of Labruzzo ocean liners."

They wandered around the three rooms set aside for the gathering. One was a hundred feet long and half that wide. It must have been the ballroom. A small orchestra played in one corner, but no one was dancing.

Drinks and hors d'oeuvres were available everywhere. A

fancy ice sculpture of a swan and a leaping fish decorated the main table. It was a small gathering of about two hundred people, but they seemed lost in the three large rooms.

Hawke found little to interest him. The windows were all secured with bars and covered with drapes. Four men constantly hovered near the Grasshopper. Hawke could see bulges under the muscle men's tailored jackets that spoke of heavy armament, probably the feisty little Ingram spitting out 9-mm rounds. They were little larger than a heavy-duty pistol these days.

Gina held on to him tightly for the first half hour or so, then she found some people she knew and told Hawke he could circulate. He did, but found nothing that would help him break down the doors if he wanted to do a silent entry. He figured this was not the time to go off on his own on a searching expedition looking for a soft spot in the mansion.

Soon a small, dark-eyed beauty attached herself to him, and they sat at a table and talked about American movies. It seemed that was her one and only subject of conversation. Hawke figured she must be part of the furniture, and maybe assigned to him by the Grasshopper to be sure he didn't get anywhere in the house that he was not supposed to.

She did a good job of that. Her dress was low-cut, and when she leaned forward to whisper something to him, the dress billowed forward just enough to show him exactly what it was supposed to be covering. No bra hid the bare facts.

Just about when Hawke figured the Colombian beauty was going to invite him into one of the lower bedrooms, Gina showed up at his elbow.

"Come on, Romeo, my fence mending is done here.

Let's go before this bimbo gets your pants off." Gina said it in English so the girl couldn't understand. The girl smiled and nodded.

"She was just getting warmed up," Hawke said.

"I bet you were warmed up too. You know she works here."

"Of course, she's part of the furniture. That's no reason I can't enjoy the scenery."

"Men! I'll never understand you guys. You all seem to think with your crotches."

"You need to try harder to understand us," Hawke said. "Hey, I'm not the one who was playing grab-the-boobs with you. As I remember, you didn't pull away all that quickly." Gina scowled at him and he grinned.

As they moved toward the door Hawke wondered out loud, "Is our limo going to be there to take us back to the hotel?"

"Of course. Señor Bocodado humors me. He will until he gets me into his bedroom. He's famous for that. He brags that he's never made love to the same woman twice."

A limo waited for them at the bottom of the steps. Once inside, Hawke stretched back and relaxed.

"I could get used to this kind of life," he said.

"I bet you could. Back home you probably drive a compact car, pay three hundred a month in rent, and go out with secretaries."

"Right. The receptionist in Miami told me that you were a secretary. You're not."

She pushed over beside him, pressed hard against him, and kissed his lips. Her breasts were tight against his chest. She eased off, then kissed him again. For just a moment he was tempted. Gina pushed away but sat close to him, touching.

"That was . . . was just an experiment. I tend to be drawn to men who don't try to come on to me in a rush."

"I haven't laid a glove on you."

She grinned. "Yeah, I know. It's my own mind-set, not yours. Don't worry about it."

"Haven't lost any sleep over it yet."

The limo stopped at the hotel. The doorman opened the door and Hawke pressed some of the funny money into his hand, and they were in the lobby and then the elevator.

At her hotel room she turned the key and paused.

"Do you want to come in for a minute?"

"Yes, and I promise not to come on to you too fast."

"Good."

Inside, she went to the small refrigerator and took out two beers.

"I'd guess you're a beer man."

"True. Strange party we went to tonight."

"It was a see-me party. The people were there to see who else was there and to be seen themselves. You'll notice there were no speeches, no games, not even a gambling table. It was just a see-me."

"And you were seen. That's the most beautiful dress I've seen in years—and so is the lady inside it."

She turned and stared at him a moment. Her mind went into an instant replay of nearly those same words, which her uncle had used the second night he had seduced her in her bedroom when she had been fifteen and lived at his house while her father was in Europe.

She shook her head to get rid of the video replay and smiled.

"Thank you, sir. Most kind. My mother tells me to stop fooling around and get married. She's very Italian. A career isn't good enough for her; she wants me to provide her with four more grandchildren."

"I'm sure you'll take care of that when you decide that you're ready. Now, I should be going—although I'd love to tear that dress right off you." He grinned so that it didn't seem a threat.

She laughed softly. "You have a way of making me feel all warm without being threatening. Nobody else has ever done that." She sighed and looked away as she sipped at the beer from the bottle.

"Damnit, Hawke, that's why it makes it all the harder for me." She looked away. "Hawke, I know who you are. I found out today in a telegram. I have contacts. I have friends in San Diego, and more associates in Houston. Your first name is Matthew, and your real last name is Hawke, and in San Diego they call you the Avenger."

A wave of surprise and shock washed over him. He didn't let it show. He was surprised she had investigated him so completely. Was it an immediate danger? He decided not.

"So?"

"I'm angry, more than angry, about what they did to your wife, even though it happened in San Diego. I have no people out there." She walked up to him and hugged him a moment, her arms around his back, her body tightly against his. He could feel the heat of her breasts and her thighs on him. Her perfume stroked him pleasantly. A moment later she stepped back.

"Hawke, I can figure out what you're trying to do, why you're in Bogota. Don't try. So one of the men who hurt your wife was from Colombia. You can't take on the whole drug operation here. It's awesome. These people control vast fortunes, billions and billions of dollars! They simply crush anyone who gets in their way.''

She hugged him again and stepped back. "Matt Hawke, I don't want you to get hurt down here. Please, take a plane out tomorrow and forget you ever came to Bogota!''

Hawke had recovered from the surprise of her announcement by then. He wasn't running away.

"I might be persuaded to go back tomorrow, if you come with me. We'll stop for a week together in the Bahamas.''

For a moment her eyes lit up with delight, then the spark faded.

"Matt, I'm sorry, but I can't go. More business to do here. I wish...oh, damn! I wish that I could...that I would go with you. Matt, you just can't know how...how damned important that could be to me. But I can't!''

She rushed to him and hugged him again, reached up and kissed his lips with passion, and caught one of his hands. Slowly she put it over the bare top of her dress and down on her breast.

"Oh, God! Oh, God!'' she whispered. She kissed him again, her tongue a hot weapon searing into his mouth.

Suddenly she broke off the kiss, pushed away from him, and walked to the door.

"Matt, I don't want to be a tease. I didn't mean to do that, but...but I know that you have to leave. Please, right now.'' Tears gushed from her eyes, and she waited with the door open. Hawke went up to her, kissed her forehead, then walked out the door. There was nothing he could say. The lady had her own private problems she had to work through.

Hawke walked slowly down to his room. She knew about him, but she hadn't tried to stop him or kill him. Or had she? It just heaped more proof on his theory that she was down there to make a drug deal. After all, her last name was Labruzzo. She was still the enemy. He had let a sexy little body and a cute face bend his judgment.

But she had put him right inside of the Grasshopper's palace. It had proved to him that he wasn't going to try to crash the fortress. So what next? He'd have a talk with his newspaperman. After ten years in town he must know somebody who would have a handle on the Grasshopper.

Hawke was up early the next morning. At breakfast in the hotel dining room, he tried to read the Spanish-language newspaper. One story interested him most. It was about a judge, Alphonso Rubbias, who had sentenced a drug smuggler to ten years in prison. It was the first drug sentence in over a year.

Hawke put down his paper and hurried out to find a taxi. He had to talk to this man, find out where he got the courage to do such an honest thing in this corrupt town. He found the name of the court and told the driver he wanted to go to that courthouse.

Twenty minutes later they badgered their way through traffic in populated streets, and the taxi driver let Hawke off.

The court did not open for another half hour. Hawke found a small coffee shop across the street and drank some of the best coffee he had ever tasted as he waited.

Judge Alphonso Rubbias had relaxed on his way to work that morning. He had a driver, a big car, and a briefcase full of case notes. Today he would have to hand down some tough decisions. He was not worried about his sentencing of the drug smuggler the day before. It had been such a flagrant case that word had gone out to the Medellin cartel leaders that it would happen.

The word to them was that this man had broken their unwritten agreement. They knew that all smuggling had to be done under the cover of some other business venture. They were rapidly losing worldwide confidence. Colombia could not officially sanction the use, processing, or sale of narcotics. It was unthinkable. The big three leaders had evidently accepted his way of thinking. This was not one of their men, anyway.

Now he felt the car stop at the front of the building. Soon there would be a more secluded side entrance for the judges and workers in the court, but today the front door was the one he used.

Judge Rubbias emerged from the big Cadillac, thanked the driver and with his briefcase in hand, then stepped up to the sidewalk and toward the courthouse.

A single rifle shot slammed through the traffic noise. It was enough to jerk Hawke's head upward. His eyes swept the street and sidewalk.

He saw the man beside the Cadillac clutching his chest. Then two men with masks on ran out from buildings. Each carried a shotgun. They fired as they ran forward.

Judge Alphonso Rubbias took the first load of double-ought buck in the side. The thirteen lead slugs, each the size of a .32-caliber bullet, riddled his new suit and blasted him back against the official black Cadillac.

Another load of buck hit him in the chest, and his arms flew up as he skidded down the side of the black vehicle to the sidewalk.

The two men ran up and blasted the body with rounds

of double-ought. Then the men calmly pulled machetes from their belts.

Hawke couldn't believe it. There, in plain sight of two or three hundred people, the killers calmly hacked the judge's body into pieces. They cut off his head and arms and legs, hacked his torso in half, cut up his arms and legs, then dropped the machetes, walked into the street, got in a light blue car that had a protective cover over the license plate, and sped away down the street.

Hawke did not need to ask who the man was he had just seen savaged. It could only be Judge Rubbias. As he watched out the window, two policemen edged toward the scene. Only after they were sure the killers were gone, did they move up. They held the people back, used radios to call in more help, and after more than an hour the area had been cordoned off with barricades and yellow tape.

There was nothing Hawke could do. He turned and walked away, found a taxi, and went back to his hotel.

For half an hour he tried to call his newspaper friend, Alex Contreras. He was out, busy. At last someone in the office told him that Alex was covering the murder of a judge.

Hawke hung up and clipped out the story in the morning paper about Judge Rubbias. He would have a follow-up story to go with it in the next day's editions.

Chapter
Ten

A little past noon, Alex returned Hawke's call.

"You're on the Judge Rubbias story?" Hawke asked.

"About a hundred of us. I got to one eyewitness, but he seems a little flaky. Says the judge pulled out a pistol and fired two shots at passersby."

"He's lying. I was in that coffee shop just across the street."

"You *saw it go down*?"

"Right. I was waiting to meet the man. He stepped out of his car, then a rifle shot sounded, and that hit him first, I'd guess. Then the two men came at him in a crossfire, taking turns chewing up his body with buckshot. Then they hacked his body to pieces with machetes."

"The men both wore masks?"

"True. Then they got into a light blue car that stopped in the street for them, and drove away."

"Christ! Now what do I file—what really happened or what the police say?"

"The two uniforms didn't come on the scene until they were damn sure the shooting was over."

"Figures. I'll file something. I was on my way to check out a freighter over in Buenaventura. That's Bogota's closest seaport, about two hundred miles west of us on the Pacific coast."

"Is the freighter dirty?"

"As dirty as they get. Panamanian registry to a New York firm, mostly coffee on board. Want to take a ride? I'll dictate the story on the judge as I go, and file it from over there."

Hawke said he wanted to go. First they stopped by at the underground arms dealer and Hawke bought four more quarter-pounders of C-3 plastic explosive and timer detonators. He had left the first chunk of C-3 in his hotel room. The explosive made Alex nervous.

"You realize that if we get caught with that C-3, it's prison for about twenty years for both of us?"

"We won't get caught. What's to suspect? You're a famous newsman and I'm a nature photographer from San Diego. The secret is never let them see you sweat. Start acting nervous and we're busted."

Hawke manned the tape recorder as Alex got his mind off the explosives and dictated his story. He used most of what Hawke had told him, throwing in some local color.

The road was fairly good, but it still took them five hours to drive through the mountains to the Pacific coast. The docks were busy, but they found the big *Georgia Peach* freighter at the end of a long wharf.

The stevedores had finished with the big freighter that was over four hundred feet long, and most of the crew was on one final liberty before they set sail at dawn. Only a skeleton team stayed on board.

Alex had a plan. "I can go on board and tell whoever we find that I want to do a story on a typical American Merchant Marine, what he does, how he works, his off-duty entertainment, the whole story."

Hawke shook his head. "Not a chance. You get down there, they remember you, you're tabbed. I'm going to blow that sucker out of the water, and I don't want you involved. Wouldn't it be better for you to go find a cozy bar and flirt with a waitress after you file your story? Keep a low profile. I don't even want the cops to know you were in town today. That way you can't get burned."

"You're right. Just make damn sure that bucket of bolts has crack or cocaine on board before you trash it. That's all that I ask." Alex stared at the C-3 again as Hawke wrapped it in brown paper and put it inside his shirt.

"You're going to use that stuff?"

"If the ship's dirty, I'll use it. The best way to destroy crack and cocaine powder is to melt it down."

"Good God! You're going to sink her?"

"If she's dirty, she goes down. That sends a signal to the ship owners as well. You get dirty with coke and you get burned where it hurts."

Hawke got out of the car at the end of the dock. He made arrangements to meet Alex on the same street corner in two hours, then every hour on the hour after that.

By the time Hawke got to the gangplank, to the low-in-the-water *Georgia Peach*, he was staggering. He looked at the name on the ship, then went up the gangplank, stumbling and swearing. At the top of the short, slanted entryway a sailor in T-shirt and dungarees blocked his path.

The man spat out something in Spanish.

Hawke stared at him, shook his head. He slurred the words but made sure the man could understand. "What the hell, don't you guys talk American?"

"Yeah, slob, and this ain't your ship. She's the *Peach*. What you looking for?"

Hawke stumbled down the deck toward a cabin door that stood open.

"Hey, asshole! I said, this ain't your ship."

The seaman grabbed Hawke by one arm. Hawke suddenly lost his stagger, swung the smaller man around, and rammed him through the opening into the stateroom.

Hawke slammed his fist into the sailor's belly, and when he groaned and bent over, Hawke brought both hands, made into one fist, down hard on the back of his neck. The man sighed and sagged to the floor, unconscious.

Hawke looked out the door, then tied up the man and gagged him. He checked the deck again, then went out and down the first ladder he found. There were eight huge holds. Which one might contain the crack and coke, he had no idea. A man shouted at him.

"Who the hell are you?"

Hawke put on his drunk act again.

"Who the hell? Jones. Ain't this the *New Bolivar*?"

"No way," the man said. He was some kind of an officer. Hawke weaved in front of him.

"Who're you?"

"I'm Blanchard, second mate."

Hawke spun the man around, put a sleeper hold on him, and eased off the pressure.

"This is a sleeper hold, Blanchard. I can kill you with it in a minute of hard pressure. It cuts off the blood supply to your brain from both carotid arteries. I have a question. You answer it and you'll live. You understand?''

Blanchard nodded.

"How many crew on board?''

"Four, five.'' Blanchard sputtered out the words.

"You've got coffee and cocaine on board. You know where the coke is hidden?''

"No coke!''

Hawke tightened the hold, his forearm bones pressed hard across the carotids. He held it for five seconds and let up. The man almost fainted. He came back slowly.

"Where is the coke?''

He waved, nodded. Hawke eased up more.

"Show you,'' Blanchard said.

Hawke pointed his .45 ACP at the man. "Any trouble and you're one dead swabby, understand?''

Blanchard nodded and took him down two ladders, into a small elevator, and down again to the lower deck. He used a forklift to push boxed bags of coffee to one side. Behind them were more boxes, but all were filled with plastic-wrapped packages of white powder, not coffee.

Hawke cut open one and tasted.

"Cocaine,'' he said. He saw other packages that showed the grayish-white crystals of rock cocaine, crack.

He took a six-inch knife off his wrist and began slashing the packages. Blanchard stood to one side.

"I'm a dead man,'' he said with no emotion. "They'll kill me slow.'' He charged Hawke. The Avenger had just finished slicing a package and turned. The knife went with him.

Blanchard slipped on the deck of the hold and fell forward, impaling himself on the blade. By the time Hawke pulled the blade free and let the man down to the deck, he was dead. Hurrying, Hawke planted two of the quarter-pounders of plastic C-3 in the middle of the boxes of coke.

Two more he took to the side of the massive hold, where the steel plates of the hull of the ship were obvious. After considering it for a moment, he taped both the quarter-pounders together and pressed them into the seam of two large plates. The timer/detonator he put in was good for five seconds to two hours. He set it for fifteen minutes and pushed the start lever.

Back in the coke boxes, he set the timer for twelve minutes and pushed the start lever, then worked quickly up the ladders toward the top of the hold, which still had the cover off fifty feet aft.

Hawke climbed out of the hatch, saw no one on deck, and sprinted for the gangplank. When he got there, he pretended to talk to someone on board, then walked down the gang-plank at a leisurely pace and up the dock. He was a quarter of a block away when he found some pilings. He sat on them for a while, watching sea gulls.

When he checked the timer on his wristwatch, it showed that ten minutes had elapsed. Hawke made sure the .45 was well into his pocket, then he sauntered to the end of the dock where it met the street. The *Georgia Peach* was the only freighter tied up at the long pier.

A moment later Hawke heard a muffled roar. Following that there were some shouts from the big freighter. Then two minutes later the second blast went off. It blew a section out of the side of the *Georgia Peach* at the waterline on the dock side. At once, water rushed into the hold. There were screams on board now, as seamen raced for the gangplank.

The big ship began to list toward the dock as the dockside

hole took on more and more water. Slowly she sank deeper in the water, then the deck began to tilt, the near side going down as the ship took water in through that side of the hold.

A two-inch hawser that tied the bow down suddenly snapped like a rifle shot. The ship heeled over, tilted beyond the balance position, and she toppled sideways in the water, her stacks crashing down on the pier. A fire gushed from the bridge, and from far off Hawke heard a fire siren.

Hawke walked back the way he had come, found the meeting place a block over from the dock, and saw Alex's car sitting there. He slipped in, and they drove toward the highway that would lead them back to Bogota.

"Hear there was some problem at the docks today," Alex said.

"That right? Might be on the radio."

Alex grinned and turned it on. There was nothing but music.

After a few moments Alex handed Hawke a cold bottle of beer and a big deli sandwich.

"Thought you might be hungry after your day at the office," Alex said. "I got my work done, the story filed and finished."

Hawke chewed halfway through the big sandwich.

"Oh, and finish that beer fast. The locals have tough rules about open bottles in a car."

Hawke drained it and tossed the bottle out the window.

"That is one shipment of crack and coke that won't get out of the harbor," Hawke said after a period of silence. "Now I'm trying to find a Miami native by the name of Vito Labruzzo. Ever seen him down here?"

"Don Labruzzo used to come down every six months

to stock up and dig out the greenbacks from his private jet. The Miami drug boss. Hell, yes, he's been around. Come to think of it, haven't noticed him the last six months or so. Heard he wasn't in the best of health.''

"Would Labruzzo carry any weight down here?"

"With the Medellin cartel? Damn little. Vito pushes maybe fifty million a year. These guys down here do that much a day. Big money is everywhere. Vito was a private buyer with his own distribution, so he'd be taken care of, but he didn't rate any special favors.''

"I went to a party last night at the Grasshopper's mansion," Hawke said.

"You lie!"

"Nope. Scout's honor. I was a guest of a little lady you probably haven't met, Gina Labruzzo, also of Miami."

"And you didn't get barbecued? Christ, how do you do it?"

"Luck and balls. What do you know about Gina?"

"No bells ring. The old man Vito had four brothers, as I recall, all in the family business. Vito had six or seven kids. He kept his wife barefoot and pregnant." The newsman worked back through his memory.

"I used to work Miami for six months or so. But I don't remember a Gina. I'll do some checking and get back to you."

"It's important."

"Yeah." Alex took a long look at Hawke. "You mean, you walked in the front door of that mansion, shook old Bocodado by his little hand, and said howdy?"

"True. But he didn't look at me; he was staring down Gina's cleavage and copping a cheap feel."

"Sounds like the old bastard. I'm amazed. I've been here

ten years, and I've never gotten closer to one of his blowouts than a preliminary press preview once. They kicked us out the back door when the guests arrived."

"You know anything about the Grasshopper's daily schedule? I saw him leave his place yesterday or the day before. He walked to the curb. Doesn't he have an inside garage?"

"Nope. They built those old buildings wall-to-wall. He'd have to tear out a whole set of rooms to get a car in and out. He won't dislodge any of his artifacts and paintings."

"Any schedule? Some routine he goes through every day? Does he ever come out of the mansion at about the same time each morning or afternoon?"

"Not that I know of. He's got everything he needs right there, and the girls are brought in the back door." Alex stared at Hawke again. "You really going to try to take him out?"

"I'm going to waste him. Somebody's got to show these bastards that they're not invincible."

"Before his body is cold, the Medellin cartel will move a new man into his slot or absorb his clients into the big two."

"If it disrupts the flow of crack and coke into the U.S. even a little, that might mean there would be a handful of men and women who don't get hooked, who don't die from the shit. That's reason enough for taking him out."

"I'll do some work on it."

"Good, you think, I'll have a nap. I plan on being up most of the night."

When they got back to Bogota, Alex helped Hawke rent a car, then left him.

"Look, be careful. I don't want to have to do a story on you the way I did on the judge."

"No chance," Hawke said. "I'm too ugly and mean to die, at least for a while."

Hawke spent half the night in his car near Benedicto Park, across from the Grasshopper's mansion. He saw the three big limos come back about midnight, and the ten-man bodyguard screen swept the Grasshopper safely up the steps and inside.

Hawke woke up grouchy and stiff in the rental car seat the next morning. After a quick breakfast and three cups of coffee he drove back to the park and found a different spot to watch. At about noon the third man in the drug syndicate came down from his mansion. He had his usual group of bodyguards around him. Bocodado looked into the park and saw a strolling musician.

The drug czar listened to the music through the traffic, sent some money to him, and the caravan pulled out. He'd done that two times! If it happened twice, the old guy would do it again, maybe tomorrow, maybe the next day. Now Hawke had to get ready.

That afternoon he found a hobby shop and bought what he needed. It was a small, free-flight model airplane with remote control. He had the salesman explain how it worked. The Spanish instructions were too much for Hawke.

He drove into the wide valley out from Bogota and learned how to fly the plane. It was easy to assemble. The wingspan was about three feet. The salesman had proved that the engine would run in the store, and had sold Hawke all the accessories he would need.

Now he practiced. It was hand-launched, and then the small hand set of controls for the engine took over. He could regulate the speed, ailerons, and rudder. Hawke had piloted some planes before, so he was a natural. Gradually he caught on, and after five or six hours he practiced bringing the small plane down over an exact spot in the empty field.

By nightfall he had it down. He could fly the little plane exactly where he wanted to. Hawke packed up the plane and all the gear, made sure he had enough of the gasoline-and-oil mixture for flying the next day, then drove back to the Casa Colombia Hotel.

He saw the note under his door as soon as he came in. It was brief: "Missed you last couple of days. Can I buy you dinner?" There was no signature.

He called Gina's room number, and she picked up the phone at once.

"So you've rented a car and everything. You planning to stay awhile? What happened to Bermuda?"

"Yes, you can buy me dinner," he said. "Maybe we can talk about Bermuda then."

Gina purred. "I'll be by to pick you up in a half hour. Make yourself beautiful."

Hawke had a shower, put on fresh clothes, a pair of slacks and matching sport shirt, and was ready when she came. Gina wore a business suit, sharp, expensive, but hiding most of her best features.

"Told you I was a working girl. Where are we going?"

Hawke tipped up her chin and kissed her lips lightly.

"You buy, your choice. Just so it's seafood."

The dinner was pleasant, a smart little restaurant where the headwaiter smiled at Gina and took them ahead of a line of waiting customers. They were at a choice table near a small combo, and next to the tank where they could see the lobster and clams and saltwater fish swimming.

They chose the fish and lobster they wanted from the tank, then saw them netted by their waiter and quickly cooked.

"What about Bermuda?" Hawke asked.

She smiled. "My business here is almost done. I need another day. I might just accept your invitation."

"You're still teasing me. That's not nice."

"I'm not teasing, I'm just not sure. I'm relieved that you're still alive. Please don't try anything stupid. If you do and you get caught, it reflects on everyone else down here."

"Us gringos?"

"Yes."

"I'll make every effort not to get killed."

"Good."

The food came then, and they talked about football. Gina had been a lifelong fan of the Dolphins. They argued football through the main course, and then concentrated on dessert. She ordered the specialty of the house, a strange concoction of meringue, coconut, a pudding base, fresh bananas, and a kind of caramel syrup that was all spread over a cake base. It all turned out to be delightful.

It was just after eleven when they got back to her hotel room. She gave him the key; he opened the door and went inside with her.

She kicked off her five-inch pumps and put her arms around his neck and kissed him. Holding him close, she pleaded again as she pressed against him.

"Please, Hawke, don't try for him, don't do anything that will get you killed. I know you've been watching the Grasshopper's mansion. Whatever you have in mind simply isn't worth it. You wouldn't get six inches onto his property before half a dozen alarms went off. He showed them to me one day when he was trying to get my bra off.''

"I'll be careful. Whatever I do, or try to do, has nothing to do with you."

"But I took you into his mansion."

"Forget it, nobody will know I'm anywhere around." He kissed her, and she clung to him a moment, then moved away. Knowing about her what he did now caused him to be quite mixed-up in his feelings about the beautiful woman.

"The other night, when you were here, I really wasn't trying to tease you. I was simply... confused, mixed-up, not sure of what I really wanted to do."

"So?"

"I guess I'm still a little confused." She took off the suit jacket and tossed it on a chair. The pure white blouse she wore strained to hold in her breasts.

"I understand. I'll allow you to be confused for another night. Tomorrow you decide if you want to come to Bermuda with me or not. Fair enough?"

She smiled.

He bent and kissed her breasts through the fabric. She made no move to stop him. Then he kissed her lips softly and moved toward the door. She watched him as he went to the door and out without a backward glance or another word. For just a moment Gina wondered if she had pushed Hawke too far.

Hawke walked quickly to his room, locked the door, and dropped on the bed. He wanted a good night's sleep so he could have a steady hand tomorrow with the model airplane. He had brought it to his room. It sat on a small table where he had left it.

It took him almost an hour to figure out exactly how to do it. He had held the plane by the wingtips to establish the center of gravity. That point must be maintained or the little plane would fly strangely and he might not be able to control it at all.

The problem was how to get the quarter of a pound of C-3 plastic explosive fitted in the fuselage of the plane—and behind the small motor, its fuel system, and control elements—without upsetting that center of gravity.

At last he solved the problem by putting a triggering roll of the puttylike C-3 directly behind the engine. Tomorrow he would place the impact detonator, pushed firmly into the C-3 there.

He made a long roll of the puttylike explosive about the size of a pencil and pinched it in contact with the triggering C-3 behind the engine. The long lead of plastic explosive extended from the detonator back to the main wad of C-3, which he placed in the hollow body slightly behind the center of gravity, so the little plane would have the same C.G. when he held it by the wingtips. He tried it, and the balance was perfect.

Hawke made one more check. The engine was in place; it would run as well as it had today. The C-3 was set, and the triggering detonator would go in place neatly tomorrow. The pencil length of plastic explosive would explode and transfer the shock to the main charge of plastic explosive for the instantaneous bang. The small fuse chain he had built would explode so quickly, it would seem to be one blast.

Yes, now all he had to worry about was flying the little plane, which was now heavier than it had been during his practice. The response and movements would be a little sluggish, slower.

He also had to hope that the Grasshopper would take a drive around noon, and this time again pause to look into the park. There would be a surprise waiting for the drug czar there.

Chapter
Eleven

Hawke stared at the radio-controlled model airplane sitting on the floor of his hotel room. It was ready. The only problem was that he had no way to disarm it. What he needed was one more radio channel to close a switch on board the craft that would push a solenoid and arm or disarm the bomb.

He had no time.

He had no equipment.

He had to go with what he had.

Hawke carried the plane down from his room, his shoulder bag filled with fuel, batteries, tools, everything he would need for the flight. He brought around his rental car and loaded the plane in it, moving it carefully. He wasn't sure how much force it would take to set off the impact-type fuse on the plastic explosive.

Hawke drove the rented car carefully to the park. He didn't want the C-3 to explode in a car accident. He parked across the street and down the block from the mansion.

There was lots of open space in the park. He had to remember that anything that the model plane ran into, like a telephone pole, light standard, or even a tree branch, would explode the bomb.

He had to make damn sure that he flew it safely until it was the right time.

Hawke spread his gear out on the grass a half block down from the car. He didn't want any immediate connection made between the rental and himself. If all went according to plan, he would not touch the car again.

He made his first flight about nine that morning, a lazy, slow circle around the treeless area of the park, bringing the plane in to land on a long, open area where there were no people around. The big tires let it roll to a stop safely.

Hawke rushed out to pick up his toy before anyone else could get there, and brought it back. He fiddled with it, watching the mansion across the street. Two cars arrived and let out passengers, but the drug czar himself did not come out.

At about ten o'clock Hawke flew the craft again. This time a small crowd gathered to watch the flight. Hawke kept the plane up longer, got more familiar with the new operating tendencies of the more heavily weighted craft, and then brought it in for a landing.

It was nearly eleven that morning when Hawke saw the three big limousines pull up in front of the mansion. The drivers got out and stood beside their large, armored, bulletproof rigs. Hawke knew the windows were made of two-inch laminated glass and did not roll down. Steel shielding in the doors and side and top panels made the rigs rolling tanks.

Hawke made final adjustments to the plane, and when he

saw the dozen bodyguards emerge from the mansion's huge door, he hand-launched the plane and began buzzing it around the park. He caught sight of the small drug king in the middle of the pack and saw him push the men aside so he could see better. The Grasshopper stood there watching the flight. He cheered and then moved toward his limo.

Hawke made another loop and waited. The drug king's car door had been opened for him, and he sat down on the seat with his feet outside, watching the plane. Hawke flew it higher, made a series of turns, then advanced the throttle to full and flew the little craft higher and out over the street.

The bodyguards were pointing at it now, chattering away. The Grasshopper was entranced for a while more, then started to push into the armored limo.

Suddenly Hawke sent the little plane into a dive. He angled it down in a sweeping curve, then, when it was just over the tops of the cars in the street, he corrected with the rudder, slipping the little craft sideways, then raced it directly for the limo. Two of the bodyguards saw it coming.

The rest of the guards were moving to the other limos, as they usually did. One muscle man jumped toward the door on the Grasshopper's rig.

The plane darted forward.

The guard caught the door and started to close it.

Hawke made a slight correction, and the radio-controlled craft slashed past the open door and directly inside the armored limo. A millisecond later the quarter of a pound of C-3 plastic explosive detonated with a cracking, muffled roar.

Much of the explosive force escaped through the open door. The windows on the limo held, intensifying the concussion within the car. The guard who almost got the door closed found that same door blasted backward against him as it was ripped off its hinges, crushed his chest, and jolted him ten feet into the street.

Inside the limo, the driver's skull exploded with the force of the blast.

Marcus Bocodado had a quick sense of danger as he heard the snarling little motor of the model aircraft racing toward him. He threw up his arms as the plane slammed through the doorway. One wing clipped the rear door post, spinning the little craft toward the back of the car.

The propeller dug into Señor Bocodado's chest, breaking a rib before it stalled. In less time than it takes to blink, the small engine jolted backward into the impact detonator on the plastic explosive, and the small connective reaction followed.

The entire interior of the limousine exploded in a fireball that gushed out the vehicle's door.

The fire consumed the upholstery, clothing, and the flesh of the two mortals inside the stretch Lincoln before any fire-fighting equipment arrived. Four of the bodyguards were stretched out on the pavement, dead or incapacitated by the blast.

Hawke dropped the radio control and walked into the crowd that had been watching. He moved into a brushy section, and the people who had watched him were now drawn to the fiery disaster across the street. Few connected the small plane with the gigantic explosion.

Hawke stopped in the brush, took a blue hat from his pocket, and pulled it on. He slipped out of the shirt he wore and turned it inside out, changing the color from white to blue. To this simple change in appearance he added his large reflectorized sunglasses and walked slowly through the park toward his hotel.

Nobody stopped him. No police were evident. He had heard many sirens, but they were concentrating on the street in front of the mansion, owned now by the heirs and the estate of one Marcus Bocodado.

It was over a mile back to the hotel, but Hawke walked all the way. He didn't want any taxi records to show a ride from this area. Once inside the hotel, he took his key and two messages from the room clerk and went up to his room. Only after he was inside his room did Hawke read the messages.

Both were from Gina.

The first said: "Hawke, Sorry about last night."

The second one said: "Double sorry about last night. We have to talk. Lunch after siesta?"

Hawke began gathering up his clothes and gear. He had little. He had left all of the model airplane equipment at the site.

He couldn't leave yet. He still had Gina to deal with. She was Mafia, was into the drug trade. He couldn't just walk away and ignore both facts. He would simply ask her, and according to her answers, he would decide what to do.

When he called, she was out. As soon as Hawke put down the phone, it rang. He grabbed it.

"Yes."

The voice was Alex's. "We have to talk. I'll meet you in the lobby, on the Bolivar Street side. We'll go for a drive."

"Right. I'm moving in that direction."

Hawke kept the .45 tucked in his belt behind his shirt. He traded the blue cap for a golf cap of soft gray, picked up his glasses, and headed for the elevator.

In the reporter's car, Hawke leaned back.

"Don't get too comfortable, you've got to get out of town. There's at least one honest cop left in Colombia. The police have a description of you. They know you were in Buenaventura two days ago; they know you bought the plastique explosive and have arrested the seller.

"They also know that you were in the park this morning. It won't take them long to tie down where you bought the radio-controlled model plane."

"So they will be checking the hotels. They know I'm an American?"

"First thing they pegged."

"Where are we going?"

"A small safe house we use from time to time."

"Safe house—that's not a journalist talking."

Alex only nodded.

"So some of you journalists do more than just report."

"Not when our paper knows about it. I felt I had to do something. This was just too dirty down here. The people I work with don't care who wants you back in the States. Right now they want you out of Colombia so this thing can settle down."

Alex relaxed a little. "Christ, I thought somebody would beat me to you at the hotel. I've been phoning every five minutes for the past hour."

Alex drove a little more slowly.

"You ever worked on a ship?"

"Not really. I was undercover on the docks for a couple of weeks, but I've forgotten the jargon."

"We'll come up with something."

"Looks like I won't be flying out in first-class comfort."

"True. You have any cash?"

"Enough."

"How much? I can get you some."

Hawke pulled out the roll of hundreds. "I'd say I have about twenty thousand left."

Alex whistled. "That should be enough for walking-around money." The car turned into an alley and stopped in a residential area. They were in a four-car off-street parking area.

"Home, sweet home," Alex said.

Hawke sat in the car. "My job isn't done yet. The girl. What do you know about Gina?"

"I was afraid you'd ask. Her father, Vito, died in Rome almost two months ago. Almost nobody knows it. A month ago, one of her uncles, Joe Labruzzo, was eliminated in traditional Mafia fashion. Three .22-caliber rounds in the back of the head. From what we can tell, Gina is running the Miami Labruzzo family."

"Can't be. The other dons would never allow it."

"What if they didn't know about it for six or eight months? Then she'd have a track record."

"She's down here setting up her new deal with the Medellin drug bosses?"

"Right. The Grasshopper was her connection."

"I've got to see her again."

Alex shook his head. "Too dangerous. She wouldn't come alone. She must know by now who took out the Grasshopper."

"I have to risk it."

Alex scowled. "I don't think they'll let you."

"Who?"

"The two gentlemen with Ingrams pointed at you just outside your window."

"Oh, shit!"

Hawke said good-bye to Alex, thanked him, then went inside the safe house with the two CIA agents. One left at once. The other's name was George. He was lean and mean, wore a crew cut, had a boyish face, and was six-two and fit.

"Mr. Hawke, we're here to help you. I can't say we disagree with what you've accomplished down here, but we can't let this be tied into the U.S. I hope you understand."

"Perfectly. I appreciate your help. When do I leave from here for the States?"

"Two or three days, after the clamor calms down. After the Medellin cartel hit men get tired of looking for you. We're thinking about a banana boat right now. Maybe the *Georgia Peach*." The agent grinned.

"You sure did a job on that one. We figure there was more than five tons of coke in that one shipment. It would have supplied the whole East Coast, dropping off the goods to coke runners in fast boats out of every small port and anchorage along the coast."

"Yeah. You have any food around here?"

There was a freezer stocked with frozen dinners, and a microwave. Hawke had one, then took a nap. Someone was always with him.

He realized he had to see Gina.

His chance came an hour later. George went to the bathroom. Since it was a safe house, it was also used for detainees, and there was a lock on the outside of the bathroom. Hawke had seen it earlier; now he slipped up, locked the door, and sprinted out the front door, setting off an alarm. By then it was too late for George to do anything about it.

Hawke looked around, memorized the names of the nearest streets at the corner, then ran for six blocks until he found a main street and a phone booth.

At last he got the number of the hotel and dialed Gina's room. She picked it up at once.

"You said something about talking?"

"Yes. I did."

"Hey, you've been crying."

"It's nothing. A death in the family. Where can we meet?"

"I'm not really welcome in this town anymore. Somewhere out-of-the-way?"

She gave him an address. "It's an apartment house, very nice. I'll be in the lobby. We've got to talk about Bermuda."

"Yes. I'll find a taxi and get there as soon as I can." Hawke put down the phone and lifted his brows. He had no idea what he was going to say to the woman. Maybe he'd get an idea on the way.

Chapter
Twelve

Hawke walked for half a mile through the mostly residential areas until he found a main street and could flag down a cab. It took him two tries to get the name of the street right. At last the cabdriver nodded.

The apartment house was well across town. It sat on the corner, was four stories high, and looked presentable enough. He had the .45 but still felt naked. Eyes watched him. He walked up to the front steps and through a heavy door.

Gina sat on a chair opposite the door. The lobby was twelve feet square. She caught his hand and led him through a door, down a short hallway, and into a room. There was a single bed, a chair, a dresser. It looked like a cheap hotel room.

"I stay here sometimes," she told him. Then she kissed him quickly and stepped back. "Hawke, I'm sorry. They made me bring you here. I didn't want to. There is no way to argue with these people."

Before he could jump toward her, Gina stepped out the

door they had come in. When he got to it, the door was locked. He saw where steel bars had slid down into steel retainers in the floor. It had been electronically locked.

He looked around. Someone made her bring him here? Where were they? Who? The room had no windows. It looked like a trap. He hurried to a door on the other side of the room. It was not locked. He pushed it open a fraction of an inch and looked out. Another hallway. This one was not carpeted. He saw several doors leading off it. There was no way out of the room but this way. He stepped into the hall.

The door swung shut behind him, and electronic locking bars slid into the floor.

The moment he hit the hall, he felt a slight motion. He stood on a pressure plate. Why? He looked at the floor. Two feet in front of him was a separation, a line of some kind. The floor beyond that looked smooth and polished.

Hawke reached into his pocket, took out a quarter, and flipped it on the floor just past the pressure plate. The coin sparkled and sputtered, then melted as a killing charge of high-voltage electricity hit it.

One more step and he would have been frying in a huge electric griddle. There was no chance of going back; he had to move ahead. The first room off the hallway was six feet down on the left side. The door stood slightly ajar, with the knob nearest him. The safe haven was still six feet away.

He had nothing to use to short out the circuit breaker to cut the power to the electrified floor. The safe pressure plate he stood on extended across the five-foot-wide hallway. It was nonconductive, wall-to-wall. Hawke had some thin, strong nylon cord wrapped around his waist, but it wouldn't help here.

The lighting fixture! Four feet from the pressure plate a

light box sprouted from the wall about five feet from the floor. The bulb burned brightly. Was there a place he could grab hold of? Would it hold his weight?

There was little use in finding out the answers to the questions, since the fixture offered his only option. He either had to make it work, or die here of a serious electrocution problem.

Once more he checked out his options. His .45 was useless. The electric locks could not be shot out. The wires were deliberately buried deep inside the door and through the hinges to prevent any manipulation of the contact points. The light fixture was his only chance.

He looked at his change and found he was down to dimes and nickels. He threw them one at a time, each six feet farther down the hallway. The first three melted and danced. After that there was no reaction. Either the juice had not been turned on that far down, or it was controlled by another pressure-plate switch. Hawke was determined to find out.

The wall light was nominated. Hawke put his toes half an inch from the seam on the floor and stretched out over the sudden death toward the light fixture. He had no ridges or doorjambs or pressure points with which to support himself. Just his flat hands against the wall. He took a better angle at it, farther from the wall, and gained another foot.

Still, with the fixture at the five-foot height, he was more than a foot away from it. He couldn't risk falling on the floor. He had to jump, grab the fixture, hang on, pray that it held, and swing his feet around and launch himself with a push into *and through* the door, another two feet up the hall.

Hawke judged the distance again, picked his spot. The

hall was too wide to grab the fixture and push off from the other wall. Damn tough.

He took a deep breath, made sure his .45 was tucked securely in his belt. He rubbed his hands together, eyed the exact spot where he would grab the fixture, crouched slightly, then sprang forward toward the light.

He caught it cleanly with his left hand; his right clawed for a grip on the far side he couldn't see, and then he swung his body, working it in midair the way a diver does, propelling his legs forward and toward the opening.

He felt his body moving, his left foot banging into the door.

Release!

Hawke let go of the light fixture and twisted his body, trying to make his torso and shoulders follow his feet. It was as if in slow motion as he crashed into the door with both feet, felt his foot hit the floor safely inside the room. Then his body tried to break in half as he whipped his torso toward the opening. His left hand grabbed the doorjamb, three feet off the floor.

Then he was dropping, heading for the hall floor and instant death! He pushed and surged with his left arm to power his shoulders forward.

His body twisted to the right, and he knew he was falling, straight down. His left hand jammed against the door frame and held on. The basic lever principle vaulted his body inward.

He fell on his back, just inside the room, but his right hand trailed and he snapped it upward just as it contacted the hall floor and daggers of fire raced through this little finger, then it was gone and he slumped against the door inside. Safe! He had made it with only a seared finger. Damn lucky.

He looked at the electrical burn on his finger. It was two inches long, from knuckle to fingertip. Hawke stared at the finger and wondered what he would have looked like if he had made it just halfway into the open door.

He turned and looked around the room. It was like a hotel room. Bed, chair, dresser, window. *Window*! He lifted up and rushed to the window, but it was locked and had strong steel bars on the outside.

He saw the connecting door into the next room and tried it. It was locked. From his pocket he took a set of picks and in a little over a minute had the simple lock open. The door swung toward him. He eased it open slowly. There was no reaction from the other side. Hawke stepped into the room and noticed a small door on the inside wall to his left—a laundry chute.

He pushed it open and looked down it. It was only one floor to the basement. The opening was two feet square and went straight down. It was Hawke's only way out.

It would be like going down a "chimney" in a rock climb. He pushed his feet inside and rested them against the far wall. Then he edged his torso in and pressed it against the near side. He had all the pressure he needed, between his feet on one side and his back on the other.

Slowly he moved downward, inching along. It had been dimly lit below. Now he could see below better. Soon he was sure he was almost down. He pulled down his feet and dropped the last yard to a pile of cardboard.

Quickly he found an outside door, checked it, then stepped out into an alley. He ran down the alley and made it to the end without being seen. Then he rushed around a building and down another street.

Now there was only one thing left to do.

A half hour later he had found a taxi, which took him to a clothing store for a new hat and a light jacket. Then he went back to Gina's hotel and up the service elevator to her floor.

He knocked. There was no response. He worked on the lock with a set of picks and soon had the door open. Once inside, he locked the door and waited.

She came in an hour later. At first she didn't see him, then her brown eyes went wide.

"You made it!" She rushed toward him, her arms wide. He caught her arms with his hands. "Darling Hawke, they made me bring you there. No one has ever escaped from there before. I thought they had killed you by now!"

"What about Bermuda?" Hawke asked.

Her smile brightened. "Yes, darling! Of course! They'll be hunting for you. The police want you, too, but I can get you out on my private jet. We'll stop at Bermuda."

Slowly she took off the light jacket covering the dress she wore. Then she unfastened the bodice and watched him.

"First I want to make love to you here. A little preview of what's in the sack, as the old saying goes." She lifted the dress over her head and wore only a soft, filmy bra and bikini panties.

Gina held out her hand and led him into the bedroom. She stood him beside a dresser and smiled.

"Now watch the rest of the show," she said.

She slid out of the bra, and he sucked in a breath. The bikini panties flew to the other side of the room as she kicked them off. She danced up to him, her breasts bouncing, her hips jolting from side to side. Her arms went around him, and her naked body pressed against his.

There was something in her eyes. Hawke pushed her away suddenly and jumped to one side.

Gina held a four-inch stiletto in her right hand. She had snatched it from the dresser. The end held a bright red fluid. Her smile evaporated in a snarl of anger. She lunged toward him. Hawke danced out of the way, did a quick-sweep kick, and caught her left ankle. Her leg gave way, and she lost her balance and fell heavily, her right hand flailing to catch herself.

For a moment Gina didn't move. She lay on the hotel room carpet, on her side. Her right hand crumpled under her. Hawke reached out his toe and turned her naked form over.

Tears spilled from her eyes.

The tip of the stiletto had punctured her right breast just over a two-inch slice that was still bandaged. The knife wound was little more than a shallow flesh wound.

"Oh, God! I've killed myself!" Gina screamed it.

"It's just a little cut," Hawke said, looking down. "You wanted me dead all along, didn't you? You sent them after me in Honduras. Then you played with me and set me up for them to kill me."

"Yes, yes! You killed the Grasshopper!"

"When did you take over the family in Miami, Gina? Was it before he died?"

"Yes! But the poison on this knife can kill more than once!"

She slashed at him with the knife, missed, tried again. She tried to throw the knife, but it sailed past Hawke handle-first.

Hawke sat down beside her on the floor.

"That was really poison?"

"Yes. I have about ten more minutes."

"You had it all, Gina. Why did you try for the moon too?"

"I didn't have it all. I didn't have love. First my father kept boys away from me. Then my uncle . . . when I was only fifteen, he raped me every day for three months! I've never known soft, sweet, tender lovemaking with a man I loved."

"I'm sorry."

"I wanted you. I . . . I just couldn't get over those three months of terror." She screamed as the first pains hit her.

"Hold me, Hawke!"

He pulled her against him and held her gently.

"We would have been great lovers in Bermuda. I really wanted to go. I did. But—"

Another pain caught at her, and she blinked back tears.

"Why does dying have to hurt so much?" Gina screamed again.

"Kiss me, Hawke, once more."

He bent and kissed her. Her body arched upward, and a moment later she fell on his lap, her eyes looking at him in a forever stare. Gently he slid from under her. He wiped his fingerprints off the doorknob. It was the only thing he had touched. With a handkerchief he opened the outside door and looked down the hall.

Clear.

An hour later Hawke walked up to the back door of the safe house and knocked. George stared out at him.

"Hawke, I think if you try, you can really get in trouble. Did you see the girl?"

"Yes."

"Did you kill her too?"

"No."

"Thank God for that."

They stared at each other a minute. George sighed.

"Hey, am I going to have to put handcuffs on you?"

"No. How do I get back to the States? I'm through here, at least for this trip. There are still three or four in the Medellin cartel I'd like to spend some quality time with."

George laughed. "How about a beer and some penny-ante poker?"

Four days later Hawke slipped quietly on board a small Dutch freighter heading for the Panama Canal. He was not listed on the crew register or as a passenger. The captain owed George a favor from times past.

George had agreed that there would be no official report made on Brian Barlow. His passport would be valid in Panama, where he could grab a flight to Texas.

"I'd avoid Miami for a while, Hawke. The Labruzzo family does have a complete report on you, and from what I hear, one of the uncles that Gina didn't have killed is taking over the family business."

"I never did get along with her relatives," Hawke said.

He settled down in the second mate's bunk on board the *Flying Dutchman #24* and thought about how he'd succeeded in wreaking havoc with the sources of the coke and crack that made it to the U.S. Now it was time to return Stateside, to deal with the druggers on the streets of America's cities. Hawke was particularly interested in the Chinese Connection in New York City. From what he had heard, Chinese immigrants had charged in and now dominated the entire New York heroin trade.

It was time the Avenger paid the big city a visit.